I0699622

LAND ON HIM

A SEQUEL

MATTHEW R. CORR

Copyright © 2024 by Matthew R. Corr
Visit the authors website at www.matthewrcorr.com
All rights reserved.
No part of this book may be reproduced in any form or by any electronic or mechanical means, including information storage and retrieval systems, without written permission from the author, except for the use of brief quotations in a book review.
This is a work of fiction. Names, characters, places, and incidents either are the product of the author's imagination or are used fictitiously. Any resemblance to actual persons, living or dead, events, or locales is entirely coincidental.

First Edition: March 2024
Edited by: Amy M. Le
Cover Art by: Kyle DePriest. Illustrations copyright © 2024 by Kyle DePriest
Interior Design by: Matthew R. Corr
Printed in the United States of America
Fiction: New Adult Contemporary
Fiction: LGBT/Gay
Fiction: LGBT Thriller
Content Warnings: Homophobia, Hate-Speech, Underage Drug and Alcohol Use, Strong Language, Forced Drug Use, Gun Violence, Blood & Gore, Death.
ISBN: 979-8-9869102-6-0 (Paperback)
ISBN: 979-8-9869102-7-7 (Hardcover)

ALSO BY MATTHEW R. CORR

Land On Me

Just For The Weekend

CAMP 1985

Blood In the Water

For my two nerds, Ryan & Kyle.
Always my safe place to land.

ONE

NEW YORK CITY

Thursday, January 2nd

My hand froze around my suitcase handle. My knuckles were red and dry as I walked through the automatic doors into the warm lobby of my dorm building. I regretted packing all my dirty laundry in one suitcase.

"Landon! Welcome back," a cheerful voice said.

I gave a weak smile. "Hey, Bernard."

Bernard was a skinny Hispanic man in his late fifties with a thin mustache who worked the night shift at the front desk. He somehow knew everyone's name, even though a thousand NYU students lived in the building.

"Long flight?"

I pushed my suitcase against Bernard's station. "Sure was."

Bernard took down a cardboard Christmas tree cutout from the wall behind the desk. "I just made some fresh coffee if you want some." He placed the cardboard on his chair, then took down the Menorah cutout.

I checked my phone; it was 11 p.m. "No, thanks. I'm beat. I should sleep."

"Might be a good idea. You look exhausted."

I scanned my student ID over a blue light. The transparent barrier opened, allowing me to step back into my life away from home. Away from my dad. Away from Caleb. I had a big, dopey smile in my picture, taken the first day I moved in. I was so ready for change but so unprepared.

I rode the elevator to the tenth floor. The heat was on full blast in my room, making my skin sticky. I unzipped my coat and tossed it on my bed.

The room was a long rectangle. Twin beds against opposite walls and desks lined up to each one. The layout made the middle of the room feel like a runway from the episodes of *Drag Race* Steven had forced me to watch. After we settled our differences last year, he'd given me a major Rupaul crash course.

A shared wardrobe lived next to the front door. At the opposite end of the rectangle, just past my desk, was a bathroom tucked in the corner.

I glanced at Josh's side of the room; it was already a mess. His suitcase was on his bed, unzipped. His clothes scattered around as if someone had burglarized his side.

I sat on my bed, feeling the bounce of the springs. It was so quiet within the cement block walls. I started a text to Caleb,

I made it back, but didn't hit send. I deleted the words, then swiped to text Dad instead.

ME

Hey, Dad, I made it back. I'm in my room now.

DAD

I'm glad. How was the flight?

ME

It felt longer than it was. I tried to read, but it was hard to focus.

The door popped open, making me jump. Josh walked in, holding an assortment of snacks from the vending machine down the hall. His black-rimmed glasses reflected every light, and his dreadlocks were pulled back with an elastic band. I knew the chip bags would end up scattered around the floor by Josh's bed, and I'd have to be the one to pick them up, but he was a welcomed sight after a rocky Christmas break.

"Oh, hey dude," he said with a sprawled smile of bright teeth.

"Hey."

Josh strolled to his bed. The bags of chips rained down from his arms onto his clothes. "Hungry?"

"Actually, yeah, kinda," I said.

The dining halls closed at 9 p.m., so the vending machines became our cheapest option.

Josh pointed to each bag. "I got Smartfood, Doritos, Funyuns, and Sunchips."

"Funyuns, always."

Josh removed the elastic from his hair, whipped around, and tossed me the yellow bag. His locks twirled with him like a dancing octopus.

The smell of onion powder greeted me as I tore open the bag. The artificial flavor against my tongue made my stomach growl for more.

Josh threw his suitcase on the floor and kicked it under the bed. He plopped down on his clothes, Doritos in hand, and pushed himself against the white cinderblock wall.

Shoving two chips into his mouth, Josh asked, "How was break?"

"It was okay," I said between crunches.

"That's it? That's all you're gonna give me?"

I shrugged. "I've had better. How was yours?"

"It was pretty dope." Josh slid off his bed and walked to the bathroom. He didn't shut the door, so I heard him peeing while he talked. "It was good to see my friends again. Stayed up late, phished a little."

"I didn't peg you as the fishing type."

Josh chuckled. "No, you rookie. Phishing, with a P H. This guy had been fucking with my friend's sister, like stalking her and shit, so we phished him through an email scheme to get some personal information, hand him some ransomware, and lock him out of his own accounts."

"Sounds illegal?"

"We didn't really do anything to him, just wanted to freak him out."

I grinned. "So you did the same thing you do here, but in Chicago?"

The toilet flushed. "Hey, you can't say I'm not consistent." The faucet turned on. "What did Caleb get you? Anything good?"

My right hand was wrist-deep in the Funyun's bag. "No." I stared at the silver ring on my finger, and a knot pulled in my stomach. Did it even matter anymore? I hopped off my bed, opened my desk drawer, and tossed the ring inside. "We aren't big on getting each other gifts." Saying the words made my chest tight. "Got some clothes from my dad, though." I sat back in my original spot.

Josh walked from the bathroom and dried his hands on his pants. "Same. My mom gets me socks and underwear every year. I have some packs I haven't opened yet if you need any."

"I'm good, thanks."

Josh shot me a look. "A black man's socks and underwear aren't good enough for you?" He smiled.

I laughed. "Shut up. Toss me the Sunchips."

Josh threw the bag at me like shooting a basketball into the hoop. I ripped it open and inhaled three chips at once.

"It must've been nice to spend time with Caleb, though. I know the distance has been hard for you guys," Josh said.

My mind replayed the last thing I said to Caleb before returning to New York, making me feel sick. I put the Sunchips down. I didn't want to talk about Caleb anymore. "Did you meet up with that girl from Reddit you were talking to?"

Josh picked his clothes up and haphazardly folded them. "I did," he said.

I playfully mimicked his tone from earlier. "That's it? That's all you're gonna give me?"

"I took her out for coffee. She was cute."

I grinned. "And?"

Josh looked over his shoulder at me. "Okay, it was bad."

My brow perked. "What, why? How?"

"I have to stop dating people like me."

"Computer nerds?"

Josh grimaced, then shouted, "Yes! This happens every time I meet a girl online. I bring my computer to the date, and she brings hers. Then we sit there, not really talking at all."

I threw myself into a lying position and laughed. "Maybe your first step should be leaving your laptop at home?"

Josh sighed. "But it's like my armor. Without it, I'm just Clark Kent." I stared blankly. Josh squinted. "...Clark Kent as in Superman's alias?"

I scoffed. "I know that!" I didn't know that.

Josh held a Dorito in front of his face to examine. "Once my eyes are on the screen, it's hard to look away. Online, I'm invincible. Offline, I'm invisible."

I propped myself on my elbow. "Josh, that's so not true. You're funny and handsome. Who doesn't love a nerd? I'm dating—" The words caught in my throat. I shook the thought from my head. "Maybe you're right, though. Maybe you should open up the girl pool a little more."

"Please don't say 'girl pool' ever again. It's creepy."

A laugh pushed from my stomach for the first time in a while. Joking with Josh made me forget everything back home, but it didn't last long. My laughter trickled off as I lay there staring at the ceiling.

My body finally catching up to how drained I felt. I reached for my backpack in search of my toothbrush. I'd usually unpack everything as soon as I returned to my room, but I didn't have the drive. It took all my energy just to leave my bed.

I stared at myself as I brushed. My hair was far from the buzz cut I was used to. I'd let it grow since graduation. It stuck out in every direction on top. When my hair was longer, it was a calmer orange, more like a burnt Cheeto than a fresh one. I closed my eyes, feeling the phantom brush of Caleb's hand through my hair on Christmas Eve.

Getting back in bed, I plugged my phone in and checked it one last time. No texts, no missed calls. I stared at the picture on my lock screen. Caleb and I were at the Ferris Wheel at Rocky Lake Park. The lights Caleb had hung up made our faces blue. I smiled at the camera, and he kissed me on the cheek.

That night was perfect.

I swiped to the settings and changed the lock screen background to a generic firework wallpaper. I didn't want to be reminded of everything that happened every time I looked at my phone.

"You okay?" Josh asked. "You look whiter than usual."

"Yeah," I lied and shoved my phone under my pillow. "I'm just wiped. I should sleep. My self-defense class is at 9 a.m. tomorrow."

"Your dad's still making you go to those?"

My head sank into the memory foam. "Yeah. I like doing it, though. They're fun."

"Huh, maybe I should take a few."

I rolled over to face the wall and closed my eyes. "Don't stay up all night talking to girls online."

Josh chuckled. "Okay, Dad."

———

Friday, January 3rd

I stepped out of my usual coffee shop, a little place called The Ivory Den. It was a four-minute walk from my dorm, just on the corner. I'd started drinking a lot more coffee during my first semester, not realizing the energy it took to keep up with college classes. I placed the cup on the edge of a trash can to zip my coat. The air was sharp and had that indescribable smell, hinting at incoming snow.

My self-defense dojo was just on the other side of Washington Square Park. As I passed under the huge marble arch, my pocket vibrated.

Lauren calling.

I stuck the phone to my ear. "Hello?"

"Hey! What's up?"

"Just got an espresso and heading to my class."

"Your classes started already? Mine don't start until next week," Lauren said.

"No, same. This is my self-defense class. The one I keep asking you to come to."

"I know, I know. I keep saying I'll think about it."

"And have you?"

She hesitated. "I'll think about it!"

I laughed. "Oh my god, you're ridiculous."

"I'm freezing my tits off. I hate going from home where it's hot to here where it's literally Winterfell."

"What does that mean?"

"Jesus, you're the only one on the planet that hasn't watched *Game Of Thrones*."

I rolled my eyes. "I'll think about it!" I moved the phone to my other ear and held the warm cup against my lobe to defrost it. As I passed by, I got a weird look from a woman sitting on a bench. I gave her a fake smile and brought my cup back down. "Where are you?"

"Columbus Circle. I need new ballet shoes, so I'm going to Capezio." Lauren's teeth chattered in my ear. "Anyway, I called to ask if you've heard from Steven yet."

"No." I took a sip—the bitter mud warmed my throat. "Why?"

"Oh. I don't know. I was just wondering."

I chuckled. "I thought you were an actress. I'm not convinced."

"Have fun in your class. Talk to you later!" Lauren said before she hung up.

What the hell?

———

The dojo was on the second floor of a duplex on Mercer Street. The building was old and had no buzzer; the front door was just always open. Nothing except a barbershop occupied the first floor, where one bald man worked.

Everything in the space was beige and glossy: shiny wood paneling on the walls, polished wood floors, and a sparkling staircase led to the second floor, where Yun Tae Kwon Do resided. The dojo reminded me of a stuffy doctor's office with its rubber smell and cramped space.

Every step creaked like I could fall through at any moment. I downed the rest of my espresso and tossed the cup in the bin at the top.

The dojo was bright from the surrounding windows. It had the advantage of being a corner building, allowing the sun to cascade over the red floormats. An office and two small changing rooms sat opposite the dojo across the small hallway. I changed into sweatpants and a tank top, then tossed everything into a locker. Usually, students wore uniforms, but our class was the only self-defense class for people who weren't Tae Kwon Do students. We learned street-level defense techniques rather than the complicated forms and kicks of Tae Kwon Do. The entire class was made up of east-side moms in yoga pants, taking an hour off from their kids. I mostly kept to myself, giving a smile or wave here and there. I wished Lauren would come with me.

The back of the dojo was where all the equipment lived. A punching bag, pads of all sizes, sparring gear, and rubber weapons. My class didn't touch any of that stuff. That was saved for the Tae Kwon Do students.

Our instructor entered the room and bowed at the Korean and American flags above the windows. "Alright, let's line up everyone." Master Jason Yun was tall and handsome. A man in his forties whose hair was starting to gray around his temples. An instructor who preferred his students to call him by his first name. Jason was the third-generation owner of the dojo and made a living teaching martial arts. According to the dojo's website, he studied Tae Kwon Do his entire life.

We started every class with stretching and breathing exercises before moving on to a few punching combos that got our blood pumping. Over the last few classes, we learned how to stop incoming attacks, take someone down, and get out of chokeholds—all things I'd learned in my class back home. But Jason had something different in mind that day.

"Today's lesson may seem a bit extreme." Jason walked to the back of the dojo. "But it's something we've been working toward." He grabbed a rubber handgun off the wall and spun it around as he returned to the front of the class. "Today, I will teach you a useful skill. One that most of you will never need. But if the situation arises, you'll want to know how to take a gun from someone." I swallowed a lump in my throat. "Landon, please join me so I can demonstrate."

A familiar pit grew in my stomach. *Say no. No thanks.* I looked at Jason but felt all the eyes on me. The public pressure pushed me forward.

"Hand, please," Jason said. I raised my right hand with my palm face up. "Have you ever held a gun before?"

My heart beat faster as flashbacks of prom night strobed through my head.

"Yes," I whispered.

"Good." Jason placed the gun in my hand, and my fingers wrapped around the handle. "This is only rubber, but it has the exact weight of a full-size Glock seventeen nine-millimeter handgun. I want you to point it at my head."

My jaw tightened. "Maybe someone else should—"

"It's okay. It's the point of the exercise."

My mouth went dry, and I did as I was told. My hand trembled. Feeling the gun's weight transported me back to my kitchen, watching Dan pummel my boyfriend to a bloody pulp. I blinked rapidly, attempting to return my focus to Jason.

"Perfect," Jason said. "Now, if the person is holding the gun in their right hand, you'll also want to use your right hand for this technique. If it's in their left hand, use your left." Jason slowly moved his right hand under the outside of my wrist so the backs of our hands touched. "You want to use your open hand as a brace against their wrist. When your arm moves, your body should also move out of the way of the gun, like this." He stepped to his right and explained the rest of the routine. He'd done everything slowly so we could study his movements before stepping back again. "This should all be one fluid move."

Jason showed the move in real-time, and it was lightning-fast. He'd taken the gun away from me within a millisecond. It made me wonder if he'd ever done it in real life, and if he had, was it that fast and that easy?

"I'll let all of you try it, and we'll go through the movements again. Pair up." Jason motioned for his assistant teacher, Crystal, an experienced mixed martial arts fighter, to come in. Crystal passed out rubber guns to each two-person team.

Jason continued, "We'll practice with it in each hand, but let's start with the gun in the right."

It was my turn to try to take the gun from *him*. The pit in my stomach boiled.

"We'll take it slow," Jason said with a smile.

He raised the gun to my head, and my stomach exploded. I clenched my eyes, and my body jerked backward.

"Landon, are you alright?" Jason asked.

I regained my focus. *It's not a real gun. Grow some balls.*

"Landon?"

My eyes popped open. "Yeah. I'm fine."

"Okay. Let's try it again."

I stood up straight and calmed my breath, but I could feel my neck pulsating.

Jason quickly raised the barrel to my face.

"No!" I screamed as I ducked away. The room fell silent. I opened my eyes to all the moms staring at me. With the embarrassment too much to handle, I sprinted from the room back to my locker.

They're gonna think I'm a freak. I ripped my coat from the shelf and sat on the bench in the middle of the room. *I can't go back in, not after that.* The thought of telling my dad I'd quit my self-defense class made me sweat.

Jason knocked on the doorframe, and his voice filled the small room. "Hey. Okay if I sit with you?"

I stared at the floor. "Sure."

He straddled the bench and looked at me. "That's not the first time someone pointed a gun at you, is it?"

The embarrassment crept up my neck again. "It's the first time someone's pointed a fake one at me," I said. "Feels the same, though."

"I'm sorry," Jason said. "That was insensitive of me. I want this dojo to feel like a safe, controlled environment."

"It's okay. You didn't know."

"But I should've made a point to ask if you were okay with the demonstration. I apologize."

I pulled my backpack over my shoulder and stood. "It's okay. I'm just gonna go home."

Jason interlocked his fingers. "I think it's important that you stay, Landon."

"You want me to freak out in front of the whole class again?"

"I have other, less triggering methods I can teach you. If you stay, I think we can make some progress."

I squeezed the bridge of my nose. "I don't know."

Jason stood. "Okay, how about I email you a training video? Much less pressure. And we can talk about the technique in the future. Is that okay?"

"Yeah." I shrugged. "That seems cool." I still wasn't convinced I'd come back. I didn't need my trauma exposing itself to strangers a second time.

"Perfect. I'll send it when I have a moment this week."

I nodded. "See ya."

I was halfway down the stairs, slipping my coat on, when Jason called after me. I looked over my shoulder to see him lingering at the top.

"I know someone if you ever need to talk things out. Think about it."

"Yeah, thanks," I said, hopping off the last step and out the door.

Jason sounded like my dad, who'd been asking me to see a therapist since everything happened. I said I didn't need one. A self-defense class was the compromise.

The cold air refreshed my lungs. I could breathe again. If I never saw a gun for the rest of my life, I'd be more than happy. I took off my bag and shuffled through it to find my phone. I had an unread text.

STEVEN

Call me!

I dialed Steven as I walked toward the park. The pulse in my neck finally calmed.

Steven's voice greeted me. "Hey, girl!"

"Hey, how are you?"

"I'm good. Whatcha up to?"

"Oh, you know, I just embarrassed myself in front of my entire self-defense class."

"Oh god, did you rip again? I told you to stop wearing swishy pants from Target."

I desperately wished I'd ripped my pants. I had a feeling the east-side moms would've enjoyed that scene more. "Don't really want to talk about it."

"You're okay, though, right?"

Not in the slightest. "I'm fine."

"Good! Now you can guess what I'm doing!"

"Jerking off to Harry Styles?"

Steven gasped. "He wishes!"

I switched the phone to my other ear and shoved my numb hand into my pocket. "Then what could it possibly be?"

"I'm booking a flight to New York!"

"For what?"

"Do you honestly think Lauren and I forgot your birthday?"

Fuck, I forgot my birthday. My dad and I celebrated with dinner before I left, so it felt like my birthday had come and gone.

"You only turn nineteen once, so we're going out tomorrow night!" Steven's mom was a flight attendant for JetBlue, which meant he could get any domestic flight he wanted for free. So, for him, booking a last-minute flight was cake.

"You really don't have to do that," I said.

"Oh, it's already booked, babe."

I chuckled. "Okay, when do you get in?"

"Nine, tomorrow morning. Text me your address, and I'll get an Uber there."

"Jesus, that's so early."

"I'm bringing you a special birthday present too! Gotta go. Love ya!"

"Wait, what? What does that mean?"

Steven had already hung up. I shoved the phone in my pocket and shook my head. How fucked up was I that I'd forgotten my own birthday? *Idiot.*

I was looking forward to doing nothing all weekend. I was gonna go over my new class schedule and maybe even read a book at The Ivory Den. Now, it was up to me to keep Steven entertained for two days.

Where is he gonna sleep? What could the birthday present be?

Steven knew what happened between Caleb and me, so he wouldn't bring him along. At least, I hoped he wouldn't. But Steven liked to play matchmaker. Knots formed in my gut. He wouldn't try to fix things between me and Caleb, right?

TWO
TEXAS

Seven Months Ago

I opened my eyes to a ticking clock on the wall in front of Caleb's bed. Barbra Streisand's face stared down at me with the second hand ticking around her. The picture was black and white. It looked custom-made and hand-painted, except it wasn't very good. It looked like something from a BuzzFeed article titled 'Top Ten Worst Portrait Tattoos.' The thought of her watching us while we slept gave me the creeps.

The smell of bacon practically lifted me out of bed. I collected my shorts, slipped into them, and then picked through Caleb's closet for a tank top.

My boyfriend's nightstand was usually a mess, and that day wasn't different. A shimmer distracted me from pulling on the tank. The key from Caleb's tin picture box—the one he showed me the night before my story about Caleb accidentally leaked, which led to my accidental outing—sat atop a stack of old magazines. I reached for it, but Caleb snuck behind me and wrapped his arms around my stomach.

"Please tell me you're coming to breakfast without a shirt," Caleb said as he kissed my neck. "You know this body drives me crazy."

His lips tickled me. I snuggled into him. "Not gonna happen."

Caleb's hands ran up to my chest and down my torso. "What're you trying to do to me then?"

"Maybe you'll find out later." I turned in his arms and planted a kiss. Caleb's forehead rested on mine, and he smiled. I gently touched his eyebrow. He'd finally gotten the stitches removed.

"The doctor said the scar will always be there."

"It's hot."

"But people are gonna think I shaved a line in my eyebrow to look cool," Caleb said.

"You look cool no matter what, so—" I touched my ear, feeling the small divot left by the whizzing bullet from Dan's gun.

Caleb smirked. "You hungry?"

"Always." I pulled my shirt on, and Caleb led me out of the room by my hand.

Caleb and Parker had officially taken residence in Miguel's two-bedroom condo. It was a safer environment for Parker and closer to his school.

Parker was friendly enough to forfeit his spot in the full-size bed when I came over to spend the night, or Caleb pulled the big brother card and didn't give him a choice. I felt awful every time, but Parker said he didn't mind the couch. I made a point never to stay over two nights in a row to save the little guy from the itchiness of the velvet.

Miguel's room was across from Caleb's, and a small bathroom was at the end of the short hallway. The kitchen was only a few feet in the opposite direction. It was big enough to fit a round table with four chairs. A half-wall separated the dining space from the living area. Unfortunately, the half-wall was just another shelf for Barbra memorabilia to live.

I sat at an empty plate, and Miguel strutted over with a pan full of scrambled eggs. "The high school graduate finally decides to join us." He scraped eggs onto my plate. Miguel wore a short, silky kimono. A strap tied over his round belly. His wrist jingled with charm bracelets as he fluttered around the kitchen.

I smirked. "I graduated three weeks ago. You don't have to keep calling me that."

"I feel like a proud mother; I'm sorry!" Miguel placed the pan back on the stove. "There's some bacon left under the paper towel, sweetie."

Caleb leaned into the fridge. "Want some orange juice?"

"Sure."

Parker sat beside me with his legs crunched on the chair and his face in a tablet.

I snatched the last stiff pieces of bacon."What're you watching?"

"Someone building a mansion in Minecraft," Parker said flatly.

"Sounds cool."

Caleb placed a cup of orange juice in front of me and sat. "Parker, please wash your plate if you're done."

Parker's eyes peered over the top of the tablet, then paused the video. He groaned, stood, placed the tablet on the seat, and grabbed his plate.

"I'm sorry," I said. "I didn't realize everyone had eaten already."

Caleb shrugged. "It's okay. I know you like to sleep in."

Miguel sat at the table, sipping from a steaming mug. "What time are you guys going to the museum?"

"As soon as Landon's ready," Caleb said.

Parker picked up the tablet, avoiding eye contact with us. He strolled to the living room and plopped himself on the couch with a few huffs. He pressed play on his video and was back in his world.

I whispered to Caleb. "Maybe we should take him."

"He's been grumpy all morning," Miguel said.

Caleb walked to the couch, kneeled in front of Parker, and placed his big hands around Parker's small, bare feet. "We talked about this, kid," Caleb said, moving the tablet away from Parker's face.

Miguel gave me a side-eyed glance and whispered, "It's just a bunch of art. You don't think Parker would be bored?"

"This weekend is different," I whispered. "There's a pop-up film exhibit. A lot of costumes and props are on display, including stuff from Jurassic Park."

"Now it makes sense," Miguel said.

"It's not fair," Parker said to Caleb.

"I promise I'm gonna take you tomorrow, okay? But I need my alone time with Landon, too."

"I know." Parker rolled his eyes. "Respect the dungarees or whatever."

Caleb chuckled. "The boundaries, yes."

Parker crossed his arms. "You owe me a milkshake for this."

"I owe you *two* milkshakes for this." Caleb poked his pinky out. "Deal?"

Parker wrapped his pinky around Caleb's and smiled. "Deal!"

———

Caleb and I parked outside a blocky building—very plain on the outside for being an art museum. It was an hour's drive south from Madison to get to Dallas. I'd been to the museum once during a middle school field trip and was bored by everything. Middle school me didn't appreciate art. My mom was one of the chaperones that year. We'd split up into groups to observe different sections of the museum. Mom's sense of direction was never great. Our group got lost, making us late for lunch with everyone else in the cafe.

A huge banner stretched above the entrance: TRAVELING HOLLYWOOD FILM EXHIBIT NOW OPEN! The T-Rex from Jurassic Park was photoshopped into the left corner of the banner.

I slipped my fingers between Caleb's. Guilt washed over me. "We should've brought Parker. Then you wouldn't have to do the drive twice."

"It's fine. Miguel texted me and said he'd come with us tomorrow. So he can drive."

"I just feel bad seeing Parker's little face all upset."

Caleb stopped to look at me. "Hey, Parker understands that you're moving in a few months. He knows how much it means to me to spend as much time with you as I can. He's fine, I promise." Caleb smiled.

I fell deep into his dimples and kissed him. "I love you."

"I love you more," he said. Caleb grabbed my hand and led me to the front door. "I'm not sure you're fully prepared to see me geek out and tell you every useless fact about movies you've probably never seen."

I groaned playfully. "Can't wait."

We paid for our tickets and moved further into the lobby, where the museum took shape. The room was massive. Even with a herd of elephants parading around, there was enough room for hundreds of people to wonder. The freshly buffed floors reflected every light. Tour guides pointed to paintings sprawled about the room.

Caleb's chin jutted to the large arrow leading to the film exhibit. "It's over here."

The exhibit was expansive and beautifully set up across two giant rooms. The chatter noise heightened as we stepped in. The tour was self-guided, so we started at the entrance. Caleb wouldn't let us miss anything.

The first section focused on film development from the early 1900s and how silent films transitioned into talkies. Screens lined the walls, showing different films. Rows of display cases featured costumes and props from popular movies. Caleb teased me for not having seen most of them. He was like a kid in an amusement park, oohing and ahhing over everything he saw.

"Wow, look," Caleb said as we approached a *Wizard of Oz* display case.

"Are those real diamonds?"

"Ruby slippers. Five different pairs were made," Caleb said. "The main ones she wore are in the Smithsonian. These must've been the ones that were stolen."

"Stolen?"

Caleb looked at me with a devilish smirk, unable to contain his excitement for telling me the entire lore of the slippers in the middle of the crowd.

I smiled at him. "How does this stuff stay in your brain?"

"That's a great question." He gave me a peck and moved on.

We came to a *Planet Wars* display case that housed a few costumes from the original films. Caleb touched the cape of a dark costume. "The sequels are better, in my opinion."

It made me smile to see Caleb smile. I imagined how much nerdier he'd be if Parker were there, too. And I'd be in the dark as they talked.

"Did you know..." Caleb started. He was about to hit me with a random movie fact. "In the original movies, they had to put a little person inside that space dog costume? So every time you see him wobbling around, a real person was in there."

"I would've quit on day two. Where do they keep all this stuff when it's not here?"

"Massive warehouses. A lot of studios have 'em. Most of it sits around collecting dust."

"Maybe we should break in and steal some stuff since no one's using it."

Caleb chuckled and wrapped his arm around my shoulders. "Yeah, why not?"

I watched him stare at the display and hoped nothing would change when I left for school. I wanted us to stay the same couple we were at that moment. I knew I'd be a wreck the first week without him, but I told myself it would only be a few months. Then, I'd be back for Christmas to see him. I hoped that would be enough to push me through.

My phone vibrated, and I pulled it from my pocket.

DAD

Will you be home today?

ME

Yeah, we're at the museum in Dallas right now, but I'll be back after. Why?

DAD

Alright, just wanted to talk something over with you.

ME

Oh god, should I be nervous?

DAD

No, son. Have fun. I'll see you soon.

ME

Okay.

I sent him a waving hand emoji and pushed the phone back into my pocket.

Caleb looked over his shoulder. "Everything good?" He'd moved on to the superhero section. A few brownstones and a storefront looked like someone pulled the New York City set from the pages of a comic book. Mannequins in their respective super suits posed in heroic stances around the set.

"Yeah," I said as I joined him. "My dad was just checking in. Who's this?"

We stood in front of a buff mannequin. His armor was yellow, black, and red. A toxic waste symbol beamed at the center of his chest. His cowl looked like a soldier's helmet.

"His name is Biohazard. He was fighting a war when an atomic bomb dropped. He somehow survived it. The radiation gave him bulletproof skin, and he can shoot toxic waste from his hands, among other things." Caleb said.

I looked the costume up and down. "Never heard of him."

Caleb turned to me, his eyes wide and chaotic. "Come on. Astonishing Comics? The ACU?"

"What's the ACU?"

Caleb rubbed a hand down his face. "I literally don't get how this is possible."

"What?" I said with a smirk.

"Where have you been the last five years? There's no way you haven't seen the toys, the commercials, kids wearing the merch?"

I shrugged. "I mean, maybe. I don't know a lot about superheroes."

"Clearly. Maybe you should put down the books and watch some screens."

I laughed. "Said no adult ever."

"I've been trying to give you the best movie education possible. I can't believe we didn't start with the ACU."

I rolled my eyes. "Okay, what the hell is the ACU?"

"Astonishing. Cinematic. Universe," Caleb said slowly, pausing between each word. I stared at him blankly. "It's only one of cinema's most ambitious feats. Five years ago, Biohazard's stand-alone movie came out. It was his origin story and kicked off a connected universe of films, with different superheroes getting their own. And last year, they finally came together for a team-up movie called *The Crusaders*."

"It sounds vaguely familiar."

Caleb sighed, seemingly losing faith in me. "Biohazard ran the team."

I counted with my fingers. "So you had to have seen six movies before seeing the newest one?"

"Ideally, yeah, and that's just *Juncture One*. There's more coming. I just read *Adam Shock* is gonna be the next one, so we gotta get you caught up 'cause he's my favorite."

"And why's that?"

"'Cause Adam Shock is gay." Caleb winked at me.

A gay superhero? And he's getting his own movie? That might be too much for the people of Madison, Texas.

"Sounds like a lot of work," I said.

Caleb playfully grabbed me by the ears and kissed my lips. "You're so lucky you're cute."

"Or what?" I said through my smile.

"You don't wanna know," Caleb said, wiggling his eyebrows before pulling me to the brownstone's stoop.

If I closed my eyes, it felt like we were in the city. "Think this is what New York is like?"

Caleb laughed. "Oh, absolutely. If you're not neighbors with Biohazard, I'm not coming to visit."

I sat on a step, next to a collection of metal trash cans. "So, you're gonna come visit me then?"

Caleb leaned against the stoop's railing. "Of course I will."

"How often?"

He hesitated, scratching the back of his head. "As often as I can. But we both know flights aren't cheap. My tips at Lucky's barely keep Parker and me fed. I'd be screwed if Miguel charged me rent."

I had to start getting used to the idea I wouldn't see Caleb as much. But it made my heart stop every time I thought about it.

"Hey." Caleb sat next to me. "We can Facetime every day. Or call, text, whatever you want."

"Promise?"

Caleb held out his pinky. "I promise."

"Save your pinky promises for Parker. I don't want to use them all up."

Caleb smiled and dropped his hand to my thigh before moving in for another kiss. I pictured us in New York, sitting on the steps of our own brownstone where we lived with Parker and two dogs. I would be a famous writer, working on my fiftieth book. Caleb would be a big-shot movie producer. The money wouldn't matter because we would have more than we could ever spend. No more relying on tips from Luckys to scrape by. That was the dream.

The last thing we saw at the exhibit was the enormous T-Rex head used in the first *Jurassic Park*. It felt as big as two monster trucks put together. We could walk around it to see it from every angle.

"It's crazy to think people controlled this thing," I said as I touched its rubbery skin. Caleb made a quick roar in my direction, making me cringe.

———

"Parker is gonna love that," I said, pulling out of our parking space. "I can see his face now. You have to take a bunch of pictures."

"Yeah," Caleb said. "He's gonna go nuts over the T-Rex. Maybe I can print some for you to hang in your dorm. I can put some in our picture box, too."

"Were you guys looking at the pictures of your dad again?" I pressed the gas onto the main road.

Caleb's brows scrunched. "No, why?"

"Oh, 'cause I saw your dad's key on your nightstand."

Caleb's eyes shifted to the road. "I've been looking at it a lot, I guess. It's been killing me lately."

"What do you mean?"

Caleb rubbed his head. "It bugs me. Did he leave it on purpose or drop it while packing his bags?"

I felt bad for Caleb, knowing he'd probably never get the answers he wanted. I didn't have much faith that he'd figure it out.

———

Dad was watching TV when I finally got home. I walked straight to the fridge, grabbed the apple juice, and brought it to the counter.

"How was the museum?" Dad asked.

I grabbed a glass from the cupboard and poured the juice. "It was awesome. Caleb loved it."

"Did Parker and Miguel enjoy it?"

"Oh, it was just Caleb and me. He's taking Parker tomorrow." I took a big gulp. The cold juice made me shiver.

"Was he driving Miguel's car again? I swear I'm gonna kill that kid. He doesn't have a license."

"I drove. I only let him drive when he goes back to Miguel's."

"Still, he could get in a lot of trouble." Dad looked tired. With elections getting closer, his campaign hours got longer.

"I told him to go slow and take the back roads. He'll be fine." I put the juice back in the fridge, placed my glass in the sink, and leaned against the counter to check my phone.

Dad stood and joined me in the kitchen. "Speaking of Caleb, I wanted to talk to you about something."

I turned my body toward him, still looking at my phone. "If this is the birds and the bees talk, I can save you some time—"

"You get your smart-ass attitude from your mother. Put the phone away."

My gaze shot over the top of my phone before slipping it back into my pocket.

"I think it would be good for you and Caleb to take self-defense classes."

I crossed my arms. "Are you serious? Why?"

Dad's face twisted a little. "Why? You know why. After everything that happened, I think it would be good for the both of you if something like that happens again."

My jaw tightened, thinking about prom night. "Dad, come on, that was like a one-in-a-million deal."

"It might've gone differently if—"

"If what? Dan had a gun, Dad. What should I have done?"

"That's something you could learn in a self-defense class."

I would've preferred the birds and the bees talk. Dad lived in a lot of what-ifs. He contemplated them all the time. "Why don't you just teach us stuff you learned in boot camp or something?" I asked.

"Jesus, that was so long ago I can barely remember it."

"Thanks, but no thanks. Plus, Caleb is still recovering. I don't think he's in the best shape to be thrown around." I started for the stairs.

"Landon, please. It would just make me feel better since you refuse to see a therapist. Give your old man a break, huh?"

I stood on the first stair, turned toward him, and leaned my shoulder on the wall. I felt awful. Dad had been a nervous wreck since prom, and I was just trying to forget. "Fine, I'll do it."

His face flipped, looking virtually triumphant. "Thank you."

"Was this another one of Grace's ideas?"

"No," Dad said. "She's not on the team anymore."

My head tilted, and I stepped back into the kitchen. "What? Why?"

Dad leaned his elbows on the island counter and put his face in his hands.

A Grinch-style grin came over my face before I rushed my dad, laughing. I pushed his shoulder. "I freaking knew it! What did I say?! I knew she was flirting with you after your speech at the church that day!"

He ran a hand through his hair and looked at me with a smile and red cheeks. "You were right, okay?" He raised his hands in defense. "I was an idiot for not seeing it."

I sat on the stool next to him, feeling validated. "So now what?"

"We hired someone else," Dad said, "a straight-laced kind of guy. He's got an aggressive work ethic and graduated from Duke. He's done good work so far."

"Think he'll fall in love with you, too?"

Dad laughed and rustled my hair, pushing my head away. "Smart-ass."

THREE

NEW YORK CITY

Saturday, January 4th

The sun was bright as I stood on the sidewalk outside my dorm. I looked like I'd just woken up from an all-night bender—wearing sweatpants, sneakers, and my winter coat over a tank top with my hood and sunglasses on. I had grabbed a Red Bull from the small store in the lobby and chugged it before waiting in the cold. Steven texted me, saying he'd be at my dorm in ten minutes. It was more like twenty.

A black sedan pulled up to the sidewalk, and my heart skipped a beat.

Please don't let Caleb be in the car with him.

The back door opened, and Steven fluttered out, holding a large tote bag around his arm with several mugshots of the same woman printed on the side. I strained my neck, trying to peek through Steven's door. I let my breath go when I realized he was the only passenger.

"Thanks, girl," Steven said to the driver before closing the door. He turned to me and squealed. "Oh my god, oh my god! My love!"

Steven rushed me, almost tackling me to the ground with a hug. "Why are you dressed like a stalker?"

"Why is your hair purple?"

"Um, excuse me? This is Lavender; there's a difference." We laughed and hugged again. Steven crossed his arms. "Fuck, it's cold here."

"I told you to bring a heavy coat."

"This is heavy!"

I raised an eyebrow. His denim jacket was far from heavy. "Let's go inside. Maybe Josh has an extra coat you can borrow while you're here."

Steven gave his ID to the woman at the front desk and signed his name as a visitor. I swiped us through the turnstiles and rounded the corner to the elevators. I expected Steven to show up with a giant suitcase, thinking he would want options.

"You packed light. I'm surprised."

"It's only one night. Sometimes, all a girl needs is her toothbrush."

I shook my head as we stepped into the elevator. "Who is that on your bag?"

Steven checked his hair in the reflection of the metal buttons. "Our Lord and Savior, Lindsay Lohan."

"Why does she have so many mugshots?"

"What, you've never made a mistake in your life?"

I chuckled. "I didn't say that."

"I will not allow you to judge Queen Lindsay in this elevator."

"You're ridiculous."

Steven followed me out, watching a shirtless guy walk by. "Is every guy in New York cute?"

I glanced over my shoulder as I unlocked my door. "Maybe you'll get lucky while you're here."

"That would be ideal." Steven gasped as we entered my room, which felt ninety degrees warmer. Most of it was a mess, thanks to Josh. "Oh my God, you didn't tell me you were living in squalor."

I smiled and proudly held my arms out. "It's home away from home."

Steven brushed the dirty clothes out of the way with his feet. "I didn't think you were this messy."

"That's Josh's side of the room. It gets annoying, but he's a good guy."

Steven placed his bag on my bed. The covers were still disheveled. "Where is Joshy poo?"

I took my coat off and placed it on the back of my desk chair. "Probably getting food. For a guy who's up half the night, he doesn't need much sleep. He's always up early."

Steven looked out our tenth-floor window. "I can fall in love with a night owl. Is he straight?"

I laughed. "Yes, one hundred percent."

"The hot ones are always straight," Steven said.

Josh walked through the door, biting an apple as if on cue. Steven whipped around and gave him the once over.

"Oh, hey," Josh said. He wiped his hand on his pants and held it out. "I'm Josh."

"This is my friend from home, the one I texted you about. Steven," I said as they shook hands.

"*Very* nice to meet you," Steven said.

Josh smiled. "You too." He sat on his bed, grabbed his laptop resting on his pillow, and opened it. "What brings you to town?" Josh didn't look up from his screen. He could converse with people and never look away from his computer.

"This little nugget." Steven wrapped his arm around my waist. "It's his birthday today."

"Holy shit!" Josh said. Apparently, he *could* look away from his screen if it were shocking enough. "I had no idea! Why didn't you tell me?"

I shrugged. "It didn't seem like a big deal."

"Of course it is. Happy birthday, my dude," Josh said, holding out his fist. I bumped it. Then he went back to looking at his screen. "Do you have plans?"

"No," I said, but Steven's voice was on top of mine.

"Yes!"

I shot Steven a confused look. "We do?"

"Lauren and I had it planned out already."

"Of course you two did." I sat on my bed and leaned against the cinderblock wall.

"I asked Tasha if she wanted to come," Steven said as he sat in my desk chair. "But she couldn't justify spending the money for one night."

"I don't blame her," I said.

Josh pulled our attention away from each other. "What's the plan then?"

"Well, we kind of have a history with gay clubs. And Landon hasn't been to one here yet."

I squinted at Steven. "I haven't had a reason to."

"Until now," Steven said with a smirk in my direction.

"Cool," Josh said. "Still got that fake ID you bought last semester?"

"Haven't used it yet, but yeah, it's in my drawer," I said.

"Wow," Steven said with a smile. "Josh, you're everything I wanted for him in a roommate." He grabbed my foot and shook it. "I'm so proud of you!" I rolled my eyes and chuckled. "So," Steven said, turning back to Josh. "Are you coming out with us?"

"I can't," Josh said.

Steven gave an exaggerated frown. "Afraid of gay clubs?"

Josh's eyebrows scrunched at his screen. "No, I've been to plenty of gay clubs," he said, causing Steven's mouth to fall open. Josh closed his computer and hopped off his bed with it. "I just already have plans. Sorry, Landon."

"No worries!" I said.

"I'll catch you guys later." Josh strutted to the door and tossed his apple core in the trash. "If I don't see you, have fun."

Steven and I said 'thanks' at the same time.

"Oh, actually," I called out. Josh popped his head back into the room. "Do you have an extra coat Steven can wear for the day?"

"Yeah, just go through the closet."

"Thanks, babe!" Steven said before Josh shut the door behind him. "Where does he go this early?"

"He's probably going to code or something with his friends," I said.

"Code what?"

I thought about it for a second and shrugged. "I don't know. You should hear him on the phone. It's like he speaks a different language most of the time."

Steven hopped to his feet, jumped onto my bed, and leaned on the wall beside me with his phone in hand. "Let's FaceTime Lauren!"

I didn't have time to respond as he was already calling her.

Lauren answered. Her eyes drooped, and her nose was red. She coughed, sounding like a frog. It was dark in her room, and she was still lying in bed.

"Hey, girl!" Steven said.

I just waved.

"Hey, guys," Lauren said with a husky tone.

I squinted at the screen. "Are you okay?"

"No. I woke up feeling so sick."

"Oh baby, noooo," Steven said.

Lauren pulled the blanket tighter around her. "Yeah, I've already thrown up twice. First, I get the shivers, and the next second, I'm sweating. I might have to go see a doctor."

"I'm devastated," Steven said. "I was looking forward to dancing our asses off."

"I know," Lauren sniffled. "I'm so disappointed. But, Landon, you have to show him around for me, okay?"

"I'm on the job," I said with a salute.

"Okay, get some rest, girlie," Steven said, blowing a kiss at the screen. "Keep us updated."

Lauren gave a weak smile. "I will. I want to know everything that happens tonight, please. It might just keep me alive."

"Of course," Steven said. "Love yoouuu!"

"Love you both," Lauren said.

We waved at her until she hung up. Steven and I were shoulder to shoulder, and we both turned our heads simultaneously.

Steven wiggled his eyebrows. "Looks like it's just you and me. The jock and the jock-strap."

"Why am I nervous now?"

Steven slapped me on the shoulder and slid off the bed before opening the closet door. I suddenly pictured a mound of Josh's trash tumbling out, crushing Steven like an avalanche, but the closet was relatively in order.

"I hope there's something cute in here."

I flopped onto my pillow and watched him. "So, where are we going tonight?"

"We are popping our New York club cherry at the gayest bar." Steven moved hangers from side to side as if he were at a department store. "Stonewall." After a moment of silence, he poked his head from behind the closet door—it didn't look attached to his body. It just floated. "In the sixties, Stonewall is where—"

"I know what Stonewall is."

Steven stepped back and clutched his nonexistent pearls. "Well, excuse me. Sports boy knows his gay history, apparently." He went back to moving hangers. "I thought it'd be the perfect place."

As Steven shopped in our closet, I wondered what Caleb would think about me going to a gay club; it'd be my first time without him. It was hard to fathom. What if I saw someone attractive there? What if someone wanted to talk to me, buy me a drink, or ask for my number? It felt weird.

"Oh!" Steven yipped. I heard some rustling before he stepped back, wearing a puffy black coat that looked filled with air. "Insulated *and* cute. It's perfect."

I smiled. "So, where do you want to go?"

"I don't care. I'll go anywhere."

I sat up, thinking. "How 'bout my favorite spot in Central Park?"

"Sound's cute." Steven smiled and zipped the coat over his denim jacket for extra warmth.

I nodded and stood. As I slipped my coat on, the breeze caught some pictures I'd taped to the wall above my desk. I stared at a picture of Parker from the film exhibit. He was pretending to run away from the T-Rex head. His face contorted with fake fear. Right next to it was the picture of Caleb driving the Delorean. I wondered what they were doing—maybe playing video games together or watching a movie. I missed them so much. It felt like a hole burning through my chest.

"You ready?" Steven asked, pulling my attention.

"Yeah," I whispered, turning on my heels.

———

We took the A train to 59th Street and then transferred to the 1. It was noticeably older than the A train, and the seats were grimier. We got off at 72nd Street. The cold was as sharp as a straight razor, cutting at our cheeks. I clutched my coat closer to my face.

The Upper West Side was somewhere I hoped to afford to live one day. It was a perfect blend of residential and bustling. I'm sure someone would disagree with me, but something about it felt special. Everyone looked kind. People walked their dogs, and joggers navigated around pedestrians while foodies dined in quaint restaurants.

Steven and I walked east on 72nd Street toward the park. I pointed out all the restaurants I wanted to try and what buildings I thought looked cool. Nothing trumped The Dakota, an ornate castle-esque building on the corner of West 72nd and Central Park West. During my first semester, I wandered the city on my days off. When I discovered The Dakota, I had no idea of its fame. Seeing people taking pictures piqued my interest enough to google the address.

I stopped at the entrance. A guard stood watch in a booth, sheltering from the cold. Two huge black lanterns hung on either side of a tall, intricately carved gate. I took it all in, wishing I could see what it looked like inside. Steven seemed unsure of what we were looking at.

I glanced at him as people cut around us. "You know who John Lennon is, right?"

"Yeah," Steven said, staring at the gate. He started singing, "Aaaall of meee—"

I laughed. "No, stop, stop. That's John *Legend*. John *Lennon* was a member of The Beatles. He sang the song 'Imagine.'"

"Oh, THAT'S who John Lennon is?"

My eyes widened. "Wait. Is this happening?"

"Huh?"

"I know something in pop culture that you don't?" I wanted to skip down the sidewalk with glee. "Me? Landon Griffin finally gets to spout some pop culture knowledge? This *never* happens!"

Steven laughed. "Alright, bitch, congrats. Spill it then."

I shook my head, looking up at the top floor. It felt like I was embodying Caleb, spouting out nuggets of trivia about John Lennon and his murder that took place just beyond the gate in front of us. "People flooded the street to pay tribute to him when he died. I should show you the pictures. It's crazy."

Steven didn't show much interest. We moved across the street into the park, where I showed Steven Strawberry Fields, a memorial for Lennon. We listened to a guy sing "Imagine" while strumming his guitar before we moved on. A path to the left led deeper into the park. We kept walking until we hit the lake.

"Where are you taking me?" Steven asked as I led him down a dirt path.

"It's right here."

We emerged from the dead foliage at a white, square gazebo called Ladies Pavilion. It was a popular spot for wedding photos. Just past the pavilion was a huge mound of rocks. Steven and I climbed to the top and looked across the surrounding lake.

"Okay, this is incredible," Steven said.

"Isn't the skyline amazing?" We could see all the tall buildings occupying midtown. Steven started taking pictures. "I came here a lot after I discovered it. It's a perfect place to sit, read, or think, ya know? It's even better in the fall when the leaves are changing."

"Yeah," Steven said. "You don't get this in Madison." The water was starting to freeze over. "Ever miss Texas?"

"Sometimes." I pushed my hands into my pockets. "I miss my dad. I feel bad I left him there alone."

"I'm sure he's too busy to miss you back. He's got a county to run."

We laughed.

"You're right. He's a busy guy. What about you? Could you see yourself here?"

Steven shot me a look. "Are you kidding? Moving away from all the racist, bigoted hillbillies sounds like a dream. Maybe tonight, I'll find myself a sugar daddy who'll move me into The Dakota."

My phone vibrated, and I took it out. My stomach fell to my feet as I looked at the screen.

Holy shit.

Steven looked at me as if he'd read my mind. "What is it?"

"Parker's calling me."

Steven hopped off of a rock and moved closer. "Answer it."

I glanced at him, feeling uneasy, before I hit the green button. "Hello?"

"Hi, Landon!" Parker's voice sang from the speaker.

I turned away from Steven and walked off the rocks, stepping onto the soft dirt that led into the water. "Hey, bud. What's up?"

"I wanted to call and wish you a happy birthday!"

I smiled. "Thank you. How'd you know it was today?"

"I heard Caleb talking about it."

He's still talking about me? I heard Caleb's muffled voice get clearer in the background.

"I wanted to say happy birthday to Landon," Parker said away from the phone.

"You're not supposed to be using your phone right now," I heard Caleb say. "Give it to me, please."

"Gotta go, Landon. I bought too many games with Caleb's card, so he took my phone away for the weekend." Parker said.

"Okay, buddy. Talk to you later!" Then I heard Caleb's raspy voice for the first time since I left Texas.

"Happy birthday, Landon." His tone was as cold as the breeze pushing off the lake. He hung up before I could get a word out. I wanted to walk straight into the water and let hypothermia take me.

Steven was behind me as soon as my phone hit my pocket. "What'd he say?"

"He wanted to say happy birthday."

"Aw, that's cute."

"Caleb caught him, though." I stared at the dirt.

"And?"

"He gave me the flattest happy birthday of all time and hung up."

Steven hugged me. The smooth fabric of his puffy jacket was cold against my chin. I hugged him back. My nose started to run. I didn't want to sniff, because I didn't want Steven to think I was crying.

"I take it you guys still aren't talking?"

"Nope," I said, pulling out of the hug. "That was the first time I've heard from him since leaving his place."

"I hate seeing you like this," Steven said, "but this is exactly why I'm here. We'll have a blast tonight, and Caleb will be the last thing on your mind. I promise."

I smiled. I missed having Steven's energy around. I don't know what I would've done without him after the New Year's party. "You hungry?"

"Starving," Steven said.

"There's this place called Dallas Bar-B-Q. They give you a lot of food, and it's cheap."

Steven's eyes lit up. "Texas BBQ in New York City?"

I laughed. "Not even close, but it's edible."

———

"Hi, Mister Griffin!" Steven shouted from the bathroom. He was applying his face for the night. I'd been on the phone with my dad for five minutes.

"Steven says hi," I said over speakerphone.

"Hello," Dad said, sounding like he was in a tin can.

I was trying on different shirts, staring at myself in the full-length mirror on the back of the closet door.

"What are your plans for the night?" Dad asked.

"Oh, it's gonna be a wild one!" Steven shouted.

Dad huffed. "Should I be worried?"

I snatched the phone from Josh's desk. "No, Dad. It's not gonna be wild. He's just being... Steven."

"Alright." Dad didn't sound convinced. "I put some birthday money in your account, so you guys have fun tonight. Make sure you text me when you're home."

"You'll probably be asleep, old man," I said.

"Hey. I used to get down when I was your age."

"Yeah? You must've had crazy parties at military college."

"We always found a way, trust me," he said. "No drinking and driving, okay?"

"Dad, we take the subway."

"Oh yeah. Well, no drinking and subwaying then."

Steven let out a cackle, which then made me laugh. "Sure, Dad. You got it."

"Alright, I love you."

"Love you too, bye."

Steven popped his head out of the bathroom, his cheeks contoured, and his eyes glittered. "Your dad is so cute."

"Are you almost done in there?"

"Come in. Let me see what you're wearing."

I stepped to the bathroom doorway and stood there awaiting his approval. I wore black skinny jeans and a marbled white T-shirt.

Steven stopped putting on his lipgloss to look at me. "Okay, this is actually a cute shirt. How can we make it gayer?"

I stood still, letting him tug at the fabric. Then he pulled it up halfway, revealing my stomach.

"Maybe we cut it into a crop top."

"Absolutely not," I said, pushing the shirt back down.

"Fine, then let me just—" Steven rolled my sleeves. "Perfect, show off those arms, girl."

"Are you almost done? I need to do my hair."

"Oh, the Queen has arrived! Okay, bitch." Steven plopped his lip gloss into his travel makeup bag and strutted out. He wore skin-tight leather pants and a black crop top with mesh sleeves.

I stared at myself. *Okay, the rolled sleeves do look cute.* My hair was so thick it didn't need any product to do what I wanted. Instead, it required a wet hand to shape it in place.

"OH!"

I flinched. "What now?"

"Your surprise gift!"

I heard rustling before Steven popped through the doorframe and into the tight bathroom. He held a standard pill bottle with no label. Three capsules were inside. The smile on Steven's face was up to no good.

"What is that?"

"Molly," Steven said. "One was for Lauren. And one each for us."

"No thanks." I tried to push past him, but Steven sidestepped, blocking my path.

"It's like a starter kit, low dose for first timers."

"I don't—"

"I remember someone floating to space after two pot brownies."

"That was different," I said.

"*This* is different."

"How do you know?"

"I've done it once," Steven said. "I told you we were gonna have a great time."

"What does it do to you?"

"It just makes everything feel... good. You feel free." Steven gave the bottle a shake and smiled again.

"No thanks, I don't need it."

"Okay," Steven said with a frown as he let me pass. "Can't stop me, though."

I heard him slurp water from the sink while I sat on my bed to tie my shoes.

"Don't forget to grab your ID," Steven called out.

My eyes widened. "Shit, thanks for reminding me!" I moved my desk chair to open the drawer. It was a mess of notebooks and pens. I lifted a folded, loose piece of paper, and my fake ID fell out of it, ricocheting to the floor. I unfolded the paper.

Don't forget about me.
I love you.
- Caleb

I sighed. *How can I?* Caleb was there in everything I did. I folded the note and buried it under as much as possible. I looked up to find Steven had been watching from the bathroom.

"It'll help you forget about him for a while," he said. "I'd never force you to do something you don't want to do of—"

"No, I changed my mind." I closed the drawer, picked up my fake ID, and extended my hand toward Steven. "I'll take it."

"Are you sure?"

"Yeah," I said. Steven fished a pill from the bottle and placed it on my palm. I pinched it between my first finger and thumb, bringing it to eye level. It was a clear capsule filled halfway with white powder. I was nervous, but I trusted Steven enough to believe him when he said it would make me feel free. There was a lot I wanted to feel free from. I popped it in my mouth and bent over the sink to sip from the tap. "When does it start working?"

"I'd give it half an hour," Steven said with a smirk. "This is gonna be fun."

FOUR
TEXAS

Six Months Ago

Caleb smiled at me as we laid the plastic covering over the table in my backyard. Lauren and Steven were in charge of blowing up balloons. Tasha came out of the house looking like she was in a circus. As the previous editor-in-chief of our high school newspaper, she was used to juggling. One arm hugged a big bowl of chips with a smaller bowl of onion dip inside, and the other hand held a stack of paper plates and napkins.

"What?" Tasha asked as she carefully placed the bowl on the table.

I took a napkin from the stack. "You have onion dip in your hair, " I said, holding some of her long curls and dabbing the dip away.

"That's what happens when you make me the chef; I make a mess."

"Making one dip hardly makes you the chef," Steven said, fluttering to us while tying a balloon.

"Do not come for me. I spent hours on that dip."

Lauren chuckled behind Steven.

"It must be so hard to open a jar and pour it into a bowl," Steven said.

Tasha grinned. "I would've taken balloon duty, but we all know you're the best at blowing."

We all laughed.

Steven snapped in the air. "Damn right! I was the best man for the job!"

Caleb put his arm around my shoulders. "Seriously ya'll, thank you for helping out. Parker's never had a real birthday party. So this is special for us."

We all glanced at Parker and his two friends. They were running around the yard, trying to keep a balloon in the air.

"You don't need to thank us," Lauren said with a smile. "He deserves it."

Caleb squeezed me tighter. "It means a lot."

"I'm gonna go grab the other snacks." Tasha turned and headed back inside while Steven and Lauren went back to blowing up balloons to stick to the fence. There were already enough around the yard, but they were determined to blow up the whole pack.

Two weeks ago, Caleb asked my dad if we could have Parker's tenth birthday party in the backyard. Dad became smitten with Parker while they were together in the hospital during Caleb's recovery. *Everyone* fell in love with Parker. I blamed it on his high-pitched laugh. It had a way of charming people's socks off.

The weather couldn't have been more perfect. It had rained the day before, so we were concerned it would carry over, but there wasn't a cloud in the sky. So, I had to put on two layers of sunblock.

I pecked Caleb's cheek. "I'm gonna go get my dad. He said he wanted to make the burgers."

"Alright. I'm gonna call Miguel and see where he is with the cake. He's never on time for anything," Caleb said.

I reached for the sliding door into the living room. The blast of air conditioning chilled the sweat on my skin. Tasha was still in the kitchen, pouring a bag of pretzels into a bowl. I stopped. "Need any help?"

"I think I got it. There are sodas in the fridge, though, if you wanna put them out."

"Yeah, I can do that." I chuckled again, watching her open another bag of chips.

Tasha let her weight drop onto her hip when she looked at me. "Boy, what are you laughing at now?"

"I'm just picturing you as a mom. Doing this for your kid's birthday party."

"Oh hell no," Tasha said, popping a pretzel in her mouth. "I ain't having a kid till I'm retired. Career first, then *maybe* a kid."

My head shook. "Till you're retired? You'll be dried up by then."

"Maybe that'll be a good thing."

The doorbell rang, making us both jump. We busted out laughing as I jogged to the front door. I opened it to a wide-eyed boy in a striped shirt, holding a gift wrapped in newspaper. The boy's mom waved at me from her car. I waved back and invited the boy in. I led him through the kitchen and into the living room. "You can put the gift with the rest on the coffee table." I pointed to the back door. "Parker's outside." The boy hurriedly placed the present down and ran out back.

Tasha grabbed the new bowls of snacks and passed through the living room. "And you picture me as a mom? It feels like you're already there."

"I'm turning into a real housewife."

Tasha raised an eyebrow. "Does it ever feel like that, though?"

I looked at her. "What do you mean?"

"You're eighteen, and you're dating an older guy who essentially has a kid. That's a lot of baggage."

"It's not like I didn't know what I was getting myself into."

"Did you?"

I stared at Tasha for a beat. "Maybe I didn't. But I do now."

Senior year was a blur. Everything was uncharted territory. Caleb coming into my life set off a chain of events that might not have happened otherwise, and Parker was a piece of that complicated puzzle. I loved the kid. I thought of Parker as a bonus, not a hindrance. "It's gotten easier, trust me."

She leaned against the sliding door. "Okay."

"Tasha, I'm fine. Everything's good."

She smiled but seemed unconvinced. "Ya'll are hella cute. I'll give you that."

I watched her struggle to open the door and rushed to help open it. "Have you seen my dad at all?"

"No," Tasha said over her shoulder as she set down the bowls.

I closed the door and started for the stairs. I peeked through Dad's bedroom door—empty. The bathroom door was open, but he wasn't there either. I barreled back down the stairs and through the living room. There was only one place left to look. Outside Dad's office was the only place I could still smell Mom's perfume. I knocked.

"Yeah?"

I opened the door to Dad sitting at his desk. Parker and his friends played in the yard through the window behind him. "You comin' out?"

Dad took his glasses off and placed them on the desk. He wore a navy blue T-shirt that day instead of his usual button-up and tie. "Yeah," he said. "Come in. I want to tell you something."

I left the door cracked and sat in a leather chair across from him. "What's up?"

"I don't mean to take you away from your friends, but I didn't want to say anything until it was official."

My heart raced. *Please don't tell me you're sick too.*

Dad closed his laptop. "And as of two minutes ago, they are."

"Okay..."

"I'm selling the house."

His words slapped me in the face. I slowly nodded, unsure what to say for a minute, as I focused on Parker's laugh piercing the window. "What? Why?"

Dad leaned back in his chair, scratching the weekend stubble on his chin. "Isn't it obvious, Landon?"

I shrugged. I didn't tell him I could smell Dan's blood whenever I entered the kitchen. I didn't tell him I couldn't look at the tiled floor —too terrified I'd see the stain Dan's insides left behind. I didn't tell him I was scared to be alone in the kitchen at night. "It's getting harder to remember the good stuff, huh?" I picked at the divet in the armchair.

"You get to start fresh when you go to school," he said. "I think it's time I do the same."

Guilt pinged me in the chest. I hated the thought of leaving my dad there by himself. "Maybe this weekend we can—"

Dad chuckled. "Landon, it's okay. We don't have to talk about this now. We have hungry kids to feed!"

I let my breath escape, nodded, and stood. "If selling the house is what you want to do, I support it. You're right. You deserve a fresh start, too."

Dad removed himself from behind the desk and wrapped his big arms around me, kissing me on the side of my head. "Sounds good to me, kiddo."

I pushed him off of me and grinned. "Come on, you said you were the grill master back in the day, right? Come show us your skills, old man!" I stepped through the door with Dad close behind.

He tried to give me a playful smack, but I dodged him. "Smartass," Dad said with a laugh.

Caleb stepped in from the backyard. "Tasha said there were sodas in the fridge?"

"Shit," I said. "I told her I'd grab them."

"It's okay," Caleb smiled as he headed for the kitchen. His dimples always caught me off guard, punching me in the heart.

The doorbell rang.

"Thought everyone was here already," Dad said.

"It's probably Miguel," Caleb called from the kitchen.

"I'll get it!" I power walked to the front door. I was about to say something snarky, but I opened the door to a man I didn't recognize. His auburn hair was quaffed, and the day's stubble sprinkled his wide jaw. The man wore a white button-down shirt tucked into his trousers. A loose tie hung around his neck, and he had rolled his sleeves.

The man looked at me with a half-smile. "Sorry to show up unannounced. I just wanted to drop these off for Curtis?" His left arm held a stack of thick manila envelopes.

"Oh, yeah, he's my dad. Come in."

"You must be the famous gay son." Tucker held out his hand.

I hesitated but shook the man's hand. "Landon. And calling me just his son is fine, thanks."

"Oh god, I apologize. Sometimes I just say things. Gets me in trouble sometimes." His southern drawl was strong. "I'm Tucker. Friends call me Tuck. I'm your dad's campaign manager."

"Oh," I said, finally able to put a face to a name. "Come in. My dad's in the living room. Sorry, we're having a ten-year-old's birthday today." I led him through the foyer and into the kitchen.

Caleb stacked soda cans on the counter while Dad took the raw patties from the fridge.

Dad looked surprised when we walked in. "Tuck? What're you doing here?" Dad placed the pack on the counter to give Tucker a handshake.

"I was in the neighborhood. Figured I'd drop these off for next week. I'm sorry to intrude."

Dad waved him off. "Aw hell, I'll grab you a beer. We can go out back and talk shop while I start these burgers."

"Great." Tucker smiled and put his hands in his pockets. "So, whose birthday is it?"

"My little brother," Caleb said, stepping around the counter.

Dad handed an open bottle to Tucker. "This is Landon's boyfriend, Caleb."

Tucker choked on his first sip. We all saw it, but he tried to play it off by straightening his shoulders. "You let them live together?"

Dad tilted his head.

"I have my own place," Caleb said. "I'd shake your hand, but—" he looked down at the cans he held and shrugged before walking away.

I gave Dad a look before helping Caleb with the door.

The others sat at the picnic table snacking. Parker and his friends moved on to kicking a soccer ball around.

"Who's the hottie?" Lauren asked, causing Tasha and Steven to turn their attention to Tucker and Dad walking toward the grill.

"Which one?" Steven asked, sucking the salt off a pretzel.

"Hey," I whispered. "Can you not ogle my dad while I'm around?"

"It's not my fault your dad's hot," Steven said.

I rolled my eyes. "Oh my god, please stop."

Tasha laughed. "Who's the guy?"

"My dad's campaign manager."

"He's an asshole," Caleb said, leaning to sit atop the table.

"You know him?" Lauren asked.

"No," Caleb said, glancing in Tucker's direction. "But he practically choked on his beer when he heard the word boyfriend."

"Classic." Tasha rolled her eyes.

Steven quickly pulled out his phone. "I bet he's on Grindr."

Lauren snatched the phone. "This is a kid's party!"

"I was just gonna peek, jeez."

The smell of the sizzling burgers made my stomach growl.

"Landon," Dad called over his shoulder. "I forgot the cheese. Can you grab it, please?"

"Sure!" I pulled the sliding door and trotted through the living room. When I touched the fridge handle, a flash of prom night cut through my mind with a jagged edge. Dan gurgling on the kitchen floor.

Parker's laugh pulled me back to reality, and I stared at my reflection in the steel door. *I can't wait to get the fuck out of here.* As I pulled the pack of cheese out of the fridge, the side door swung open, and Miguel stumbled in from the driveway with the cake.

"Finally!" I hurried over, took Miguel's cake, and placed it on the island.

"You know I like to be fashionably late to every party." Miguel breathed as if he came from running a 5k.

Caleb stepped inside. "Fashionably late would've been an hour ago. You're *late*, late."

"The cake is here. That's all that matters," I said.

With the cake and pack of cheese in hand, I led Miguel to the backyard. Parker hugged the latecomer as I set everything on the table.

"Happy birthday, sweetie!" Miguel said.

Caleb opened the lid, and Parker's eyes lit up like a cartoon character seeing a chest full of gold. "Whoa! A Crusader's cake!"

The cake had the Crusaders team on it, which Caleb told me about at the film exhibit. Biohazard was front and center with a text bubble from his mouth that said, 'Happy Birthday, Parker!'

"I love it!" Parker hugged Caleb and Miguel again before running to his friends, screaming about the cake.

"What'd you get Parker for his birthday?" Lauren asked Caleb as I jogged back from cheese duty.

"I hope it's a pony," Steven joked. "I asked for one for my birthday every year."

"My brother isn't a horse girl," Caleb said, ruffling Steven's hair. Everyone laughed except for Steven.

"I resent that, bitch." Steven cracked a smile. "And Parker still has time to figure that out!"

"I got him an iPhone. He thought it was a prank."

"Best big brother ever," Tasha said.

Caleb shrugged. "It's two generations old and used. I can't even remember when I started saving for it."

"But it's something," Lauren said.

"Paying for two plans will be tough, but it was time he got a phone," Caleb said.

I slid my fingers between Caleb's. "You're incredible."

Dad popped up with a plate piled with burgers and sat them on the table.

Caleb shouted to the running boys. "Come eat!"

They all rushed to the table. Everyone got up so the kids could sit. They were like ravenous chipmunks, grabbing for the buns, burgers, and ketchup. It was a surprise the plates weren't devoured, too. The rest of us were a little more patient.

Caleb touched Parker's shoulder as he chomped into his burger. "After we eat, we can do gifts, okay?" Parker nodded. Ketchup already stained his shirt.

One of Parker's friends leaned over and said, "You're gonna love my gift." This started a verbal war about who gave him the best gift.

We moved from the table and huddled up with Dad and Tucker, all eating over our paper plates under the blazing sun.

"These aren't half bad," I said to Dad.

"I told you," he said.

"What else do you cook, Curtis?" Miguel asked.

"Not much else. Landon can tell you I'm not much of a chef."

Tucker cleared his throat and looked at my Dad. "I was in the same boat last weekend for my nephew's birthday... grill man." We all nodded silently. Tucker continued. "It's a real nice day you put together for that boy, Caleb."

"I try my best."

Tucker pointed his beer at me. "You two raising him together?"

"Nope," Caleb said. "Just me."

"Your parents don't help out?"

"They aren't really in our lives anymore," Caleb said, staring at his plate.

Miguel jumped in. "He gets all the help he needs from us."

We all nodded in solidarity.

"They live with me," Miguel said. "Parker sees me as his auntie."

Everyone smiled except Tucker, who looked confused.

"But you're a guy," Tucker said.

Miguel's eyebrows jumped.

Tucker sighed. "Let me guess, your pronouns are some form of plural?"

"Excuse me?" Tasha asked with a furrowed brow.

"It's ridiculous wordplay invented by your generation. A lazy attempt to make everyone feel included."

"Tucker—" Dad said nicely.

"What's wrong with including people?" Lauren asked.

"It's just not how life works," Tucker said, sipping his beer smugly.

"Says the privileged white man," Miguel said. I wasn't sure if he wanted to say that under his breath, but we all heard it.

"Nothing in my life has been handed to me because I'm white," Tucker said.

Tasha groaned while Steven said, "You're missing the point."

My wide eyes locked on my dad, trying to give him a signal to make his friend shut up.

Tucker turned to Steven. "What point?"

"We should go inside," Dad said to Tucker with a forced smile. "Let them watch the kids for a while."

Tucker didn't acknowledge him. Instead, he continued his word vomit. "The point that a little kid ain't being raised, right? That he's surrounded by people who will change who he is? It's gonna confuse the kid."

Caleb spiked his plate to the ground and stepped to Tucker. "You don't know jack shit about what he's been through." Caleb pointed a finger in Tucker's face. "If you did, you wouldn't try to tell me how to raise him."

Tucker swigged his beer, talking into the lip of the bottle. "A faggot shouldn't be raising kids to begin with."

Caleb decked Tucker across the jaw, sending him to the grass. Miguel and I quickly lunged for Caleb's arms to keep him from doing more harm.

Dad rushed to put a hand on Caleb's chest as he looked down at Tucker. "Get the hell up," Dad said with an intense growl. Tucker got to his feet, holding a hand to his face. Dad looked him dead in the eye. "You got a lot of balls using that word in my house. You're fired."

Tucker let out an embarrassed laugh. "Are you serious? You need me! Your career is gonna tank because of these people. I didn't want to say it before, but everyone knows it."

"These people are my family, and they're a hell of a lot more important to me than my career. Now, kindly get the *fuck* out of my house."

Tucker shook his head, stumbled to the fenced gate, and let himself out onto the driveway. The gate slammed behind him, wobbling the fence.

We let go of Caleb, who'd finally relaxed his shoulders. He glanced at the table. Parker and his friends stared.

"Everything's alright," Caleb called out. "Go inside once you're done eating. We'll do gifts, okay?"

Dad rested a hand on Caleb's shoulder. "I'm sorry he said those things. I'm gonna make sure he's gone."

Tasha followed close behind as Dad left the yard. "Mr. Griffin, I'm taking a modern journalism class during my first semester. I know this is awkward, but I was wondering if I could interview you." Her voice trailed off as she followed him to the front of the house.

"That was all way too familiar," Steven said. Lauren wrapped her arm around him.

"Yeah, it was," I whispered, still shocked by everything. "You okay, Caleb?"

Caleb chewed his bottom lip. "I ruined Parker's birthday, didn't I?"

I put his chin in my hand, making him look at me. "You could never do anything wrong in his eyes. He adores you. I promise you didn't ruin anything."

"Pinky swear?" Caleb held up his hand with his pinky sticking out. His knuckles were red. Then, he smiled, and I thought about the rest of our lives, knowing I'd never be able to say no when Caleb's dimples were on full display.

I wrapped my pinky around his. "Pinky swear."

FIVE

NEW YORK CITY

Saturday, January 4th

Steven and I thought filling our stomachs would be a good idea before any potential alcohol entered our system. We grabbed a slice of pizza for $1.50 from a place at the top of the subway's entrance. We'd spent almost an hour sitting at the shallow counter, eating, chatting, and showing each other dumb TikTok videos we saved since I left Texas.

Stonewall was a short walk from the pizza place. And the molly didn't kick in until we walked out on the street. I was suddenly very aware of my legs feeling full of air. It swirled around my ankle, honing in on how the joints propelled me forward. The air twirled up my shin and pushed through my knees. A bounce formed in my stride. Then, the breeze tickled up my thighs and through my hip sockets.

Steven looked at me. "Feeling anything yet?"

I glanced at him. His eyes shimmered under a streetlight. Steven's pupils took up most of his eyes. "Yeah, I think so," I said.

Google led us to a short line next to the big window looking into the bar. A red neon sign read: 'The Stonewall Inn.'

Steven peered through the glass. "I can't believe we're here!"

I was gonna make a joke about police raids being part of the full experience but decided against it. Was Molly making me think clearer?

The bouncer stopped us and shined his flashlight on our IDs. My heart pounded, wondering if he could spot a fake.

It's real. You don't have to study it. It's real, I promise. Who'd bail me out if I get caught? Steven can flirt his way out of jail time, but me? Have I mentioned it's real?

The bouncer handed our IDs back. "Have fun, guys."

Thank you, gay gods of Stonewall!

We stepped inside.

"I can't believe that worked," Steven said.

"What worked?"

"I was totally flirting with him so he wouldn't pay attention to our IDs!"

Neon signs and Edison bulbs lit the long, skinny room. The left side housed a bar, while tables and chairs hugged the opposite wall. A small stage in the back corner was where a Drag Queen with big hair spoke into a microphone—the faint beat of a song thudded from upstairs. We gave our coats to a small woman with green hair sitting on a stool in a closet.

I passed Steven some cash and followed him to the bar. I didn't want to use my card and risk Dad finding out we'd gone to a club. Steven leaned against the bar before waving to the drag queen. She noticed him and said, "Who let that fetus in here?" Everyone laughed and turned to us. Steven took in all the attention and then twirled to the bartender.

My eyes focused on one of the bulbs hanging from the string lights. It gave off a yellow hue, and the longer I stared at it, the more I swore I heard its hum get louder.

Steven grabbed my arm and handed me a drink. "Happy birthday, love!"

"What is it?" I asked.

Steven clinked my cup with his. "Vodka Red Bull! It's delish. You'll love it!"

I sipped from the skinny straw. The cold filled my throat. If there was a burn from the alcohol, I didn't notice it, only the carbonated tartness of the Red Bull. I leaned into Steven's shoulder. "Hey, I'm not sure this is our crowd."

"I was thinking the same!" Steven chugged his drink, leaving a glass of ice on the bar. "Let's check upstairs. If it's dull, we can go somewhere else."

"Okay." I downed the rest of my drink before following Steven through the crowd. The stairs and the walls were all black, and red light washed over everything. We passed the bathrooms before we found the dance floor. A younger crowd glistened under the disco lights. A small bar and DJ booth sat at the back of the room. *This is more our speed.*

The lights were incredible and sent me into a spin as Steven led me to the middle of the floor. Different colored circles rolled around my feet, up the walls, and danced on the ceilings. I couldn't take my eyes off them as I swayed, doing tiny circles in place. My arms were like ribbons, gracefully cutting through the air.

Someone wrapped their hands around my waist as I floated with the colors on the ceiling. I smiled, assuming it was Steven. I put my hands over his, amazed by his skin's softness. I continued up his arms. It's what I assumed a dolphin felt like. His skin was magical against my palms. I moved my fingers up and down his arms and through his fingers.

I turned to face him, wanting to ask if his entire body felt like that, but my words got caught in my throat when I saw a pair of familiar blue eyes behind thin glasses. "Holy shit!" I yelled over the pounding music. "Blake?"

He looked just as shocked as I did. "Landon?"

Steven was spinning in place. I grabbed his wrist and clumsily pulled him into me. I cupped his chin, forcing him to look. Steven gasped. "Oh my god, Blake!"

"That's what I said!" I shouted.

Blake motioned for us to move off the dance floor toward a couple of big black squares and gestured for us to sit. "What the hell are you guys doing here?"

"I live here now!" I shouted.

"And I'm visiting for his birthday!" Steven said, barely able to keep his eyes off a bearded man in a tank top dancing nearby. He was a moth to a flame. No thoughts, just lust pulling him into the man's hairy, bulging chest.

"Sorry, we're kind of all over the place tonight," I shouted.

"Yeah, I can tell! Your pupils are huge. What'd you take?"

"Molly."

"How does it feel?"

"Like nothing I've ever felt before. So amazing!" I said, staring at him. His club attire was more relaxed than the suit and tie he wore to our first date at the coffee shop in downtown Madison, and his blonde hair was in his face. Whenever Blake pushed his hair back, my hormones kicked me in the groin. "Wait, what are *you* doing here?"

"I'm working for my uncle now. He runs an agency here."

I tried not to let the lights distract me. "What kind of agency?"

"It's kind of an all-in-one place. They represent actors, models, singers, writers, dancers."

My eyes widened. "Maybe I'll be sending a query letter someday!"

"Oh yeah, you said you were a writer, right?"

"I'm surprised you remember that." The beat of the music matched my pulse.

Blake moved closer. "What do you mean?"

"You were all business the first time we met."

"I was?"

"You said 'that's cute' after I told you I wanted to be a writer. You were kind of a dick."

Blake laughed. "You're right, that was a dick move. I'm sorry."

"At least you admit it."

"Is that why you took off so fast?"

"No, I probably could've tolerated you for a few more minutes."

"What was it then?"

I sighed. "My boyfriend called. His little brother got into a fight with their stepdad, and—"

"If you had a boyfriend, why'd you go on a date with me?"

I stood to get the blood back to my feet. "We were kind of on a break? It's complicated. Can we talk about something else?"

Blake smiled, stood, and moved closer, pressing himself against me. He touched my lower back, helping me sway with the music. "Can I talk about how sexy you are?" His warm breath against my ear tickled my groin. Blake's lips grazed my neck, sending an intense tingle down my back. Something was coming over me that I didn't want to control. Steven wasn't lying when he said the molly would make me feel free. I didn't have a care in the world, and how Blake touched me felt amazing. My hands made their way back to Blake's arms. *How is he so smooth?*

My heart beat quickened. Maybe it was the Red Bull, but my blood pumped straight to my crotch. Blake and I were cheek to cheek, dancing carelessly.

"Are you single now?" Blake asked.

I closed my eyes. I was transported back to my bed, laying shirtless with Caleb, feeling the goosebumps his touch left behind on my torso. I could almost taste his lips. *Stop.* I couldn't let my thoughts drag me down. I grabbed Blake's hand and pulled him off the dance floor. Instead of taking the stairs, I led Blake into the bathroom. Graffiti and stickers covered the walls.

"Are you okay?" Blake shouted over the heavy music.

I pushed open a stall and pulled him inside. I made quick work of the lock and leaned against the door.

"Landon, are you—"

"Shut up." I yanked him into me. Blake's lips were thinner than Caleb's. It felt like kissing a cardboard box. Blake moved his wet mouth to my neck, and I let out a small moan. I gripped his hair with one hand, and suddenly, Blake was on his knees, unbuttoning my jeans.

The molly heightened every sensation. Every touch, every kiss, every thrust. With my eyes closed, I pressed my head against the door, reveling in everything Blake was doing. Luckily, the music drowned out the moans escaping me.

I flinched from a loud thud in the beat. *It's just the music.* Another thud transitioned into a bang. My eyes popped open, and I focused on two small holes in the wall above the toilet. *Bullet holes.*

The music pumped again, and I heard more shots. My heart jumped into my throat. I pushed Blake aside to pull my pants up.

He stood and wiped his mouth. "Was that okay?"

I didn't want to see him anymore. I fiddled with the lock before I pulled the door open and ran for the stairs. I knocked into a guy's shoulder on the way down, spilling his drink.

"Sorry!" I yelled as I hopped off the bottom step, fled past the Drag Queen, and ran out the front door. Every streetlight beamed like the sun. I rubbed my eyes, but it didn't help.

A motorcycle whizzed by. It was so loud I covered my ears. When the exhaust popped, I threw myself to the side of a parked car and sat on the cold sidewalk. I clenched my eyes and hugged my knees. The ground vibrated around me.

"Landon!" Steven's voice called out. He kneeled when I finally opened my eyes.

"He's here," I whispered.

Steven held my arms. "Who?"

"Dan."

Blake appeared behind Steven, watching us.

"That's impossible," Steven said. After a beat, he cupped my face. "You're just overstimulated. I'm gonna get our coats. You're freezing." Steven didn't take long; he wrapped me in my coat in less than a minute.

Blake got closer as Steven lifted me to my feet. "Is he gonna be alright?"

"Yeah," Steven said. "It's been fun, Blake, but I'm gonna get him back home."

"DM me later?"

We started for the street corner. "Sure, Blake. Byeeee." Steven said.

My arm draped over Steven's shoulder as we rounded the corner. "I'm sorry."

"Why are you sorry?"

"I ruined our night," I said.

"Not even close."

"Fine, I ruined *your* night. You were making out with that guy."

"I got his number. I'll sext him later."

The fog started to clear when the warmth of the subway train engulfed us, and we sat in front of a map of New York City. Only a few stops and we'd be home.

"You give me one pill, and I'm suddenly letting Blake blow me in the bathroom."

Steven gasped. "You didn't!"

My head fell. "I did."

"Landon!" Steven playfully slapped my leg. "Was it good?"

I rested my head on the map behind me. "Yeah, until it wasn't."

"Oh god, too much teeth?"

"I saw two—" I squeezed my legs. "I got freaked out. I heard something, and suddenly, I was convinced Dan was there."

Steven held my hand and sighed. "Landon, if I can promise you one thing for the rest of our lives, it's that Dan can *never* hurt either of us again."

If that was true, why was he still haunting me?

———

Sunday, January 5th

I woke up groggier than usual. The sun reflected off the white walls and into my eyes. I turned to my other shoulder only to see Steven's drooling face fast asleep on my pillow.

Typing echoed. "Morning," Josh said, his eyes glued to his screen.

I swung my legs over the edge, noticing Steven and I were both only in underwear. "Oh god. Did we?"

Josh's hands shot up. "Don't ask me."

I shook Steven. He groaned and rolled to his other side. If I'd hooked up with my best friend during a horny molly-fueled night, I'd never take another drug again. I remembered everything that happened at the club, but was hazy post-Blake.

I brushed my teeth and rubbed on some deodorant. I pulled on my pants from the night before, then grabbed a blue sweater hanging in my closet. "I need coffee. Do you want anything?" I nudged Steven, but he swatted me away. I looked over my shoulder. "Josh?"

"No, thanks," he mumbled.

I nodded, collected my coat from the floor, slipped into my shoes, and was out the door.

Something about the city streets made me move faster. Was it the cold or the power-walking nannies with their strollers? I reached The Ivory Den at record speed, pushing the glass door open and enjoying that bitter smell I was used to. Two baristas worked the marbled counter, speeding around each machine as if they had extra hands and feet. Jazz played overhead. I immediately felt relaxed. The Ivory Den was my home away from the dorm, a serene place I used to study and write. I stepped to the counter and ordered a caramel latte.

As I waited for my drink, scenes from the club played in my mind. I rubbed my forehead as if it would help release my thoughts.

The barista called my name. I grabbed the cup from the counter and lingered by the cream and sugar station, reaching for a brass thermos of milk.

A hand entered my peripheral, placing a cell phone down. The brightness caught my eye, but the wallpaper on the screen kept me there. I stared at a symbol that looked a lot like Caleb's tattoo. It was an 'A' in a bold circle, but this one had a white lightning bolt through it. I squinted, so perplexed by the similarity that I hadn't realized I was still pouring the milk.

"Shit!" I let go of the thermos entirely, and it crashed onto the table, knocking my cup over and drowning the cell phone in a caramel latte. "Oh my god!" I raced for napkins and tried to catch the liquid from dripping onto the floor, but it was too fast. I snatched the phone from the puddle; its screen went dark. "I am so sorry," I said, wrapping napkins around the phone.

"You're good," he said, looking at me with eyes so emerald green they glistened like jewels under the fluorescents. I'd never heard a British accent in real life, just in the movies Caleb showed me. "It was an accident."

The guy's skin was flawless, and his jaw led to a rounded chin with a dimple at the end. A dirty blonde mop of curls rested on his forehead. He was a bit shorter than me and wore a thin, black sweater that hugged his round shoulders and showed off his chest, where my eyes lingered for too long. His light wash jeans led down to a pair of black Converse.

I gave him his phone back, wondering how long I'd been staring, then sopped up the coffee on the floor. My arms flailed everywhere. Thankfully, one of the baristas relieved me of clean-up duty.

I popped the lid on my cup again. With a quarter of my latte left, I took my defeat to the corner table and stared out the window, hoping no one would notice I was still alive.

"First, you spilled coffee on my phone. Then you steal my table?"

I looked up to see Curly-Head standing there with a smile. There was a tiny gap between his two front teeth. I hadn't noticed the coat on the other chair. "Jesus," I said and stood. "I'm the worst."

"I'm kidding," he said calmly. "You stay." He grabbed his coat. "I can move somewhere else."

"It was your table first. I should go."

He smiled again. "Let's share it then."

I wasn't exactly in the mood to share a table with someone. Before kicking Steven out of bed, I wanted to wallow in my lousy decision-making. But I might have killed Curly-Head's phone, so I felt obligated to stay.

"Sure," I said with a single grain of enthusiasm. Curly-Head finally sat when a girl approached our table.

She stood behind him, holding her phone in her mittened hands, barely holding back her smile. "Oh my god, can I get a selfie?"

My tablemate slipped me some side-eye. He licked his lips and took a short breath before turning on his smile. "Of course," he said. He wrapped his arm around her shoulders as she pushed her cheek to his and snapped the picture. She forced a hug on him before jogging out the door.

The whole interaction was awkward to witness. Curly-Head placed his phone on the table—the screen was still black—and sat in the wire chair across from me.

"Do your friends always randomly ask to take pictures with you?"

He chuckled. "Kind of, yeah." He sipped his drink. "I think I've seen you in here before. Do you go to NYU?"

"Yeah. First year."

He nodded. "I'm in my second. What's your major?"

I rolled my eyes and smiled. Everyone I'd met so far asked that question. "I'm in the creative writing program."

"Very cool."

I took the remaining gulp of my latte.

Curly-Head's eyes passed between me and the window. "I should buy you another coffee. I feel bad."

"*You* feel bad? I'm the one that drowned your phone."

"I'll put it in some rice or something. It'll be fine." He smiled again, showing the small gap in his teeth. It was cuter each time I saw it. Finally, he twisted to reach into his coat pocket, pulling out a gray beanie that he slipped over his curls, but they couldn't be contained. For a college student, he seemed too okay that I'd damaged his phone. I wasn't sure I'd be so nice if he'd done the same.

His bright emerald eyes glanced through the window again. I turned in my chair; the selfie girl stood on the street corner with two other friends. They giggled and waved at us with their phones out.

"I think she likes you," I said.

"I think so, too."

"Want me to go out there and ask her out for you?" *That was weird. Why offer that? What if he says yes? That would be terrifying.* My shoulders tensed.

"Thanks, but no thanks," Curly-Head said. "She's not my type." He tried to turn on his phone, but it didn't light up. "I gotta find some rice." He stood and collected his coat again.

My chest tightened. I needed to offer something before he left. "I'm sorry about your phone," I blurted out. "Let me..." I racked my brain. "Okay, I can't pay for a new one, but maybe I could pay your phone bill or something this month." I swallowed my embarrassment. Dad would flip if he found out I offered to pay a rando's phone bill.

"It's really okay." He pushed his arms through his earth-toned coat, looking like he could blend into a forest floor. "Just pay for my coffee next time."

"That works for me. Just call out my name if I don't notice you. I can be in my own world sometimes."

"Typical writer," he said, shaking his head. He zipped his coat. "What should I call you?"

"I'm Landon," I said, reaching over the table. He shook my hand. "What should I call you?"

Curly-Head's lip twisted, and his eyebrows strained, but everything quickly melted into a smirk. "Isaac."

"Alright, Isaac. I'll see you around."

I was lucky to see Isaac's tooth-gap again before he turned and jetted out the door. I watched through the windows. He waved at the girls on the corner before crossing the street.

I stood and tossed my cup in the trash. I wasn't feeling particularly energized, but I wanted to get back to the room before Steven woke up.

SIX

TEXAS

Five Months Ago

I leaned against a tree to catch my breath, the trunk thick enough to hide me. I peeked over my shoulder to a sea of green trees. Leaves and sticks covered the ground for miles. I had no idea where I was, but I was so out of breath it felt like I'd been running for an hour straight. My throat burned, and my head ached. I touched my left ear. It was wet, with blood trickling down my neck.

A stick snapped, and I pressed myself against the tree again. I needed a next move, but everything looked the same; there were so many trees. No caves or caverns. No rivers or streams. No shacks or houses. Just acres of trees. Another snap made my heart thud. I pressed my hands against my chest to stop the sound from echoing through the woods. All I could hear was my heartbeat and his footsteps inching closer.

I clenched my eyes, listening for the leaves to stop rustling. Maybe he would walk by and miss me completely. Or maybe he would turn around and walk the opposite way. I opened my eyes as my heart calmed. I rounded the tree, thinking I was safe.

There he was—sticking out in his white tux. I blinked, and

suddenly, he was closer. I crunched my eyes to get rid of him, but when they opened again, he was there, pointing his gun at my face. I screamed, yet didn't produce a sound. I desperately pushed and pushed, but I had no voice, no air. A gunshot rang through the trees.

My eyes popped open, propelling me out of the sheets, gasping for a breath.

"Landon?" Caleb sat up in bed next to me. We were in his room—safe. He touched my shoulder. "Jesus, you're soaked." He hopped out of bed and reached for a towel in the closet. Caleb blotted my neck. "Bad dream?"

"Yeah," I said, fixing my eyes on the Barbra clock.

"Was it Dan again?"

I kicked my legs off the bed and leaned on my knees. "It's always Dan."

Caleb dabbed the towel against my back before kissing my shoulders. His fingers grazed up and down my arms. "You're okay," he whispered. "We're okay."

It was the third time that week Caleb would have to wash his sheets. I sighed, twisting to look at him. "I'm sorry."

Caleb pressed his forehead to mine. "Don't be."

I closed my eyes. "Is this ever gonna stop?"

"Are you ever gonna tell your dad about the dreams?"

I wiped my forehead on my arm. "No."

"Why?"

I looked at Caleb. "He's stressed enough. And more worrying about me isn't gonna help. If he knows, he'll force me to go to therapy."

"Maybe it's not a bad—"

"I don't want to talk about it, okay? Can we just focus on today?" I stood, knowing he felt the pain as much as I did. "You still want to come today, right?" I asked, pulling my shirt on.

"Of course," Caleb said, bouncing off the bed like a trampoline and pulling on a pair of jeans.

"You told your friends to vote, right?"

"I told everyone I know, babe. By this time tomorrow, your dad is gonna be Mayor."

"Don't jinx it," I said, zipping up my backpack.

Caleb knocked on the wooden closet door three times while I tried to shake my nightmare. *Just focus on today.*

We left the bedroom to find Miguel and Parker at the kitchen table, in their usual spots. Miguel had dressed for the day, but Parker sat in his underwear, eating a bowl of cereal.

Miguel had his car keys in hand. "I'm going to the grocery store. Need anything?"

"Actually," I said. "Mind dropping us off at City Hall? My dad's making a speech."

Miguel shrugged. "Yeah, sure."

"You're voting today, right?"

"I never thought I'd vote for a Republican, but yes," Miguel said. "Your dad isn't the usual crazy we get from that side, thank God."

I hugged him. "That means a lot."

"He better not let us down," Miguel said, playfully slapping me away.

"Oh, and we're having everyone over tonight for the results. My dad said they'll be drinking no matter what."

"You know I love a party, but unfortunately, I have dinner plans. Sorry boo."

"It's okay. You're voting. That's what matters."

I pulled my backpack onto my shoulder as Caleb kissed Parker on the head. Then we were out the door.

———

City Hall was a colonial-style building in Madison's downtown square. Local news crews were setting up their cameras as we pulled up. A podium was set up on the front steps. Knowing my dad had a strong chance of becoming a leader in our community made me smile. It was weird at first when I started seeing his face on buses and on signs in people's yards, but seeing all the camera crews made it feel global.

Caleb and I weaved through the crowd and walked up the steps. The pillars at the front of the building felt like skyscrapers.

"This is where your dad's office would be?" Caleb asked. His voice echoed through the empty foyer. Everything glimmered, and the room's centerpiece was the marble staircase leading to the second floor.

"Yeah. It's pretty wild."

Caleb held my hand as we ascended the stairs, but I pulled away. He was quick to call me out. "What was that?"

"I'm just not sure who knows and who doesn't," I whispered. "We don't need another Tucker situation."

We stopped and leaned against the railing, looking into the foyer below.

"Why does it matter? Our story was all over the news. Pretty sure everyone already knows."

"I'm just thinking about my dad. Reading about us or seeing pictures is different from seeing us in real life." Caleb huffed and looked back toward the foyer. I stared at him. "I'd rather be safe than sorry."

Caleb pursed his lips. "Fine."

"Landon!"

I turned to see Dad poking out of a doorway, motioning for us to come in. We walked into a large room with too many desks to count. People hustled everywhere, making calls, writing things down, and typing. Dad leaned against a desk, going over his speech on note cards. His suit jacket was slung across a chair.

"You ready?" I asked as we approached.

Dad removed his glasses to look at me. "Ready as I'll ever be." He smiled. "I wanted to tell you guys I'm mentioning you in my speech."

"Wait," Caleb said. "Both of us?"

Dad nodded.

I looked between them. "Like, as a couple?"

"Yes, son."

Caleb smiled.

I shifted my weight to one side. "Dad, it's voting day. Maybe you should wait until after."

Dad stood. "Look, I didn't make a statement after your prom night because I feared what guys like Tucker might advise me to do or say. And I regret that." He pocketed his glasses. "I'm proud of you guys. Why would I want to hide you?"

"Maybe you shouldn't take a stand just yet? Remember the comments on the article after prom?" I asked.

"I didn't read the comments," Dad said.

I sighed. "It wasn't all nice."

Dad shrugged. "Landon, it's already been in the press. People know everything."

"Sounds familiar," Caleb said under his breath as if he wasn't standing inches from me.

I rolled my eyes. "If you do this, it'll change people's votes."

Dad's face twisted. "If this small thing changes someone's vote, then they didn't fully support me to begin with."

I crossed my arms. "Who told you this was a good idea?"

"I did," a voice called from behind.

I snapped to see Steph walking through the door, holding a folder close to her chest. I'd only seen her wearing a Lucky's uniform, so seeing her in a pantsuit was jarring.

"Oh my god," Caleb yipped. Steph hugged him.

"Steph is my campaign manager," Dad said.

I turned back to Dad. "This is who you've been talking about for a month? Why didn't you tell me?"

"I wasn't aware you two knew each other," Dad said.

"We don't, really," Steph said. "I was only his waitress a couple of times. But Caleb told me all about you." She held out her hand, and I shook it. "It's nice to meet you formally, Landon."

Caleb was still smiling. "Why didn't you tell me this is what you left Lucky's for?"

A smile tugged at Steph's lips. "I wasn't sure if I was allowed to."

"Why were you at Lucky's if you could've been here?" I asked, feeling Caleb's eyes on me. "Not that working at Lucky's is bad."

"I had to pay for grad school somehow. Unfortunately, that meant two jobs, Lucky's and bartending on the weekends. It was hell, but I thought I'd be a perfect fit after Caleb told me what happened with Tucker. So I reached out to your dad's team."

"She's been a breath of fresh air," Dad said. "And the kind of diversity that's needed around here."

"Dad, this is all amazing, but do you really think you can change Republicans' minds?"

Dad reached for his jacket. "Maybe it's time to change the definition of Republican."

I couldn't believe the words coming out of his mouth. He was a cooler guy, a much more relaxed guy. I'd even dare to say a more confident guy.

"Everyone is ready for you outside," Steph said.

Dad nodded, slipped on his jacket, put his note cards in his inside pocket, and headed out the door.

Steph briefed us on where to stand during the speech.

"Wait, we're gonna be on camera?" I asked

"Awesome!" Caleb said.

I wiped my palms on my shirt. "Are you sure that's a good idea?"

"Yes," Steph said. "The public needs to see you guys together. You'll be great."

I glanced at Caleb as we approached the stairs at the front of the building. He looked overjoyed. Too overjoyed if you asked me. Then I freaked out about what I was wearing. If someone had told me I would be on camera, I would've worn something nicer than my ripped jeans and baseball T.

We walked out into the heat to a much bigger crowd than when we arrived—a mix of news stations and townspeople. My heart raced. Caleb and I stood on a higher step to Dad's left. Steph had stayed back by the building's entrance.

I looked at Caleb one last time. His arms were in front of him with his hand clasped around his wrist, looking like a proper first gentleman or something, just glowing. I followed his lead and stood as he did, putting on my best attempt at an enthusiastic smile.

Everyone's cheers calmed as Dad spoke. "Hello, everyone!" His voice boomed across the square as he leaned into the microphone on the podium. "Thank you all so much for showing up to vote on this beautiful day. Whether you're here to vote for me or not, if I win tonight, I can assure you that I will fight tooth and nail for this community. Strengthen our bond as neighbors. I want to help people on our streets without homes by introducing more aid and food programs. I want to make our town more accessible for our disabled patrons. I want to represent you, no matter who you vote for today.

"I've learned a lot from this campaign and grown as a person. I feel like the things I've learned and the people I've met have added years to my life. That's when I realized that this country, this state, and this town is built on diversity. We as Republicans must stop looking at every situation as this or that, with no middle ground in between."

I tried my best to avoid eye contact with anyone watching. But as Dad spoke about diversity, I noticed the gay couple holding hands at the crowd's edge. I even spotted a pack of people wearing pride shirts.

"We as Republicans have to start standing up for the people different from us. The people with a different skin tone, the people with different voices, the people whom society has deemed less than. There are a lot of Republicans in this state and even in the building behind me who are shaking their heads right now. Well, I'm here to tell them it's time for change."

The crowd erupted into applause.

"There have been a lot of people along my campaign trail that have changed me for the better, and I want to thank one of them now." He gestured to me. "If you don't already know, this is my son, Landon."

The crowd clapped.

Caleb nudged me. "Wave, so they know which one of us is Landon."

I waved awkwardly, feeling like a walrus in a beauty pageant.

Dad continued. "He's taught me more about life in the last six months than I've learned in all my forty-nine years, most of which was spent on an army base. When Landon came out to me, I thought my life was over. Everything I'd envisioned for him shattered. But it didn't take long to realize that it wasn't about me or what I had planned for him. It's his life, not mine. All I can do as a father is support him and make sure he's happy, and that's exactly how I want to run things as Mayor. I am proud of my son and his boyfriend, Caleb, for being true to who they are. Let me show you who I am so you can be proud to call me *your* Mayor."

The crowd exploded again. Cameras lit up the scene from every direction. The response was overwhelming. I couldn't believe they were all cheering for *my* dad. The nerves washed away, leaving pride in the sand.

As the applause died, a man shouted, sending his words over the crowd. "Your son murdered that boy!"

My heart hit my stomach, falling like a snapped elevator. I scanned each face in the crowd.

Another voice yelled, this time a woman. "They BOTH murdered that boy!"

"We want justice!" Someone else yelled. "We want a trial!"

That sent the crowd into a frenzy as people screamed their thoughts at each other. I gripped Caleb's hand. It was exactly what I was afraid of.

"Excuse me!" Dad yelled into the microphone, nearly knocking everyone to their knees. "I've said enough about the vicious attack on my son and his boyfriend." Dad's hands gripped the edges of the podium. I could see his fingernails digging into the wood. "Dan Wilson was a trespasser and an aggressive intruder in my home." Dad's expression softened when he looked at me, then turned to the mic one last time. "What matters is that my son is safe." Dad crossed the steps to us and wrapped his arm around my shoulders, smiling as the flashes continued. The crowd cheered, but I could still see the angry people trying to shout over the applause.

Steph stepped to the podium to address the crowd and point them toward the voting stations.

Dad led me back into the foyer. Caleb stepped in behind us. "Are you okay?" Dad asked.

The knot in my stomach loosened. "I wasn't expecting that."

Dad huffed and gripped his hips. "They know the damn law. You did *nothing* wrong."

"And they'd do the same if it were them," Caleb said.

I scratched at the chill in my arm. "I had hope for this town when I saw the pride shirts, ya know? I should've known it wouldn't last long. I can't wait to leave Madison." Caleb's eyes hit the floor, and I bit my tongue. "Caleb, I didn't mean it like—"

"I'm gonna go vote," Caleb said. "I'll see you guys in there. Good luck, Mr. Griffin." He patted Dad's shoulder before trotting off.

Dad's eyes met mine. "Sometimes you have to think before you speak." He buttoned his jacket. "Don't let that linger, son." Dad hooked his arm around my shoulders. "Let's go vote, huh?"

Think before I speak. What a concept.

———

Everyone gathered at our house for the election results. I never saw the place so packed. Almost everyone from my dad's team was there. Some even brought their families. Parker played with other kids in the backyard while several bottles of champagne sat in buckets of ice. Caleb looked to be feeling the effects of two drinks Steph made him. My dad said I shouldn't be seen drinking since people he worked with were around, so I let Caleb enjoy himself. His buzz showed in the form of butt squeezes when no one was looking. He tried the fifth secret squeeze when I pulled him into the stairway.

"Hey."

"Hey," he mimicked my tone.

"When I said earlier that I couldn't wait to leave, I didn't mean that about you."

Caleb sighed. "I know. It just makes me sad. And I don't want to be sad, because Steph's got a *heavy* pour. I am feelin' it!"

"Oh wow, okay."

Caleb leaned to whisper in my ear. "How hot would it be if I took you upstairs with all these people here? I want to taste you."

I laughed. "Keep dreaming, drunky."

"I'm not drunk. I'm buzzed," he said, grabbing me by the hips.

"Babe, I love you, but it's not gonna happen. There's too many people here. My dad would kill me if I disappeared."

He huffed. "Fine. You're no fun." He hopped off the step and joined Steph on the couch.

Tasha popped up next to me, shoving her phone in my face. "You have to see this! Your dad is blowing up on Twitter, Or X. Whatever. Doesn't matter. Look!"

"No way," I whispered, scrolling through the feed and seeing pictures of us. People were commenting in support of my dad's speech.

Dad stood by the TV, glued to the screen, biting his nails.

I jogged to him. "Dad, look." I held the phone out. "You're all over X."

He scrolled for a few seconds before his eyes returned to the TV. "The votes are what matter, son." He handed me Tasha's phone. "And Henley is ahead right now."

"I don't see any mention of him. You're literally going viral right now. There's no way you can lose!"

"Don't jinx it," Dad said.

Caleb knocked three times on the coffee table, and winked at me.

I moved back behind the couch with Tasha and returned her phone. Lauren and Steven joined us, sipping from plastic cups.

"Your dad looks so nervous," Steven said. "It's cute."

"It's like when we used to stare at the computer waiting for a cast list to go up," Lauren said.

Steven gripped Lauren's arm. "Oh my god, yes! That was so stressful!"

"Or like football tryouts," I said. Lauren and Steven gave me a blank stare.

"We wouldn't know what that's like." Steven pantomimed a hair toss.

"Speaking of football," Lauren said, "I saw Chris at Shop n' Go yesterday."

My stomach seized just hearing his name. I hadn't seen Dan's brother Chris since we spoke in the church parking lot before Dan's funeral. "How was he?"

"He seemed okay."

"Did you guys talk about anything?"

"A little," Lauren said. "Him and his parents are moving back to North Carolina. Said he's gonna try to get into college there."

The guilt crawled up my spine again, as if everything happened yesterday. I'd ruined his family, and now they'd move so they didn't have to see me around town. "That's great," I said, plastering a smile. "He'll have a lot of opportunities there."

Tasha was still staring at her phone. "People are *loving* your dad."

Lauren peeked over.

Steven pushed his way to Tasha's other side to look, too. "Oh my god."

Caleb, now sitting alone on the couch, stared at the TV. I spotted Steph in the kitchen talking to a tall man wearing glasses. To me, most of the people there were strangers.

I slid onto the couch next to Caleb and kissed him on the cheek.

He was slumped into the cushions with his arms crossed. "You're dad's trending, huh?"

"Apparently."

"I just wanna know the results already."

I nudged him. "Are you mad at me?"

Caleb stared at the TV.

"Oh my god," I said, turning to face him. "You're mad I wouldn't go upstairs with you?"

Caleb struggled to fight the smile tugging at his lips. "I'm drunk. I don't remember anything."

I laughed. "Oh, *now* you're drunk. I thought you said you were buzzed?"

"Perfect example."

I snuggled close to him, wrapping my arm around his. "How bout I make you a deal?"

Caleb looked at me with drowsy eyes. "Go on."

"If my dad wins, we can go upstairs while everyone celebrates."

Caleb bit his lip. "Are you trying to take advantage of me while I'm drunk?"

I put a hand on my chest. "I would *never*."

"What if I gave you permission?" Caleb flashed his dimples with an enticing smile.

My jaw tightened. It took everything I had not to straddle him and make out in front of everyone. "Do we have a deal then?"

"I think we do."

"This is it!" Dad shouted, getting everyone's attention. The chaotic chatter of the house settled as everyone moved closer to the TV. The local news channel had been keeping track of the results all night.

A woman wearing a red blazer sat behind the desk on screen. "I'm just getting word that the ballots have all been counted."

Caleb and I stood, and his hand grabbed mine. Tasha and the others came close to us. Lauren wrapped her arm around my waist. The whole house was silent except for the laughs from the kids playing out back.

"Bear with me while I get the final results," the newswoman said.

"Oh, come on already!" Dad shouted.

I squeezed Caleb's hand. It was like waiting at the top of those death drop rides at an amusement park.

"Okay," the newswoman said. "It's just been said that the people have voted...Curtis Griffin as mayor of Madison."

The cheers that erupted should've blown the roof off my house. Everyone rushed to my dad, squeezing him in one big group hug. Caleb and I jumped and hollered. Tasha, Steven, and Lauren danced in circles.

"Speech! Speech!" Someone yelled out over the chaos.

Dad looked out of breath when everyone settled back to their spots. His hands hugged his hips. He shook his head and smiled at the floor. "I couldn't have done this without any of you." Dad pointed around the room. "This team has worked so hard. We all felt it. Many, many late nights and missing out on time with our families. But God damn, was it worth it!"

Everyone clapped and hollered again.

Dad continued. "We went through two campaign managers! After I got rid of Tucker, I honestly thought that was it for me. So, I want to thank Steph for being one of the most dedicated, hard-working people I've ever met. She set us on the right path." He pulled one of the champagne bottles from the ice bucket and pointed it at Steph. "We won because of you. Tonight, we celebrate. Tomorrow, we go to work."

I leaned my head back to see Steph in the kitchen, crying and smiling. Her girlfriend hugged her from behind.

Dad shook the champagne before popping the cork. A blast of fizzy liquid shot across the living room. Everyone cheered and danced. It had been so long since I saw my dad ecstatic.

I wrapped my arms around Caleb and kissed him. His smile was equal parts cute and seductive. I pressed my forehead to his and whispered, "We have to be discreet. We can't let everyone see us go upstairs together."

"You're right, split up. I'll head up first and pretend I'm going to the bathroom, and then you come up a couple minutes later?"

"It's a date." I winked.

Caleb stood and drunkenly announced, "I'm going to the bathroom!" No one heard him over the music except my friends, each raising an eyebrow at the news.

My face fell into my hands. Caleb stormed up the stairs as I looked around for my dad. I wanted to make sure he was busy before I slipped upstairs. My house wasn't big. I could see most of the first floor just by doing a spin. But I didn't spot him.

I peeked out the sliding door but only saw the kids playing tag. Then it hit me—*Dad's office.*

I knocked and poked my head in. Dad sat at his desk, holding the picture of Mom in the chrome frame. A small lamp lit his face. I tiptoed in and shut the door. The room was almost silent. I sat in the chair across from him. "You've been escaping to this room a lot lately," I said.

"It's where I feel your mom the most," Dad said. "I talk to her here. I guess I've been doing it more now that we're selling."

"Is everything okay?"

Dad sighed. "I wasn't done living my life with her." My heart shattered. "I wanted her here more than I wanted that win."

"She would've been really proud, Dad."

He placed the frame back on the desk and looked at me. "She would've been proud of both of us."

I nodded. "Yeah, she would've." He wanted to smile. I saw his mouth twitch, but it never came. "You sure you want to sell?"

"It'll be good for all of us." He sat up in his chair. "I'll be back out in a minute. I just want to talk to her a little longer." I smiled and stood. "I love you, son."

"Love you too, Dad. Congrats on the W. You deserve it."

He shook his head. "Still can't believe it."

"Believe it!" I said, walking out the door and shouting over the music. "You did it, old man!"

My phone vibrated as I closed the door behind me. Caleb texted me a shirtless selfie from my bed. I smiled at the screen and bolted up the stairs. *A deal's a deal.*

SEVEN

NEW YORK CITY

Sunday, January 5th.

When I got back, Steven was up, but he was in Josh's bed. He managed to put on his pants, but he remained shirtless.

"Josh is teaching me how to code... or something!" Steven said with a chipper tone.

I sat on my bed. "Oh really?"

"It's very fascinating."

I laughed. "So fascinating you didn't have time to put on a shirt?"

Steven shot me a look. "I'm thinking of switching majors."

"From fashion to computer science?" I laughed again. "I'd love to see that."

"Hey," Steven said as he slid off Josh's bed, "don't you dare put me in a box. It's offensive!" Steven dramatically paced around the room, looking for his clothes and putting his theater experience to good use. He swiped his shirt from under my bed and shoved it into his Lindsay Lohan bag before pulling on a clean one. "While I'm very satisfied with my stay in this prison, I must go."

I made a fake frown. "Aw, already?"

"Walk me down? I'll call an Uber on the way."

I smiled and hopped off the bed. "Sure."

"It was lovely meeting you, Josh," Steven said. I half expected him to hold out his hand so Josh could kiss it.

"You too, man," Josh said with his eyes locked on his computer screen.

———

Steven sighed when we stepped into the elevator. "Josh is so straight."

I laughed. "I told you he was."

Steven's phone dinged as we hit the lobby. "It'll be here in three minutes."

I nodded. "They're a lot faster here than in Texas." Steven suddenly hugged me and held on tight. I chuckled. "This feels a little premature. We still have two minutes!"

"I know but... Are you okay?" He whispered.

"Yes. Why?" I said, still wrapped in his hug.

Steven looked at me. "To be honest, you kinda scared me last night."

I shrugged. "It was just the molly. Overstimulation."

"Was it? I mean, it hasn't even been a year yet."

"I told you during Christmas break, I don't have the dreams that much anymore."

"That doesn't mean everything's fine." Steven's arms fell to his sides. "I know I asked you about it during break, but you should talk to someone."

"Who are you, my dad?"

"I'm just saying... if I had gone through—"

"Well, you didn't. You didn't go through it."

"I didn't, but I know what it feels like to be tormented by Dan."

I rolled my eyes.

"What?" Steven asked.

"It's different. I told you I don't have the dreams anymore. I'm not gonna be the kid who went insane after high school. I can deal with it on my own."

Steven crossed his arms, staring out at the street. "It's obvious you're going through some shit, especially now with Caleb. But don't push away the people who want to help."

I never wanted Steven to think I wasn't grateful to have him as a friend. The night we spent in my car in the Barnes and Noble parking lot flashed through my thoughts.

A black SUV parked at the sidewalk, and Steven shouldered his bag. "That's my limo." I followed Steven to the chilly sidewalk. He opened the car door and looked at me one more time. "I had a blast. But I'm worried about you, girl. Please call me if you need to, okay?" He looked up at all the tall buildings. "Who knows, maybe I'll end up here someday, and then you won't be able to get rid of me."

I half-smiled. "New York City isn't ready for Steven Mori."

Steven wrapped his arms around my neck. "Love you." He plopped into the seat and closed the door.

I waved through the window, watched him drive off, and ran back inside before I got hypothermia.

———

Monday, January 6th

My first day back to class was filled with Gen-Eds. I wanted to get through them early in my college career. I trudged through the day, pushing through the boring stuff to get to my last class, screenwriting.

The professor was a middle-aged man who wore thick glasses and clearly dyed his hair black—his grays still showed in the back. He set his laptop on his desk and projected his screen onto the whiteboard. He'd written Pat Virta in the top left corner of the board.

The class was in a small, second-floor room that felt like a dorm. Twenty desks fit in a semicircle around the room. When I started a new class, I liked to sit as far away from the teacher as possible, just to get a feel for everything.

I opened my laptop. A few people scattered around the class, but a guy in a striped shirt sat beside me. He opened his computer and stared at me, bouncing in his seat.

"This guy is a legend," he said. "You know he wrote *Reaper's Dawn*, right?"

I glanced at him. "Haven't seen it."

"Shit, really? I figured everyone here has, or else why take his class?"

"I'm trying to dip my toes in a few different writing styles, see if anything sticks."

He nodded. "You must be a movie buff, then."

"Not really," I said, hoping it wasn't required. "But my boyfriend— I mean, one of my friends is. He tries to keep me up to date."

"He'd probably flip if he knew your teacher was Pat Virta."

"Yeah, probably." I booted up my computer.

"I heard he's kind of a hardass."

My brow perked. "Oh?"

"He's notorious for ripping up people's papers in front of the whole class if he thinks something isn't good."

I gulped. "Sounds intense."

"Totally. I can't wait!"

I pulled out my phone and opened my text thread with Caleb. He still hadn't responded to my last three messages.

ME

> I'm taking a screenwriting class. Pat Virta is my teacher. Thought maybe you'd think that was cool.

Surprisingly, I sent the message, and the three dots popped up. My heart jumped, and I stared at the screen, eagerly waiting to see what he would say. Just as quickly, though, the dots disappeared. My eyes lingered on the screen, but I gave up hope.

Pat Virta spent half the class going over his career. While inspiring, it felt gratuitous. The class picked up when Pat told us the basics of the three-act structure in storytelling. So much of what we discussed made me think of Caleb. I was tempted to call him after class but knew he wouldn't answer.

I stopped at the Ivory Den on my way home. It was a warm place to land after a full day, and the smell never got old. I planned on binging a few of Pat Virta's movies, starting with *Reaper's Dawn*, so I needed caffeinated fuel. I got to the shop a half-hour before closing as the baristas cleaned up. They probably hated me. I put several dollars in their tip jar before ordering to get on their good side. "Can I get a medium mocha, please?"

"Sure thing," a petite blonde girl said with a smile. She looked young. I assumed she went to NYU, too. Her name tag said 'Jenna.'

Being the only one in the shop, standing in silence was awkward. I glanced over my shoulder at the corner table where Isaac and I sat. I wondered if he'd been back since then or if he'd remember I owed him a coffee. An idea hit my thoughts. I pulled a napkin from its metal holder and took a pen from my bag.

"Hey, Jenna," I said. "This might sound weird, but can you do me a favor?"

She looked at me with squinted eyes as she poured my drink. "Depends what it is."

I placed the napkin on the counter and slid it toward her. She looked down at it, rolled her eyes, and slid it back to me when she saw my phone number. My cheeks warmed. "Oh. I'm not hitting on you."

"That's not what it looks like," Jenna said.

I scratched the back of my head. "I really should've given more context." I stared at the napkin. "There's this guy that comes here—"

"Isaac, right?"

My brow tightened. "How'd you know?"

Jenna laughed. "You're probably the fourth person to leave your number for him this week."

Just this week? "What is he, like, the hottest guy at NYU?" I asked.

She stared blankly, then pressed the lid onto my cup. "He usually tosses them."

"Oh. Forget it then." I reached for the napkin, but Jenna grabbed it first.

"I'll throw it out," she said.

"Wait. Will you tell him I still owe him a coffee if he comes in? My name's Landon. He'll remember. Who doesn't want free coffee, right?" I chuckled, but Jenna seemed unamused. I reached for my cup and exited back into the chill.

———

I was lying in bed with my computer on my chest when my phone vibrated.

UNKNOWN

You shouldn't give your number out to strangers. They could be psycho murderers.

I paused *Reaper's Dawn*.

ME

Very funny, Jenna. Are all your co-workers gonna troll me now?

UNKNOWN

Trolls are the worst kind of people. This is Isaac. :)

I shot up, almost sending my laptop crashing to the floor. *Holy shit!*

ME

OMG, seriously?

ISAAC

Seriously. You owe me a coffee. And I like free stuff.

ME

I was at Ivory Den like an hour ago. Jenna said she'd toss the napkin.

ISAAC

Jenna is a dirty liar, then, haha. Luckily for me, it was the last napkin available before closing.

Thank you, Jenna!

ME

She told me you get a lot of numbers.

ISAAC

I was surprised this one was from you.

ME

I wasn't sure when you'd be back, so I thought leaving my number was my best shot.

ISAAC

I'm in there a lot, actually. I only live three blocks over. Best coffee in the village.

ME

Oh, definitely! I'm glad I didn't destroy your phone.

ISAAC

A bag of rice can work wonders.

ME

Haha good. So, I take it you don't live in the dorms?

ISAAC

Haha no, I don't.

ME

Lucky. I like my roommate, but my own place would be better.

ISAAC

It can get lonely, but I've adjusted.

So, what're you up to?

ME

I'm watching a movie called Reaper's Dawn. My screenwriting teacher wrote it, so I thought I should watch.

ISAAC

Ah yes, Pat Virta. It's a classic.

ME

It's kinda fucked up. Lol.

ISAAC

Every revenge movie is fucked up. That's what makes them so good!

ME

Haha, I haven't seen many.

ISAAC

I can leave you alone then. Didn't mean to interrupt.

ME

You didn't! It's totally fine. I'm glad you texted me.

Don't sound too desperate.

ISAAC:

> I'm glad you left your number. :) I know this is last-minute, but I'm meeting a friend for dinner on the Upper West Side. Would you maybe want to meet me after, at the pier, around 8:45ish?

My anxiety showed its ugly head again as I read his text. Part of me doubted I was talking to Isaac and that it was one of Jenna's co-workers setting me up for a laugh. But if it wasn't that... *No, a date would be dinner or coffee. This is just a hang-out.*

ISAAC

> I know it's cold, so it's okay if you don't want to.

ME

> No, that's fine. I'd love to meet up.

ISAAC

> Cool! Meet me at the pier on 70th Street.

ME

> Alright, I'll be there. :)

I finished the movie before stressing over what to wear. I opened the wardrobe and shuffled through the hangers. I kept turning to the mirror, holding shirts against my body like I was in a dressing room.

My sigh caught Josh's attention, sitting at his desk on his laptop. "What're you doing?"

"I'm figuring out what to wear," I said, pulling a sweater off a hanger.

"For what?"

"I met this guy at the Ivory Den, and he asked me to hang out."

"Whoa, what's Caleb think of this guy?"

I wanted to avoid the question, but bringing Caleb up wasn't his fault. I hadn't told Josh anything yet. "Caleb doesn't have to approve everyone I hang out with. And also, this guy's just a friend. It's not a date or anything. We're just meeting at the pier." I put the sweater back on the hanger and stared at all the clothes, feeling lost.

"Okay," Josh said. His fingers tapped the computer keys. "It's gonna be freezing at the pier. Does it matter what you wear if you have a coat on the whole time?"

Damn, he's right. "You're so smart, Josh."

"That's why you keep me around," he said.

"I just need to layer up." I removed the sweater from the hanger and pulled it over my T-shirt.

———

When I got off the 1 train, I walked west towards the Hudson River. With all the exploring I did during my first semester, I'd yet to make it to the pier. I loved the city at night; everything was bright. I liked looking up at random buildings, seeing the lights in apartment windows, and thinking about what it might look like inside.

The pier at the western edge of Manhattan ran down the island. A quick Google search on the train showed I had to cross the busy Riverside Boulevard to get to the grassy area leading down to the pier.

Tall lamp posts lit the whole strip of the boardwalk. I imagined an array of flowers blooming in the soil in warmer weather, but that night, everything was dead, except the grass that looked like it was trying to get a peek at the small waves. As I approached the guardrail, Isaac came into focus under the light post. His curls jumped off his head. I approached Isaac and smiled. "Hey."

"Hey!" Isaac took out a pair of earmuffs from his coat pocket and slipped them on. "Thanks for meeting me."

I squinted at him. "You kinda look like someone." Isaac deflated. " You look like this guy who goes to my coffee shop."

Isaac straightened up and laughed. "Oh, *your* coffee shop, huh? I've been going there since I was fifteen."

"Really? So you grew up here? I never would've guessed from the accent."

"I'm originally from this small town outside of London called Newbury. But I moved here when I was young, so the accent comes and goes." Isaac pushed off the guard rail and started walking.

I stepped with him. "That's so cool! I always wondered what it would be like to grow up in a big city."

"Where are you from?"

"Texas. So, very different," I said.

Isaac smiled. "How do you like New York so far?"

"I love it! I've never felt more independent." I zipped my coat up to my neck. The wind flew off the river like a jet plane crashing into us.

"Getting around NYU, okay?"

"Yeah, it's pretty easy once you know where every building is. The flags help." Isaac chuckled, and I looked at him. "You said you were a second-year, right?"

"Kind of. I haven't officially started my second year."

Huh? Classes started today.

Isaac cupped his hands and blew into them. "I decided to take the year off to work."

I thought of my dad—he'd never let me take a gap year. "Where do you work?"

Isaac looked at the ground as we walked. "I'm still in training, so I haven't officially started yet." He looked at me. "Is this your first time here?"

"At the pier? Yeah." I said.

Isaac stopped to admire the skyline across the river, so I leaned on the rail beside him.

"I love it here at night," Isaac said. "Not too many people bother you. Just the sound of the river on one side and traffic on the other."

I took a moment to close my eyes and listen. Waves smacked the rocks below us. A bus blared its horn. When I opened my eyes, Isaac was looking at me.

He showed off his tooth gap. "Nice, right?"

"Yeah," I said. "Did you come here a lot growing up?"

Isaac faced the street and leaned back on the rail, resting his elbows. "Not really. I learned to appreciate it more as I got older when I learned to take things a little slower."

"Can't relate," I smirked. "I feel like there's a constant checklist in my head. I'm always thinking about the next thing I have to do."

"We should meditate together sometime. It might help."

"I've never tried it."

Isaac faced me. "Really? We'll need some crystals, then. Do it right."

"Crystals?"

"I have crystals for everything. We can totally balance you out."

I laughed. "Do they really work?"

"Hell yes, they work. You'll see." Isaac smiled and faced the water again. My phone vibrated. I pulled it out and unlocked the screen. Isaac glanced over. "Everything okay?"

The scene in the dojo replayed in my head as I stared at my phone. "Yeah." I locked the screen. "My self-defense teacher just sent me a training video."

"Oh, cool. Can I see it?"

His question took me aback, but I didn't want to reject him. "Uh, yeah. Sure." I pulled the phone out and touched the notification. We watched Jason demonstrate the same move from class.

Isaac's eyes were glued to the screen. "That's so cool. You can do that?"

"I haven't really tried... yet."

"Let's try it!" Isaac pushed away from the rails and hopped into the grass off the boardwalk.

"Wait, really?"

Isaac bent and grabbed a stick. "Yeah!"

I stepped into the grass with him, feeling unqualified to teach. Isaac pointed the stick at me. I held my breath, waiting for Dan to assault my thoughts. What the hell was it about Isaac that made the panic stop?

"You okay?" Isaac asked.

I shook my head. "Yeah, sorry. Okay, depending on which hand the gun's in determines how you move." I slowly walked through the movements from the video as best I could.

Isaac pointed the stick at me again.

Don't panic.

"Now try it faster," Isaac said.

I got into position and did my best to perform the move as fast as Jason had, but instead, I knocked the stick in the air, flying toward Isaac's face. It might've taken his eye out if he had weaker reflexes. "Oh my god!" I rushed closer to him. "I'm so sorry!" I cupped my cold hands around his face to steady him for a look at the mark I'd caused. His emerald eyes were like beams of light staring into my soul.

"What's the damage?"

"Barely a scratch," I said, examining his cheek before our eyes met.

He placed his hands on mine. I swear they were as hot as the earth's core. "So you're saying I'll make it, Doc?"

I stared at him for a moment, stuck in his eyes. His hands thawed the thin layer of ice around mine, or at least that was what it felt like. The cloud from his breath floated between our faces, inches apart. My hands fell, and I stepped back like I'd broken his spell. "Yeah. You're still hot," I said before my eyes widened. "I mean your hands! They're really warm."

Isaac laughed, shoving his hands back in his pockets. "Thank you. I'm glad I won't be deformed for the rest of my life." He stepped onto the boardwalk, and again I followed.

"Check this out," Isaac said. He stopped and pointed. We'd arrived at a section of the pier that wasn't protected by guard rails.

Instead, massive cement steps led into the river. "Mind if we get closer?"

"Okay," I said. We took it one step at a time, but neither noticed the low tide. We were two steps from the water when we both slipped. It was too dark to see the thin layer of algae that had accumulated over the cement. Our instinct was to grab each other for balance, but we were both destined for the water. Isaac somehow turned into a graceful ballerina—able to twist his body mid-air and land in the water standing. The tide reached just above his knees.

My experience was very different. With all my flailing to catch myself on Isaac's arm, my body turned into a rag doll. Every limb flung itself into the air, and I crashed into the water headfirst, completely submerging myself in the Hudson River. The water felt like a thousand knives piercing my skin. I popped through the surface with a gasp of air as Isaac pulled himself from the water. I had fallen so far out I had to swim back to the cement steps. Isaac helped me out of the water and held onto me until we reached the grass again. Not only was I the most embarrassed I'd ever felt, but all of my clothes were covered in green goo.

Isaac looked at me before touching my shoulder. "Are you okay?"

I pulled out my phone and tried to turn on the screen. Nothing. My hands shook, and my teeth chattered. "I think my phone's broken," I sighed. "My dad's gonna kill me."

"It's my fault. I shouldn't have—"

"I have to go home." I couldn't even look at Isaac.

"Let me call you a car."

"No," I said a little too aggressively. "I'm just... I'm gonna go." I slipped on the grass, hurried to the street, and left Isaac without a goodbye.

I got to Riverside Boulevard and hailed the first cab I saw. My teeth wouldn't stop chattering. Luckily, Dad gave me a credit card for emergencies, and I considered the cab ride home a major one. I ripped my coat off as soon as I stepped into my room.

Josh looked at me with shock. "What in the hell happened to you?"

I wrapped my coat around the radiator, still dripping with river water and goo. "I don't wanna talk about it." I slammed the bathroom door behind me and turned on the shower, making the water as hot as possible. I peeled off my wet clothes and placed my soaked wallet and dead phone on the sink. As I tried to regulate my body temperature, I kept thinking about how I'd never be able to see Isaac again. He's probably texting all his friends about the idiot who fell in the Hudson River.

EIGHT

TEXAS

Four Months Ago

"Now strike him in the throat!" Sam shouted at us. Everyone in the class hit the throat of their rubber dummy. "Rake his eyes!" We went for the dummy's eyes. "Knee to the chest!"

My dummy was too tall, so he got a knee to the stomach instead.

Sam paced as he watched us. "Everything I've taught you thus far can be used in succession."

I'd been taking Sam's self-defense class for two months at that point. At first, I just wanted to appease my dad. But as the weeks went on, I started to enjoy it. It kept me active. Otherwise, I'd be on the couch watching movies with Caleb all summer. The class was specifically for young adults. We were lined up, facing a bust of a bald rubber man on a pole with a weighted bottom.

Sam stood behind my dummy and grabbed its shoulders. They looked like twins. "These moves will be vital for moving to New York."

I could feel the sweat dripping from my hair. "Been talking to my dad again?"

"Elbow to the jaw!" Sam yelled to the class. "I don't consider that a bad thing. New York is riddled with crime. You have to have eyes in the back of your head."

Sam dodged my elbow, crashing into the rubber jaw. I wanted to roll my eyes but was afraid of the repercussions. Sam was a former bodybuilder. You felt it when he tossed you around the mat. "Plenty of people there'll take advantage of a newbie," Sam said, digging his fingers into the rubber. "Uppercut to the chin!"

I sent an uppercut to the rubber chin, bobbing it's head. "Have you ever been to New York?"

"No," Sam said. "But I've heard plenty of stories. And I watch the news." He walked to someone else, and I rolled my eyes when he wasn't looking to get it out of my system. Of course, I was nervous about navigating New York City, but I'd have Lauren and Google Maps. I don't think Dad or Sam realized how much New York had changed since they were kids.

———

I dabbed at my neck and forehead with a towel after class when Sam popped up next to me. For such a big guy, he moved like a ninja.

"It's been great having you in class, Landon. You've made a lot of progress."

I let the towel fall on my shoulder before picking up my water bottle. "Thanks. It's been great. I'm glad my dad talked me into it."

"Glad you were able to learn a few things." He held his hand out. "Good luck in New York. I'm sure you'll do great."

I shook his hand and smiled. "I appreciate it."

"Don't forget about us small-town folk. You're welcome to stop by anytime you're home. And tell your dad I said hi. He's gonna do great things for this town."

I grabbed my backpack and pushed my water bottle inside. "I will, Sam, thank you."

He nodded and walked off as I zipped my backpack. I snatched my phone from my bag's side pouch and opened the screen. One unread text from Steven: *Call us!*

Once inside my dad's car, I clipped my phone into the mount on the dashboard. "Hey Siri, FaceTime Steven Mori." He didn't answer until I pulled out of the parking lot.

Steven popped up on my screen, shirtless. "Landy, where are you?"

I glanced at him as I pushed through a four-way intersection. "I told you I had my last self-defense class."

"Oh yeah. How's the defense man?"

"He told me New York City is riddled with crime and that I had to have eyes in the back of my head. So, ya know, the usual."

Lauren pushed Steven out of frame. "That's bull shit! What does he know?" She held up a makeup brush before moving out of frame.

Then Tasha's face peered at me. "If he's done any research, he would know crime in New York has dropped dramatically over the last five years."

My eyes moved back and forth from the road to the screen. "Are you all in the bathroom?"

"Yes," Tasha said. "We're doing our make-up for tonight."

Steven rotated into frame, and Tasha moved to the mirror. They were like a three-person circus. "Are you meeting us here? You need some glitter on your face."

"I'm gonna get ready at home with Caleb, so we'll meet you at Paradise."

Steven batted his mascara'd eyelashes at me. "Okay, girl. Don't be late!"

I smiled. "I promise I won't be late."

Steven blew me a kiss and hung up the phone.

———

Caleb was in the kitchen when I got home. Dad had given him a key in case he or Parker ever needed anything. Caleb stood from the stool and scooped me in a bear hug. He pecked kisses all over my neck and face before licking his lips. "Salty."

I laughed and pushed him away to start up the stairs. "Yeah, I need to shower before we go."

Caleb followed behind. "Cute butt. Maybe I'll join you."

I tossed my backpack on my bed and removed my shirt. "It has to be a quick shower, though, nothing else. Steven wants us there on time."

Caleb pulled off his shirt before pressing his torso against mine. "What're you trying to say?"

My hands drifted to the tight muscles around his tailbone. "You seduce me every time we shower together. I'm saying there's no time for that."

Caleb bit his bottom lip. "I promise I'll be on my best behavior." He untied my basketball shorts and pushed them down before giving his lips to mine.

Showering with Caleb was one of the most intimate things I'd ever done with anyone. I loved being wrapped in his arms as the hot water covered us, wishing we could stay there for hours, swaying back and forth. Seeing Caleb Montes naked was a privilege I never wanted to give up.

I passed the bar of soap across his chest and down his side. "The bruises are gone."

Caleb wiped his eyes to take a glance. "Yeah, they said the ribs healed up nicely. I'm ready for the self-defense class now."

I chuckled. "It's a little too late for that."

Caleb wrapped his arms around my neck and pressed his forehead to mine. The water trickling off his nose landed on my lips. He closed his eyes. "You leave in two days," he said. "What am I gonna do without you?"

His words pierced my heart. I pulled him close. "If it were my choice, I'd take you with me."

"Then who'd take care of Parker?"

"Exactly," I said.

"But I won't have you to kiss."

"We'll FaceTime every night."

"I know. It's just not gonna be the same." Caleb squeezed me a little tighter. "I don't want to be here without you."

I cupped his face and kissed him. "Maybe the days will fly by, and I'll be home for Christmas."

"And then you're gone again."

"I'm sorry." I couldn't think of much else to say as we stood under the water, clinging to each other. NYU was something I wanted so badly, and it was finally becoming a reality. But I worried for Caleb. I hoped we could handle the long distance.

———

We pulled into the parking lot of Paradise. The usual eighteen-plus crowd lingered around their cars, pregaming since they couldn't drink inside. Lauren, Steven, and Tasha stormed our car once I killed the engine.

We got out and hugged each of them. They were all dolled up. Each wore a different color around their eyes but had matching glitter streaks across their cheeks.

Steven approached me after hugging Caleb and pulled out a chapstick. "We need to gay you up." Steven wore a white crop top with a unicorn on it. "This shorts-and-tank-top look just isn't enough." He raised the chapstick.

I reared back a little. "What is that?"

"It's my glitter stick. Can I put it on you, please?"

I glanced at a smiling Caleb.

"Oh, he's getting it too, don't you worry," Steven said.

I didn't love the idea of wearing glitter, but it was our last night together. "Fine."

Steven drew a line across one cheek and then the other and smoothed it with his thumb. He moved on to Caleb, who was more than willing to offer his face.

Tasha played with her hair in the reflection of a car window. "Is Miguel coming too?"

Caleb eyed Tasha as Steven smoothed the glitter into his cheeks. "No, he's having some of our other friends over for dinner tonight."

"There," Steven said. "You're pretty now."

Caleb laughed. "Thanks."

Lauren walked backward. "Can we go dance our asses off now?"

Steven's tongue popped. "Yes!" He locked arms with Tasha, and we followed Lauren around the building.

I locked my fingers between Caleb's. "You didn't tell me your friends were doing dinner. You didn't have to miss it."

He looked at me. "If you think I'll miss a waking second with you this weekend, you're nuts." He squeezed my hand as we hopped in line.

Lauren eyed the bouncer, then turned to us. "What's with the black X he's drawing on people's hands?"

"That's so the bartenders know we're under twenty-one," Steven said. "You have so much to learn, you poor naive girl." He stroked her hair as a grandmother does to a child. She slapped his hand away.

Caleb looked at Lauren. "Is this your first time at a club?"

"Yeah," Lauren answered.

Tasha slowly raised her hand. "Mine too."

"I never thought I'd say this, but," Steven put a hand to his chest. "I'm so honored to be popping your cherries tonight."

We all laughed, and the girls said a simultaneous 'ew.'

The bouncer drew an X on my hand, and I followed Caleb through alcohol-soaked air. We immediately fled to the dance floor, passing a sitting area of red leather couches. We pushed through the bodies, following Steven to the middle of the floor. He liked being the center of attention. His dance moves were erratic but somehow attracted the moths to his flamboyant flame. A disco ball spun, plunging us into an ocean of colors.

I felt awkward dancing, but being with my friends made it easier. And the fact that I wasn't trying to impress Caleb anymore helped. He was mine, and I was his—no need to act cool anymore.

Caleb grabbed my waist and danced against me. His smile could've lit up the room even without a disco ball. Steven was locked in a dancing sandwich between Lauren and Tasha. Everything we'd been through seemed like a distant dream on that dance floor.

We must've danced for an hour before Tasha pulled us away for a break. We all held hands, letting her lead us to the couches in a single-file line while Caleb stood at the bar.

"I can't believe you're all leaving me here," Steven shouted over the music.

Tasha wrapped her arm around Steven. "We'll all be back for Christmas at the very least."

Steven pouted. "What if you love DC so much that you never want to come back to Texas?"

Lauren laughed. "That's never gonna happen. All our families are still here."

"And you," I added. The three of us looked at Steven and then crowded him with a group hug.

"It's not like you're staying in Madison," Tasha said as we sat. "Dallas is very different."

I put my hand on Steven's knee. "You're going to art school. Think of all the gays you'll meet there!"

Steven smiled. "I *am* excited about that part."

Lauren nudged him. "Who knows, you might meet the love of your life."

"I don't know," Steven said. "New York and DC sound much more exciting."

"You know you can visit us any time," I said.

Caleb approached with teetering cups of water. I grabbed one from him and passed it down until we all had one.

Caleb plopped next to me. "What're we talking about?"

I leaned into my boyfriend. "Steven's sad we're all leaving him."

"Hey," Caleb said, pointing to himself. "I'll still be here! We can hang out. We're friends."

Steven smirked. "With benefits, right?"

Water almost sprayed from my nose, trying to hold in my laugh.

By the look on Caleb's face, he might've thought Steven was serious.

"I'm kidding!" Steven held his hand out to Caleb with a limp wrist. "Of course we're friends."

Caleb leaped to kiss Steven's hand as if he were royalty. "Let's go fuckin' dance then!" Caleb pulled Steven off the couch.

Steven's eyes widened when he looked at me. "He's so strong!"

I laughed, guzzled the rest of my water, and followed them to the dance floor. We couldn't get the smiles off our faces as we moved around each other, grinding to every song that filled the room—letting the sweat pour. A remixed version of "We Are Family" played as Caleb pulled his shirt off, catching the eyes of the surrounding guys, but Caleb's gaze stayed on me.

I smiled and shouted, "What are you doing!"

Caleb's dimples beamed at me as he put my hands on his chest and slid them down to his waist. His skin was warm and damp. Then, he spun around to grind on me. Caleb leaned his head back on my shoulder. "I'm having fun. That's what I'm doing."

"You look sexy as fuck!" I shouted. "Every guy here is looking at you!"

Caleb's grinding stirred excitement behind my zipper. He turned and wrapped his arms around my neck. "Let 'em' look. You're the only one that matters!" He pushed his lips to mine while our hips moved as one. "Let's show 'em' how hot *you* are." Caleb pulled my shirt over my head, revealing my pale skin to the entire club, but I didn't care. Caleb made me feel sexy, and I liked the idea of everyone watching us. Touching his glistening shoulders made me think of the first time I saw him in the courtyard at school, daydreaming about what his skin would feel like against mine.

I brought my lips to his ear. "I love you."

"I love you more!" He shouted. "I never want this to end!"

This is heaven.

———

We stepped outside and gasped for air, feeling like we'd been stuck in a rocket, drifting in space for years. I put my shirt back on as the wind chilled my damp skin. Caleb followed suit.

Steven whipped out his phone. "Oh my god, how is it almost midnight already?"

Caleb's face scrunched. "Shit." He pulled out his phone and started texting someone. "You guys mind if we dip? We have that thing."

I tilted my head. "What thing?" I looked at the other three. "What's going on? Why are you all smiling?"

Steven hugged me tightly. "I'll see you soon."

I was hesitant to hug him back. "Wait, so this is it?"

"Yeah, girl," Steven said. "Your man has something planned."

"And you all knew about it?" I asked.

Tasha hugged me. "Of course we did."

I squeezed her. "I'm so confused."

"Just go with it," Lauren said as she piled on another hug, wrapping her arms over Tasha's. Steven added his hug, too, and my eyes welled.

"I'm gonna miss you all," I said. "A lot."

They backed off of me, and the girls' eyes sparkled.

Tasha wiped a tear from her cheek. "We'll see each other for the holidays."

"Yeah," Lauren said. "It's only a few months."

I nodded and wiped my eyes before any tears could escape. "Love you guys."

We hugged again before going our separate ways. It was official: high school was over. My friends headed off to their independent lives. Every high school memory played out as I walked to the car. Laughing with Tasha in the library and throwing fries at Lauren during lunch. Bathroom gossip sessions with Steven, wishing I could go back and make a different choice that didn't include Dan.

———

I started putting the pieces together as Caleb directed me where to go. The familiar dark and dusty roads gave it away. I parked in front of a chain link fence. The car's high beams lit up the 'NO TRESPASSING' sign.

I killed the engine and looked at Caleb. "Why are we at Rocky Lake Park?"

His dimples appeared. "Get out. I'll show you."

We passed through the break in the fence and walked through the foliage littered with empty beer cans, finally arriving at the end of the path. Caleb opened the white door for me, bowing as if it were some grand gesture. I smiled, walked through the game booth, and hopped the half-wall into the park.

Caleb held my hand and led me down the hill toward the Ferris wheel. The night's moon was so bright we didn't need our flashlights. I saw everything much clearer than the first night Caleb showed me the abandoned park. It was easy to see the spray-painted dragon on the floor of the bumper car pit and all the smashed beer bottles in front of the hot dog stand.

As we inched closer to the Ferris wheel at the end of the park, I noticed a blue hue against the cement. I thought it was coming off the lake, but it was too vibrant to be natural. Then I saw it. It was like something out of a fairytale. One of the carts of the Ferris wheel glowed. Caleb pulled me closer, and I couldn't stop smiling. A string of lights wrapped around the cart, the seats, and the rods that kept it in place. Everything was blue. It looked magical.

"Oh my god, babe."

Caleb released my hand and reached for a paper bag on the cart's seat. "I hope the food's still warm."

"How'd you do this?" The cart wobbled as I sat, feeling like we'd be lifted over the lake at any moment.

"Miguel and Parker may have helped." Caleb pulled two take-out containers from the bag.

"Wait. So, was there a dinner at Miguel's tonight with your other friends?" Caleb shook his head. I smirked, "You're real slick."

He passed me a warm container and a plastic fork. I could smell it, but opening the box confirmed it: sesame chicken with pork fried rice. My stomach growled. Caleb turned on some music.

"You know," I said with a mouth full of chicken. "I thought you were gonna murder me the first time you brought me here."

Caleb chuckled and sipped from a bottle of water he pulled from the paper bag. "I'm glad you trusted me."

"I was so nervous. But I was even more nervous when you kissed me."

Caleb put the cap on the bottle, stood, and took my food away to sit on my lap. He wrapped his arm around my shoulders. "Still nervous about kissing me?"

"Maybe."

Caleb leaned and kissed me deeply, slipping his tongue between my lips before pulling away. "How 'bout now?"

"No nerves, but I'm definitely feeling something."

Caleb laughed. "Yeah, I can feel it against my leg." He tried to return to the other bench, but I clung to him. I pulled out my phone and held it up for a selfie. Caleb kissed me on the cheek just as the camera snapped.

Caleb stared at my screen. "It's hideous."

He flailed back to the other bench. We ate our food, laughed, and talked about what we would do in New York when he visited. Caleb wanted to see all the tourist attractions: the Empire State Building, the Statue of Liberty, and even Macy's.

I tossed my empty container into the bag. "Kissing at the top of the Empire State Building? Isn't that a little cliche?"

"I like cliche. It's romantic."

"It's in a million movies!"

"How would you know?"

I stuck my tongue out at him, and he did the same.

He reached for his phone and switched the music to a peaceful piano. Then, he put his hand out in front of me. "May I?" He guided me to the overview of the lake. He kept his hand in mine, and the other went to my hip as we swayed. "How's this for cliche? Slow dancing under the moonlight."

"You're right. Cliches *are* romantic." I rested my head on his shoulder. I could see the houses lit up across the water. "Thank you for doing this. It's the best last night I could've asked for."

"I wanted it to be perfect," he whispered.

I looked at him before planting a light kiss. "You're perfect."

We pressed our foreheads together, closed our eyes, listened to the music, and swayed side to side, slowly spinning. I wished I could freeze time. Everything I needed was right there with him.

We stayed silent, wrapped in each other's arms for a few minutes before he spoke. "You must be excited to finally get to New York tomorrow."

"Yes and no," I whispered.

"What do you think it's gonna be like?"

"A lot louder." I chuckled. "Maybe that's what I need to drown out the bad dreams."

"You can leave all that behind on the plane."

"Sounds impossible."

"Don't let Dan ruin your fresh start." Caleb cupped my face and looked at me. "I know it's easier said than done, but you gotta let him go."

It was as if Dan's soul was trapped in my consciousness, screaming to be set free. Maybe leaving Madison was the only key to that lock. "I want to."

Caleb kissed me. "You will."

NINE

NEW YORK CITY

Wednesday, January 8th

After my third and final class, I tried to turn my phone on again. My thumb hurt from holding the power button for so long. I charged it all night, but the screen stayed dark.

"Come on, work," I whispered. I hadn't texted Dad in almost two days—the panic was setting in.

Walking home from class, I tried to think of an excuse to tell Dad why I needed a new phone. We didn't get insurance because I'd never broken a phone before. I never expected to fall into a river with it.

"Dad. Don't be mad. I fell in the Hudson River." I pulled my hood over my head. *No, he'll ask what I was doing there, and I don't want to tell him I was with a new guy.* "Dad, I dropped my phone down the elevator shaft." I sniffled. *No, too far-fetched.* "Dad, I dropped my phone, and it shattered." *Simple. Done.*

My internal GPS led me to The Ivory Den. I considered getting a latte but decided on a hot chocolate instead.

"Landon!"

I flinched as Isaac appeared next to me.

"Sorry, didn't mean to scare you," he said.

I couldn't look at him. The events from the pier filled my thoughts. "Hey."

"I wanted to apologize for the other night. I've been waiting around, hoping you'd show up."

I gave in and looked at him. His curls were too damn cute. "It's the middle of the day. How long have you been waiting?"

"Five hours yesterday, and like, three today."

"Jeez, really?" Was that creepy or endearing?

Isaac was swimming in an oversized knit sweater. "I tried to call you, but it kept going to voicemail."

"Yeah, my phone's completely dead."

"I figured. Which is why I wanted to say I'm sorry. Everything was my fault."

Okay, it was endearing. "It's fine." I looked at Isaac and pointed a thumb to the counter. "I still owe you a coffee—"

"I'm okay. I had two coffees while waiting."

I ordered my drink and pulled out my wallet.

"I got it," Isaac said.

"You don't have to."

"I want to."

I looked at the barista. Annoyance was written over her face as she looked back and forth between us.

I shrugged. "He insists, I guess."

The barista lazily flipped her screen, and Isaac tapped his phone to it. A green check mark appeared with a ding.

I moved to the waiting area. Isaac returned to his table to grab his coat and put it on as he approached me again.

"Thanks. Now I really owe you."

Isaac winked. "We can call it even."

"All that waiting around just to pay four dollars for a drink?"

He smiled. "It was worth it." My cheeks warmed. Isaac pulled his usual beanie over his head and pushed the curls off his eyes and under the hat. "I was actually hoping I could take you somewhere."

I crossed my arms.

"I promise we'll stay away from water," Isaac said.

His charm made the embarrassment fade. I couldn't help but laugh. "Seems dangerous."

"I'll make sure we stay on the sidewalk and only cross the street when there's a walk sign." He wrapped a scarf around his neck that covered the bottom of his face.

I grabbed my hot chocolate from the barista and turned to Isaac. "Lead the way then."

————

We walked through Washington Square Park—the wind bit at my nose. Isaac's scarf was a good call.

We passed a fenced-in dog run, unfortunately without any dogs, just random, muddy-looking toys left behind. Isaac pointed. "I love watching the dogs there. When it's not negative three degrees."

"Do you have a dog?"

"No, but I have a cat! His name's Potato."

"I love animals with food names. I met a dog named Cheddar once."

"That's a perfect name for a dog. I used to make my ex-boyfriends stop every time we walked by. It's fun to sit and watch."

Bells rang as if I just won a game show. *He's gay! He's gay!* When the thoughts dimmed, his words registered in my brain. "Wait, boyfriends?"

"Yes, plural. Boyfriends. I was dating them at the same time."

"Did they know you were dating the other?"

Isaac chuckled. "Yeah, because they were also dating each other."

We turned out of the park. "Oh, like a throuple situation?"

"Not my favorite word, but yeah, I'm polyamorous. You sound familiar with it."

"I've read about it. But I've never seen it in real life."

Isaac smiled. "You make it sound like a myth."

"How does it work? I mean, how did it work for you and your boyfriends?"

We turned onto Greene St.

"It's pretty easy once you open your mind to it. You love all your friends, right? And all your family members?"

"Of course."

"It's just as easy to love multiple partners just like we do with friends and family."

"But what about jealousy?"

Isaac huffed. "That's the tricky part. I think there will always be jealousy, but that gives you a reason to stop and think, why am I feeling this? Mine came down to my insecurities and what society deemed normal. It can work as long as everyone involved is in the same mindset and willing to try." The fog of his breath floated from behind his scarf. "Communication and honesty are important. Talking about how you feel is everything. Think of how many relationships are ruined by cheating, temptation, or even attraction to someone else."

"True."

"If we were taught about free love when we were young, I feel like everyone would be a lot happier and maybe more confident."

"I've never thought about it like that," I said.

Isaac chuckled. "Of course not. Because everywhere we turn, we're told that one man and one woman are normal and how things should be. Even gay couples depicted on TV or in movies are looking for their one soulmate—true love. But in my experience, the heart can do so much more than that."

"You know, with all your talk of crystals and free love, I'm starting to think you're some kind of hippie."

"Don't knock it till you try it!" I laughed as Isaac came to a halt. "We're here."

I peeked through the glass door. An underwhelming surprise. "This is an Apple Store. You know we have these in Texas, too, right?"

"Listen, I feel terrible about what happened at the pier. So I want to buy you a new phone."

I almost spit my drink on his coat but gulped hard. "I'm sorry, that's ridiculous."

A smile pulled at the corner of Isaac's mouth. "It's really not. I should be the one to replace it."

I shook my head. "I have a credit card for emergencies. It's fine." I hadn't planned on getting a new phone at that moment, but we were standing there, so why not?

Heat blanketed us as we passed the threshold. Just as Isaac unwrapped his scarf, a petite woman approached us wearing a blue shirt with the Apple logo on her chest.

"Oh... Oh my god. Um, hi," she said to Isaac.

"Hey," Isaac chirped. "We're here to get my friend an iPhone."

Her eyes widened. "Sure, which one?"

I waved at her. "Me, he's talking about me."

She giggled. "Sorry, I meant which phone."

I suddenly wanted to jump off the Brooklyn Bridge.

Isaac shrugged. "The newest one is fine."

She beamed at Isaac. "Great. Do you want to pay with cash or card?"

Isaac reached for his wallet. "Card, please."

I let out a nervous laugh. "Hold on," I said to her, putting up a finger before pulling Isaac to the side. "That's an eleven-hundred-dollar phone. I'm not letting you do that."

"Don't worry about it, Lan."

A chill shot down my spine. I closed my eyes and was sent back to the day of the school shooting drill, sitting on my front lawn the first time Caleb called me Lan. I blinked at Isaac. "Please don't call me that."

"I'm sorry, I didn't mean—"

"It's fine, but I can't let you buy me that phone. You're a college student. You can't afford that."

"I'm taking a year off to work, remember? So technically, I'm not a student." Isaac looked over his shoulder at the woman. "We'll take the black one, please."

She nodded, then strutted off before I could say anything.

I stared at Isaac with wide eyes. "Are you serious?"

"Yeah," he said smoothly.

"I'm leaving."

Isaac jumped in front of me before I could grab the door. "Please don't."

"Please *move*." I stepped to the side, but he blocked me again. "You're really stubborn, aren't you?"

"I'm not the one declining a gift." He winked at me.

Stubborn and smug. Bastard. "A gift, huh?"

"I was the one who damaged it, so yes, a gift."

"*You* didn't damage it. The water did."

"But who asked you to get closer to the water?"

I rolled my eyes. "No. I don't want it."

"It's too late. That nice girl is already getting it."

I pinched the bridge of my nose. "You're extremely frustrating, you know that?"

"Look, you can take the phone and never talk to me again if that's what you want. But let me make this right."

"You're not gonna let me leave, are you?"

"Not unless you want me to cause a scene in front of all these people." His smile was laced with evil.

I sighed and moved away from the door. "Fine." I crossed my arms like a toddler about to have a tantrum. "What are you, a trust fund baby or something?"

The petite woman approached from behind me. "Isaac?"

He never told her his name.

She held up a rectangular box. "It's all set." She presented the card reader.

I pushed Isaac's arm down before he could pay. "Is there, like, a payment plan or anything?"

Isaac's arm weaved around mine, quickly tapping his phone to the card reader. It was done.

She handed Isaac the box. "Anything else I can help with?" Her eyes practically bulged out of her head, looking at him like a puppy begging for food.

"Nope. You've been really helpful," Isaac said. "Thank you."

"Come back any time. My name's Maxine if you need anything."

"Thanks." Isaac smiled and started for the door. He wrapped his scarf around his face just before stepping outside.

I gave the woman a weak smile and jogged after him. The wind sliced at my face. "Wait, did you know her, or?"

"No, why?" Isaac shoved the box into my hands.

"I'll pay you back," I said.

Isaac walked backward, staring at me. "Please don't."

I glanced at the plastic-wrapped box, then back to Isaac. "Where are you going?"

"You agreed to take the phone and never talk to me again!" He shouted before twisting around. "Enjoy it!"

Pretty sure I never agreed to that. I cupped the side of my mouth with one hand. "You're so annoying!"

He waved but didn't look back.

I huffed and walked back toward Washington Square Park. I needed to set up the phone and text Dad before he thought I'd been kidnapped.

———

Friday, January 10th

I sat at my desk finishing a short story for my creative writing class when Josh busted through the door.

"Dude, we're going to a party!"

I let out a sigh. "I'm not going to a coding party again. Nobody talked to me."

Josh threw himself onto my bed and propped on his elbows. "It's not a coding party. It's a real party. Like in a real apartment. Not a dorm."

"Oh, how'd you find out about it?"

"This girl, Allison, in my economics class, we're working on a project together, so she invited me. Said I could bring friends."

"You have other friends."

"They're computer nerds. I need a wingman."

"It's almost nine."

Josh let his head fall into my pillow, then shot up again. "Come on. It's a Friday night, and I need you. I can't talk to this girl by myself."

"You know I'm gay, right?"

"Get dressed." Josh hopped up and ran into the bathroom.

"We're leaving now?" I shouted.

His voice was muffled behind the door. "Get dressed!"

I closed my computer. I hated having to stop writing in the middle of an idea, but I pushed myself up, opened the closet door, pushed some hangers aside, and my *Jurassic Park* T-shirt stared me in the face. I smiled and took it off the hanger.

———

Josh and I took the A train uptown to Harlem. A lot of college students who didn't live in the dorms lived in Harlem for cheaper rent, or so I'd heard. That night was the first time I'd ventured to upper Manhattan. We got off at the 145th St. stop. Allison's apartment was on Nichols Street, five doors from a corner barber blasting music outside the shop.

Josh checked his phone. "This is it."

We stepped to a door with foggy windows. Josh pushed a button labeled 5L.

A woman's voice yelled at us from the crackling speaker. "Who is it?"

"Allison? It's Josh."

"Oh, hey boo, come on up."

The door made an awful buzz before Josh twisted the handle. The entryway was narrow and fluorescent. A few Amazon packages rested at the base of the stairs. There was no elevator, so by the time we'd gotten to the fifth floor, still wearing our coats, it felt like we'd just climbed Mount Everest.

"I'ma wait before I knock," Josh said, holding onto the railing.

"Why?"

"I ain't lettin' this girl see how out of breath I am from four flights of stairs."

I laughed and leaned against the wall, feeling just as winded. "Fine with me. I'll wait."

Josh huffed and composed himself.

"Slow breaths," I said.

"Fuck you."

I smiled, shaking my head before Josh knocked on the door.

A beautiful girl answered, wearing ripped jeans and a halter top. Her dark skin sparkled under the fluorescent lights, and long braids flowed down her back. "Hey, guys!"

"Hey," Josh said as he hugged her. He gestured to me. "This is my roommate, Landon. Landon, this is Allison."

"Nice to meet you," I said with a wave.

Her smile widened. "You too! Come in."

We stepped into a long hallway that led down to the kitchen. People were shoulder to shoulder, music blasted from an unknown source.

I leaned into Josh. "I thought you said it was just a couple of people."

"Word got out, I guess."

Allison shut the door behind us, revealing a living room area. The place was a lot bigger than I thought. She gestured to follow her down the hall. Squeezing through the bodies, I noticed two doors on the way to the kitchen.

Allison stopped at the farthest door and opened it. "You can throw your coats on the bed."

We dropped our coats and followed Allison to the crowded kitchen. My back was still moist from the jog up the stairs. Everyone had a drink in their hand, and a few people were smoking at the one open window.

Allison poured vodka into two shot glasses and handed them to us. "Everyone who shows up has to take a shot."

Josh gulped it immediately, but I was hesitant. I took it in two small sips, smiling through the pain. *Fuck, that burns.*

My phone vibrated.

LAUREN
Hey! How're your classes so far?

ME
Enjoying them. You?

LAUREN
My ballet teacher is a creep, but other than that, I like them.

I sent a GIF of kids running away.

LAUREN
Haha what're you doing?

ME
I'm at a party in Harlem.

LAUREN
Booo I'm jealous! Take me next time! I'm so bored.

ME
I'll make sure Josh knows next time haha.

LAUREN
How is it?

ME
They just made me take a shot.

LAUREN
JEALOUS!

"Did you get a new phone?" Josh asked.

I closed my screen. "Yeah. My other one wouldn't turn on after I fell in the Hudson."

Allison looked at me with a loose jaw. "You fell in the Hudson? How the hell did that happen?"

I scratched my head. "I was oblivious, per usual." I didn't need to relive the embarrassment.

Allison chuckled before turning to Josh, striking up a conversation about their economics teacher. I looked at my phone again. Isaac hadn't texted me at all. I didn't think he was serious about the agreement.

ME

Hey. I never said thank you for the phone.

To my surprise, Isaac's response was instant.

ISAAC

You're very welcome.

ME

I'm sorry for being a dick. What you did was really generous. I should've been more appreciative.

ISAAC

I'm glad you texted me because I was about five minutes from breaking the agreement.

ME

Damn, I should've held out :) What are you up to?

ISAAC

Just sage-ing my apartment. Potato hates it.

"Landon."

I looked up; Josh was in a circle around the kitchen table. "Play this game with us," he said.

I slipped my phone into my pocket and slithered into the circle.

A guy across from me pointed at my shirt. "Best movie of all time!"

I glanced down, remembering I was representing *Jurassic Park*, and smiled. "You're not wrong."

Allison held up a joker card from a playing deck and did her best to explain the rules over the music. "Has everyone played suck and blow?"

I hadn't, but I didn't want to be the only one who raised my hand.

Allison snickered. "Good. If you fuck up, you take a shot."

Shit.

Allison placed the card to her mouth and leaned in to let Josh take it with his. He kept it moving—passing it to the girl on his other side. She was five people away from me, but they all passed it like pros. Suddenly, I blinked, and I was next.

Fuck, what do I do? The game is 'suck and blow,' so just do one of those, I guess?

I leaned into the girl beside me but blew instead of sucking air in to grab the card. I clumsily grabbed at it before it fell to the table. Everyone groaned.

Allison pointed at me. "Shot!" She pushed the bottle of vodka toward me. I didn't even get a glass. I downed a gulp from the bottle and tried not to show the discomfort on my face.

I placed the card against my lips and sucked in. I leaned to the guy beside me and blew out before he could even lean in. The card fell and we almost kissed. Everyone laughed as I took another gulp. By the time the game was over, I'd taken nine shots.

The card had passed around the circle ten times before Allison took Josh by the hand and led him down the crowded hallway. I lazily watched them disappear as I sat at the table. The circle had dispersed, and I grabbed my head as the room spun. I rubbed my temples and glanced down the dim hallway. My heart dropped. Dan stood still among the dancing crowd, glaring at me.

No.

I stood and rushed to the sink, quickly splashed my face with water, and looked again. Dan's neck gushed blood, but no one batted an eye at him. My jaw clenched. *He's not here. I'm awake. He's not—*

Suddenly, Dan spun and ran through the crowd.

"Hey!" I shouted. People around me stared and laughed. I bolted through the crowd as the front door slammed. "Dan!"

Bumping every shoulder through the horde, I opened the front door and stumbled down the first flight of stairs. The next three weren't much smoother. I ran out onto the street, panting, looking left and right, but I couldn't spot Dan's white tux.

A taxi honked at me, taking me out of my trance.

"Sorry! I'm sorry." I returned to the sidewalk, cupping my forehead. "What the fuck is wrong with me?"

I'm drunk. Drunk people see things sometimes, right?

My heart raced as I reached for the door—locked. I couldn't remember Allison's apartment number, so I sat on the stoop with my back against the door. My breath fogged as I tried to control it. I pulled out my phone and called Josh. No answer. I decided to text him, but my eyes caught Caleb's name, and I quickly hit the green button.

The phone rang twice before going to voicemail and beeped in my ear. "Hey, it's Landon." My words were elongated. "I know you don't want to hear from me, but I didn't know who else to call. I... This is gonna sound—I saw Dan. But it wasn't a dream this time." I raced through the maze in my mind, unable to find the words to explain what I'd seen without sounding insane. "I know how that sounds. It's impossible and ridiculous. But, I really fucking thought I left him in Texas." My voice cracked. "You're the only one who understands." I sniffled, wiped my eyes, and took a breath. "I'm sorry I called. I'm a little drunk, I think? I knew you wouldn't answer, but—" My voice trailed off. "Jesus, I'm sorry. Okay? I've said it a million times, and you're probably sick of hearing me apologize. But I know I shouldn't have said what I said on New Year's Eve." My hands trembled. "I'll... I'll leave you alone. sorry I called. Fuck, I miss you." I hung up, popped to my feet, and buzzed every apartment until someone let me in.

TEN

TEXAS

Four Months Ago

"It's seven!" Parker bounced, shaking the bed like an earthquake.

Caleb tossed a pillow at his brother, hitting him in the face. "Go shower and get dressed, you demon."

Parker made one more jump, this time off the edge. The thump of his feet hitting the floor made my heart drop. He pulled open a dresser drawer, swiped some clothes and a towel, then rocketed away.

Caleb plopped an arm over me and gently kissed my cheek. It was my wake-up call every time I stayed over. I loved it. I pulled the blanket up as he cuddled me.

"Morning," Caleb whispered. His warm breath on my neck pulled me into him. The cotton of his underwear brushed my arm. He tried to kiss me.

"Don't. I have morning breath."

Caleb pressed his nose against my cheek. "So do I. It's fine."

I kissed him just as the shower turned on from down the hall.

"We probably have ten minutes before Parker's done," Caleb said, rubbing his hand over my chest. "If you're up for it again."

A smirk pulled at my lips. I'd been *up for it* every morning since I was fourteen. My hand covered Caleb's and pushed it down my torso and under the waistband of my underwear. A smile took over Caleb's face as if he found a hidden treasure. Caleb pushed the covers over his head, navigating his way to collect his findings. He was a magician between the sheets, somehow removing both my underwear and his own with little effort. He straddled me, and the blanket fell away. My hands explored the curves of his back and settled on his naked hips.

I took all of him in, knowing it would be the last time I'd see him like that for a while. I didn't want it to end. I didn't want to leave his bed. He made it easy to forget I was moving that day when he pushed against me, setting fire to my insides.

———

I crouched beside the bed, rifling through my backpack. "I think I forgot clean underwear."

Caleb pulled on his pants. "Grab a pair of mine." He said as he stepped out of the room.

I hopped to my feet, afraid Parker would run into the room any second. I reached for the first pair in Caleb's top drawer but grazed something hard. I slipped on the underwear before searching through the other pairs.

My jaw tightened as I picked up a handgun from the bottom of the drawer. It was silver with a black grip. I touched it as if it were a spoiled diaper. Flashes of prom night hit me all at once, and I dropped it back in the drawer, landing softly on the stacks of underwear.

"Caleb," I whispered, still staring at the gun. "Caleb!" He jogged into the room, licking something off his fingers. I pushed past him to close the door. "What the *fuck* is that?" I didn't need to point. Caleb saw the drawer was open. He covered the gun with his underwear, closed the drawer, and ran a hand down his face. I stared at a shirtless Caleb, awaiting a response that never came. "Caleb, are you serious?"

He looked at me with wide eyes, like a kid who'd been caught with porn under his bed. "It's not loaded." I rolled my eyes. "I bought it legally," he said. "It's just not registered yet."

I kept my voice low for Parker's sake, but my heart pounded. "I don't give a shit where you got it. Why is it in your drawer?"

"I got it after I left the hospital."

"For what?"

"For protection." Caleb leaned on the dresser, crossed his arms, and stared at the wall across the room.

My hands slapped my legs. "Protection from what?" Caleb's gaze hit the floor. I stepped closer. "What if Parker had found it?"

"Parker knows about it. We watched a whole lecture on gun safety. He knows it's not a toy."

"Jesus, Caleb. And you leave it in your top drawer? What if he decides to handle it when you're at work or something?"

"I'm getting a safe for it. I just don't have the money yet."

"Then how did you afford it in the first place?"

"Miguel, let me borrow—"

I shook my head. "After everything—you know how I feel about—"

"What do you expect me to do, Landon?" Caleb pushed himself from the dresser—his brow furrowed. "Let another psycho point a gun at us? Let him beat me close to death again? If I can't protect you, Parker, or Miguel, then what fucking good am I?" Caleb sat on the bed with his head in his hands.

I stared, so wrapped up in my own trauma that I hadn't paid much attention to Caleb's. I sat on the bed, tucked one leg up, and looked at him. "Caleb, I'm sor—"

"I'm not stupid, okay?" His eyes latched onto me.

I squeezed his hand. "Babe, I never said you were."

"I got the license, and Miguel paid for the classes. I started shooting lessons when it didn't hurt to raise my arm anymore."

"Why didn't you tell me?"

"I knew you wouldn't like it."

"We could've talked it out, at least. If I knew it was this important to you."

"I can't let that happen again."

I pulled Caleb into a hug and kissed his neck. "It won't, babe. I promise." I looked into his beautiful hazel eyes. My hands cupped around his face. "Okay?"

Caleb nodded.

I should've been checking in with him. I was an idiot not to. He protected me without thinking of his own safety. If he hadn't pushed Dan's arm away when he did, the bullet would've killed me. "Can we talk about it from now on? And please tell me when you get the safe."

The door creaked, and Parker poked his head in. "I don't mean to be a time goblin, but—"

We laughed. Caleb looked at his little brother with narrow eyes. "I'm guessing that means you're ready to go?"

Parker pushed the door open and gestured to his fully dressed body. "Uh, yeah."

"Okay, sass goblin. We'll be right there," Caleb said before Parker rolled his eyes and walked out. "When did he become so responsible?"

"Hey, he's in the double digits now. He's grown."

———

I tossed my backpack into the backseat of Dad's car. Caleb lifted my suitcase into the trunk.

Dad stood at the side door. "Is that everything?"

It was a tricky question. I'd mostly packed clothes—two suitcases worth, with a few books shoved into the zipper pockets. "Yeah, I think so," I called back.

"No Miguel?" Dad asked.

"He's visiting family out of state," I said. "He's letting Caleb use the—"

Dad poked a finger into his ear and clenched his eyes. "Caleb doesn't have a license. I'm not hearing this..." Caleb shrunk behind the car a bit. "I'll give you guys a few," Dad said. He stepped through the screen door back into the kitchen.

"He's right. You shouldn't be driving," I said.

Caleb closed the trunk. "This is a special occasion."

The screen door squeaked again, and Parker waltzed out. "There's actually one more thing."

My forehead tensed, and I gave Caleb a look. Parker held out a neatly wrapped box in front of me.

"What's this?" I asked.

"Your going-away present!" Parker's voice squeaked. "Me and Caleb picked it out. Miguel wrapped it. And your dad kept it hidden."

"A real group effort," Caleb said smoothly. Parker bounced to his brother and wrapped an arm around his waist.

"Aw, that's so sweet. Thanks, you two." I placed the box on the trunk and ripped the corner of the wrapping paper, revealing a white cardboard box. I glanced at the two of them. Their smiles barely fit on their faces. I pulled the lid off. Inside was a folded *Jurassic Park* t-shirt. My lips wrapped around my teeth. I ran my fingers over the logo as butterflies crowded my stomach.

"You're officially part of the club," Parker said.

I pulled Parker into a hug. "Thanks, bud! This means so much."

I felt Parker's chest rise, and a small whimper caught in his voice. "Do you have to go?"

I pulled away and kneeled. His cheeks were already wet with tears. Seeing his eyes fill up crushed my heart. "Unfortunately, I do. But you'll see me soon. I'll be back for the holidays, okay?"

Parker nodded as he wiped his eyes dry. I squeezed him tight before standing.

Caleb rustled Parker's hair. "Go wait by the car. I'll be there in a second."

My stomach flooded with doubt as I watched Parker shuffle to Miguel's car. I finally looked at Caleb with teary eyes. "I don't know if I can do this."

Caleb's big hands wrapped around my face, and his thumbs wiped my cheeks dry. "You were made for this."

"Yeah, but what if my dad needs me for something?" My voice

cracked. "What if *you* need me? Maybe I could take classes at the community college for a while and—"

"Babe," Caleb whispered. "Just breathe, okay?" I closed my eyes. Caleb pressed his forehead against mine. "You're gonna own New York City." He planted a long kiss on me. "I'm always gonna need you, but somebody's gotta be here when you get back." Caleb hugged me tightly. My face lingered on the nape of his neck, making it damp with tears. When I finally looked at Caleb again, he was crying too. "Only a couple of months, yeah?"

I nodded and wiped my nose on my sleeve.

Dad tried to lock the side door as quietly as possible. I could see him staring at us from the corner of my eye. "Ready, kiddo?" Dad asked.

I tried not to sob as I studied the details of Caleb's face through blurry vision. I hugged him again, squeezing as tight as I could. "I love you."

Caleb looked me in the eyes. "I love you more." He smiled, but I knew he'd forced it. We kissed one last time before I finally got in the car.

Seeing Caleb and Parker in the passenger-side mirror made my chest hurt. If we were in a movie, this would be the part at the end where I realized I'd made a mistake and told the driver to stop so I could dramatically run back through the street. I closed my eyes to imagine it. I'd run into Caleb's embrace, and he'd pick me up with his strong arms and spin me around with my legs wrapped around his waist. But that hadn't happened. When I opened my eyes, the car had already turned the corner.

It was a strange feeling, leaving the town I had lived in my whole life. We moved into our house across from the high school when I was three, so I never knew anything else. My parents and I never had a reason to leave Texas since all of our extended family was there, some only an hour's drive away. My stomach was a mix of butterflies and sludge.

I'd never been on a plane before. Dad made sure to get me a

window seat to see how differently the world looked from above. Big Texas felt so small from up there.

I smiled, thinking of the night before when Caleb and I explained to Parker how I was technically traveling back in time by an hour. Of course, that made him want to watch *Back to the Future*, so that was what we did.

I pulled my laptop from my bag and then glanced at Dad. He was already working on his emails for the day. I glanced at my phone; Caleb's text lingered there.

Text me when you land. I love you too!

I had close to three hours to spare, so I leaned back in my seat, put on my headphones, and watched *Back to the Future Part II*.

————

Dad and I followed a bubbly girl named Savvy down a bustling hallway. Her red hair led the way through hordes of kids from around the world, all gaining their independence simultaneously. The excited chatter was freedom calling my name. We passed a closed door that shook from loud music on the other side. Dad cocked an eyebrow at me. We both caught a whiff of skunky air seeping from the room.

We arrived at a door displaying two name tags. 'Landon' and 'Joshua' were printed on white squares surrounded by a blue border of construction paper. We rolled my suitcases into a tiled room. It was narrow and felt cramped with two beds and desks. It reminded me of a prison cell. Cold and quiet, void of personality.

"You'll have to share the closet," Savvy said. "But the drawers under the bed are for your use only. And the bathroom is back there." She pointed to the door in the back left corner.

I nodded, scanning the walls and exposed pipes. Finally, I hoisted my suitcase onto one of the beds, claiming the left side of the room.

Savvy handed me a few sheets of paper stapled together. "Those are all the dorm rules you'll need to follow. If you have any questions, I'm the RA on this floor, just two doors down. You'll see my name on the door." Her smile was like the sun—bright and warm. "Just let me know if you ever need anything."

"Thank you, Savvy," Dad said.

Savvy stopped before stepping out. "Oh! Orientation starts tomorrow morning. Just keep an eye on your email for the details."

I nodded. "Awesome, thanks!"

Savvy closed the door behind her, and the room went silent.

Dad looked at me. "Must be the concrete walls."

I sat, bouncing on the bed. "It's smaller than I thought it'd be. Tasha said her dorm has a whole kitchen." I was curious to see the other rooms, wondering if they all looked identical.

Dad pointed to the paper in my hands. "Is there anything on there about the dining hall?" He sat next to me and eyed the printed words.

"No hot plates are allowed in the dorm rooms as it could be a fire hazard." My brow creased. "What's a hot plate?"

"Did you learn anything during your twelve years in school?"

A knock echoed against the concrete slabs. Then Savvy walked in again. This time, three people followed behind her. Dad and I stood.

"You must be Joshua." I held out a hand to the youngest-looking of the three.

"Josh," he said, returning my handshake. His dreadlocks were tied up, but one was left out, hanging in front of his glasses.

"Nice to meet you, Josh. I'm Landon. This is my dad, Curtis."

Josh pointed a thumb over his shoulder. "My parents, Melissa, and Rodney." Josh's dad was so tall he had to duck through the door. I never had to crane my neck so much to speak to someone. Savvy left us to exchange pleasantries. We swapped where we were from and our majors, but eventually, my dad suggested we explore the neighborhood.

———

The city felt overwhelmingly huge. Walking the busy streets and being amongst the skyscrapers made me feel like an insignificant bug. The air was different. Everywhere in Texas, it smelled like grass and straw, with a bit of barnyard now and then. New York City smelled industrial, but as we walked, it turned into this kaleidoscope of scents. The smell of falafels and hot dogs blended with freshly brewed coffee and florals from a boutique. Then we would turn a corner and get hit by the smell of dog pee and trash bags baking under the sun. I didn't mind that though, because to me, New York City air smelled like freedom and independence for the first time in my life.

I couldn't say I wasn't anxious, though. The city was everything I hoped it would be, but navigating it was a different story. A subway map looked like a foreign language made of colors. *Thank God for Google Maps.*

The streets overindulged with every type of person, every skin color, every body type, and every age. And everyone somehow looked confident in their skin. Pride flags were everywhere, too! Every time Dad spotted one at a shop or a restaurant, he'd point and say, "Oh, there's another one," with a smile. I think he was glad I'd have so much support around me.

Dad spotted another pride flag, this time in the window of a dojo. "Hey, look! Maybe we can get you some classes that work around your school schedule."

I huffed. "Come on, Dad. I don't need more self-defense classes."

"The hell you don't." He crossed his arms. "I'm letting you move halfway across the country. The least you can do is give me some peace of mind."

I had no choice but to sign up.

———

We found a small Italian restaurant with outdoor seating. I was slurping up a mound of spaghetti carbonara when it dawned on me that it was the last meal I'd share with Dad for a while. A wave of emptiness washed over me. I'd never been as far as a few hours from him my whole life.

I stared at the black and white checkered tablecloth. "What was it like when you had to leave Mom to go overseas?"

Dad cleared his throat. He was mid-chew and cutting into his chicken parm. He wiped his face with a napkin. "It was tough. Really tough. Having to leave my wife felt like a spear through the heart."

"How did you do it?"

"Technically, I didn't have a choice. I had to." His fork scraped the plate as he cut another piece. "But that was also a time when the U.S. was fired up. Everyone was eager to fight for their country after they'd hit us." His eyes wandered down the street. "I imagine not too far from here."

I could only count a handful of times Dad told me anything about his military days. I had seen more pictures than I had heard stories. I knew he was medically discharged from a shot to the shoulder, as he could no longer hold a gun steady.

"What was it like being without everyone you knew?"

"It was lonely at first, but you find your people. You eventually settle into a group of friends. Makes it easier when you're missing home."

I stabbed the pasta and spun my fork, wondering if I'd find a new friend group.

Dad reached and placed a hand on my arm. "Luckily, you and Caleb aren't oceans apart. You can call him every day."

I looked at him. "I know. It's not just that." My eyes shot to my pasta again. "You're going back to that house alone. I know it's going on the market soon, but I still feel like I'm just leaving you behind." I took a deep breath. "And I'm leaving you to deal with all the baggage that came with what I did. You're the one having to deal with the dirty looks on the street because your son shot someone. Those people at your speech—"

"—Are the exact reason I want you in self-defense classes. Those people don't know you, Landon. If someone wants to give me dirty looks or support an opponent of mine, then the hell with them." My shoulders slumped. "I know what it feels like to squeeze a trigger when you don't want to. I know what it feels like to protect someone you care about. And you know what? I'm *proud* of my son."

I gave a weak smile. My stomach curled as I thought about prom night.

Dad might have seen it on my face because he tapped the table. "Buddy, this is your fresh start. No one here judges you for that because no one needs to know unless you want them to. You have all the control now."

He was right. I wasn't going to get the weird looks walking through NYU. I was an untouched canvas, free to paint a new picture. "It helps to think about it that way."

"Your mom would be proud."

I laughed. "No, she'd be a crying mess."

Dad smiled. "Oh, buckets! But she'd know this was right for you. We can't keep you forever. This is your life now."

———

Dad held it together until his Uber pulled up in front of my dorm. He tried not to let me see, but I could hear his sniffles when he pulled me into the tightest bear hug. He looked at me with red eyes. It made my chest feel empty.

"Just because you're on your own now doesn't mean you can stop calling. Okay?"

I nodded. "Text me when you're on the plane."

He hoisted a leg into the car and looked at me again. "I love you."

Tears flooded my eyes. "Love you, too."

He closed the door before the car drove off. I watched it go until I couldn't see it anymore. I was glad to have the elevator to myself returning to my room. The emptiness pushed its way up my chest, and I sobbed into the bend of my arm. I was officially alone.

My sleeve wiped away the tears as the elevator door slid open. I took a breath. *Fresh start.*

My room was empty. Josh's things were strewn about his side of the room. He and his parents had probably left to explore. The only thing to do was unpack. I hoisted my fat suitcase onto my bed and unzipped it.

What the—

A note stared up at me, perfectly balanced on my winter coat.

Don't forget about me
I love you
- Caleb

I smiled and reached for my phone. I needed to hear my boyfriend's voice more than ever.

ELEVEN
NEW YORK CITY

Friday, January 10th

The screeching stop of the train pierced my eardrums, forcing my sleeping eyes open. My tired gaze focused as the doors stretched open. I'd have missed my stop if I hadn't woken up. I jumped out of my seat and through the doors, rubbing the kink in my neck.

Luckily, it was a short two-block walk to my dorm. I shoved my hands in my coat pockets, keeping them in a fist to retain warmth. I scanned every face on the sidewalk, looking for Dan. My jaw tightened every time I saw someone wearing white. *I'm fine. I'm just drunk.* I convinced myself it was the drugs when I saw the bullet holes in the bathroom stall, so it was easy to do the same with the alcohol.

I crossed the vehicle-littered street and stepped through the automatic doors. My sneakers squeaked against the tile of the lobby. Bernard sat behind the front desk, smiling at something on his phone. He gave me a nod before I tapped my ID.

My phone vibrated in the elevator. *Isaac Calling.*

"Hello?" I answered.

"Hey."

"What's up?"

"I think you drunk texted me?"

My eyes widened as the elevator opened. "Wait, what?" I stomped down the hall, rapidly swiping through my texts.

"I mean, I assumed because of the typos," Isaac said.

Shit.

I pulled out my phone and read the texts.

ME

I'm soryyy I clled. I wish I cold see ypu.

ISAAC

I don't have a missed call from you. And you can see me anytime! You okay?

I wanted to facepalm so badly, but I feared I'd knock myself out.

"You didn't respond, so I just wanted to make sure you were okay," Isaac said.

"I'm okay. But after tonight, I'm done with drinking for a while."

"Did something happen?"

"Yeah. No. I'm... Sorry if I worried you or anything."

"No problem. I assume you're home now?"

I sat on my bed. "Just walked in."

My chest warmed, but it wasn't the alcohol. Isaac checked in because I spelled a few words wrong. Did he really care that much?

"I thought about coming to the dorm, but thought that might be creepy."

I smiled. "I never told you which one I live in."

"If it's close to The Ivory Den, I know which one. Does Bernard still work the front desk?"

"You know Bernard? Who don't you know around here?"

"I lived there first semester last year."

"Didn't like it?"

Isaac's voice hesitated. "Got too crowded for me, I guess." My head tilted. "Can I ask you something?" Isaac spouted. "And feel free to say no... don't feel pressured or anything."

I chuckled. "What is it?"

"Can I take you out to dinner? Tomorrow night? I know a great Italian place." His voice got a little higher as he finished his sentence.

My cheeks warmed. "Like a date?"

"I mean, maybe? Yeah? Yes. A proper date since we fell in the Hudson last time."

I smirked. "Oh, *that* was a date?"

"Okay, maybe not, but I know I need to see you again. So let's try for real."

I hesitated to answer, which was dumb because he had been nothing but sweet to me. I didn't have anything to lose. Caleb seemed to be out of my life for good. "Okay. Sure."

"Great! It's an amazing place on the Upper East Side. The owner and I used to work together. He can get us a table."

I wondered where Isaac could've worked with someone who I assume was in their 40s if they owned a restaurant in New York City. "Sure. I mean, you're the local, so I trust you."

"Great! I'll text you the address!" His voice piqued with a squeak, reminding me of an excited ten-year-old I knew. "I'll talk to you in a bit."

"Okay, see ya."

"Bye!"

I stripped down to my underwear and plopped onto my bed. I could still feel the buzz running through me. I smiled into my pillow.

An actual date—finally, something to make me feel normal again.

I reached for my phone, thinking maybe I should tell Caleb. I'd want to know if he was going on dates with someone else. I swiped to my texts, but my fingers didn't move.

I already left him a drunk voicemail. A text might be overkill.

He doesn't care about me anymore.

Just as I was about to close my phone, Isaac texted me.

ISAAC

Do you own a collared shirt?

I flipped onto my back and held the phone above my face.

ME

Yeah, why?

ISAAC

This place has a dress code. Is that okay?

Do I have a choice?

ME

Of course.

Isaac texted me the address, and I Googled it. La Vista was a restaurant on East 70th Street. I skimmed the menu before bringing my phone to my chest.

How the hell am I gonna afford this place?

———

Saturday, January 11th

I turned onto East 70th Street between Lexington and 3rd Ave. A gold awning jutted across the sidewalk. I would've assumed it was a hotel if it hadn't said La Vista in cursive.

Isaac spun around as I approached. His curls now slicked back away from his face. The streetlights lit up his eyes, making them look like emerald stars against the night sky.

"You found it!" Isaac wrapped his arms around me. He smelled like an expensive Macy's cologne counter. "Come on." Isaac held his hand out, and led me through a set of heavy, mansion-sized glass doors.

A gray-haired woman offered to take our coats as soon as we entered. Now that our winter shields were gone, I gave Isaac a once-over. Seeing him so dressed up made my heart flutter. He wore a black suit—with sparkling lapels resembling a galaxy—and a bow tie. I suddenly felt very underdressed, looking more like Isaac's valet.

"You look... Just wow. Dashing." My face scrunched, and I closed one eye. "Do people still say that?" My mouth tasted like dust. "I'm sorry I didn't have anything nicer to wear."

Isaac gave me a once-over and winked. "You look *dashing* as well."

My eyes shot to the floor. I would've passed out if I stared into his eyes any longer. Isaac touched my lower back and led me to the host station.

A golden theme carried throughout the restaurant. The room was a large circle, and the white-clothed tables made a spiral leading to the middle. Small chandeliers hung above every table. The ceilings were high, and murals stretched across them, reminding me of old Italian architecture I'd seen in history books. A string quartet played soothing sounds from a small balcony.

A woman with straight black hair smiled as we approached her podium. "Chef Souza will be right out, Mr. Matthews."

I glanced from her to Isaac. *He must come here often.* It was all much more formal than I was used to.

"Thank you." Isaac tugged me off to the side. His eyes scanned the room. "Incredible, right? This place used to be a bank."

Everything sparkled, from the crystal chandeliers to the diamond earrings around the room. Even the marbled floors were squeaky clean.

Isaac's eyes met mine again. "Lee Souza makes incredible food. All organic, nothing processed."

"How do you know him again?"

"We worked together for a while."

"Where?"

A low voice hit us. "Isaac, my friend!"

Isaac's eyes focused on the voice behind me. "Chef!"

I moved to avoid getting squished between their hug. A stocky bald man in a white chef's coat rocked Isaac back and forth in a tight squeeze. His big smile accentuated the wrinkles around his eyes.

"It's been too long," Chef said with an accent I couldn't place. He grabbed Isaac by the shoulders. "How've you been?"

"Fantastic, you?" Isaac's smile widened like Lee was a best friend he hadn't seen in years.

"Hey, I'm doing what I love, my friend." Lee gestured to the dining room, seemingly proud of his golden palace. "Speaking of, I read about that part you got—"

"I'm so rude," Isaac said, gesturing to me. "This is my friend Landon." Lee and I shook hands. "I wanted to bring him to the best restaurant in New York," Isaac said.

"The place is stunning," I said.

Lee's hands came together as if he were praying. "Thank you, Landon. I'm so grateful you're both here. I've picked out the perfect table for you." Lee gestured to follow him. We zig-zagged through tables, our heels clacking against the marble.

We sat at a table against a colossal square window facing 70th Street. The chairs were cushioned and sturdy. A tall white candle flickered at the center of our table, surrounded by a clear vase. My stomach growled as a server walked by, holding two plates of sizzling steaks.

Lee smiled at Isaac and patted his shoulder. "Please enjoy."

"Thank you, Chef," Isaac said, looking up at the bald man. "I owe you one."

As soon as Lee stepped away, a slender waiter appeared. I ordered a Coke, and Isaac started with water.

I grazed the menu. The steaks that sizzled by our table cost more than every football uniform I've ever worn.

I could stick with a salad. I could afford a salad.

I glanced over the top of my menu and noticed a table of four looking in our direction, watching Isaac read. Had they never seen two men on a date before?

Then, a bright flash caught my attention from the corner of my eye. I placed the laminated menu down and stared out the window, scanning the parked cars, until I noticed a man across the street with a camera strapped around his neck. My gaze shot to my menu as soon as the man looked at us again.

Fuck.

My heart fell. The same tightness squeezed my chest as the day Dad gave his speech. My thoughts raced. I was sure the cameraman was someone from Texas. A Private Investigator sent by one of the people who thought I should be in prison. What if they wanted to post something about me at NYU? "I'm sorry." I said.

Isaac's brow pinched. "For what?"

"I just— I have to go." I stood. "The food is much more expensive than—"

"Landon, it's my treat."

I knew more people were staring now, but I didn't want to look. Isaac's puppy dog eyes bore a hole in my heart. "With the phone thing, this isn't fair, so—"

Isaac opened his mouth to speak, but I started for the door. The gray-haired woman was already holding my coat. She must've been watching, too.

Isaac caught me at the bend of my arm as I stepped outside. His cheeks were already red. He kept me in place, but my eyes wandered across the street. There were three men with cameras now. All pointed at Isaac and me.

"Please come back inside," Isaac said with warm words I could see in the cold. "You don't have to spend anything, I promise."

I stared at him, wishing I could tell him, but I didn't want to throw all of my bullshit on him at a fancy restaurant, especially when he wanted to foot the bill.

A flash went off across the street, finally catching Isaac's attention, and his face changed. He let go of my arm, pinched the bridge of his nose, and closed his eyes. "I just wanted one night."

What?

"I'm really sorry, Landon."

I sighed. "For what? I should be the one—"

Isaac held a finger up. "I'll take care of it." He walked backward. "One sec." He swiveled, crossed under the awning, and passed the window we were sitting at. He looked across the street and waved the camera people over. "Hey, everyone!"

My heart shot into my throat.

What the hell is he doing? They're gonna tell Isaac I'm a murderer.

I wanted to bolt to the subway.

"I'll do you guys a favor if you do one for me." Isaac's tone stayed calm. Three men in sweats stepped closer, all varying heights. "If you delete all the pictures of my friend, you can take more of me."

What? They're here for Isaac?

The men glanced at each other before agreeing to Isaac's deal. "Thanks, Isaac." The shortest man said.

He knows them?

Isaac looked at me and mouthed, 'I'm sorry,' before pocketing his hands and smiling for the photographers.

The cameras resembled lightning, assaulting Isaac every two milliseconds. He somehow knew how to stand, where to look, and how to keep his smile from fading. He was a natural.

"When do you start shooting?" The tallest man asked.

"A few weeks," Isaac said.

"How does it feel to take this on and join something this huge?"

Just as Isaac started to speak, it dawned on me. The memory of my mom reading her tabloid magazines hit me as if she had sent it straight from heaven.

They're paparazzi. I laughed at the thought. *There's no way.*

I remembered the girl in the coffee shop asking Isaac for a selfie. And it was strange when Jenna told me people left their numbers for him at the coffee shop. The girl at the Apple store seemed so giddy around him.

No fucking way.

The camera people went their separate ways, and Isaac crossed back to me, knocking the thoughts from my head. "Can we talk inside?" Isaac asked, rubbing his hands together.

I nodded and followed Isaac back to our table. We sat, and I couldn't take my eyes off him.

"I'm sorry," he said. "I know how weird this is."

I chuckled. "Uh, yeah. What are you, like, a celebrity or something?"

Isaac winced. "I hate that word, but... yeah."

I sat up in my chair so fast that one of my knees hit the top of the table, causing the dining room to go silent for a second.

I leaned forward, trying not to notice the stares again. "Wait, really?"

Isaac nodded. "Really."

Holy shit, don't freak out, don't be weird. I sat back. "Why didn't you tell me?"

Isaac leaned his arms on the table. "It's hard to explain how refreshing it feels when someone treats me like a normal person."

I squinted one eye. "This might be a dumb question, but what made you famous?"

"I moved to New York City when I was nine, I was on a TV show called *Little Chef*. I played a kid named Cameron Little, a prodigy chef running his own kitchen at a hotel. It was ridiculous and badly written, but everyone loved it for some reason. The show was my life for seven years."

I stared at him with wide eyes, soaking in the new information.

Isaac's head tilted. "You've really never heard of it?"

"Nope."

Isaac rubbed his chin. His eyes darted around the room. "People called it *Hell's Kitchen* meets *Suite Life*."

I shrugged.

Isaac raised an arm and started drawing an invisible shape in the air. "Hey, I'm Isaac Matthews from *Little Chef*, and you're watching—" His arm flailed as if holding an invisible wand casting a spell. "None of that rings a bell?"

"No, I'm sorry. I guess I was more of a cartoon kid."

Our server stood at our table again. I scrambled for the menu.

"Actually," Isaac said, looking at me. "Do you mind if I order for us?"

"Please."

"Do you eat meat?" I nodded. Isaac looked at the server. "May we have the rack of lamb, the truffle filet, medium, broccolini, carrots, and the bean risotto?" The server nodded and reached for our menus. "Thanks," Isaac said.

I leaned on the arm of my chair. "How do you know I'm not lying?"

"What do you mean?"

"How do you know I wasn't lying about not knowing you."

Isaac's shoulders bounced when he laughed. "Oh, people have tried it, but I can always tell." He sipped his water. "I can count on one hand the number of times I've properly introduced myself to someone since the show aired."

"Is that how you met Lee?"

Isaac nodded. "He was my mentor and teacher for the show because I had to cook on screen."

Now I was interested in seeing the show. I wondered if it was streaming. I made a mental note to Google it on my way home. "Wow. What was that like? Being on a TV show, I mean,"

"It was weird. And it all happened so fast. We were filming all the time, and I was doing all these appearances. It was nonstop. It felt like my face was everywhere for seven years straight. It changed me, but maybe that isn't the best chat for a date."

"Oh. We don't have to—"

"No, it's okay. Maybe we'll get there. But after all that time, I needed out."

"Did you keep acting?"

Isaac nodded. "After the show, my agent suggested I do an underwear ad. People got a little too intense after that, so I laid low for a while."

My fingers itched to Google him—something I couldn't do with Caleb when we first met. It was all kinds of insane to wrap my head around. I was sitting across the table from a real-life celebrity. How could I have been so oblivious?

Throughout the meal, Isaac spoke about growing up in New York City and visiting family back in the UK around the holidays. It was obvious he wanted to talk about anything other than being famous, and I didn't want to push him into an uncomfortable topic. But I'd be lying if I said I wasn't interested in those sections of his story.

Isaac scooped up the last bite of risotto with a spoon and held it out. "Last bite?"

My stomach bulged, but who knew if I'd ever taste it again? "Sure." The risotto was so creamy, and the black beans added the perfect balance of textures. "So, you know how to cook like this, then?"

Isaac chuckled. "Not to this level of expertise. Lee is a beast. I'm pretty good, but not *this* good." Isaac crumpled his cloth napkin and tossed it over the empty plate. "Maybe I could cook for you sometime."

My whole body warmed.

Isaac paid the bill and didn't let me look at the price. I assumed it was in the triple digits—more than I had in my bank account.

Lee met us at our table before we left. He shook my hand, and I thanked him for the best meal I'd ever eaten.

"That's very kind. Thank you," Lee said. He and Isaac hugged one last time. "Don't be a stranger. You know you're always welcome here."

Isaac smiled. "I'll be back soon."

When we collected our coats, Isaac handed the gray-haired woman a cash tip before I pushed the glass door, stepping back into the cold.

"I can't thank you enough," I said. "You've been so generous. I'm not sure I deserve it."

Isaac pulled his hood over his ears. "I'm usually more lowkey than this. I might have been trying to impress you a little."

I laughed. The steam from my warm breath assaulted the air. "Consider me impressed."

"It would've been perfect if those guys hadn't shown up. I know how weird that can be, so again, I'm sorry."

"Were you ever gonna tell me if they hadn't shown up?"

"I was getting there." Isaac smiled. "Got any secrets you wanna get out?"

A flash frame of a bleeding Dan in the middle of the party last night cut through me. I was desperate to avoid his question. "Why haven't I seen paparazzi around you before?"

"They get bored when you do the same thing every day, so they move on. And like I said, I've been laying low."

"Then why did they show up tonight if they moved on?"

Isaac's eyes wandered. "It was announced today that I got this part in a movie."

The air was dry and cold on my throat. "That sounds like a big deal."

"We've been talking about me all night."

"No, it's okay. I wanna know."

Isaac let out a breath, and I watched the steam dissipate above his head. "I got the part of Adam Shock."

I smiled as my mind reeled. I'd heard that name before but couldn't remember how or when. Isaac may have noticed my blank eyes.

"Adam Shock, the gay superhero? He's a member of the Crusaders. He has electricity powers?"

My eyes widened, and my smile stretched even farther. "Yes!" I shouted. "I knew I'd heard that name before!" Isaac threw his head back and laughed. "That's huge news, Isaac! Congrats! That's amazing!" I hugged him tightly.

My memories shifted. I was suddenly running around the

museum, kissing Caleb after every behind-the-scenes fact he shared with me.

When I pulled back from the hug, Isaac leaned in to kiss me. My mind was so cluttered I turned away, and Isaac's lips landed on my cheek.

He recoiled. "I'm so sorry," Isaac said. "I should've asked. I didn't mean—"

"No, *I'm* sorry." My jaw tightened. "I'm kind of dealing with a lot, and—"

"I didn't mean to rush into anything." He buried his hands in his pockets, and I fought the urge to reach for them. "It wasn't the right time."

It was, though. It would've been the perfect time to kiss any other person in any other circumstance. I wanted to, but it was like an invisible wall kept me from moving on. I kept smashing into it like a fly trying to escape.

I stared at his beautiful face, watching him frown as I started to walk backward. "I gotta go. I'm so sorry."

"Landon, just talk to me."

"Thank you for dinner. You were so generous. I—" I turned and power walked away, forcing my mouth shut. How was I supposed to move on without any resolution?

Caleb can't even give me the courtesy, so why do I still care?

"You don't always have to run!"

Isaac's echo followed me around the corner, leaving a print of guilt with every footstep. I had said those exact words to Caleb.

TWELVE
TEXAS

Three Weeks Ago

My plane home from NYC landed two days before Christmas. Caleb and Parker waited for me by the baggage claim. My eyes teared up seeing them. Parker drew a big sign in different colors that said, 'WELCOME HOME LAN!' I ran as fast as I could. I was an addict who'd gone too long without his drug of choice. My arms wrapped around Caleb's neck so tight I'm sure he could barely breathe. His arms wrapped under mine and lifted me.

"I missed you so much!" Caleb said, putting me back on his level.

I furiously kissed his face before landing on his lips. I stayed there and took in his smell. I hadn't been able to touch my boyfriend in months. Kissing Caleb felt like home. It was hard to pull myself away.

Parker wrapped his arms around me and then poked at my coat. " Aren't you hot in this?" He and Caleb wore shorts and tank tops. I peeled off New York's winter, my lower back drenched in sweat.

Caleb grabbed my suitcase off the conveyor belt. "Everyone's meeting us at Lucky's."

"Who's everyone?" I asked as we started for the exit. Parker's homemade sign dragged behind him.

Caleb smirked. "The usual suspects."

The Texas heat surprised me. It had gotten colder by the day in New York and had just started snowing when I got on the plane. Yet, even in December, it still felt like summer in Texas.

Miguel leaned against his Jeep when we reached the parking lot. Caleb still hadn't gotten his license back and wouldn't until his probation finished at the end of the month. Miguel's face lit up when he saw me. He wore a long, baby blue sundress that bellowed in the wind. A white silk durag wrapped around his head. His dark skin glistened under the sun, and his many gold bracelets clinked as he threw his arms around me. He smelled like a tropical breeze.

"Hey baby, how are you?" Miguel asked, beaming at me. "How's New York treating you? You look fantastic."

"New York's been really great, but I missed everyone a lot." My eye caught Caleb smiling as he put my suitcase in the trunk.

"We missed you too, love." Miguel stepped back with a hand on his hip. "If I had to see Caleb moping around the apartment for another day, I was gonna move out."

Caleb shut the trunk. "I was not moping."

"Whatever you say, honey." Miguel winked at me. "Let's get in before I get heatstroke. My ass don't need to visit the ER today."

———

We parked at Lucky's, and I sent my dad a quick text to say I was safely in town. I stared at the little white building. Those few months away felt like a lifetime, but Lucky's had stayed the same, except for the Christmas decorations. Stickers of Santa and reindeer flew across the windows, and a giant wreath with a red bow hung on the front door. This time of year meant every kid that came in got to cut out a paper snowflake that the owner hung from the ceiling with a fishing line. It was the closest thing to snow Madison, Texas got.

Steven barreled toward me before I could even step out of the car. His hair was white. He tackled me against the Jeep and squeezed the breath out of me.

I squeezed him back. "I missed you, too."

"It's been the worst without you," Steven said. "I'm coming to New York next semester to visit you. I don't care. I need to get out of this town. It's just breeders everywhere."

Miguel popped his head out the driver's side window. "And what are we? Gay chopped liver?"

Steven gave Miguel some side-eye. "Okay, I see these queens sometimes—"

Miguel gave Steven the finger and a smile. "You love me, bitch."

Steven did a hair toss and looked back at me. "But it's not the same without you!"

Parker made his way around the car and looked up at Steven. "What's a breeder?"

Steven laughed behind his hand. "I'll tell you inside," Steven said.

"Please don't!" Caleb called out.

"Mama's got some Christmas shopping to do," Miguel said, his arm draped over the open window. "I'll be back in an hour to pick ya'll up."

Caleb wrapped his arm around me, his hand held onto my hip. "Please don't get me anything," Caleb said to Miguel before glancing at me. "We even agreed not to get anything for each other this year to save money."

When I had called Caleb a few days before leaving school, he asked if skipping Christmas gifts for each other was okay. His tips at Lucky's hadn't been great, and paying two phone bills was starting to add up. I didn't have much money either—no gifts was A-okay with me. As long as I was with Caleb on Christmas, cuddled up on the couch watching a movie, that was all I needed.

Miguel rolled his eyes. "Fine. I'm getting something for Parker, though."

Caleb chuckled. "I'll allow it."

Miguel blew us a kiss and put his Jeep in reverse.

Parker and Steven stepped into Lucky's ahead of us. I stopped Caleb and faced him before walking in. "My dad wants to get something for Parker, too. We know how tight money is for you right now."

His eyebrows popped up so fast I thought they might sling shot off his forehead. "Really? He'd do that?"

"Of course, babe."

Caleb opened the door, seemingly unable to wipe the dopey smile off his face. "He hasn't had a good Christmas in years. Thank you." He kissed me as I walked through the door.

We were lucky enough to sit at Parker's favorite table, the retro video game theme. He was already giving Steven a lesson on who Mario and Sonic were when Caleb and I finally sat. The diner felt cheerier. Christmas music played over the radio on the counter, and it smelled like fresh apple pie. A Christmas tree stood by the restrooms, wrapped in colored twinkling lights. Most of the ornaments looked made by elementary schoolers—boxes wrapped in white and red striped paper clustered around the tree.

Lauren and Tasha walked in, squealed, and ran to us. Steven yipped as he jumped from his seat. Caleb and I greeted our friends with tight squeezes. Even though it was eighty-five degrees outside, we all still ordered hot chocolate to feel festive.

Steven leaned over Parker to tap Tasha. "Did you get the internship yet?"

Tasha's face scrunched a bit. "No. Probably won't hear til after Christmas."

Lauren grabbed Tasha's hand over the table. "Don't worry. You're literally the perfect candidate."

I noticed a man and his wife sitting side-by-side in a booth at the diner's corner, watching us. Both had white hair and wrinkled foreheads. The man wore a black cowboy hat. They pointed at us and whispered to each other. My stomach turned sour.

"I don't know," Tasha said. "There's a lot of competition in DC. Every journalism major is trying to get an internship."

"But there's only one muthafuckin Tasha Morgan!" Steven said, making Parker bust out laughing.

I tried to pay attention to the conversation, but my eyes fluttered to the couple again. Did they think we were being too loud? What was their deal? The old man stood and left a twenty-dollar bill on the table. His wife hobbled out of the booth and flanked her husband. The man's gut bounced when he walked, and their beady eyes bored into me. The man finally landed at our table, his belly inches from Steven's shoulder.

"Um, hi," Steven said. "Can we help you?" Everyone at the table looked up at the older man, but his eyes locked on me.

The man crossed his arms, resting on his stomach. "Aren't you the one who killed that Wilson boy?"

I opened my mouth, but nothing came out. I stopped breathing altogether.

"Excuse me?" Lauren asked, breaking the tension.

The white-haired man never acknowledged her. Instead, his eyes stayed on me. "I voted against yer daddy 'cause you shot that boy in cold blood."

"It was self-defense," Caleb said with fire in his voice.

"Not what I heard!" The wife shouted. I could hardly see her behind her husband.

Did people think I was the bad guy? The facts were in the news. The police reports were filed. My hands trembled, so I pushed them under my legs.

The older man struggled to catch his breath just standing there. "That boy's family deserved a trial."

Tasha whipped around in her seat to face them. "Oh, come on. Dan Wilson attacked them in *their* home. The law states that if someone threatens your life in your own home, you have every *legal* right to shoot them dead."

It was weird to hear Tasha talk about Dan as if he wasn't our friend once. I glanced at Steven, who looked at me with sympathetic eyes. I flashed back to all the times he and I played video games with Dan for hours, wasting all the daylight on Saturdays.

"That's fake news if I ever heard it," the woman chomped at Tasha.

"You know what you're saying makes zero sense, right?" Lauren scoffed.

The white-haired man continued to stare down at me. His black cowboy hat almost covered his eyes. "Where've you been? People say they haven't seen you around in a while."

The woman slapped her husband on the shoulder. "He's been hidin', Jim."

"I've—" My voice was hoarse, and my breathing picked up. "I've been away at college."

Jim snorted like a pig, and the corner of his mouth turned upward. "You hear that, Luanne! The Wilsons get forced out of town while the murderer roams free at some fancy school. "

Caleb's fists slammed the table, and everyone flinched. He stood so fast his chair fell backward. The slam made everything in the diner go still. "I'm getting real tired of hearing you rednecks accuse my boyfriend of all this bullshit."

Luanne snickered from behind her man. "Oh, Jim, the fairy's gettin' upset. This town would'a been just fine without ya'll. That Wilson boy had every right—"

"That's enough!" The voice was strong and deep from behind the counter. Dale Connors, Lucky's owner, wiped the sweat from his brow. Grease from the grill stained his white apron. "We don't need any of that in here. Take your business outside. All of you."

Caleb looked at his boss. "You're gonna let them talk to me like that?"

I could feel Caleb wanting to lunge, so I stood and faced him with my hand on his stomach. "Can we go?" My voice quivered. "Caleb, please."

"Fuck this place," Caleb said.

The others stood and collected their things.

"I'll give you a ride," Steven said. "I'll text Miguel to let him know I dropped you off."

I looked at Steven. "Thank you."

Parker took Caleb's hand and led everyone out. The old couple stayed, watching us with everyone else as if we were headed to the electric chair.

My hands trembled as I hugged Lauren and Tasha goodbye in the parking lot.

"You sure you don't want us to come over?" Tasha asked.

I shook my head. "I'm pretty tired from the flight."

Lauren looked at me with glistening eyes. "You know what they're saying isn't true, right? You did nothing wrong."

"It's not like they wouldn't do the same," I said.

"They're only saying shit because we're gay," Caleb said. "They don't want us here; they'd rather see us dead—fucking bigots."

Parker hugged his brother.

Steven tugged my arm. "Lets get you home and settled."

Everyone hugged and said their goodbyes as I got into the backseat of Steven's car. Parker sat next to me and rested his head on my shoulder. Honestly, it made me feel a little better. I tilted my head to rest on his, reminding myself that Caleb, Parker, Dad, and my friends knew the truth. They knew *me*, and that had to be enough. But it was hard to stop Jim's words from replaying in my head.

———

Steven pulled onto my street, and everything from the past four years came rushing back like I was on a nostalgic acid trip. As we pulled into my empty driveway, I glanced at Madison High—one place I didn't miss.

Parker and Caleb jumped out first. I promised them I'd do a Crusader's marathon, so they were eager to start.

"Um, okay, bye!" Steven scoffed. Caleb and Parker waved before heading inside. Steven swiveled in his seat to face me in the back. "You doing okay?"

I stared out the window. "I thought I missed being home. But that just reminded me why I left."

Steven sighed and turned to fix his hair in the rearview mirror. "Girl, you are *not* missing anything. It's the same shit-town it's always been."

"The guilt was just starting to fade."

"Leave it to two hillbillies to screw it up. Are you seeing a therapist yet?"

I had used the football field to work out my feelings for most of my life. And now I was hitting punching bags instead of tackling other guys. "No, I haven't had a single dream about Dan since being in New York. I'm getting better. I don't need it."

Steven's mouth formed a pouty smile. "Still, it might not be a bad idea," he said.

"Thanks for the ride." I hugged Steven, squeezing the driver's seat between us. "I love you."

"Love you, too," Steven said as he squeezed me. "Let me know what you're doing for New Years Eve."

I sat back. "I think Miguel is having a thing at his place if you want to come to that?"

Steven smiled wide. "I'm already planning my outfit."

———

As soon as I stepped into my house, I got a strong whiff of pine. Dad got our Christmas tree from Welch Farms every year because they let him cut it down himself. The six-foot tree stood in the corner of the living room. It was already decorated, but Dad left the topper on the coffee table. Since I was five, it was my job to put the star at the top of the tree.

It was our second Christmas without Mom. Dad tried to fit every ornament from the storage bin on the tree since she died. So many of them weren't even pretty; they were passed down to the women on my mom's side for generations. My least favorite ornament was always hanging front and center. In fourth grade, I made a paper machete heart ornament in art class, and at the center of it was my school picture from that year. My smile fully displayed my braces, and my bangs swooped to the side.

Caleb snuck up behind me and wrapped his arms around my waist. "Hey." He rested his chin on my shoulder.

I leaned into him. "I'm glad you didn't hit that guy."

Caleb pushed air through his nose. "My probation is over in a week. I wasn't gonna fuck that up." He kissed my neck, then noticed my fourth-grade ornament. "Who's that nerd?"

I elbowed Caleb and chuckled. "I look like a ginger Justin Bieber."

"I'm surprised you know who that is," Parker said from behind us. Caleb and I turned to see him sitting on the couch.

"Okay, you need to stop hanging out with Steven," Caleb said. He poked at Parker's side, making him giggle. "His sass is rubbing off on you."

———

Dad always made cinnamon rolls on Christmas morning—the only thing he looked forward to cooking all year. After opening gifts, the sweet bakery smell made my stomach growl. Biting into one was like chewing a cloud. The fluffy bun melted into my mouth, and the sugary glaze coated my tongue.

Dad and Parker chewed away on the couch, flipping through the channels, and eventually landed on *A Christmas Story's* twenty-four-hour marathon. Caleb wrapped his arms around me from behind and sniffed into my neck. I nuzzled him. He looked at me before running his fingers through my hair. "I like it long. It's cute."

"You're cute."

Caleb grinned. "Come upstairs. I wanna show you something."

I followed him to my room and sat on the bed as Caleb ruffled through his backpack.

"I know we said we weren't doing gifts," Caleb said. He sat next to me, holding something behind his back.

"Caleb, I didn't get you anything."

"That's okay. This is kind of for both of us." Caleb's arm floated from behind his back and presented me with a small black box. "Your dad offered to help. Since it's our first Christmas together, I think we should have something to remember it."

The way he looked at me made me think of Parker. There was so much innocence in his eyes it hypnotized me. As soon as the dimples appeared, my insides turned to mush. I couldn't hold back kissing him anymore. My lips were crafted to fit his, making me warmer than the Texas sun.

"Open it," Caleb whispered into my lips.

I swiftly removed the lid. Inside were two chrome rings with an equality sign stamped into the top. I smiled and glanced between Caleb and the rings. "Oh my god. They're perfect, babe."

Caleb slipped the metal circle on the ring finger of his right hand. "I figured we'd wear them on the right so people don't think we got engaged or something."

I pushed my ring onto my finger. "Would that be such a bad thing?"

Caleb kissed me again. "I missed you so much."

"This means we're together forever, right?"

"Forever and ever."

———

That night, Dad stood at the counter slicing chunks off a glazed ham he had cooked with Parker's help. He placed the plate of meat at the center of the kitchen island. "The next house will have a dining room, I promise.".

The first bite of ham melted in my mouth, and a whirlwind of sweet and salty danced across my tastebuds. "You're getting pretty good at this whole cooking thing, Dad."

Dad scooped a dollop of instant mashed potatoes onto his plate. "It was mostly Parker. There's a tutorial for everything on YouTube, apparently."

Parker shrugged before filling his mouth with a slice of ham almost as big as his face. "It's true."

"Which Christmas has been your favorite?" Caleb asked, mid-chew. He wasn't looking at anyone in particular, so I assumed he wanted to start a conversation.

"Remember the time Mom almost burned the house down?" I asked.

Dad choked on his water as he laughed.

Caleb smiled wide. "What happened?"

"Yeah, tell us!" Parker said.

I put my fork down as if it would help me remember. "I think I was ten?"

"Eleven," Dad said.

"Yeah, I was eleven!" I wiped my mouth with my napkin. "Mom bought a huge turkey that year, even though it was just the three of us. And she planned out this entire spread from, like, three different cookbooks."

Dad shook his head. "She was really into the food channel back then."

"She did this crazy brine with all these herbs and fruits, and it soaked for, like, two days," I said. "Then she smeared her homemade herb butter all over it and cooked it all day."

"Then we started playing Monopoly," Dad said.

Caleb eyes widened. "Oh no."

My brows hopped. "It was probably the most intense game we'd ever played. And we were so into it that Mom forgot to check the turkey. We were so locked in we couldn't even smell it burning."

"Until we noticed the black smoke," Dad said.

"Mom screamed at the top of her lungs."

Dad laughed a wheezing belly laugh. "Scaring the hell out of both of us."

I hopped out of my stool to reenact the story as I told it. "She ran to the oven and opened it. It was like a chimney. Suddenly, the whole kitchen was filling with smoke."

"So I start running around the house, opening every door and window I could," Dad said between laughs.

"So, Mom grabs two hand towels to take the turkey out, but one of the towels touches the hot rings and immediately catches on fire. So now Mom is screaming bloody murder as she sets the turkey down and is flailing around the kitchen with a dish towel on fire." I ran around the kitchen island and waved a small towel around my head. Parker's high-pitched laugh floated over the others. I finally tossed the towel in the sink and turned on the faucet, just as she had that day. I plopped back into my stool, breathing heavily. "Meanwhile, Dad and I couldn't stop laughing."

Dad wiped his eyes clean. "She was so mad at us at first, then started laughing."

I took a bite from a chunk of ham as my laugh calmed. "Best Chinese food Christmas ever!" I turned to Caleb. "Which Christmas has been your favorite so far?"

Caleb reached for my hand and held it between our plates. He glanced at Parker and smiled. "This one."

Parker smiled at his brother, then beamed his freckled face at us. "Mine too."

I squeezed Caleb's hand and drew a circle in his palm with my thumb. The only thing that could've made the night more perfect was if Mom had been there. Two Christmases without her, and it still wasn't easy... probably never would be. But retelling that story almost made it feel like she was there.

"She would love this," Dad said. "All of us here together."

"She really would have," I said.

Then Parker chimed in. "Think she would've liked our ham?"

Dad threw his head back with a laugh. "Absolutely!"

Our laughter cut out when we heard a loud knock at the front door. Each of our eyes met with the same puzzled look.

"I'll get it," I said as I crept off my stool. They all laughed and chatted again as I turned down the hall. I opened the door, and a breeze made its way inside. If I had blinked, I would've missed Chris starting his car and speeding away. A breath hitched in my throat, seeing him for the first time since Dan's funeral.

I stepped out, and my foot bumped a thin gift box left on the top step. I bent to pick it up and pulled the envelope taped to the top. *Landon* was written in Chris's chicken scratch. I glanced down the street again; Chris's car was gone.

I stepped inside and closed the door. The echo of Parker's laugh penetrated the wall. I leaned back against the door and opened the envelope, balancing the light box on one arm. It was a letter.

Landon, I'm sorry to leave this at your door, but it's too weird being at that house, and my parents don't want me around there. I hope you can understand. I hope you're doing okay. I see your insta posts. New York seems to be treating you good. I hope it's everything you wanted. I know this is random, but I found this in Dan's closet when I was cleaning out his room. I thought you might want it? I want you to know I read every story you published in the school paper. Dan didn't, but I always did. I knew that story because I'd heard Dan tell it a hundred times. If it's too weird, you can always throw it away, but since we're going back to North Carolina, I thought you should have it. And I think moving will help my parents. I'm sorry everything happened like this. Please don't reach out. Space will be good for a while. Maybe I'll see you down the road.

- Chris

I slid to the floor and placed the letter down. The box's lid was loose when I removed it. Pushing the tissue paper away revealed the frayed purple shirt Dan wore after my embarrassing picture day in elementary school. It was huge on him back then, but now it looked so small. I touched the fabric, hoping it would transport me back to the lunchroom the day Dan solidified himself as my best friend.

The lump in my throat pushed through, and I tried to stop my eyes from watering. It was the best gift Chris could've given me. I wished I could hug him. Guilt bubbled in my stomach again. I ruined his life. I ruined his parents' lives.

I sat on the floor with my back to the door and the box in my lap. My jaw tightened, and I clenched my eyes. The guilt felt like a spider creeping up from my stomach, clawing to my chest. I knew what it was like to clean out someone's stuff who had passed. I learned how hard it was to throw things away or donate them. I suddenly cherished everything my mom left behind. Even something as dumb as a hairbrush. I wondered if Chris was as gutted looking at the purple shirt as I was. That was probably why he wanted to get rid of it.

I unfolded the shirt and lifted it to my face. It still smelled like Dan's room—Axe body spray with a hint of mildew. I kept my face there and finally let the tears go. The newer, scarier memories had pushed aside the older ones. The new Dan blocked out who the old Dan used to be. God, I wanted to be back in that elementary lunchroom so badly. Our responsibilities were minuscule, and all we cared about was video games.

———

It was close to midnight on New Year's Eve, and we packed ourselves into Miguel's apartment. Everyone wore something shiny on account of the 'sparkle' theme. Several disco balls were placed throughout—the biggest one hung above our makeshift dance floor in the living room. People were everywhere. It was shoulder-to-shoulder traffic. Even though the AC was cranked, my lower back was as damp as it ever was on the football field.

Steven danced and mouthed the words to a Whitney song. He wore a sparkly blazer unbuttoned with nothing underneath. His chest was sprinkled with glitter, acting as the hair he'd never grow. It amazed me that no matter how much he flailed around, he never once dropped an ounce of alcohol from his cup. Lauren and Tasha sang the words in each other's faces in sparkly bras and metallic yoga pants.

Caleb was shirtless and glistening, per usual. Some of Steven's sparkles had rubbed off on him. I didn't mind swaying with Caleb's hips grinding against me. Touching his sweaty, bare skin sent the same fire down my stomach as the seven vodka shots we took. My fingertips dipped under Caleb's waistband. He twirled to face me—a grin spread across his face. He wiggled a finger at me.

Caleb danced in the middle of our circle, holding a vodka bottle. "Drink!" He shouted.

Steven and Lauren screeched with excitement. Tasha puffed her cheeks.

Caleb popped the cap and poured the alcohol into Steven's open mouth. He swallowed hard and checked his phone. "Omg, Landon, Blake just snapped me."

"Ew, why?" I shouted.

Lauren and Tasha got down on one knee. Caleb touched the bottle to their lips and poured. Then Caleb gulped a shot and unsteadily spun to me. "Open up, pretty boy."

I could count on one hand the amount of times he said that to me, and I always obeyed. My throat went numb at that point, the nerve endings singed by the 80 proof. My metallic tank top stuck to my back. "We should do New Year's in New York sometime!" I shouted over the music. Everyone smiled and cheered except Caleb.

"OMG, yyuuuuussss!" Lauren screamed.

"I can't wait to go back!" I shouted.

Caleb stopped dancing and pushed past me. "I need a break!"

Tasha eyed me. "Go talk to him."

I shrugged. "What did I do?"

"I caught the look on his face. Just go check on your man!"

"Okay, okay." I turned to a sea of sweaty bodies, everyone grinding on each other as if it were our last night on Earth. My vision blurred slightly, but I knew I could spot Caleb's sweaty shoulders in any crowd. I pushed through the dancing, leaving my friends in the eye of the storm.

The kitchen was overcrowded with people refilling their cups, but no Caleb. I skipped down the hall and knocked twice before entering Caleb's room—it reeked of booze, making my stomach flip.

"Hey," I said, closing the door behind me. The walls barely held back the music. "You okay?"

"God damn it!" Caleb chucked his phone across the room, and it crashed against the wall.

"Whoa! What's going on?"

"I wanted to call Parker, but my old ass phone is dead."

"Here, you can use mine."

Caleb waved me off and paced in front of the bed. "I just needed to cool off."

I opened the only window in the room. "Maybe that'll help."

Caleb followed and slammed the window shut. "I don't need your help, Landon." He stepped back and found the half-empty bottle of vodka again, taking two swigs without flinching.

"Okay? Did something happen?"

He huffed. "I'd rather not talk about it."

"Okay, we can talk about New Year's Eve in the city. Maybe next year we can go to Times—"

"Stop." Caleb pinched the bridge of his nose.

"Stop what?"

"Talking about New York every two seconds!"

My heart dipped into my stomach.

"All summer, you couldn't wait to leave."

I wobbled on my feet. "Okay. I'm here now."

"For how long? You've been home for, like, a week? And already you can't wait to leave. Do you know how shitty that makes me feel?" The music seemed to get louder as Caleb raised his voice. "You got out, lucky fucking you."

"Do you want me to apologize for going to college?"

"Why did it HAVE to be in New York? Why did it have to be halfway across the fucking country? There are good programs at plenty of schools here." Caleb swallowed another shot. "It was an easy out."

"You're acting like I wanted to get away from you."

"That's what it felt like!"

My arms shot out, and I almost lost my balance. "Why didn't you say anything!"

"Then what? It wouldn't have changed anything!" Caleb sipped from the bottle and paced again. "You get to move on from everything while I'm stuck."

"You're not stuck. You have your brother and Miguel. Your job."

Caleb touched the tip of the bottle to his temple and chuckled. "My job? You think I'd stay at a place where no one has my back?"

"What are you saying?"

Caleb glared at me.

"Did you quit? Caleb, that's so stupid! You have Parker to worry about. You have bills to—"

"No shit."

"You need *something*. When were you gonna tell me?"

"When were you gonna tell me about Blake?"

"What're you talking about?"

"I overheard Steven talking about setting you up on a date. Made me feel great that you went all summer without telling me."

Damn it, Steven.

"Did you actually go on a date with him?"

My face burned as if Caleb's eyes shot flames. "Yes, but that was before prom. After my story came out in the school paper. You were ignoring *me*, remember?"

"Were you into him?"

"That's a stupid question."

"Stop fucking calling me stupid." Caleb wiped a hand down his face and finished off the vodka. He tossed the bottle on his bed and started for the door. "I need another—"

I stepped in his path. "You're being an asshole."

"I'm the asshole? You don't realize how self-involved you are? Every time we're on the phone, we talk about you in New York or you and Lauren in New York. What you did this weekend *in New York*."

"Sorry I don't look forward to hearing you say the same thing every day. You hate your job. You can't afford anything. It's always the same, and now that you quit, you're just gonna bitch even more about the things you can't afford, when it's your own damn fault!"

"Yeah, I'm always thinking about how I'm gonna pay my bills. I don't have the luxury of a dad who pays for everything."

I crossed my arms. "At least mine stuck around."

"Oh really? With all his campaigning, your dad's been around? Why have you spent more time here then?"

"You know why."

"You're too much of a coward to stay in that house?"

I chewed my cheek. "Yep, you nailed it. I'm surprised you could figure that out."

"Oh, fuck you. You think you're so much smarter than me, but not smart enough to go to fucking therapy. Which, again, your dad will pay for."

"Oh my god, you're so fucking jealous of my dad! Yeah, he pays for shit. You know why? Because he loves me!" I poked Caleb's chest. "That's a hell of a lot more than you can say about your parents. At least my dad wants something to do with me."

"Stop fucking talking!" Caleb shoved my shoulder with his and reached for the door.

"Look what you turn into when you drink. I left to fucking do something with my life! I have goals. I want to be someone. Your dad left for a fucking reason, maybe he didn't want kids. Or maybe he did, but he just didn't like the one he got. He knew you'd be a fuck-up with no drive for anything. Maybe things would've turned out differently if you didn't get drunk and crash a fucking car. Who the fuck is Parker supposed to look up to? It sure as hell shouldn't be a convicted felon, your coked-out mom, or your runaway dad. Parker's better off without all of you!"

Caleb's shoulders fell, his face deflated, and his eyes hit the floor. "Leave. I don't want you here," he whispered.

"Wait. Caleb, I didn't mean—"

"Get the fuck out, Landon! Now!" His aggression pierced my chest, stopping my heart.

"But—"

"Fucking GO!"

I pushed by him and pulled the door open so hard it smacked the wall.

Everyone in the apartment was shouting as I passed through the kitchen. "Five! Four! Three!"

I slammed the front door behind me just as midnight hit. I raced down the carpeted hallway, hearing celebrations from other apartments. When I made it outside, I opened my phone to call an Uber. I could hardly see the screen with tears welling in my eyes.

"Landon?" I whipped around to Lauren, walking through the glass door of the building. She stepped toward me. Her heels clacked across the sidewalk. "I saw you bolt. You okay?"

The floodgates opened as every word I said to Caleb caught up with me. Lauren hugged me, and I broke. She held me as I sobbed into her shoulder.

———

I spent the next day packing up my room before heading to the airport the following afternoon. My lungs were void of air the whole time. I had lost my boyfriend and had to pack up all my childhood memories, all within twenty-four hours. Dad caught me crying on my bed, so I had to confess what had happened.

He rubbed my slumped shoulders. "Couples fight, son."

"Not like this."

"Sure they do. Your mom and I said some awful things to each other in our day. People get emotional when they love someone. You love hard, and sometimes you fight hard."

I wiped my damp cheek. "This seems impossible to come back from."

Dad patted my knee. "Give it time. It'll heal." He stood and stretched his arms behind his back. "You got everything?" I nodded. "I don't know why NYU needs you back so early. Kids at A&M get most of January off."

I shrugged. "Classes start next week."

"Mayor Griffin will be sending a strongly worded letter to the dean about this."

I appreciated Dad's attempt to make me laugh, but there wasn't a glimmer of light in my soul that day.

———

I checked my group text with Steven, Lauren, and Tasha as Dad and I merged onto the highway.

STEVEN

Did he text you yet?

ME

He smashed his phone against a wall last night. I don't think he could text me even if he wanted to.

TASHA

He will. I promise.

LAUREN

He's still on my shit list.

STEVEN

Same.

TASHA

Oh, I'm not happy with him. If I see him, he's gonna hear it.

ME

Thanks, but it's okay. I don't need you all to fight my battles. He's probably done with me now anyway.

TASHA

Nah, that boy's an asshole, but he loves you, believe me.

LAUREN

WE love you, Landon! I'm sorry, I have to go but have a safe flight. I'll see you back in the city!

ME

Thanks.

STEVEN

<3

TASHA

Safe travels, bb!

I couldn't stop crying when I hugged Dad before passing airport security. I would've shelled out my life savings to get Dad to come back to New York with me. It felt like I needed him more than ever.

———

Thursday, January 2nd

My hand froze around my suitcase handle. My knuckles were red and dry as I walked through the automatic doors into the warm lobby of my dorm building. I regretted packing all my dirty laundry in one suitcase.

"Landon! Welcome back," a cheerful voice said.

I gave a weak smile. "Hey, Bernard."

Bernard was a skinny Hispanic man in his late fifties with a thin mustache who worked the night shift at the front desk. He somehow knew everyone's name, even though a thousand NYU students lived in the building.

"Long flight?"

I pushed my suitcase against Bernard's station. "Sure was."

THIRTEEN
NEW YORK CITY

Saturday, January 11th

After I ran from my date with Isaac, I returned to the dorm, immediately took everything off, and got in bed. The only way to avoid the guilt taking up ninety percent of my body was to get under my covers with my laptop on my chest. I propped my head on my folded pillow and Googled Isaac Matthews, and every article on the first three pages was about him getting cast as Adam Shock.

TOTAL CINEMA: BREAKING, Openly Gay Actor Isaac Matthews Set To Play The ACU's First Gay Superhero, Adam Shock.

SHOUT FILM: SPECIAL REPORT: Former Child Star Set To Make His Come Back As Gay Superhero In The Wildly Popular ACU.

Come back?

One article shared a link to Isaac's Instagram account. My eyes widened. *700K Followers.*

Isaac's latest pic had a black background and white text in all caps.

I AM SO HONORED TO TAKE ON THIS CHALLENGE AND TO BRING MY FAVORITE SUPERHERO TO LIFE. THANK YOU FOR YOUR SUPPORT! *LET'S SHOCK THE WORLD! #AdamShock.*

I scrolled through the comments. So many people were happy to see a gay actor get the part. Of course, the trolls had something to say, too, criticizing that a gay superhero didn't belong in the ACU. Some fans had created art with Isaac in Adam Shock's costume. It was black armor with a red A on his chest and a white lightning bolt through the middle.

I Googled the character Adam Shock. In 1962, he was introduced in Astonishing Comics as a billionaire who threw a lavish party for Biohazard in 'The Crusaders' #44. However, he wasn't seen again until reintroduced in 2010 with his own title series. He was the arrogant, gay son of a steel tycoon. His father owned half the buildings in the city. A lightning storm during Adam's twenty-first birthday party knocked out the power at his eighty-first-floor penthouse. He braved the rain, stepping onto the terrace to mess around with the fuse box. When his fingers touched the first switch, a lightning bolt hit the roof, sending all its electricity into Adam's body. The bolt hurdled Adam off the balcony and into the rain clouds. His body was hit by two more bolts, sending him smashing through the windows of his building on the seventy-fifth floor. Paramedics found him with no pulse and used a defibrillator to jolt him back to life, fusing his cells with the electricity and giving him the ability to manipulate it.

I clicked away from Wikipedia and back to the fourth Google page on Isaac. An article caught my eye.

· · ·

TOTAL GOSSIP: EXCLUSIVE, Former Child Star Isaac Matthews Suffers Panic Attack Outside NYU Residence Hall.

Isaac publicly came out of the closet in tandem with the release of his underwear ad, pushing him from the boundaries of his innocent image. More fans bombard him on the street. NYC teens of all shapes, sizes, and genders flocked to Isaac's dorm daily. They waited outside for hours, hoping to get a glimpse of him, a selfie, or an autograph. "It made me not want to leave," Isaac was quoted saying in a brief interview. Fans rushed Isaac one morning on his way to class when he collapsed from panic. One doctor quoted in the article called it "sensory overload."

The article concluded with a tweet from Isaac the day after his incident. *I am doing much better today. I love you all, but I need my space for a while. Please respect that.*

I clicked back to Isaac's Insta. The last post before his Adam Shock pic was from a year ago—of him sitting in bed with his cat. I caught myself smiling as I scrolled through Isaac's Instagram. His dirty blonde curls made my heart flutter. Getting the part of Adam Shock was a massive event in his life that he'd seriously downplayed. I'd crumble under the pressure.

I wanted to text Caleb so badly. I was sure he already knew Isaac was cast, but a part of me wanted to hear him nerd out about it. I clicked Caleb's name and stared.

He's not gonna answer.

I turned to my side and swiped my phone's screen to call Isaac.

He answered after two rings. "Hello?"

"Hey, it's Landon."

Isaac chuckled. "I know."

I shuffled under my covers, trying to poke my feet out. "Sorry, I hope I didn't wake you up."

"I'm in bed, but I was just scrolling."

"Me too," I said as I stared at the ceiling.

We fell silent for a moment, then spoke at the same time. "I wanted to—"

"Oh," I said. "You go ahead."

"I wanted to apologize, so I'm happy you called."

I sat up and pushed the covers off my bare legs. "Wait, apologize for what?" I giggled. "*I* wanted to call to apologize."

"Apologize for trying to kiss you. That wasn't cool. I should've—"

"I should've kissed you back."

"What?"

I smiled in the darkness. "I had an awesome time. You were so sweet all night, and I should've kissed you back. A lot is going on in my head, so it's hard to process sometimes."

"I get that," Isaac said warmly. "I have a lot of shit going on in my head too." He stopped to take a deep breath. "Maybe we can talk about it sometime?"

I pulled my legs to my chest and rested my forehead on my knees. "Okay."

"Maybe brunch tomorrow?"

"I have class. Oh! And I'm meeting my friend Lauren for coffee. And then I have a writing session planned."

"Okay. How about you come to my place for the writing session? I'll cook."

"Is this an 'I'll show you my skills if you show me yours' situation?"

"Sounds fun," Isaac said. I could hear the smile in his voice. "Text me after your coffee, and I'll send you my address."

"Okay," I hugged my knees, feeling like a middle schooler again. "Can't wait."

"I'll see you tomorrow then."

"Bye." Nibbling my lip, I tried not to smile. I hung up and let the phone fall between my legs. My stomach fluttered as I lay back. I couldn't stop thinking about Isaac's voice and his adorable accent. I reached for my laptop and scoured YouTube for any episodes of *Little Chef* I could find.

————

I looked at my phone as 2:00 a.m. approached. I watched five episodes of Isaac's show and didn't want to stop. It was campy, loud, chaotic, and fun, with enough slapstick to keep me laughing throughout every episode. It was interesting seeing smaller Isaac. He was naturally funny, his timing impeccable, and at the same standard as the adult actors. His American accent was so perfect. If I had watched the show when I was young, finding out Isaac was British would've blown my mind. He was shorter, obviously, and his face rounder. But his eyes were still bright, and his hair was just as curly.

I shut my laptop and set it on my desk behind me. I could still hear Isaac's laugh as I closed my eyes. Isaac deserved more than what I was giving back. How long was I supposed to wait for Caleb to accept my apology? We'd fallen apart. Maybe I needed to start accepting that. I just wished he'd talk to me, even if it were to say he never wanted to speak to me again. At least then, I'd have closure.

————

Sunday, January 12th

Lauren and I picked at a chocolate croissant at The Ivory Den. The shop was overstuffed with college students taking shelter from the cold.

"I already have to write three papers by the end of the week," I said, licking the chocolate filling off my fingers.

"Not only do I have to write two papers, but I also have performances at the end of the week. So, two dance combos, two monologues, and a song from friggin' *Les Miz* to memorize."

"Jesus," I said before sipping from my cup. "Why are you even here?"

"I needed a break, believe me." Lauren ripped the end off the croissant. "These musical theater girls are bat shit."

I laughed.

"Has your roommate started to clean up after himself yet?"

I rolled my eyes. "Nope."

"Hey, I've seen your room at home. You aren't exactly Mr. Clean."

"Yeah, but this is next level," I said. "I've already used an entire bottle of Febreze since being back. And I have to wear headphones to bed because he stays up late on his computer."

"Doing what?"

"He's really into coding and hacking and stuff. He types so fast. I swear I can hear it in my dreams."

Lauren laughed, taking a sip from her cup. "How's your dad doing? He must be crazy busy since he got elected."

"Yeah, it seems pretty nuts. But you should hear what people suggest at council meetings," I said.

Lauren chewed, shaking her head. "Christmas break went by so fast. I feel like I barely got to see anyone."

"I know," I said, checking the time on my phone.

"Still nothing from Caleb?" Lauren asked before finishing her hot chocolate.

I sighed and crossed my arms. "I've texted and called him since I've been back, but he hasn't responded. He gave me a half-assed Happy Birthday when Parker called me, but that was it. I fucked everything up," I said, looking at my lap.

Lauren's voice got soft. "You both said shitty things. And you were drunk. He can't hold that against you forever."

Lauren unhooked her purse from the chair. "It's not like he hasn't gone dark before.

"It's different this time."

Lauren laid a hand over mine across the table. "He's being an asshole. Maybe I'll text him." She stood and slipped on her coat.

"I don't want to get you involved." I stared at my phone's dark screen.

"Okay, but I'll send him a text if you want me to."

"Thanks."

"I should stop procrastinating and get back to memorizing." She struggled to slip her backpack on, so I stood to help her. "What're you up to for the rest of the day?" She wrapped her long scarf around her face.

"I have a writing session with Isaac, so I'm heading to his place next."

Lauren pushed the scarf under her chin and raised an eyebrow. "Who's Isaac?"

I shrugged, slipping my hands into my pockets. I could feel the chill whip in whenever someone walked out of the coffee shop. "This guy I met. He's a year ahead of me at NYU." I didn't want to spill all the beans about Isaac just yet.

"Is he cute?"

I smirked. "Yeah, I guess."

"Is he single?"

"Why? You want me to hook you up?"

"Hey, straight guys are hard to come by at my school. A girl has needs."

I laughed before pulling her into a hug. "He told me he had two boyfriends once, so I think you're out of luck."

"Two boyfriends? At the same time?" Lauren pulled back, leaving her arms around my waist.

I looked down at her. "They were a throuple, apparently?"

"Oh." I could tell the gears were turning in her head. Then she looked up at me with sincerity in her eyes. "Caleb will come around, okay?"

I nodded, forcing a smile. "I'll text you later."

Lauren flung open the shop's door, entering the human current along the sidewalk. Just as the door was about to close, I caught a glimpse of Dan standing in the middle of the sidewalk in his bloodied tuxedo, unnoticed by the people walking by, wrapped up in their winter garb. I scrunched my eyes closed and took a deep breath.

Fuck, not again.

FOURTEEN

S *nap the fuck out of it. He's dead!*

    I opened my eyes, and Dan was gone. My hands clammed as I collected my things and walked out the door. My heart rate quickened as I searched the sidewalk, afraid of seeing him in another crowd.

Why is this happening now?

Before, I chalked my visions up to being drunk or high. But I was stone-cold sober.

It won't happen again. If I focus on Isaac, it won't happen again.

I checked Isaac's text to remind myself of his address. Luckily, it was a short walk. The wind whipped down the sidewalk, feeling like a personal attack. My eyes frantically scanned the faces of every person who walked by.

I spotted the black awning with *The Mercer Building* printed in cursive along the side. It matched the picture Isaac texted me. I walked through a revolving glass and met a doorman with a white mustache behind a desk. His gray uniform had 'Carl' printed on his chest.

Carl stood and clasped his hands in front of him. "How may I help you?"

I stared blankly for a second. "I'm here to see Isaac?"

Carl squinted. "Ah yes, he told me he'd be having a visitor. I have to ask your name, though."

"Landon."

"Last name?"

"Griffin."

Carl slapped his hands together. The echo in the empty lobby made me jump. He smiled. "You passed the test!"

I let out a breath I didn't know I was holding and faked a laugh. "Oh, okay."

Carl's smile didn't fade as he picked up the phone and punched some numbers. "Mr. Matthews, Carl here. Landon has arrived. Should I send him up?" He paused. "Great, thank you." Carl returned the receiver and looked at me. "Head on up. Eighteenth floor."

I nodded and passed the desk.

The elevator door opened, and my reflection met me as I stepped inside. The black carpet sparkled like a night sky. Eighteen was the top floor. I figured Isaac's place would be nice, but I hadn't expected the elevator doors to open inside his apartment. There was no hallway to walk down and no numbered doors to search through.

The whole place had wood floors and was open without dividing walls. Tall exposed support beams, painted black like the ones on subway platforms, scattered around the room. Stepping through the threshold, I could finally hear something other than my heartbeat racing—something sizzling.

Large square windows and a few massive skylights let the sun in, lighting the entire apartment. Plants were scattered everywhere, some hanging around the windows—in every shade of green, with a few blasts of reds, pinks, and yellows.

The living space was to my right. A glass coffee table sat snuggly into a substantial L-shaped couch. A projector screen hung from a lowered ceiling. I noticed the metal stairs leading to the loft above the living room. It was a balcony space that overlooked the entire apartment. Folk music played softly from the speakers that hung in every corner.

"Hey!" Isaac stood behind a marbled island, moving—what smelled like onions—around in a pan. Even the countertop behind him was marble. Isaac washed his hands before gliding to the fridge. He bent down to reach for something on the bottom shelf, and his T-shirt hiked up, exposing his lower back. "Here's a water if you want one," Isaac said, placing it on the counter. He wore loose jeans with frayed strings at his bare feet. He rounded the counter and hugged me through my open coat. He was so warm. "I can take your coat." Isaac's smile was so inviting that it was easy to forget I'd seen a vision of my dead best friend twenty minutes before.

I wiggled out of my coat. "Thanks."

Isaac took it, reached for my bag, and brought it to a closet near the elevator.

I did a three-sixty to take everything in. "This place is insane." Framed posters hung on the wall leading up the stairs. One of *Little Chef*, one of the *Adam Shock* logo, and finally, Isaac's underwear ad that I'd seen all over Google—of him sitting back in a velvet lounge chair wearing only white briefs. His curls were slicked back, and he was touching his thumb to his bottom lip.

Isaac's bare feet clunked their way back to me. "Thank you. I spent a lot of time making it feel like me."

"Everything looks incredible," I said.

Isaac smiled wide before hustling back to his smoking pan.

I sat on a cushioned stool at the counter and then glanced back at the logo. "Are they gonna put your face on the *Adam Shock* poster?"

Isaac crushed a piece of garlic under his knife and peeled it. "Maybe? That's just the teaser poster."

"Where do you sleep?" I blurted, sounding like a creeper. "There just aren't any walls here, and I don't see a bed." Isaac arched an eyebrow. "Not that I *need* to see your bed. That'd be weird..."

"My room's upstairs. The bathroom is too, in case you need it."

I'd love to go flush myself down the drain, I thought.

"Wanna help me cut the yams? They're already peeled over there." Isaac asked.

"Sure!"

"Just wash your hands, then you can use this knife."

I hopped off the stool. My mom had taught me better manners. I should've offered to help before I sat down. I set myself in front of the cutting board after washing my hands. "What are we making?"

"Gumbo. I figured it'd be perfect for this cold day." He hopped to the pan again and moved the garlic and onions around. I wanted to taste the air.

I stared at the knife, realizing I never chopped a yam before. It couldn't be that hard, but I didn't want to look like an idiot in front of a guy who probably knew how to chop yams fifty ways.

Do I chop horizontally or vertically?

"Mind if I show you how?" Isaac asked.

I tried not to cringe at my ineptness. "Please." I flipped the knife, handing him the blunt end. Instead of taking it from me, he wrapped his hand around mine. Isaac held the knife for both of us, planted himself behind me, guided my hand to the vegetable, and wrapped his other arm around me to hold the starchy tube. His chest leaned against my shoulder blades. His breath tickled my neck. "Just hold it like this," Isaac said softly next to my ear. "And grip the knife like that." His hand tightened as mine tightened around the handle. "Just let the knife do the work. Glide it down and through. You'll want to repeat the movement like this." His weight against me made me feel safe.

I nibbled my lip, trying to focus on the cutting. Isaac's chin grazed the side of my neck, and the tingle it caused pulsed down my body. There was no way I could focus if he kept the lesson going. I took a breath, then felt his cheek against mine. He smiled. And I had a feeling he knew what he was doing.

Letting out a chuckle, I rocked my head back on his shoulder. Isaac saw an opportunity and took it. His lips grazed my neck. Our hands let go of the knife and instead locked fingers. I leaned into his soft lips.

Isaac gripped me by the waist, and suddenly, I was facing him, locked onto his sparkling eyes. He cupped my face with his smooth hands, and our lips met just as fast as he'd spun me around. Our tongues danced, and my chest felt as tight as my jeans. My hand wrapped around his lower back and under his shirt. His skin was like silk.

The vision of Dan from the coffee shop intruded my mind, and I gasped.

Isaac pulled back. "I'm sorry. Did I hurt you?"

My hands swiped down my face. "No, no," I said through clenched teeth. "It's—I'm sorry." I turned around and gripped the counter. "My head is all fucked up," I whispered.

Isaac's hand lightly scratched my back as he leaned against the counter to face me. "Hey, it's okay. Let's pause the food for a second and talk."

"We really don't—"

"Go sit on the couch," Isaac said, turning off the burners. "I'll bring your water."

The small flame of a red candle flickered on the coffee table. The scent of apple crisp danced around the air, reminding me the holidays weren't far behind us. A tiny meow surprised me as I sat on the couch. I swiveled on my cushion to see a dark-striped cat lounging on the top part of the couch.

"That's Potato." Isaac sat next to me, holding two water bottles. "It's a good sign if he lets you pet him." He handed me a bottle. "He didn't like my exes. Wouldn't give them the time of day."

I'll keep that in mind.

Isaac put a hand to his mouth, eating a small pill before cracking open his water.

"For your panic attacks?" I asked.

He grinned. "Did Google out me again?"

I sat up straight and cleared my throat.

"It's cool," Isaac said. "Why wouldn't you?"

I rolled my eyes. "Okay, yes, I googled you."

Isaac threw his head back and laughed. His mop of curls bounced. "Now you know how much of a mess I am."

"You turned out okay, I think."

Isaac blew a puff of air to move the hair dangling close to his eyes.

"After one or two public panic attacks, people tend to leave you alone —most of the time."

"You're about to star in a massive franchise. Aren't you nervous that the panic attacks might come back?"

Isaac nodded slowly and took a breath. "That's what the pills are for."

I wasn't sure I shared his confidence in a single pill. If I did have anxiety, mine seemed different. I leaned an elbow on the couch and rested my head on my hand. "Can I ask you something?"

Isaac pulled his other leg onto the couch and faced me criss-cross style. "Always."

"Can people with anxiety, like, hallucinate?"

"I think so?" Isaac reached into his pocket. "Google knows every-thing... As you know." He winked at me before looking at his phone. Isaac's thumbs bobbed in and out. He nodded as he read his screen.

"What's it say?"

"It says people with anxiety and depression may experience peri-odic hallucinations. The hallucinations are typically very brief and often relate to the specific emotions the person is feeling."

"Have you ever felt that?"

"Not exactly," Isaac said as his eyes scanned the room. "My anxiety always feels like the walls are caving in on me, which triggers panic attacks." With his hands, Isaac demonstrated a ceiling forcing its weight onto him. "I know it's gonna turn into a panic attack when I see little flashing lights. It sends me to the ground."

I could definitely relate. The past year felt like one big, crippling ceiling. And I folded under its weight. But I never saw any flashing lights.

"Have *you* ever felt that?" Isaac asked.

Lost in my thoughts, it took me a second to respond. "Felt what?"

"Any of it. Anxiety? Panic attacks?"

"No." The word shot from my lips so fast that Isaac arched an eyebrow.

"Did something happen in the kitchen? Is that why we stopped?"

I lied again. "No." Isaac's entire life was plastered on the internet.

He couldn't hide his trauma. And it wasn't fair to hide mine from him. I leaned an elbow on the couch again and rubbed my forehead.

Isaac's warm hand touched my knee.

I looked at him and leaned my temple against my fist. "I've spent a lot of time saying the wrong things. I don't want to do that anymore."

"Okay," he whispered.

I sighed. "Yes, I've felt a lot of those things. It happened in the kitchen. It's like flashes of certain memories hit me all at once, and it's hard to focus. I'm sorry, I must sound—"

"Hey," Isaac said. "You *never* have to apologize for the way you feel. Especially to me, and especially about mental health."

My fingertips traced little squares over Isaac's hand.

"Do you wanna talk about it?" Isaac asked.

"I never really have."

"It's totally up to you."

I scratched the back of my neck. "It's kind of *a lot.*"

"It could feel good to get it out. Or we can talk about something completely different. No pressure."

My shoulders relaxed. "It's hard to know where to start."

Isaac gently squeezed my leg. "I have all the time in the world." His smile was intoxicating. How did his little gap-toothed grin have so much power over me? "How about I do the cooking, and you do the talking?"

I tugged at my earlobe. Did I really want to unload all of my batshit baggage onto a guy I was just getting to know? How do I tell someone I've killed another person? "Sure."

As Isaac clicked on the burners, I sat across the island from him. "Let's start with your parents," Isaac beamed. "What're they like?"

"I guess everything started with my mom."

———

My planned writing session never happened because I spent two hours telling Isaac my life story. By the time I got to Caleb in the hospital after prom night, Isaac and I had already cleared our plates and were back on the couch. I curled up in the corner, and Isaac faced me, sitting cross-legged again. Both his hands rested on my thighs this time, and Potato slept in Isaac's lap.

My fingers swept through my hair. "I told you it'd be a lot to take in." Isaac didn't say anything. "If this changes things, I totally understand."

"Nothing's changed, Landon." He flipped his hands, and I held them. "I know you did what you had to. If anything has changed, it's that I feel more connected to you now than I did a few hours ago." His thumbs stroked the back of my hands. "It couldn't have been easy to tell me all that. You've been through more than most people ever will," Isaac said.

After telling him the whole story, I was emotionally drained. I prayed it was the last time I'd ever tell it.

"Have you heard from Caleb yet?"

"Not since my birthday," I said. "It's been weird not talking. I went to him for everything. Every time I fell, I could land on him, you know? Now, it's like he's a stranger."

Isaac pouted. "I shouldn't have been so forward. I wouldn't have kissed you if I knew your wounds were still fresh."

"Honestly, having you around has helped."

Isaac sat up straight like a kid on Christmas morning. "Happy to be the best distraction I can be."

I slapped my knee. "Okay, we've been talking about me for hours. Can we switch it up?"

Isaac chuckled. "Sure."

"What about you? Why aren't you still with your two boyfriends?"

Isaac's eyes scanned the floor. "Oh, it's time to air my dirty laundry now. Got it." I laughed. "My panic attacks kept me in the house for a long time. I became manic. And then NDA's got involved—"

"NDAs?"

"Non-disclosure agreements." Isaac rubbed his neck. "The press started to wonder where I was after my meltdown. I was so scared my boyfriends would go to the paparazzi that I forced them to sign

NDAs. I wouldn't leave the house because I didn't trust the public. It bled into my relationship. Even though I had no reason to doubt them. Our life together was a secret outside this apartment, and they hated it." He gave a weak smile. "That's the abridged version."

I gently squeezed his hand. "I'm sorry, Isaac." My phone vibrated on the cushion next to me, and I noticed the time. *Holy shit!* It was almost nine, and I still had homework to do. I bounced up and reached for my shoes. "I'm so sorry. I didn't realize how late it was."

Isaac looked at his phone. "Let me get you an Uber."

I stood and walked around the couch. "Isaac, my dorm is like six blocks from here. It's okay. Really."

Isaac hopped over the top of the couch and jogged to the closet. "It's freezing outside."

"I kinda like it."

Isaac handed me my coat and bag. "At least let me walk you out?"

I zipped my coat and pulled my bag over one shoulder. "Sure."

We rode down the elevator and stood on the sidewalk facing each other with our hands in our pockets.

"I'm sorry again," Isaac said.

"For what?"

"My timing sucks."

"I don't know. It feels like I spilled coffee on your phone right when I needed you." A smile tugged at Isaac's lips. "Like a real-life superhero."

Isaac chuckled. "Yeah, one who's too afraid of rejection to ask before kissing someone."

"Adam Shock isn't a mind reader?"

"Isaac Matthews definitely isn't."

"Isaac Matthews should try again. Maybe third time's the charm."

He smiled and stepped closer, wrapping his arms around my lower back. "May I kiss you?"

My hands found the back of Isaac's neck before pressing my lips to his. When Isaac's tongue found its way to mine, I thought about how it would look to people walking by. I was sure New Yorkers had seen weirder things than two boys making out. His lips were like a magnet. I had to force myself to pull away. We couldn't stop smiling at each other.

"Text me when you're home safe," Isaac said.

"Will do." I watched him go through the door before I started walking. My stomach was so full of butterflies I could've floated home.

Later that night, I sat at my desk, finishing a paper about plotting a story.

Josh popped his head out from the bathroom next to my desk. His dreadlocks swung in every direction. "Can I use your bar of soap? I'm all out."

I peered at him. "Sure," I said. He smiled and shut the door while I made a mental note to open a new bar of soap the next time I showered. Josh was cool, but coexisting with him in a small space wasn't ideal. I started typing again as I heard the squeak of the shower knob and the water hitting the porcelain.

I was on my last paragraph when a loud knock rocked my door, causing me to jump out of my skin. With a grunt, I pushed myself out of my chair, kicking a pair of Josh's boxers under his bed.

I opened the door, and my blood went cold when I saw Caleb. He wore his tight jeans and leather jacket.

"Caleb..." I muttered, barely able to speak.

He held a backpack that looked like it'd been through a tornado. One strap was missing, and the fabric was torn and ruffled. He entered my room and tossed the backpack on my bed.

My tongue dried up. "How... How did you get through security?"

"I snuck in," Caleb said, sounding raspier than usual as he rifled through his bag.

"That's impossible. How?"

"Doesn't matter."

Caleb manically dug through the backpack.

I stepped closer with a huff. "What are you doing here? I've been calling you."

"Can't afford a new phone."

That's right, he smashed it on New Year's. "So you didn't hear my voicemail?"

"No."

I was relieved he hadn't heard of my mental break. "How did you get here?"

"Two buses. It was the cheapest way." Caleb finally pulled his hands from the backpack and opened them in front of me, revealing his numbered key. He looked at me, his eyes worn with bags. "He wanted me to find it," Caleb said.

"What?"

"The numbers. I figured it out."

"What about them?"

"I asked around some hardware stores, and one guy recognized it. Said someone came in asking to make a copy but said he couldn't because it was technically a federal key."

"What does that mean?" Staring Caleb in the face felt like a dream.

"He said it belonged to a safety deposit box. It took me a few days, but I finally found the bank it belonged to."

My jaw fell agape. "Holy shit."

"It gets weirder."

Caleb paced between the two beds in the room. My mind raced with questions. I hadn't been that close to Caleb in so long. I wanted to hug him and tell him I was sorry.

"The woman at the bank said I was the only person authorized to open the box. I had to show my ID," Caleb said.

"Why are you *here* then? It sounds like your dad might be in Texas."

"He isn't. There was a New York address in the box with some other stuff. I've been looking for it for almost two days, but without my phone, it's been hard to find."

"Caleb, you've been here for two days! Why didn't you come here first?" The thought of Caleb alone on the cold city streets shattered me.

"After—I thought I could do this alone, but I'm realizing I can't. I need you."

His words pierced my chest. I heard the shower turn off, and my eyes shot to the bathroom door.

"Landon," Caleb said with a whimper in his voice. My gaze returned to his hazel eyes. "I need to figure out what happened," Caleb said. "My dad is here somewhere. If I'm gonna find him, I need your help."

FIFTEEN

I'd wanted to hear those words from Caleb's mouth for so long. My chest warmed. But, honestly, I'd started to give up on the idea I'd ever see him again. Him standing in my dorm room was the last thing I imagined happening. After what I said, I didn't think he'd want anything to do with me. My jaw tightened. "Um, okay. Sure, I'll help." My brain struggled to process being in the same room with him.

Caleb sat on my bed. "Mind if I use your phone?" I pointed to the desk. Caleb grabbed my phone off my notebook. He remembered my password, and after a few swipes, he pressed the phone to his ear. "Hey, Parker, it's me." Parker's voice muffled against Caleb's head. "Yes, I know. Listen, okay? I'm fine," Caleb said. He pushed himself further onto the bed to lean against the wall. "I'm sorry, kid." Caleb's eyes looked heavy. "I'm at Landon's now. I'm safe."

I leaned forward. "Hey, bud."

"See?" Caleb said. Parker's mumbling lowered. Caleb rubbed his forehead. "No, I haven't found anything yet. I'll let you know as soon as I do." Caleb paused and let out a chuckle. "Yes, I pinky swear. Okay, get some sleep. And call Landon's phone if you need me." Caleb rested his head against the wall. "Love you too. Bye." Caleb's arm fell, and he sighed.

I sat on the edge of the bed. "He okay?"

"He was worried when I didn't call."

"I don't blame him," I said. "Why didn't he call me?"

"I told him not to."

I pushed myself further on the bed and leaned a shoulder against the wall. "What the hell? Why?"

His eyes shot to me. "Because your dad isn't the one missing."

The bathroom door creaked open, and Josh stepped out in his underwear, a towel hung around his neck. "Oh, my bad," Josh said. "Landon didn't tell me he was having someone over."

Caleb quickly stood. "I'm sorry, that's my fault. I surprised him." He held out his hand. "I'm Caleb."

Josh glanced at the pictures pinned on the board above my desk, then back to Caleb. He smiled wide, gripped Caleb's hand, and pulled him into a one-armed hug. "Shit, man! I've heard so much about you. It's nice to meet you finally!"

Caleb chuckled softly. "Same."

Josh stepped to the closet. "Sorry for the mess."

"I've seen worse." Caleb shuffled toward the bathroom. "Excuse me for a sec." He closed the bathroom door and turned on the faucet.

Josh turned to me and pushed his head through a black T-shirt with a green binary code printed on the front. "Why do ya'll look like someone just killed your dog?" Josh whispered.

I sighed. "We kinda broke up, I think."

Josh pulled on a pair of jeans but stopped short before buttoning. "Shit. Want me to kick him out?"

I scooched to the edge of the bed and planted my bare feet on the floor. "No, but thank you."

Josh's shoulders relaxed, and he finally buttoned his pants. "Okay, good, 'cause I hate confrontation. Gives me an upset stomach and shit." He picked two random socks off the floor and sat on his bed to put them on. "Are you okay?"

I blew air from my nose. "Oh, I'm fine," I lied. "We broke up on New Year's Eve."

Josh stopped tying his shoe to look at me. "Wait, what? Why didn't you tell me?"

"Because it was my fault. I wasn't ready to talk about it, I guess."

Josh stood, reached for his computer, and placed it in his backpack. "Do you want to talk about it now?"

I shrugged. "Not really."

"Okay, good, 'cause I give terrible advice."

I couldn't tell if he was serious or trying to make me laugh.

Josh walked to the closet again. After pulling a shirt from its hanger, he shoved it into his backpack and hung it over his shoulder. "I was going to a friend's place, so I'll stay there tonight. You guys need your space."

"Josh, you don't—"

"It's cool, I swear."

I took a breath. "Okay." Josh held out his fist, and I bumped it. "Thanks."

Josh was already halfway out the door when he said, "Text me if you need anything."

The shower turned on, so I tiptoed to the bathroom door, grabbing my used towel off the back of my chair. A shirtless Caleb opened the door as I was about to knock. It might've been the steam from the shower, but I suddenly felt sweaty. I couldn't help but look him up and down. His jeans clung to his hips as if painted onto his skin. His torso was just as smooth as the last time I saw it. But it was his necklace my eyes got stuck on. A thin rope tied around the ring from Christmas dangled in the middle of his chest. Caleb snatched the towel from my hand, pulling my focus up.

"Thank you," he said before closing the door in my face.

My stomach sank. I slumped into my desk chair and opened the long drawer. Shuffling some papers aside, I found my matching ring. I snatched it, closed the drawer, and placed it on my notebook. Was I wrong for not wearing it? Caleb wasn't exactly wearing it, either. But if he didn't want to wear it, why make it a necklace?

My computer screen was black. How was I supposed to focus on school with all the questions about Caleb flying around my head?

The shower turned off, and Caleb shut off the light before tiptoeing out of the bathroom with the towel wrapped around his bare waist. He looked around. "Where's Josh?"

"He said he'd stay at his friend's tonight."

Caleb rubbed his hands dry on the towel. It was hard not to notice how low it sat. Caleb caught me looking. "Sorry, but can I borrow some underwear?"

"Yeah." I crouched and pulled one of the plastic drawers from under my bed. I tossed Caleb a pair of grey boxer briefs.

Caleb turned away from me and slipped the boxers on under the towel.

A pit formed in my stomach. "I've seen it before, ya know."

Caleb ignored me and hung the towel on the bathroom door. He fixed the blankets on Josh's bed, fluffed the pillow, and climbed under the covers. We were five feet from each other, yet oceans apart. And it was cold on my island.

"Where did you stay last night?"

Caleb tucked an arm under his pillow. "A subway station."

I stood to take my pants off. "Jesus. Did anyone bother you?"

"A guy tried to take my bag but just ripped the strap off."

Why did he say that like it isn't terrifying?

"Parker always calls it my lucky pack. Guess he's right," Caleb said.

"Caleb, I wish you would've come here first."

"Stupid, I know."

"I didn't say that."

The room went quiet as Caleb turned to face the wall.

"So that's it?" I spat out.

Caleb peered over his shoulder. "What?"

I gestured to his bag. "You show up here out of the blue and want to sleep?"

"Landon, I'm exhausted. We can talk in the morning."

"I have class tomorrow morning."

"It's fine, Landon. You don't have to help."

I rolled my eyes. "That's not what I meant. I want to know what the hell's going on."

"It's great that you suddenly care."

"Caleb, I've always—"

"Please, I'm too tired to do this."

My jaw clenched. I waited this long, and he wanted to torture me for one more night. "Fine." I got up and hit the light switch—a reflected beam from a streetlamp cut across the ceiling. I reached for my phone to plug it into the charger but saw Isaac had texted me thirty minutes before.

ISAAC
Hope you had a productive night. Sleep tight.

A kissing face emoji followed his text.

ME
Not as productive as I'd hoped. Night.

I sent a kissing emoji back and huffed. Isaac's lips provided all the warmth I needed standing on that cold sidewalk. I wondered if I was cursed with bad luck. Who did I piss off so badly? I closed my eyes, comforted by Caleb's breathing.

What the hell do I tell Isaac now?

———

Monday, January 13th

Something slapped me on the face, jolting me awake. The sun beamed in, making my eyes sting. I thought I was dreaming, but Caleb's voice pulled me into the real world.

"Can you explain this to me?" Caleb said, sitting on Josh's bed.

I wiped the sleep from my face and looked at him with one eye open. "What?"

Caleb pointed to the floor. "Is that you?"

I peeked over the edge of my bed. A magazine was face down next to my jeans. That must've been what slapped me awake. I grabbed it and sat up in my bed before flipping it over. My stomach lurched, and my arms stiffened. It took every ounce of willpower not to vomit all over my blanket.

At the center of the TOTAL GOSSIP magazine cover was a picture of Isaac and me kissing outside his building from the day before. The big yellow headline read, 'Isaac Matthew's Night Out With New Mystery Boy.' The picture was taken from a low angle as if the person was behind a mailbox or something. It showed us in profile, but my fiery hair was unmistakable, and the image was so high quality I could see the freckles on my neck. There was no denying it, and Caleb's tone told me he already knew.

"Oh fuck!" I flipped through the pages. *Holy fucking shit, people are gonna see this!* My eyes scanned the words. They'd written a speculative article about my dinner date with Isaac. And those asshole paparazzi never deleted the pictures of us, even after Isaac was so friendly to them.

Caleb popped to his feet. "I fucking knew it!." Caleb paced, running his hands through his hair. "Holy shit."

I blinked at the cover. "Where did you get this?"

"I stole it from the corner store."

I couldn't stop staring at the picture. A silent 'fuck' escaped my lips again, and I wondered if Isaac had seen it yet. I reached for my phone.

Caleb looked down at me, his coat still zipped. "You move on quick, huh?"

"It's not what you think."

Caleb paced again. "Isaac *fucking* Matthews? How the fu—I don't know if I should be impressed or pissed off."

My brow furrowed. "That's not fair! You haven't spoken a word to me since New Year's, Caleb!"

"I didn't have a fucking phone!"

"You could've used Parker's or Miguel's! Anything would've been better than silence."

Caleb stomped to his tattered backpack on my desk chair and zipped it. "I shouldn't have come here." He slung the bag over his shoulder and started for the door. "I can do this on my own."

I flew off my bed and caught Caleb by the elbow. I hadn't moved that fast since my final football game. "Stop doing this!"

Caleb looked over his shoulder at me. "Doing what?"

"Shutting me out! You've done it too many times. I'm not letting it happen again," I said. The tension in his arm settled. "Let me fucking help you." I dropped my aggressive tone. "Please."

Caleb sighed before turning to me. He looked me up and down, and I realized I was standing there in nothing but my underwear.

My arms fell to my sides. "Can we just pause for a second?"

Caleb's jaw flexed, and his eyes stayed on me.

"Please tell me what's going on."

Caleb turned, placed his bag on my bed, unzipped it, and pulled out a white index card with crumpled corners. He passed it to me. *143 E Houston St. NYC*, was written in black Sharpie. "My dad's there," Caleb said. He had so much hope in his voice.

"How do you know?"

"Because it's all I have."

I stared at the index card. "Why now?"

"You said I needed to do something with my life. This is it."

"Caleb, what I said that night, it—"

Caleb pointed to the index card, "Do you know where that is?"

"No, but I can map it on my phone." I grabbed my jeans off the floor, slipped them on, and searched for my socks and shoes. "What else was in the box?" I reached for Caleb's backpack, but he quickly snatched it and searched inside. He handed me a picture from a disposable camera, just like the ones Caleb had in his tin box back home. He and his dad smiled at me with squinty eyes from the Texas sun. They were standing in a driveway in front of a beat-up silver car. Caleb had to be Parker's age. His arm was wrapped around his dad, only standing as tall as his pop's shoulder. His smile was so big it barely fit on his face. Caleb's dad looked different from the older pictures I'd seen in Caleb's box. In this one, he had a dark beard and shaved head. I flipped the picture—someone had drawn a circle with a pen at the bottom left corner.

"That was my first day of school the year he left," Caleb said. "I remember my mom taking it, but I'd never seen it until I opened the deposit box." Caleb reached into his bag again. "This was the last thing in the box." He held a silver key attached to a stretchy coil bracelet.

"What the hell is that one for?"

"No clue," he said before dropping it back into his bag. It clinked against something at the bottom.

I passed the picture back to Caleb and reached for my coat. What the hell did it all mean? If Caleb's dad decided to leave them, why would he leave clues behind? "Well, I guess the address is a start."

Caleb nodded, zipped his bag, and started for the door. I glanced at my desk and snatched the magazine. I didn't need Josh to see it, so I folded it vertically and shoved it into my coat pocket. My phone vibrated just as I locked the door. I pulled it from my jeans. *Isaac Calling. Fuck.*

"You comin'?" Caleb's voice grabbed my attention. He was holding the elevator.

I silenced my phone and jogged to Caleb.

———

The address wasn't far from my dorm. I had typed it into Google

Maps before zipping up to brace the cold. Caleb walked with his hands in his pockets. I hoped his leather jacket was warm enough.

"Which way?" Caleb asked.

"It's just south of here. Like, a ten-minute walk."

Caleb nodded, and steam escaped his mouth. "This isn't anywhere near where I was looking," Caleb said. "New York's confusing."

We crossed Lafayette Street, just making it before the light changed. "It's a numbered grid. It's easier if you think of it like that. Except for this area, the grid doesn't apply here."

"See, confusing," Caleb said.

What did people do before GPS? We followed the map and took a right on Bowery Street. I couldn't stop thinking about the tabloid folded in my pocket. It made my stomach flip. I needed to focus on something else before I spiraled. "What do you think it'll be?"

Caleb's gaze stayed straight. "What? The address?"

I looked down at my phone again. "Yeah."

"I'm hoping he lives there."

"And if he doesn't?"

Caleb blew out a puff of warm air. "I find a new purpose, I guess." Caleb looked up, taking in a thirty-story high-rise blocking the sun as my words from New Year's Eve replayed in my head.

My phone vibrated. A text popped onto the screen.

ISAAC

Can we talk?

I eyed Caleb before texting back.

ME

Kinda busy right now, later?

ISAAC
Sure.

I needed to stall a little longer. If I didn't mention the tabloid, then maybe Isaac would assume I hadn't seen it yet. I promised myself I'd call him after Caleb saw his dad. "Maybe the other key is for his apartment."

"Maybe," Caleb said. He eyed the street signs.

As we approached 143, I could read the white letters on the glass door. *Lewis Law Firm.* We stopped, leaving the whole sidewalk between us and the building. Neither of us said anything. Maybe we didn't want to accept the disappointment.

"I don't think he lives here," Caleb said.

I turned to him and shrugged. "Maybe he works here?"

Caleb started for the door. "Only one way to find out."

"Wait, we can't just—"

Caleb was too quick, already passing through a blast of warmth that tousled his hair. I tentatively followed him inside. The lobby was an off-white rectangle with a marble desk at the center of a wall of elevators.

My phone vibrated in my hand again. *Lauren Calling.* I rolled my eyes.

The bald man behind the desk stared at us with pursed lips. I looked at Caleb. "Lauren's calling me." I turned away and hit the green button. "Hey."

Lauren's voice assaulted my ear. "You didn't tell me the Isaac you were seeing was ISAAC MATTHEWS!"

"I didn't want to make a big deal of it," I whispered.

"There are pictures of you kissing a celebrity. This IS A BIG DEAL! And don't say it isn't you. I know your hair."

My heart raced. Lauren wasn't helping. "Listen, I can't talk about this right now."

"Are you in class?" she asked.

"No." I swallowed hard. "Caleb's back."

"I'm sorry, what?"

I leaned a hand against the cold wall. I needed to brace myself because the words were hard to believe, even for me. "Caleb's with me right now, in New York."

"What the hell, why?"

"It's a long story, but we're looking for his dad."

"Jesus, Landon."

"What?" I looked over my shoulder. Caleb was still chatting with the doorman.

"Did he explain why he's been M.I.A?" Lauren asked.

"Yes—kind of. I forgot he smashed his phone on New Year's."

"Still, it's been over a week, and then he just shows up?"

"Lauren, he's been wondering what happened to his dad for, like, half his life. What was I supposed to do? I gotta go, okay?"

"I'm so confused. You need to call me soon to explain this." Lauren said sharply.

"Okay."

"Steven is gonna die when he finds out."

I scratched the back of my head. "Please don't tell him yet. Or Tasha. I don't need my phone blowing up right now."

"They're gonna see it online."

"Fuck." I massaged my forehead. "Just don't say anything, okay? Please."

I glanced at the front desk. Caleb looked at me and shook his head. Then, I noticed a large framed picture on the wall behind the doorman. "I gotta go," I said to Lauren. I hung up and stepped to the front desk, slipping the phone into my coat pocket.

Caleb's eyes stayed on me. "This guy knows everyone who's in and out of this building. I even showed him the picture. He doesn't know my dad."

My focus stayed on the frame. It was a picture of 143 E Houston St. I recognized the skinny trees on the sidewalk and the yellow fire hydrant we stood next to outside. But the building with 143 on the door was not Lewis Law Firm. It was a different structure entirely. I pointed to the picture. "What's that?"

The bald man looked over his shoulder and smiled before looking at me again. "That's the old movie theater."

Caleb's attention perked up like a dog who had heard someone pull into the driveway. "Movie theater?"

"The original 143 Houston. They demolished it about seven or so years ago after it closed down."

Caleb looked at me. "That means it was still here when my dad left," Caleb said.

I placed a hand on the marble desktop. "Is there a record of anyone who worked there?"

The man shrugged. "Probably not."

Caleb sighed and walked backward. "Thanks, anyway."

I met Caleb at the door before he could open it. "Hey, it's okay. I'll see what I can find online."

"Hold on a second," the doorman called out to us. He unhooked a walkie from his belt. "I think one of our custodians used to work at the theater." The static from the speakers pulled us back to the desk. The bald man held the radio to his mouth. "Hey, Richie."

Seconds later, a frog-like voice came through. "Yep, go 'head."

"A couple of kids are here asking about the old movie theater. You worked there, right?"

The crinkled static echoed. "Ten years. What'a they wanna know?"

Caleb leaned against the desk. "Ask him if James Montes worked there."

The doorman held the button down. "Did you know a James Montes who worked there?"

The static went silent, and the air had never felt thicker. I wondered if Caleb's heart was beating as fast as mine.

"It's not ringin' any bells," Richie said with enough confidence to shatter my hopes.

"Sorry, guys," the bald man said.

The radio clipped again, and Richie continued. "Pretty sure the owner still lives above that Indian restaurant on the corner of Allen Street. Maybe he knows somethin'?"

Caleb's face lit up. "Where is that?"

The bald man pointed behind us. "Go out the door and make a right."

Caleb nodded and jogged to the door. "Thanks!"

I was able to stop him on the sidewalk. "Caleb, wait. Are we really gonna go knock on some rando's door?"

"Why not? He might know something."

"Or he'll call the cops on two kids harassing him."

Caleb tugged his arm from my grip. "Go home then. You found the address, that's all I asked you to do." Caleb turned and walked away.

I watched him go, then quickly caught up. "I'm not gonna let you go by yourself."

"It's really fine," Caleb said, still walking and keeping his eyes forward. "I'm sure you wanna go see your celebrity boyfriend."

Of course he was thinking about the cover too. I sucked my teeth. "He's not my boyfriend."

"Sure looked like it."

We stopped in front of an Indian restaurant, its yellow sign wrapped around the corner of the building.

"You're jumping to conclusions again," I said.

Caleb slapped his hands together. "Jumping to conclusions? You're kissing him on the cover of a magazine. The conclusion is pretty fucking obvious."

"I thought we were over, Caleb. You kicked me out. It felt like a breakup."

"Now who's jumping to conclusions?"

"You made no effort to make me think otherwise!"

"Maybe I didn't want to talk to the guy who used my probation against me. Ever think about that? Saying Parker was better off without me—the one person who cares about him? That fucking hurt, Landon. What did you expect to happen?"

My mouth went dry, and I couldn't swallow. His words came at me like a firing squad. My teeth ground together. What was I supposed to say? He was right.

Caleb glanced at the restaurant. A woman exited a door with a stained glass window. We both saw a set of skinny stairs leading to the second floor above the restaurant. Caleb scuffed across the sidewalk and looked at me, holding the door open. "Thanks for getting me this far. I'll let you know if I find anything."

"No." I jogged to grab the door from Caleb. "I have to keep an eye on you... for Parker's sake."

Caleb huffed. "Fine. Let's go."

SIXTEEN

The stairs were so skinny we had to go up single file. Various spices wafted up from the restaurant. It looked as if they hadn't updated the hallway in decades. The brown carpet was scuffed and faded. Chipped honey-mustard-colored paint covered the walls. All four doors on the second floor were numbered. Apartments one and three were on the left—directly across the hall were apartments two and four.

I turned to Caleb. "Now what?"

Caleb shrugged. "We're looking for an old man. We'll knock until we find him." Caleb knocked on apartment #1 before I could say anything. No one answered. His knock was polite but weighted. If someone were in there, they'd hear it. Caleb moved on to apartment #3. The door wasn't as sturdy as apartment #1 as it shook in its frame.

The door was yanked open, and a woman with frizzy hair answered, holding a toddler against her hip. "What?" Her eyes flickered between us.

Caleb straightened. "So sorry to bother you—"

"What do you want?" she asked.

Caleb cleared his throat. "We're looking for an older guy who—"

"Right there." She pointed to the apartment behind us and slammed her door.

We looked at each other before turning to apartment #4. Caleb knocked.

"I'm coming. I'm coming!" A muffled voice said. Once the door popped open, a short old man wearing an oversized T-shirt and sweatpants greeted us. He shuffled forward in black slippers, pulling an oxygen tank behind him. The man's cheeks sagged into dog-like jowls. Sunspots peeked through his thin white hair. He pointed a shaky finger at us. "It's about time you showed up. I've been waiting all damn morning."

Caleb tilted his head. "I'm sorry?"

"You should be." The old man said. "Now come in. I don't have all day."

"Come in?" I asked. "I'm sorry, I think—"

Caleb shoved me with his shoulder before my wide eyes shot to him. He pointed his chin at the door. I pursed my lips, knowing Caleb would go in with or without me. I followed the old man inside. Caleb stepped in, closed the door, and dropped his bag with a hard thud.

The apartment was a perfect rectangle. An open floor plan, with a floral couch and coffee table on the right and a kitchen lined the wall on the left. Beige carpet covered the entire apartment, except the few feet of the white tiled kitchen. Across from the couch was a boulder of a TV. The air was thick and smelled of stale cigarettes.

The man's slippers scratched the tile as he moved to the sink. He turned the knob, but the faucet stayed dry. The old man looked at Caleb. "Stanley, com'ere."

"Stanley?" I whispered.

Caleb strolled to the sink.

"The damn thing doesn't work. I thought you fixed it already?" The old man asked.

Caleb looked over his shoulder at me with a raised brow. "I thought so, too." Caleb took a knee and opened the cabinet doors under the sink. "Let's see what the issue is."

"And hurry up." The old man leaned an elbow on the counter. "I didn't raise you to be a slow poke." The man noticed a half-empty pack of cigarettes beside his arm and clumsily shoved them into his pocket.

Caleb unloaded the various cleaning supplies from under the sink. The old man shuffled by, assumingly headed for the couch, but stopped before me. The closer he got, the more I could smell the cloud of smoke that clung to his presence.

"Who are you?" The old man asked me with saliva collecting around his jowls.

Caleb poked his head out from under the sink. "He's my... apprentice. Remember?"

The old man's eyes narrowed, still on me. "Right, right," he said before hobbling to the couch and plopping down. The man coughed into a handkerchief. It was the wettest, phlegmiest cough I'd ever heard. I needed out of there before I threw up.

I crouched next to Caleb. "What're you doing?" I whispered.

Caleb reached into the cupboard without looking at me. "He's obviously confused."

"Right." I glanced at the couch. "So what are we still doing here?"

Caleb twisted a knob. "I'm stalling. He still might know something. Maybe we can remind him."

My face soured. "And how should we do that?"

Caleb finally looked at me. "I don't know. Look around?"

"Look around? He's right there, and you want me to snoop?"

Caleb shrugged. "You said you wanted to help. This sink isn't attached to anything, so I'm gonna keep pretending to fix it." Caleb leaned into the cupboard again.

I huffed. "Fine." The man's coughing stopped, but snoring kicked in instead. "That was quick," I mumbled as I stepped off the tile. Old newspapers and ashtrays covered the coffee table, so I steered clear.

I stepped to the dusty display case in the corner of the living room and could see through the glass on closer inspection. Old trophies sat on the top shelf, but I could only read the inscription from a baseball trophy. *Most Home Runs In A Season: Stanley Marsden.*

I crouched, scanning the bottom shelf—home to an array of

knick-knacks, all guarding a dusty frame behind them. I squinted—it was the deed for 'Moonlight Theater.'

The snoring continued, so I tiptoed back to Caleb and crouched. "There's a deed over there for a theater."

Caleb looked at me. "We know we're in the right place then." He gestured with his chin. "Check over there."

The wall opposite the front door was crowded with framed pictures, mostly tinted yellow. One frame held a picture of the old man in a Navy uniform, probably in his twenties. 'Marsden' glistened on his silver-plated name tag. My eyes fluttered from frame to frame, learning who the man was in his younger years. A gold frame held a picture of Marsden standing in front of the movie theater, smiling ear to ear. And right next to it…

"Holy fuck."

I heard a thud from behind me, and Caleb groaned. "What?"

I pulled the frame off the wall and rushed to hand it to Caleb.

My finger met the picture. "That's your dad, right?"

Caleb's voice was barely a whisper. "That's him."

The photo showed two men standing behind a bar. The neon sign behind them said 'Moonlight Theater.' The man on the left was pale, with a round face and deep-set eyes—his arm wrapped around the shoulders of Caleb's dad.

The front doorknob jiggled, making us jump to our feet.

"Dad, I told you to keep the door locked when—" The pale man spotted us and let the door swing open. He was the same guy from the picture frame in Caleb's hand. "Who the fuck are you?" His eyes searched the room before landing on his dad, then back to us once he realized the old man had gone unharmed.

"We're with building maintenance," I blurted out. The vein in my neck pulsed.

"I own the building, asshole. Try again!" The pale man slammed the door behind him.

The older man jolted awake and sat up on the couch. He looked over at all of us before focusing on the pale man. "Stanley! It's about time you showed up. I've been waiting all damn morning."

Caleb held his hands in the air, still holding the picture frame. "We don't want any trouble."

Stanley's eyes narrowed. "What the fuck are you doing in my father's apartment?"

I pointed. "We heard he used to own a movie theater down the street," I spat out, afraid Stanley would rush us.

"What was the name of that place?" The old man said to himself. He scratched his head, looking forward. "Sunrise Theater? Somethin' like that."

Stanley pulled out his phone. "I'm calling the cops."

"Hold on! I think you worked there with a guy named James Montes," Caleb said.

"Don't know anyone with that name. Now, get the fuck out." Stanley said.

Caleb stepped forward to show Stanley the frame. "He's in this picture with you!"

Stanley's fingers stopped swiping his screen, and his deep-set eyes squinted. "That's... not his name."

Caleb and I exchanged a confused look.

"What do you want with him?" Stanley asked.

Caleb looked at the pale man. "I'm trying to find him."

"Why?"

"He's my dad."

"What?" Stanley asked.

"I'm trying to find him. That's why we're here."

Stanley's brow furrowed. "I worked with the guy almost every day. He never mentioned having a kid."

Caleb placed the picture frame next to the kitchen sink. "He left when I was young and apparently started working at the movie theater."

"How the hell did you know to come here?"

"He left the address of your dad's theater in a safety deposit box. Someone who works at the new building guided us here," Caleb said. He crossed his arms and shrugged. "I was hoping for answers, but now I just have more questions."

"If you could just tell us his name," I said with a voice crack, "we'll get out of your—"

"I have no idea who the fuck you are. You're trespassing. I don't have to tell you shit," Stanley said.

"He told us his name was Thomas," the old man said. "Tommy Flynn."

"Dad!" Stanley called out.

Caleb perked up and took a step toward the couch. "Do you know where he is?"

"Actually, yeah," the old man said. "I remember Tommy said he got another bartending job, something fancy. How's Tommy doin'?"

Stanley looked at us. "My father can't remember how to tie his shoes. So, take that with a grain of salt. Now get the fuck out." Stanley opened the door.

Caleb passed through. "Sorry for intruding."

We were in the hall and down the stairs before Stanley slammed the door.

The wind whipped across my cheek like an unexpected slap, forcing me to pull my hood up. I followed behind Caleb, trying to figure out where we were going.

"What am I supposed to do now?" Caleb asked.

I trailed behind him. "Can you stop power walking?"

Caleb stopped to face me. His cheeks were beet red.

"We know something about your dad we didn't know this morning," I said, guiding Caleb to the sidewalk's edge.

"Yeah, and he obviously wanted nothing to do with me. So congratulations. You were right."

"If he didn't want anything to do with you, why leave the address?" Caleb stayed silent, but his breath left evidence of a sigh. "Exactly. That's what we need to figure out. Come on." I held his hand, pulled him through the automatic doors of Duane Reade, and huddled near a fifty percent off Christmas candy display. I pulled my phone out.

"What're you doing?"

My tongue instinctively poked out as I scrolled through my

phone. "Back when I was trying to figure out who you were, Steven suggested I check Facebook or Grindr. And I think we can eliminate one of those options already." Caleb leaned against the window and stared at my phone. I clicked the Facebook app. "Tommy... What did he say the last name was? Floyd?"

"Flynn."

About fifty Tommy Flynns popped up on my screen, and most didn't have a profile picture. "Do any of these guys look like him?"

"No," Caleb said flatly.

I refined the search to New York, and six Tommy Flynn profiles surfaced. Each one had a profile picture. I opened every page, but none belonged to Caleb's dad.

"This is a waste of time," Caleb said.

Seeing him disappointed made my heart sink. Part of me, maybe most of me, hoped he wouldn't give up and return to Texas. I didn't want to go back to being strangers. "I have an idea." I dialed Josh.

He picked up after one ring. "Why are you calling me?"

"Too urgent for text," I said.

"I've literally never talked to you on the phone. This is weird."

"I agree, but I have a question. I don't even know if it's possible."

Josh grunted like he was sitting up. "I'm intrigued."

I looked at Caleb and took a deep breath. "If we were to give you someone's name, is it possible to find out where he works?"

"What's the name?" Josh asked.

"Thomas—Tommy Flynn."

"Occupation?"

"Uh, bartender?"

"Age?"

I looked at Caleb. "Fifties, maybe?"

"Picture?" Josh asked.

"Caleb has one in his bag. I'll text it to you."

"Give me ten minutes," Josh said before hanging up.

Caleb looked at me. "What'd he say?"

"To give him ten minutes."

"What does that mean?"

I shrugged. "I'll text him to meet us at the dorm."

———

We made it back to the room before Josh. Caleb slouched into my desk chair. His head hung over the back as if he'd melted into it.

I hung up my coat, hopped onto my bed, and scooched close to the desk. "We're gonna find your dad."

Caleb stared at the ceiling. "What makes you so sure?"

"If anyone can help, it's Josh."

Caleb massaged his forehead, sat up, and leaned an arm on the desk. "I appreciate the optimism, but it's all been a disappointment so far."

"All of it?"

"Seeing you kissing another guy on a magazine cover didn't help."

A rock of guilt hit my stomach. "I'm—"

"Found him!" Josh proclaimed as he bolted through the door and onto his bed.

Caleb shot off his chair. "How?"

"There's a database for everything. Just gotta know where to look."

Josh and Caleb sat side by side on Josh's bed. Josh opened his laptop just as I sat with them. The computer flashed awake, and a picture of Caleb's dad was there front and center. It was a picture of an ID badge. Caleb's dad was clean-shaven, but the slicked-back hair was all too familiar, and his eyebrows were thick like Caleb's. The ID badge had 'Thomas Flynn' printed under the headshot and a barcode at the bottom.

"Is that him?" Josh asked

"Yeah," Caleb whispered.

Josh minimized the picture to a screen with a list of names. "He was the only Flynn listed."

I peered at the screen. "Wait, what is this?"

Josh pushed his glasses up his nose. "Do you know how many bartenders are in this city? A million, but not all of them are unionized. So I started there. Once I found his name on the union list, I cross-checked where union bartenders work in the city."

Caleb glanced at Josh, one eyebrow quirked. "Unions are allowed to post members' names publicly?"

"Not exactly." Josh's tone stayed casual. Josh pointed to the screen. "This is the basic backend of their system, which means very basic information. Right now, I can see every person who scanned into the Union building over the past year. Luckily, I found him. Otherwise, I'd have to find their corrupted files to go back further, as they seem to auto-delete that info."

"Okay, simple info. Does that include his address?" I asked.

"New privacy policies make that a little harder to find," Josh said.

"But not impossible?" Caleb asked.

"Yeah, what does that mean?" I asked.

Josh's attention was our ping pong ball, and we were hitting every serve. He clicked his trackpad again. "Firewalls. And I'm talking layers and layers of firewalls before someone could find his address." A small black box popped onto the screen, and Josh's fingers went to work. "Getting through this would take skill and finesse." He paused. "Discipline."

I watched as random numbers, letters, and symbols appeared in the small box on his screen. Coding was a completely different language my brain couldn't grasp.

"How long would something like that take?" Caleb asked Josh.

Josh hummed. "A day. Maybe two?"

"Jesus." Caleb stood and stared out the window.

I looked at Josh. "Can you do it?"

Josh scoffed. "Of course. But before I commit another felony, who the hell is this guy?"

Caleb still watched the street below. "My dad. He left when I was a kid."

Josh pushed up his glasses, sighed, then looked at me.

"I'll owe you," I said. "Whatever you want."

Josh's jaw clenched, and his eyes shot to the screen. The way Josh's fingers danced across the keys was almost pornographic. "Give me two days, just to be safe."

Caleb turned to us. "Is there anything else we can get sooner than two days? What about where he works right now? You said you cross-checked a list."

Josh clicked to maximize the picture of Tommy and zoomed in on the barcode.

"What're you doing?" I asked.

Caleb rushed back to Josh's other side.

"I'm sending the barcode to someone I know. He can tell me where it's registered in the city. Assuming Tommy's using it to scan into a building."

"How can he look that up?" I asked.

"He's got it," Josh said.

"Holy shit!" Caleb and I said at the same time.

Josh clicked a link, which opened a new window. "Pearson Suites: Luxury Events Space," Josh read off the screen. "It's on the corner of West Seventy-second and Central Park."

I sat taller. "The Dakota?"

Josh's fingers moved at warp speed. "Nope, Pearson Suits is across the street."

"He must be one of their bartenders," Caleb said softly. "When's their next event?"

"Uhhh." Josh's fingers revved up again. "Tonight. Seven p.m."

"Perfect!" Caleb jumped to his feet. "We'll go see if he's bartending then."

Josh looked at Caleb. "Yeah, it doesn't work like that."

"What do you mean?" Caleb asked.

Josh read his screen. "Says here it's a private fundraiser. So that means security, and it's two thousand dollars a ticket."

"Two thou—" Caleb plopped himself next to Josh on the bed and laid back. His hands covered his face. "Perfect."

Josh continued to type. "I can try to forge a pass for ya'll, but security is unpredictable. I don't know if we should risk it."

A lightbulb shattered in my mind. "We don't need a pass. I know someone who can help." I popped off the bed, opened the closet, and reached into my coat pocket.

Josh scoffed. "Oh right, 'cause you know someone with two thousand bucks lying around? Riiiight."

"Actually." I tossed the TOTAL GOSSIP magazine. It landed next to Josh with a slap. "I do."

SEVENTEEN

J osh snatched the magazine. "The fuck?"

Caleb sprung up. "No." The chill in the room wasn't just coming from the window. "Outta the fucking question."

Josh squinted. "Is that you? Kissing Isaac Matthews?"

Caleb rolled his eyes.

I sighed. "He can help, Caleb."

"I'm not asking your new boyfriend for money," Caleb scoffed. "No fucking way."

I couldn't help but suck my teeth. "Oh my god, I've said this already—he's not my boyfriend. What other choice do we have?"

Josh stared at Caleb as if watching a movie on a big screen.

Caleb paced between Josh's bed and the bathroom door. "I don't know. Wait outside until he comes out?"

"It's like negative two degrees. Who knows how long we'll have to wait," I said.

Josh chimed in. "And the staff could use a different entrance."

"I don't care. I'll wait," Caleb said.

I stepped closer. "Think about it. If you were him, who would you rather talk to? Two guys approaching you on the street or two guys ordering drinks from your bar?"

Caleb stopped to look at me. His jaw tensed. "There's gotta be another way." His cheeks were every shade of a sunrise.

"I know it's awkward, but it's the easiest option," I said.

Caleb deflated into the windowsill and rested his head against the glass. "Fine."

My shoulders relaxed. "I'm gonna give him a call. Be right back."

"I have so many questions," Josh said as I stepped out.

I leaned my back against the door and gently knocked my head a few times, hoping I'd hit some ideas loose. A guy turned the corner, making me stand upright and whip my phone from my pocket. I stared at Isaac's name, my thumb hovering over the call button.

Okay, how do I ask him to help?

The phone rang twice before Isaac answered. "Hey, are you okay?" He sounded out of breath.

I stared at the gray carpet. "Hey," I said softly. "Yeah, I'm okay."

"Are you sure? 'Cause I never meant for this to happen."

"I'm not gonna lie. It's weird."

Isaac sighed. "I should've been smarter about it."

I wanted to talk about the picture, but Caleb pushed at my thoughts. "Actually, I didn't call about that."

"Okay," Isaac said, the suspicion weighed in his tone. "So, what's going on?"

I let go of a breath. "Caleb showed up at my dorm last night."

"What? Is he okay?"

"Kind of?"

"Are you okay?"

"Sort of?"

A beat passed before Isaac spoke. "So, what's going on then?"

"It's kind of a long story, but... Can we come over?"

"We?"

———

Caleb was lying on my bed when I entered the room again, still wearing his coat. Josh hadn't moved, but Caleb propped himself up to look at me. "What'd he say?"

I opened the closet door. "I didn't ask him yet."

Caleb's brow wrinkled at the center. "Why not?"

I pulled my coat off its hanger and slipped it on. "Because this isn't the kind of thing you ask someone over the phone. So we're going to his place."

Caleb whipped his legs off the bed to sit up. "We?"

"Would you do a favor for someone you've never met?"

It was written all over Caleb's face. He wanted to debate and fight, but deep down, I think he knew I was right. Finally, he reached for his shoes and slipped them on.

"I'll keep working the firewalls as our backup plan," Josh said. "His address is here somewhere."

"Thanks," Caleb said over his shoulder as he followed me out the door.

———

Caleb hadn't said a word until we turned onto Isaac's street. "I can't believe I'm doing this." I almost wished he stayed quiet. Caleb stopped short of walking into Isaac's building. "I don't want to be someone's charity. He's never gonna agree to it anyway. Who the fuck am I compared to him?"

I groaned, stepping in front of him. "Can you forget your pride for two seconds and let someone help you?"

Caleb's lip curled. "Why would he care?"

"Maybe you'd find out if you gave him a chance."

"A chance?"

"Yes! He's not what you think he is."

"An entitled rich asshole?"

"Love when you jump to conclusions."

Caleb's hands balled. "Whatever."

"He's a nice guy, Caleb. And genuine, I promise."

Caleb pushed through the door, and I met him at the front desk, where a tall woman sat. Her blonde ponytail poked out the back of her hat.

"We're here for Isaac," I said.

She smiled. "Yes, he told me to expect you. Go on up."

We were silent in the elevator. A new batch of butterflies formed in my stomach with each floor. I never thought my ex, or whatever he was, would be meeting my new, whatever Isaac was. The elevator rocked a bit, making my hand brush against Caleb's. My left arm suddenly turned into a sparkler. Then, just as we caught each other's glance, the elevator door opened.

Caleb's eyes widened as we stepped inside. "I didn't think New York had apartments this big."

"Me either," I said.

Isaac must have lit a candle because it smelled smokey with a hint of pine, that same smell that clung to your clothes after a campfire.

Isaac's bare feet slapped the stairs one by one as he came from the loft. He wore gray sweats and a white tank top so tight you could see his stomach muscles moving as he strode toward us. Isaac held out a hand. "You must be Caleb. I've heard so much about you."

Caleb's body went still, and his eyes locked on Isaac, staring. I couldn't tell if he was starstruck or thinking about punching him. Caleb crossed his arms.

Say something.

My palms clammed. The silence felt like an eternity, and butterflies turned to rocks that sank to the bottom of my stomach.

Caleb finally shook Isaac's hand. "Yeah."

The air was thick, and I didn't know how to break it.

"Bathroom?" Caleb asked, pulverizing the rocks in my stomach to dust.

Isaac smiled. "Yeah, it's upstairs. You'll see it. Ignore the crystals; I was just cleaning in there."

Caleb shuffled toward the stairs as Isaac hugged me. Caleb watched us before disappearing. The bathroom door slammed, making Isaac and I flinch.

"Is he always this brooding?" Isaac asked.

"Not until recently." I strolled further into the apartment, finding my resting place at the back of Isaac's couch.

"He saw the picture, didn't he?"

"Before I did."

Isaac's gaze hit the floor. "Damn. Is that why he came to New York?"

I shook my head as Potato brushed against my legs. "No, that's a longer story."

"Are you back together?"

It was an interesting question, one I wondered myself because we never technically said the words, but Caleb's cold shoulder routine gave me all the context clues. "Honestly, this is all really confusing for me."

Isaac moved closer to my outstretched legs. "That's understandable."

"These feelings are all kind of new for me. I really like you."

Isaac showed his tooth gap. "I feel like there's a 'but' coming."

My shoulders hugged my ears. "*But,* since Caleb showed up again, all my feelings for him came rushing back."

Isaac leaned on the edge of the couch next to me. "Of course they did. You haven't been apart that long. Love doesn't go poof. It might get placed elsewhere, but it never goes away."

Isaac wasn't much older than me, but his grasp on his emotions felt beyond his years.

"Then how do you explain the feelings I have for you?" I asked.

"Have your feelings for Caleb negated your feelings for me?"

"Should they?"

"That's something you gotta figure out."

I smiled at him. "How did you get this way?"

"What do you mean?"

Our fingertips grazed between us. I tickled the soft spot between his thumb and pointer finger. "I don't know. Like, why you feel things the way you do?"

Isaac chuckled. "Years of therapy."

He made me smile so easily. Our eyes met. Isaac's forehead hid behind his blonde curls. He was so fucking cute.

"I really am sorry about the pictures," Isaac said softly. "I should've just paid those guys off."

"Nah, it would've come out regardless. We didn't even know the guy was there."

"I know, but I could've been smarter about it. I wasn't thinking."

"Okay, that's the second time you've said that today. What does that even mean?"

Isaac traced my hand now. "My therapist likes to use the phrase 'old tapes.' So when I saw the pictures of us kissing, my paranoia hit again. I thought if you saw it, you might get weirded out and cut me off."

My heart sank hearing his words. "That wouldn't be fair of me. It's not like you asked for this."

I hadn't noticed Caleb descend the stairs, and his sudden voice startled me. "I'm guessing you haven't asked him yet?"

Isaac looked at me with a furrowed brow.

"Can we sit?" I asked.

"I'll stay right here, thanks," Caleb said.

Isaac steppped away from the couch. "Listen, I know this is weird. But whatever it is, I wanna help."

Caleb's sigh sounded more like a growl. I could see the gears moving in his head. His shoulders finally relaxed as he moved to the couch.

Isaac stepped toward Caleb. "Want me to take your co—"

"No."

"Okay," Isaac said, stepping back and around the other side of the couch.

I sat in the corner of the L while Caleb sat to my right and Isaac to my left. Both faced me—my two worlds colliding.

"So?" Isaac asked.

I blinked a few times to center myself. "Sorry."

"We're looking for my dad," Caleb shot out. "He left outta the blue when I was a kid."

I raised a finger. "I want to preface this with sa—"

"He left a key behind," Caleb said.

I looked at Isaac. "You don't have to agree to any—"

"It took me until a few days ago to figure out what it unlocked."

I brought a leg up on the couch. "We can think of other solutions too—"

"Landon," Isaac said with a smile. He placed his hand on my knee. "Let him speak."

I glanced at Caleb before sitting back in the corner. My lips wrapped around my teeth.

Caleb's eyes left me for Isaac. "The key unlocked a safety deposit box with a New York address in it. I think my dad left it behind for a reason. Long story short, we were led to a company he bartends for. And—" Caleb sighed, glanced at me, and stood. "Forget it, Landon. I'm not doing this."

"Not doing what?" Isaac asked.

Caleb swiftly rounded the couch. "I can do this on my own."

I hopped the back of the couch and jogged to stop Caleb. "No, you can't."

Caleb leaned toward me. "I'm not asking him," he said softly.

Isaac was suddenly behind us. "What's going on?"

Caleb looked at the floor, but I looked at Isaac. "There's a fundraiser tonight that Caleb's dad might be bartending for. We were hoping to show up and talk to him."

"That's a great idea," Isaac said.

"One thing, though," I said. "It's a private event."

Isaac crossed his arms. "I'm sure I can pull a few strings. Where is it?"

"We're good," Caleb said. "Come on, Landon." Caleb tugged my arm toward the elevator.

"I can make a phone call." Isaac shouted.

Caleb stopped before pressing the elevator's down button. He looked over his shoulder. "We'll figure it out."

"Please," I whispered to Caleb. "Let him try."

"Why?" He asked me before turning fully to Isaac. "Why do you want to help? What's in it for you?"

"Who wouldn't want to spend more time with their dad?" Isaac asked. Time slowed for a moment as Isaac's words washed over us.

Caleb swiped a hand down his face.

"He's the best chance we have, Caleb," I said. He side-eyed me before nodding. I looked at Isaac. "The fundraiser's at Pearson Suites on the Upper West Side."

Isaac pulled his phone from his pocket. "Be right back." He started up the stairs and placed the phone to his ear. "Hey Jeffrey, can you do me a favor, please?"

Caleb looked at me with wide eyes. "This is a bad idea."

I squinted. "Why?"

"I don't know, it just—something doesn't feel right. He's gonna want us to pay him back or something, and—"

"Isaac isn't like that."

"Oh really? How long have you known him, again?"

Isaac landed on the first floor again. "Amazing, thanks Jeffrey. I owe you." He hung up as the elevator doors opened behind me. Isaac beamed. "I hope you brought a suit."

Caleb and I shared a confused glance.

The words trickled from my lips. "Does that mean—"

"We're going to a fundraiser tonight? Yes, it does." Isaac said.

"*We?*" Caleb asked. "You're coming too?"

Isaac nodded. "Is that a problem?"

"We don't have suits!" I spat out before Caleb could answer.

"I know a place on Prince and Sullivan. It's not far." Isaac jogged to the closet by the elevator.

Caleb stepped toward me. "I can't afford to buy a new suit," he whispered.

"Me either," I assured him before shouting to Isaac. "Do you have any here? Maybe we can—"

"This is a fundraiser for the environment," Isaac called back as he slipped his coat on. "I've been around rich people enough to know you don't show up to one of these things wearing a suit that doesn't fit perfectly." Isaac gestured for us to join him in the elevator.

I had to push Caleb to get him to move an inch. The doors closed, and I texted Josh on the ride down.

ME

Hold off on searching for the address. I think we found him.

JOSH

Copy that. Keep me updated.

———

'Cuffs & Tails Tailor Shop' was printed on a big glass window that took up the whole width of the storefront. Several suit jackets were on display, tightly fitting over three mannequin busts. An 'Open' sign hung in the door's full-length window.

"This is giving serious *Kingsman* vibes," Caleb said.

Isaac smirked. "If you're lucky, I'll show you the secret room full of spy gadgets." Isaac held the door open for us, and Caleb finally cracked a smile before we stepped inside.

The store was big enough to fit my entire dorm but small enough to fit snugly in Isaac's living room. Dark wood shelves and closets lined the perimeter, displaying hundreds of suit jackets in every style and color. The place smelled like mahogany and crisp, freshly printed money. Caleb slowly circled a table at the shop's center, eyeing the neatly folded pants.

Isaac closed the door, setting off the small bell that teetered above.

Behind the cashier's desk, a woman poked her head out from behind a black curtain at the back of the store. She looked to be in her sixties. Her plum-colored hair was pulled into a messy bun, with a knitting needle holding it all together. She pushed the wire-framed glasses up the bridge of her nose. "Is that my Isaac?" She smiled before rounding the desk and into the store to greet us. She wore ballet flats and black leggings. A thin gray poncho hung off her skinny frame.

Caleb and I stole another glance before Isaac hugged her tightly. "Guys," Isaac said, facing us with his arm around the woman's shoulders. "This is Zelda. She's been fitting me since I was a kid." He looked at her with adoring eyes. "We're going to a fundraiser tonight."

Zelda stood a few feet shorter than Isaac, but that didn't stop her from pinching his cheek. With the way she beamed at him, anyone would assume she was his grandmother.

Caleb planted himself next to me. "Nice to meet you, Zelda."

"Isaac always brings me the handsome ones." Zelda detached herself from Isaac to circle Caleb. She closed one eye as she surveyed his backside. A small *hmm* vibrated from her throat. She gave Caleb another once over with a hand on her hip and the other cupping her chin. "Five ten. Thirty-two waist," she said to herself.

"How'd you know that?" Caleb asked.

"I've been at this a long time, kid," Zelda said with her eyes on Caleb's shoulders. She grabbed the tape measure hanging around her neck and stretched it across Caleb's back before patting his shoulder. "Take off the coat, and meet me by the mirrors." Zelda trotted to a corner and moved hangers from the closets.

I followed Caleb to a trio of floor-to-ceiling mirrors. Two of them angled out off the middle one. "What is she doing?" Caleb whispered.

I glanced over my shoulder at her. "I think she's fitting you."

"I didn't ask for this."

Isaac sat in one of the two leather chairs facing the mirror. "You didn't have to. I got it covered."

"No," Caleb said. "I don't need to owe anyone else any favors."

"You won't owe me anything," Isaac said.

"Sure," Caleb responded, turning toward the mirror. He watched me take the seat next to Isaac.

Zelda strutted past us, holding two suit jackets on hangers. She hung them on a hook, then reached for a hidden curtain between shelves. The curtain swooshed across a quarter of the room, shielding us from the large window. "Isaac, take his coat, please."

Isaac popped from his chair as Caleb slid his backpack off his shoulder. He removed his coat and handed it to Isaac, who reached for Caleb's bag.

Caleb gripped the strap. "Bag stays with me."

Isaac raised his hands. "That's cool." He returned to his seat, placing Caleb's coat over the arm.

Zelda handed Caleb a thin white button-up shirt. "Put this on." She stepped outside the curtain.

"I'll give you some privacy." Isaac stepped outside the curtain.

I got up, too.

"Stay," Caleb said to my reflection.

"You sure?"

He nodded, and I sat. Caleb lifted his T-shirt over his head, letting the ring necklace fall against his bare chest. He swiftly slipped on the button-up.

Zelda glided in as he finished the top button and handed him a pair of black slacks with a shiny black stripe down the leg. "These oughta do it. I might have to bring the legs up, but try 'em on and see while I get the tie." Zelda zipped away again, leaving us there.

Caleb held onto the dress pants as he kicked off his sneakers. He unzipped and revealed the underwear I'd lent him. I tried my best not to stare, but he filled them out much better than I did. Caleb tucked in the shirt and struggled to find the clasp at the waist.

Zelda returned with Isaac, and she helped Caleb into the first of the two suit jackets. The jacket was fire engine red with black lapels. "It's a little tight in the shoulders," Zelda said as she poked and prodded the fabric. She danced around Caleb, fine-tuning his frame with pins and needles. Finally, she buttoned the first button of the jacket and spun him around to face Isaac and me in our seats.

Caleb wouldn't make eye contact with us.

Isaac leaned forward in his chair. "You hate it, don't you?"

"Red isn't usually my color," Caleb mumbled.

Isaac cleared his throat. "Zel, this is a classy fundraiser. Can we get something a little less... loud?"

Zelda glared at Isaac over the rim of her glasses. "Well, excuse the hell outta me." She turned Caleb's body to face her again and unbuttoned his jacket. "Take it off. Try the Prada instead." Zelda pointed to the other blazer on the hook. She folded the red jacket over her arm. "Less loud," she said in a low tone, giving Isaac a playful slap on the shoulder before exiting the curtain.

Caleb carefully slipped on the new jacket and stared at himself in the mirror. His back straightened, and he almost smiled.

Isaac stood and circled Caleb, stopping in front of him. "Now, *this* is sexy!" He said, fluffing the lapels. Isaac spun Caleb to face me. He looked even more handsome than he did on prom night.

I stood and closed Caleb between us, smoothing his lapels. "It's a perfect fit."

"It needs one more thing," Isaac said before shuffling past the curtain.

"Is this really Prada?" Caleb whispered.

"I think so," I whispered back. I couldn't help but touch the shimmering lapels again, smoothing them over Caleb's chest. My eyes suddenly met his, and the world stopped spinning, just as it had in the middle of the dance floor at prom.

Isaac rushed through the curtain again, sending me back a step. He stopped behind Caleb, popped the button-up collar, then wrapped a black tie around his neck. Isaac twisted and thumbed the fabric into a perfect bow. "This will make the whole look," Isaac whispered; the words barely traveled past Caleb's ear. Isaac leaned his chin on Caleb's shoulder to look at me. "What do you think?"

I straightened the tie, pressing Caleb between Isaac and me.

"I've never worn anything like this before," Caleb said with a slight pull at the corner of his lips.

"You look incredible," I said.

Isaac turned, making all of us face the mirror. "See for yourself,"

Caleb's eyes widened. He smoothed his hands down the front of the jacket and clasped the middle button. He shook his head as if trying to wake himself from a dream. "I look... rich." Caleb twisted his body to see his backside and smirked. His shoulders dropped. "Still, I can't afford this."

"Don't worry," Isaac said, still looking at Caleb's reflection. "It's on me. You gotta look your best when you see your dad."

Caleb glanced at me in the mirror.

"Isaac, I have something new for you!" Zelda called from across the shop.

Isaac pushed his way between us, wrapped his arms around our shoulders, and led us back to the leather chairs facing the mirror. "Just sit in it and see how it feels."

Zelda rushed in with gray pants and a forest green jacket. "Here, put this on. I'm thinking just the jacket, nothing underneath."

Isaac smiled. "I love it."

Zelda spun and zipped away like a mouse on the hunt for cheese.

Isaac hung the clothes on the mirror and untied his sweatpants.

Caleb massaged his forehead and stood. "I'll be outs—"

"It's okay," Isaac said. "Stay. Both of you. I'll need your opinion." Isaac pulled his shirt off with one hand. The front of his pants hung loose, exposing the band of his underwear.

"Oh." Caleb eyed me, then Isaac, and slowly sat. "Um. Okay."

Isaac's sweatpants hit the floor. His underwear ad had come to life in front of us. I glanced at Caleb, whose jaw tensed. I didn't need telepathic powers to know what he was thinking.

Isaac faced the mirror, giving us a perfect view of his front and back simultaneously. I squirmed in my seat. What the hell was he trying? He ran a hand down his stomach as the other reached for the suit jacket. He slipped it on and buttoned it in the middle. He spun to us and smiled. "Think they'll let me in like this?"

"*Risky Business*," Caleb said.

"Nineteen eighty-three," Isaac replied. "Tom Cruise was my gay awakening. My mom had the DVD. Watching him dance around in those undies really did something for me."

Caleb's lip curled into a half smile.

Finally.

EIGHTEEN

We stood at the corner of 72nd and Central Park West, across the street from Pearson Suites. The venue's entrance was packed with photographers.

"Mind if we wait it out?" Isaac asked.

Caleb shoved his hands in his coat pocket. "In the cold?"

A playful group of teenagers exiting the park caught my attention. "The park has heating lamps."

We passed the rowdy group and into the warmth of the Imagine Mosaic. A man on a stool lightly strummed his guitar.

Isaac looked at his watch as the park lights flickered on. "They'll be gone soon."

It was cold enough to see our breath, and Caleb's were few and far between. His eyes glazed as he stared at the roses resting on the mosaic.

I looped a hand around Caleb's elbow. "Think you're ready?"

Caleb shook himself from the trance and looked at me. "Think he'll recognize me?"

"Of course he will." My suit jacket was thick, and my lower back moistened under the heat lamps. I removed my coat, and people started to notice Zelda's best.

Caleb stuck with the Prada jacket with its shimmering lapels and bow tie. I settled on almost the same, but my lapels were a matte black, and I wore a skinny tie. Isaac strayed from the pack with a white jacket with black lapels and a white bow tie. Our shoes shined, with heels that click-clacked against the sidewalk. Zelda had suggested a pop of color for our pocket squares. Mine was red, Caleb's blue, and Isaac's green.

Caleb's lips smacked. "My mouth is so dry."

Isaac checked his watch. "Let's go inside, we can get a drink."

"You sure?" I asked.

Isaac took a deep breath. "Yeah. It's okay. Gotta test these meds at some point, right?"

Caleb's brow furrowed.

I nodded. "Okay. Let's go."

Only two photographers sat outside the venue when we finally crossed the street. Luckily, they were too busy looking at their phones to notice Isaac speed by.

Josh was right. Once we walked into the building, two large security guards dressed in fitted black suits were posted at the elevators. They checked Isaac's phone for our tickets before letting us through.

"Which floor?" Caleb asked.

"Penthouse," Isaac said.

Caleb pressed the button. The elevator sped to the top floor, and the doors opened behind us to a giant chandelier reflecting every light in the room. It was hard to believe we were still in the same gray-brick building that looked like every other one on the block. We stepped out onto a red carpet, split in three directions like a trident. The middle carpet stretched out in front of us and down a marbled staircase wider than my dorm room. The right and left sides of the carpet extended up curved staircases, which met in the middle at the top, leading to a balcony. I couldn't see the roof but felt the cold breeze slinking down the stairs.

Three men dressed like butlers quickly took our coats, handing us each a numbered ticket before we took the path of the middle carpet. We looked down into the crowd of strangers mingling at tall, skinny tables wrapped in tight white cloth. Everyone was dressed to the nines. The steady chatter filled the room, as if every rich person spoke at the same pitch. The air was a mix of floral perfumes and a hint of bacon.

Paintings, sculptures, and even a few sparkling jewelry pieces were scattered around the room, all taking up their own tables with clipboards nearby for a silent auction.

The wall under the left staircase was entirely floor-to-ceiling windows overlooking the warm glow of the street lamps and winterized foliage of Central Park. Men in matching navy blue suits played piano, and upright bass, and two others played violin on a raised platform in front of the glass wall.

A long bar occupied the wall under the right side staircase, with no one working it.

I hoped we didn't make Isaac do this for a dead end.

My hand glided smoothly against the gold railing, not a single crack or divet. Just as we reached the bottom of the steps, Caleb stopped, turned around, and ascended the stairs again. Isaac and I glanced at each other before I grabbed Caleb's arm, stopping him two steps up.

"I can't do this," Caleb said. "It's too weird, showing up at his job? I don't even know what I'm gonna say."

I stepped up to Caleb's level. "Hey. You *can* do this. Think of how long you've waited."

Caleb looked at me. "Everyone here is rich and white. Clearly, I don't fit in."

Isaac joined me in front of Caleb before he could get further up the steps. "These people's heads are so far up their own asses. They won't even notice we're here. Believe me."

I smiled at Caleb. "See? It'll just be us."

Caleb's eyes shot back and forth between us before he sighed. "Fine. Just don't leave me alone, okay?"

Isaac flashed his tooth gap. "Never."

Caleb turned back toward the crowd. "Okay, I'll hit the bathroom quick, then I'll be ready."

"Good idea," I said, following close behind. We made it off the steps and veered right to the alcove under the curved stairs. The restrooms were tucked in the corner. "We'll wait here," I said before Caleb disappeared behind the door.

The room was louder now that we were on the same level as everyone else. The hum of chatter filled the space. More staff walked around with trays of finger foods and cocktail napkins. It was the first time I'd been surrounded by wealth. I regretted not asking Dad for some pointers on mingling with strangers. My visual sweep of the room ended on Isaac biting his nails. "You okay?"

Isaac's hand fell from his mouth. "Yeah, why?"

"If it's too much, I'm sure Caleb would understand."

Isaac huffed. "I don't need to give him another reason to hate me."

"He doesn't hate you."

"The only time he cracks a smile is if I make a movie reference."

"Yeah, that's kind of his thing."

Isaac leaned a shoulder on the wall to face me. "How do I show him I'm not, like, a threat? Should I apologize for kissing you?"

"No. Caleb and I were—I don't know what we were, but it's not like I didn't want to kiss you back." My head pulsed with overcrowded thoughts. It was like I was in purgatory, facing an impossible choice.

"Every time he looks at me, I feel like he wants to rip my head off." Isaac watched the bathroom door. "Not that I blame him."

"Why are you so willing to help then?"

"I want him to like me."

"Why?"

"Because he loves you."

My heart skipped. I leaned on the wall and let my shoulder slide closer to Isaac.

"I'm realizing I want to be in your life in whatever way I can, and after hearing the history between you guys, I feel like I need Caleb's blessing to do that."

The back of my hand grazed Isaac's. "He's put up a lot of walls. It takes time to break through."

"You think he'd ever—"

A camera flashed at us. A short man lowered it from his face and smiled. "Good to see you out, Isaac!" He shuffled away and snapped another picture of a woman posing with a necklace up for auction.

Isaac massaged his forehead. "Fuck, I'm sorry. I'll ask him to delete it."

I blocked Isaac with my arm. "It's okay. If you're gonna be in my life, I guess I gotta get used to people taking our picture."

Isaac half smiled, and his emerald eyes glistened as bright as the chandelier.

The bathroom door swung open. "Okay," Caleb said. "All good."

I scanned the bar, but still no bartenders. I caught the attention of a server who held a silver plate full of skewered meats on toothpicks. "Excuse me. Will there be alcohol served tonight?"

"Yes," the server said. "The bar was having issues with their taps, but they should be out shortly. Bacon-wrapped scallop?" The server held the plate out, and Caleb was the only one to partake before the server walked away.

"I know we just got here," I said, "but can we get some air? I'm really warm."

"Let's check out the balcony," Isaac suggested.

We follow Isaac back up the center steps. By the time we were at the top, Caleb had grabbed two more scallops and shoved them into his mouth. We pushed through double-glass doors at the top of the curved staircase, leading us out onto the balcony. The air cooled my insides. Once the doors closed, they completely shut out the sound. The music and chatter had faded into a symphony of New York City sounds, honking horns, barking dogs, and clacking horse-drawn carriages totting tourists around Central Park.

Three tables were placed evenly along the half wall closing in the balcony. Two men chatted softly while smoking cigars in the corner. We hustled to occupy the opposite end.

I leaned against the wall with my hands hanging over the edge of the building. "Wow." Looking out over the park, I became envious of every pigeon that soared over the trees, not realizing how lucky they were. The wind whipped harder, enough to knock Isaac's curls from their product-induced coma. I liked it better when his curls fell over his eyebrows anyway.

I glanced to my left, curious to see the view through Caleb's expression, but he wasn't looking at the park. Instead, he peered over the edge to the street below.

Isaac leaned an elbow on the wall and faced Caleb. "Landon told me you're a fan of the ACU?"

Caleb stared straight ahead at the building across the street, hunched over the edge of the wall. "Maybe."

Isaac's brow perked. "Maybe a bigger fan than most?"

Caleb shrugged. "I guess."

"You've seen every movie, right?"

"Obviously."

"Did you catch the Adam Shock easter egg in The Crusaders movie?"

"Duh." Caleb finally turned his attention to Isaac and mocked his tone. "Did you?"

"I saw it in the theater like everyone else," Isaac said.

Caleb stood up straight. "Wait, really? Did you know you were gonna play Adam when you saw it?"

"I got the call about auditioning the day before the Crusaders movie came out."

Caleb paced away from the balcony wall. "Holy shit."

"By the end of the audition process, it was either gonna be Troye Sivan or me," Isaac said.

"I'm sorry, WHAT?" Caleb shouted, causing the two men in the other corner to glance toward us. "Are. You. Kidding. Me? Troye can't act for shit. You're lying."

"Pinky swear," Isaac said with a chuckle.

Caleb stopped pacing, and his eyes caught mine. I was sure he was thinking what I was thinking: Isaac's words hit a soft spot in Caleb's chest.

The men at the other corner finished their cigars and walked back inside, leaving the entire balcony to the two nerds and me.

Caleb leaned his back against the balcony wall. "When is the movie coming out?"

Isaac scrunched the left side of his face. "Can't answer that."

"Will Adam fall in love with Jacob in it?"

"Can't answer that either."

"How connected is the movie to the rest of the franchise? Any cameos from Biohazard?"

"Okay," Isaac said with a laugh. "Maybe we shouldn't talk about the movie since my NDA is pretty intense."

Caleb nodded. "Fair enough. Favorite Adam Shock comic?"

Isaac's cheeks filled with air before letting it out into the cold. "That's a tough one. But issue eighty, probably?"

There was no way Caleb would know which—

"No fucking way!" Caleb's eyes got as bright as Times Square. "The one where Terranox crashed Adam and Jacobs's wedding?"

"Yes!"

"Who is Terranox?" I asked.

Caleb looked at me again. "Terranox is Adam's main villain. He can control earth and rock."

Isaac looked at me, too. "It was a two-part event."

"Everyone who read part one thought Jacob was killed off at the end," Caleb said. "And they made us wait TWO weeks for the next issue."

Isaac's eyes were on me, but he pointed at Caleb. "He knows his stuff."

I smiled. "He knows pretty much everything."

Isaac grinned and rubbed his hands together. "Alright, let's test your knowledge then. I'll give you a quote. You tell me which movie it's from. No inflections, no acting, just words."

Caleb puffed his chest. "Easy. You go, I go?"

"Deal."

My hands started to cramp from the chill, so I slipped them into my pockets. I had gotten the air I wanted, and my body was beginning to adjust. I wondered how long the boys would compete before I turned into the fundraiser's newest ice sculpture.

Caleb focused, ready to pounce at the first word.

Isaac started with, "You had me at hello."

Caleb scoffed. "C'mon. *Jerry Maguire*, don't go easy on me." Isaac laughed. "You're killin' me, smalls," Caleb said.

"Talk about easy," Isaac said. "*The Sandlot*."

These were easy ones?

"I drink your milkshake," Isaac said next.

"*There Will Be Blood*," Caleb said calmly. "'You better lawyer up, asshole.'"

"*The Social Network*. 'Come in and have a tea with the misses.'"

"*Labyrinth*. 'Death by stereo.'"

"*The Lost Boys*. 'No more wire hangers.'"

"I'm gay," Caleb said, tilting his head. "You think I don't know the most famous quote from *Mommy Dearest*? 'Open the pod bay doors.'"

"*2001: A Space Odyssey*. 'I know, funny. I'm a clownfish.'"

"*Finding Nemo*. 'One does not simply—'"

"*Fellowship of the Ring*. 'Molly, you in dang—'"

"*Ghost*. 'There are certain rules one must—'"

"*Scream*. 'Yippe K—'"

"*Die Hard*. 'Come with me if you—'"

"*Terminator*. 'You guys wanna go see a dead b—'"

"*Stand By Me*. 'I was twelve going on thirteen the first—'"

"Also, *Stand By Me*," Isaac said.

It was like a tennis match. My eyes bopped back and forth. Their mouths were the rackets, their words the tennis ball. They were the star athletes, and I was just the tired kid on the sidelines running after the stray balls until Isaac gave his next quote.

"'Hold onto your butts,'" Isaac said.

"JURASSIC PARK!" I shouted so loudly I was convinced the people on the sidewalk fifteen floors below heard me.

"Yes, babe!" Caleb said, beaming a smile at me that faded just as quickly once he'd realized what came out of his mouth.

We all went silent, and Caleb's gaze hit the floor. It felt like the building had cracked up in the middle, and we were waiting to crumble into the park. My chest was as tight as my jaw.

Isaac sighed before pushing his hands into his pockets. "I'm gonna go check the bar. See if anyone's working yet." Isaac glanced over his shoulder at us before stepping back inside.

Caleb leaned against the ledge and stared down at the concrete. He rubbed the back of his head. "Sorry. Old habits, I guess."

"You don't have to apolog—"

"I do, though." Caleb's eyes caught mine.

My teeth chattered. "Can we talk inside? My face is going numb."

Caleb nodded and followed me in. I parked us against the railing overlooking the stairs leading into the main hall. I could hear the music better from up there. Caleb didn't look over the edge. Instead, he leaned against the rail, crossed his arms, and stared at his feet.

I stood to his right and rubbed my hands together, hoping they'd combust and thaw me out. "I'm the one who should be apologizing. I said a lot of shitty things."

Caleb turned, gripped the railing, and looked at me. "You were right. I'm an asshole when I drink. I had already quit Lucky's, and didn't know what to do."

"Why didn't you talk to me about it?"

"You were excited to get back to New York. I didn't want to admit I was jealous that you knew what you wanted for your life. Telling you I'd quit would've made me feel like an even bigger loser."

I touched his hand. "Caleb, you're not a—"

"Everything you said was true. My choices got me where I am." He scratched his cheek. "Finding my dad felt like the only place to start. Maybe if I find out why he left, I can finally—I don't know, not feel so stuck anymore." Everything was coming into focus. "I was so scared you'd slam the door in my face as soon as you saw me."

I mimicked his stance and leaned my arms on the rail. The middle of the chandelier sparkled in front of us. "I don't think I could, even if I wanted to."

"What do you mean?"

"I thought about you every day," I said. "Wishing I could take back everything I said."

"I convinced myself you didn't need me. But it was too late when I realized how much I needed you." Caleb's eyes hit the floor. "It felt wrong to keep wearing the ring after you left. But I still wanted a piece of you close, so I made the necklace."

A searing pain pierced my chest. Suddenly, all the times Caleb and I laughed together flashed through my thoughts like a montage from one of those cheesy '80s movies he loved. "Caleb, it's not too late."

Caleb rubbed a thumb over the A inked onto his right hand. "Why would you ever choose me over a celebrity?" Guilt washed over me. "It just feels—"

"Like I have to choose?"

Caleb sighed. "No. It feels like you really like him."

"If I did, how would that make you feel?"

"Like I lost."

"This isn't a competition."

"So you do like him?"

"I don't know."

Caleb scoffed. "C'mon, I see the way you look at him."

"And I saw the way *you* looked at him in the mirror at the suit shop."

Caleb crossed his arms. "He's a literal superhero who was practically naked in front of us. Sorry for being human."

"I never said I had a problem with it."

Caleb eyed me and cocked his head. "Then what are you saying?"

I glanced over the rail at the bodies below, searching for Isaac.

Caleb huffed. "If you like him, then just—."

"Yes, I like him. Okay?" Caleb's shoulders fell. "I'm starting to realize that not everything is black and white. I really like Isaac, but —" My throat tightened as I gripped the rail. "I never stopped loving you."

Caleb's face calmed, and he looked at me with big eyes. "What?"

"My head has been so fucked up since New Years Eve. I didn't know if we were done, if I should forget you. I thought you'd never talk to me again after what I said. Talking to Isaac helped, and somehow along the way, I caught feelings. But that doesn't mean I love you any less than I did dancing with you at prom."

Caleb stared at me in silence. The music had lowered. His Adam's apple bounced with a hard swallow before he cupped my face. He stepped closer—his breath warmed my chin. My hand relaxed its grip on the rail and fell to my side. I craved his stubble tickling my upper lip.

"Guys!" Isaac called out. Caleb jerked backward, and I looked over my shoulder. Isaac stood at the base of the staircase, waving at us. "The bartenders are all set up!"

I glanced at Caleb. "C'mon."

Our shiny shoes clunked down the carpeted steps with barely any traction. We met Isaac at the main landing. The bar was crowded now.

"Can you see him from up here?" Isaac asked.

Caleb's head bobbed. "No, I don't see him."

Isaac took Caleb's hand and led him down the stairs. "Let's get a closer look."

I swiftly followed behind as the crowd engulfed us.

Isaac guided us to the bar and found a space between two couples waiting for their drinks. Isaac gently nudged Caleb to the bar. "Maybe you can ask if he's working tonight?"

"Good idea," Caleb said. He leaned over the counter.

I flanked Caleb. "Anyone look familiar?"

"Not yet," Caleb said over his shoulder.

A muscular bartender approached Caleb. His arms bulged from his tight button-up. A thick vein ran up the bartender's neck, looking like it could burst if his shirt were any tighter. "What can I get ya?" he asked Caleb.

Caleb leaned in again. "Actually, I'm looking for someone who bartends here."

The man looked unamused. "Okay."

"His name's James, uh, I mean, Tommy. Tommy Flynn?"

"Never heard of him," the man said flatly before moving on to the next person's order.

Caleb turned to us. His eyes looked heavy. "That was helpful."

"He didn't have to be so rude," Isaac said.

"Hey!" A voice called to us.

Caleb spun around. It was the other bartender. He was a short, stocky guy with only hair on the sides of his head. "You lookin' for Tommy?"

"Uh, yeah," Caleb said. "You know him?"

"You with Victor?" The bartender asked.

Caleb glanced at us, his brow furrowed. He turned back to the bartender. "No? Who's Victor?"

"Meet me by the bathrooms in five minutes," The bartender said before filling a glass with ice and turning to the shelf behind him.

Caleb looked at Isaac and me. "Okay?"

"Hopefully, he knows something," I said.

Isaac smiled. "I have a good feeling about this."

Caleb huffed. "That makes one of us."

"Isaac Matthews?" A woman in a short red dress stopped us before reaching the bathrooms. She wrapped her arm around Isaac's waist. "It's so good to see you out. Come take a picture with us."

Isaac caught my glance over his shoulder. "I'll be over soon." He was swept into the crowd before I could respond.

Caleb paced up and down the alcove outside the men's room, tucked away from the crowd. I leaned against a wall, watching silently, anxious to hear what the bartender knew. Five minutes felt like thirty seconds.

The bartender casually entered the alcove, wiping his hands with a small towel before placing it over his shoulder. He and Caleb shook hands. "Name's John."

"Caleb."

"Do you know the other guys?" John asked.

Caleb's head shook. "What other guys?"

"A couple of guys were here last week asking around for Tommy. One kinda looked like that guy Stalone fought in Rocky Four."

"Did they say what they wanted?" Caleb asked.

"Just said they were looking for him. I should've asked why."

Something about what he said pulled my intestines into a knot. Of course, it could have been a coincidence, but it still felt strange.

"I was behind the bar, so I didn't really have time to chat," John said.

But you do now, during a big party? I thought.

"So, what'd you tell them?" Caleb asked.

"Told 'em Tommy didn't work here anymore. He quit like a month ago."

Caleb wiped a hand down his face. "God damn it. Of course." Caleb paced for a second before leaning against the wall. I felt awful. He couldn't catch a break.

"What happened next?" I asked John.

"They were asking more questions, but I was too busy. I ignored them, and they moved on. I probably would've done the same to you if this wasn't the second time someone asked for him. So now I'm curious."

"Tommy is my dad. We haven't seen each other in a while, so I wanted to surprise him."

John stared. "Tommy has a kid?"

"Two, actually," Caleb said.

John sucked his teeth. "Well, shit."

"Yeah, we'd really like to see him," I said. "Would you happen to know where Tommy lives?"

The balding bartender crossed his arms. "What's in it for me?"

Caleb sighed and reached for his wallet, taking a peek inside. "My last twenty bucks?"

John smirked. "Make it forty."

"I said it's my last twenty." Caleb pushed his wallet in his pocket and held the twenty between two fingers. "Take it or leave it."

John snatched the bill and pushed it into his pocket. "We only hung out a few times, but I remember his building. Kinda grungy lookin' place, small.".

"Where?" Caleb asked.

"West seventy," John said, scratching his chin. "One-seventeen, I think?"

"Apartment number?" I asked.

John's bushy brows wiggled. "That'll cost ya an extra fifty bucks."

Caleb launched himself at John, grabbed fistfuls of his vest, and pushed him against the alcove wall.

I rushed to block the view of any passersby.

Caleb squeezed his grip. "I gave you all the money I have, you greedy piece of shit. Now stop bullshitting me." Caleb pressed again, pushing John's vest closer to his neck.

"Okay! Jesus!" John shouted before Caleb let him go. "Apartment five oh five," he said between breaths, frantically tucking his shirt back in.

"Thank you," Caleb said calmly. He shoved John away before walking back into the party. I caught up to Caleb, giving a staff member his coat check ticket. I gave mine as well. The elevator doors opened just as we got our coats back.

"Hey!" Isaac called out, skipping every other step until he reached us. "What happened?"

"We got the address," I said, slipping on my coat.

"Great! Where is it?"

"West Seventy," Caleb said.

Isaac smiled. "That's so close! So, what now?"

I looked at Caleb. He zipped his coat and said, "I'm going there."

"Now?" I asked. "It's kinda late. Should we wait til tomorrow? We got the address. That's what we wanted."

Caleb glared at me. "Seriously? After everything we went through today, you wanna wait? It's so close. I'm not waiting another day. You guys can stay. Enjoy the party."

"You shouldn't go alone," Isaac said.

I looked at Isaac. "Since this is more your scene, I'll go with Caleb."

Isaac pushed his hands in his pockets. "You're right. I should sit this part out. I don't want to be a distraction." His eyes caught mine. "Let me know what happens, okay?"

Caleb looked at Isaac. "Thank you. We couldn't have gotten this far without you. I promise I'll find a way to pay you back."

Isaac smiled. "It's really okay. I'm glad I could help. Hopefully, I'll see you again soon." Isaac hugged Caleb and kissed him on the cheek.

Caleb scratched the back of his head with a slight smile. His cheeks had gone red.

Isaac did the same for me, giving me all the warmth I needed to face the windy sidewalks. "Be safe. Text me when you're home."

"We will," Caleb said. We stepped into the elevator just as Isaac was swept into another photo-op.

I pulled out my phone. "I'll update Josh."

ME

Hey, Caleb's dad wasn't there, but we got the address.

JOSH

Nice. How?

ME

A bartender who knows him.

JOSH

That'll do it. What now?

ME

Caleb and I are headed there now.

JOSH

Good luck, my dude.

NINETEEN

The wind collected the aroma of the Nuts 4 Nuts cart on the corner of 70th Street and Columbus Ave.

"John said one-seventeen, right?" Caleb asked.

"Yeah." I sniffled.

We crossed Columbus Ave, and Caleb jutted his chin toward the corner building. "That's one-oh-one. We're close."

We walked half a block further before we hit the address. It was a large apartment building with an AC unit in every window. We stood in front of a large glass entryway. Two large arch-like windows were fixed on either side. A man exited with his small, scruffy dog, so we squeezed through the door. The place looked as if no one had swept it in years. The paint on the walls chipped every few feet. The main desk in the lobby was unoccupied.

The elevator doors were painted the same puke-green color as the rest of the walls. Stepping inside, I felt a sudden grasp of claustrophobia take hold of my throat.

The elevator doors opened on the fifth floor. "This is it," Caleb said.

A light flickered as we stepped off, and the entire hallway smelled like cheese. I followed behind Caleb. My thoughts raced. *What if*

Caleb's dad is asleep? What if he isn't home? What if he doesn't want to see us or care that Caleb came all this way?

Caleb and I hadn't discussed any possibilities of what Caleb's dad might do or say. He could easily slam the door in our faces, and all the trouble would be for nothing. What then?

Caleb stopped at a white door with numbers stickered haphazardly on the door. *505*. Caleb was about to knock when I grabbed his arm. He looked at me with a tight brow. "What?"

Something felt off, but who was I to stop the reunion Caleb had been waiting for since he was a kid? I sighed and let go. Caleb gave three solid knocks.

Indistinguishable whispers, footsteps, and furniture sliding around seeped through the door.

"Who is it?" A hoarse voice asked from inside.

Caleb crossed his hands in front of him and squared his shoulders. "Hi, my name's Caleb. I'm looking for—"

The door swung open, and a haze of smoke floated by us. A man with shoulder-length, greasy black hair stood in the doorway. His clothes looked two sizes too big. The sleeves of his t-shirt hung off his toothpick-like arms. The man's cheeks were sunken, his eyes bloodshot. The skin on his face was scarred and droopy. The man's tongue slapped and sucked whatever he was chewing, giving us a perfect view of his chipped yellow teeth. He looked us up and down.

"Jasper, who it is?" A deep voice with a thick Russian accent called from behind the greasy man.

"Two snobby rich kids, from the look of it," Jasper said between gum smacks.

Caleb and I glanced at each other.

"Who was it you're looking for?" Jasper asked.

"Actually," Caleb said, "we have the wrong apartment. Sorry to bother—"

"Don't act rude!" the Russian voice said. "Invite in!"

I took a step back. "We're okay."

Caleb stepped away, too. "Thanks."

"Now, hold on," Jasper said, pulling our focus. He lifted his shirt, exposing the gun handle tucked into the waist of his baggy jeans.

My heart jumped into my throat, and I closed my eyes. *No, not again. This is a dream, another vision.*

Caleb grabbed my hand. "Listen, we don't want any trouble."

"Then don't give us any," the greasy man sneered. He cleared his throat and spat his phlegm at our feet.

Most of my body hid behind Caleb. "We just want to go."

The man pulled the gun from his waistband and scratched his scalp with the barrel. "If the boss invites you in, you take the offer."

Caleb squeezed my hand. "Okay, okay. Whatever you want."

Jasper stepped aside, allowing us to look into the apartment for the first time.

Straight ahead, against the back wall, a man sat on a tattered brown couch, counting money on the coffee table in front of him. The Russian voice was his. "Please, come."

My breath staggered as Caleb stepped forward, still holding my trembling hand. I focused on Jasper's gun, and my feet cemented themselves to the floor.

Caleb slowly turned to me and touched my face. "I won't let anything happen to you. I promise," he whispered.

"I can't do it."

"We don't have all day!" Jasper shouted.

Caleb glanced over his shoulder. "Alright! Okay." He turned to me again. "We have to. Just stay behind me." Caleb turned and led me through the door. The sour stench hit me on the way in.

The apartment was one square room, just a little bigger than my dorm. The walls were stained yellow.

A tall, broad, blonde man leaned against the sink. He looked like a giant compared to the size of everything in the kitchenette. His red and white striped shirt was tight around his muscular frame. He didn't say a word but crunched a bite of apple as he stared.

I scanned the rest of the space, attempting to devise an escape route. The only window in the entire apartment was behind the

Russian man, who hadn't bothered to get up off the couch. Even if the window was an exit option, we were still five floors up. There was a door tucked in the right corner of the room. Maybe that was an option.

The Russian boss wore nicer clothes than the other two men. His slacks and button-up looked pristinely kept. He tossed a few hundred dollar bills next to the two stacks of cash on the coffee table. His hair was silver, and his face looked freshly shaven. "Jasper, get chairs for guests."

The door closed behind us, and Jasper slumped by, shoving the gun back into his waistband. He grabbed two metal chairs leaning against the wall and set them on the opposite side of the coffee table. His eyes glued to us as he stepped aside.

Another crunch from the giant behind us made me flinch. Caleb guided me to a chair and then sat to my left. We stared at the Russian, and my hand continued to tremble, so I slipped it under my thigh. My heart pounded against my chest, and I tried to steady my breathing.

The Russian scooched to the edge of his seat and straightened his back. "Do you know who I am?"

Caleb's jaw clenched. "No, sir."

"You know what I do?"

"No, sir," Caleb repeated.

The Russian sucked his teeth, pulled a lighter from his pocket, then lit a cigarette. He let the smoke slowly escape his mouth. His demeanor was the calmest in the room. "Very interesting to me."

"Why's that?" Caleb asked. Was he trying to antagonize him?

The boss held his cigarette between the two middle fingers of one hand. "People dressed like you knock at my door, not often."

My teeth ground together.

Caleb adjusted in his seat. "Like I said, we had the wrong apartment."

The Russian leaned back into the couch. "Right." A chuckle escaped with the next puff of smoke. "He said, didn't he, Jasper? I forget, almost." He glanced at Jasper, who nodded furiously. The boss looked at Caleb. "You have excellent memory..." He raised an eyebrow

"Caleb."

"...Caleb," the Russian finished. "Your memory good. I think you know apartment you look for. So, who is it?"

"A friend."

"Friend? You don't know where friend lives?"

"A new friend. This was our first time here."

"Our?"

"Me and Landon."

The Russian pointed to me. "Is this?" Caleb nodded. "Landon?" My eyes shot up and across the table. "Look nervous," he said. "You nervous?"

My cheeks burned. I shook my head, keeping my eyes on him.

"Is true? What Caleb says?"

My lips pushed together. "Mmm."

The Russian leaned to flick his cigarette into a glass ashtray on the table. "That *very* interesting to me." The counter squeaked under the weight of the man behind us. The Russian slowly adjusted his posture and crossed one leg over the other. "Do you believe fate, Caleb?"

"I'm not sure," Caleb responded.

"I do," he said. "Fate bring us together. Start of new friendship." A throaty laugh came from Jasper. The Russian placed his cigarette on the edge of the ashtray, then extended his hand across the table. "I'm Victor." The smile on his face sent a chill up my spine. His teeth were too perfect. The more his silver, slicked-back hair caught the fluorescent light, the more he looked like a ventriloquist dummy.

Caleb reluctantly returned the handshake. Both of my hands made their way under my thighs at that point, so Victor didn't attempt another greeting.

Victor gestured to Jasper. "You meet Jasper." He then gestured behind us, but neither Caleb nor I looked. "Big man is Mikhail. No

English." Victor shot out something in Russian, and Mikhail grunted back. "Muscle. No brain," Victor said. Jasper snorted and spat on the floor. "Him? No manners," Victor said. "Jasper, get drink for new friends." Victor looked at us again. "In home country, we toast new friends."

The back of my neck dampened. Buried under the suit jacket and winter coat, it started to bake me alive.

Jasper appeared in front of us, slamming a whiskey bottle down on the coffee table, then returned to his spot against the wall.

Another wooden smile stretched across Victor's face. "This special bottle. Friends only." He twisted the top off. "We drink from bottle. Please." He gestured to the whiskey as Caleb and I glanced at each other. Neither of us moved. "What?" Victor asked. "Don't trust friend?" He snatched the bottle and chugged as if drinking water. Victor slammed the bottle down, making me jump. He unbuttoned his sleeves, pushed them up his arms, and wiped his moist lips across his forearm. "See?"

Caleb took a deep breath, reached for the bottle, and took a quick swig. His lips tightened when he swallowed. Caleb handed me the bottle. His still eyes fixed on VIctor.

I took the bottle with two hands, hoping to steady the trembling. I touched the bottle to my mouth and tilted it. The liquid touched my lips, but I didn't let any in my mouth. I pretended to swallow before returning the bottle to the table.

Victor clapped. "Ah, you see? Friends trust! Right, Landon?" I pushed my hands back under my thighs and nodded. "Now I show gesture. Good faith. I like same from you."

"What do you mean?" Caleb asked.

Victor smiled. His eyes widened. "We play game."

Caleb tugged at his coat. "Actually, I think we should go."

Victor's smile faded before he slammed his fist on the coffee table. "YOU STAY!"

I jumped in my seat, and my breath stopped. Caleb sat up straight.

Victor sighed, shook his head, then displayed his wide smile again. "Friends play games." He reached into his pocket, pulled out something shiny, clicked a button, and released a switchblade from its sheath. "A simple game. Prove you not cop."

Caleb leaned against his thighs. "A cop? No, no, no. We aren't cops."

Victor swung and stabbed the knife into the table, forcing Caleb back into his chair. "Is easy, then," Victor said. He snapped his fingers at Jasper. Jasper tossed a baggy of white powder into Victor's hand.

"This is ridiculous," Caleb said. "How can we prove we aren't cops?"

Victor opened the baggy, pulled the knife from the table, and gently stuck the point of the blade into the opening. "One of you snort." Victor slowly pulled the knife from the bag. A small mound of powder sat at the tip. "In Russia, we call this Hell Dust." Victor brought his eye closer to the blade and smiled, tilting his head. He slowly pointed the knife in Caleb's direction. "Eeny..." Then at me. "...Meeny..." Back to Caleb. "Miney." The blade pointed at me again. "Moe."

Terror crept through my nervous system. I froze in my chair.

"Mikhail will help," Victor said.

"No!" Caleb shouted. "I'll do it."

My eyes shot to Caleb.

Victor cupped his hand under the blade and laughed. "*Good* friend you have, Landon!"

Caleb's jaw tensed. "Let's get this over with."

Victor's brows perked as he held the knife out over the table. Caleb plugged one nostril, snorted the powder off the knife, and jolted back. His eyes clenched, and he pressed his palm to his forehead.

My heart slammed against my chest. I wanted to yell for help, but I was too scared Mikhail would hit me before I could let out a second scream.

Victor said something else in Russian. Mikhail shuffled through the drawers before presenting a black pencil case to Victor. Mikhail's thick arm brushed my shoulder as he returned to the kitchen. "How you feel, Caleb?" Victor asked as he unzipped the pencil case.

Caleb sniffled. "Fan-fucking-tastic. We did what you asked. Now, can we please go?" His fingers twitched.

Victor stared at us with hollow eyes. He sucked his bottom lip, using his teeth to scratch the stubble. "Game not finished."

Caleb rolled his eyes. "Yes, it is. We proved we weren't cops."

Victor pointed the knife at Caleb. "You proved." Victor pointed the knife at me. "Not proved."

Caleb stood. "Lan, get up. We're leaving."

I started to move.

Victor reached behind his back and casually placed a handgun on the coffee table. "You leave when I say."

My chest rose and fell rapidly. My eyes locked on the gun sitting there. I thought about my dad and how I wanted to hear his voice one more time. I thought about Parker growing up without a brother. I'd never get to graduate college. I wanted to hold Caleb's hand through to the end, but every bone in my body was stiff.

Victor stabbed the knife into the wood again, then pulled a blackened metal spoon from the pencil case before sliding it into the baggy of powder. Victor scooped up a small mound, grabbed a lighter from the case, and lit the flame under the spoon.

"What're you doing?" Caleb asked.

I couldn't take my eyes off the gun. It was black with a brown grip on the handle.

Victor looked at me as the powder crackled. "You want gun, don't you?"

I slowly raised my gaze.

"Go on," Victor said.

My eyes scrolled to the gun, then back to Victor. Was it a test—another game? What if I tried to shoot Victor, but the gun wasn't loaded? Jasper would take me out with a bullet of his own before I even realized Victor's gun was empty.

"TAKE IT!" Victor screamed.

My heart jumped into my throat. I clenched my eyes, forcing a tear down my cheek. I shook my head, praying Victor wouldn't shoot me where I sat. My eyes shot open when I felt a hand on my thigh. I flinched before realizing it was Caleb's. My trembling hand grabbed his.

Caleb glared at Victor. "What do you want us to do?" He said through his teeth.

Victor placed the spoon on the table, and some brown liquid spilled over the edge. The boss pulled a needle from the case.

"No fucking way!" Caleb yelled. "Who knows where the fuck that needles been!"

"I sanitize," Victor said with a cheery tone. He flicked the lighter and moved the flame back and forth over the needlepoint. "See? Clean."

I tried to speak, but even my voice was stuck.

Caleb wiped his nose repeatedly, and his words slurred a bit. "You can't expect him to do that. We don't know what that is. It could kill him."

Victor laughed, then dipped the needle into the liquid. He pulled the syringe back. "Small amount," Victor said. "Won't last long."

I had never been afraid of needles until that moment. Growing up, I never looked away when getting blood drawn. It never phased me. But this was different.

My eyes were the only part of me that moved. "I... I can't."

Caleb looked at me, then at Victor. "Please, Victor. We will do anything else."

Victor frowned, holding the needle in the air. "No."

"We have money," Caleb said. He was getting desperate enough to lie. "How much do you want? We can get it."

"No," Victor said again with an even tone.

Caleb rubbed his eyes and then his nose again. "Jesus fucking Christ, fine! I'll do it then! I'll take it. Just leave him alone, please."

Victor smiled and looked at me. "Landon, you hear? Caleb willing to take for you. Such good friend. Like love birds."

Jasper let out a phlegmy laugh.

"Please let me do it. I don't care what happens to me," Caleb said.

I squeezed Caleb's hand. He had done enough for me already.

"I have idea," Victor said. He looked at Caleb. "You give Landon needle."

Caleb let go of my hand. "What?"

"You inject Landon." Victor laughed and turned to Jasper. "Is that right word? Inject?"

Jasper nodded and smiled, exposing his rotting teeth again.

"No," Caleb said. "I'll take what's in the needle."

Victor sat back and spoke in Russian. Suddenly, Mikhail was on me, gripping my shoulders, trying to remove my coat.

"Don't touch me!" I screamed, thrashing in my seat. But Mikhail overpowered me and pulled me off my chair.

Caleb jumped to his feet, but Jasper quickly stepped to him, pointing his gun at Caleb's head. Everyone in the room froze. Caleb stared at me and slowly raised his arms.

Mikhail easily picked me up off the ground and removed my coat and suit jacket, tossing them toward the front door. Mikhail squeezed my shoulders and forced me back in the chair across from Victor.

Victor clapped. "So brave." Victor snapped his fingers, calling off his henchmen. Jasper and Mikhail stepped back in their usual spots. Jasper uncocked his gun and pushed it back into his waistband. Victor looked at Caleb. "Sit."

Caleb did what he was told. His jaw was tight, his breath heavy, and snot leaked down his face. He was sweating, still fully dressed in his suit and coat. Caleb wiped his nose across his coat's sleeve and stared daggers at Victor.

"Americans. Dramatic," Victor said. He sat up and leaned across the table, holding the needle. Caleb carefully took it from him. Victor cleared his throat and sat back. "You inject him. Game over." Caleb stared at the needle in his hand. "If you don't, Jasper shoot you both," Victor said.

Jasper's hand gripped the handle poking out of his pants.

I unbuttoned my sleeve, pushed it above my elbow, and looked at Caleb with wet eyes. "Do it," I whispered.

Caleb squinted. His lips rolled over his teeth as if trying not to cry, and he gently pulled my arm straight. He swallowed hard. His finger grazed my palm, drawing a circle. I stared into his eyes before clenching mine.

"I'm sorry," Caleb whispered. The quiver in his voice was the last thing I heard before the needle poked through my skin.

TWENTY

Time slowed as lava flowed through my veins. The burn ripped through my arm to my fingertips. Caleb was still holding my hand, but I couldn't feel it. I unraveled our fingers. Pins and needles shot up my arm and across my chest like an alien wreaking havoc on my insides. My head swayed.

Caleb faced me in his chair. I looked at him, but my vision was underwater. I wiped my wet eyes with my wrist. Victor's shoulders bounced with his maniacal laugh. Jasper snorted.

The walls in the apartment bowed as if made of flimsy plastic. My chair turned into a spinning carnival ride. I tried to plant my feet on the floor, but the pins and needles had spread past my knees and through my toes. Bile sloshed in my stomach, each splash sending a burn up my throat.

I stood but instantly hit the floor. Muffled voices circled me. Hands gripped at my shirt. I pulled myself free and crawled to the only door in the room, using the knob to hoist myself up to push through. Slamming the door behind me, I twisted the lock. Everything was blurry. I dropped to my knees at the toilet and flipped the lid up.

I heaved into the bowl with clenched eyes, then pitched again. My body wanted everything out. I lurched over and over until my stomach was sore. I finally pushed myself from the toilet and sat against the opposite wall. Keeping my eyes closed, I leaned my head back. Flashes of colors erupted from the darkness behind my lids. My right hand reached for anything solid to try to stop the spinning. I finally gripped the porcelain of the tub.

A thud passed through one ear and out the other. A muffled voice traveled along with it. I wanted to stand. Maybe if I drank some water from the sink, it'd settle my stomach. Another thud pulsed through me. The voice sounded three apartments away, barely able to push through the walls.

"Landon," the whisper fluttered into my ear. Unlike the muffles from behind the door, the voice was crystal clear. I watched the door, but no one was there. My head flopped against the wall again. Gravity pulled at my eyelids. Then, the whisper grazed my ear again. "Landon, help."

I blinked the blur away, and my heart sank when I saw Dan lying in the bathtub. He was propped next to the faucet, staring at me. He wore his white prom suit, and blood gushed from his neck, but his face was neutral, unfazed. He blinked at me. "Help me, Landon," he whispered again.

"Oh my god, Dan!" I pulled my weight over the edge of the tub. My knees knocked against the tile as my upper half hovered over him. I cupped Dan's face. "It's gonna be okay. You're gonna be okay!" My hands were slick with blood. I pressed my palm against his wound, but the gushing didn't let up. "You'll be okay," I mumbled as tears wet my cheeks.

I glanced around the room, desperate to stop the bleeding. The toilet paper roll on the sink was the closest, but the thin paper disintegrated whenever I tried to wrap it around my hand. My heart raced. I needed to save him somehow. A white towel was crumpled up in the corner by the door. I splayed across the floor to reach for it, smearing Dan's blood around the tiled squares. Bunching the towel, I pressed it against Dan's neck.

Blood trickled from the corner of Dan's mouth. "Am I going to die?"

"No, it's gonna be fine," I said scratchily. The white towel dripped red. There was no stopping the flow. "I'll call for help."

Dan reached for my arm and grasped me with weak fingers. "Tell my family I'm sorry."

"You'll tell them yourself, okay?" I said, barely able to see through the blur. "Help!" I screamed over my shoulder. Using my arm, I wiped the tears from my face. Dan's eyes drooped. "Stay with me, okay?" I applied as much pressure as possible, but the tub filled with blood. "Please, Dan! I'm sorry!" The towel, now completely soaked in red, fell from my hands and sunk into the pool of blood that rose above Dan's waist.

Two more thuds sounded from behind. Each one made the room shake. A snap followed the next thud. A breeze brushed my neck, and I was suddenly ripped from the tub. "No!" I reached for Dan and screamed. A pair of arms wrapped underneath mine and hugged my chest. "He needs help!"

Caleb's voice was in my ear. "Landon, it's me!"

I resisted, trying to make my way back to Dan. But Caleb was too strong. He pulled me through the bathroom threshold, and we tumbled to the carpet. He must've kicked the door in because the wood around the frame was splintered. I crumbled into Caleb's chest. My face wet with tears. "We have to help him!"

"Shh," Caleb said, rubbing my chest. "It's okay."

"No!" I cried. "He's not okay!"

Caleb squeezed me a little tighter, but his voice was calm. "Landon, there's no one there."

I shook my head. "That's impossible. I know what I saw. He's right there! Look!" I tried to get away again, but Caleb held me tight. My vision blurred as I tried to fight, and my head got heavier. The laughter from Victor and the others echoed through me as if my body was hollow until the sounds bounced around my skull.

"We proved what you wanted. Is that enough?" Caleb yelled.

Victor's laugh calmed. "Mikhail, let them leave. They don't know to have fun."

Caleb hoisted me to my feet, wrapped my arm around his neck, and guided me through the front door. We were moving so quickly, yet I could barely feel my legs. The last thing I remembered was the musty smell of the elevator and Caleb wrapping me in my coat before my eyes became too heavy to stay open.

———

"Landon, sweetie," a voice said from the void. "You're gonna be late for school."

My eyelids were sticky. I had to blink a few times to pull everything into focus. A familiar stucco ceiling hovered over me, reflecting the sunbeams cascading through a window at the foot of the bed. I closed my eyes again and took a deep breath. Something else was familiar. A fruity mist hung in the air. It smelled like mango, like...

The mattress dipped. The light was too bright initially, but as my eyes adjusted, the silhouette on my bed became clear. My mom smiled down at me, looking completely different from the last time I saw her. Her cheeks were full and rosy, no longer sunken and pale. The scarf she wrapped around her bald head was now draped over her shoulders, letting her long, wavy red hair flow down her back.

I shot up to sit against the headboard and blinked rapidly. "Mom?"

She smiled. "Yes?"

I reached for her hand. "It's really you?"

Mom gently squeezed my grip. "Who else would it be?" She chuckled.

A voice echoed above us as if over the house entirely. *"What did he take?"* The voice's volume lowered. Words faded in and out of my consciousness. *"Prep Narcan... We don't know if..."*

· · ·

"Oh my god!" I pushed the covers away and scooped Mom into a tight hug.

"What is this for?" she asked into my shoulder.

I studied her face. "I... thought... I'd never see you again."

"What do you mean? I'm right here."

I glanced around my room. Everything was as I left it. Everything in the room still existed except her.

She patted me on the leg. "Now get dressed. I don't want you to be late." She tried to stand, but I held her arm, keeping her on my bed. "What is up with you today?"

I glided two fingers through a lock of her hair. She looked at me like I had three heads. "Can I skip school today?" I asked.

Her brow furrowed. "For what?"

"Let's spend the day together. We can get ice cream and... and buy all the tabloid magazines. Maybe watch some reruns of *Will and Grace*?"

"You know how Dad feels about that show." She looked me in the eye. "But it can be our secret," she whispered. "But what about your game later?"

Another voice trickled down from the sky. *"He'll be okay, right?"*

I shook my head. "I don't care. I'll skip it."

"All this just to spend the day with your old mom?"

I held her hand again. "I'd do anything to spend one more day with you." My eyes welled.

"Sweetie," Mom said, gently cupping my cheek. "Is everything okay? Is there something you want to tell me?"

My breath caught in my throat, and my lip quivered. "There are so many things I want to tell you."

"Landon, honey, you know you can tell me anything."

• • •

A voice faded through the walls. *"They said... Only a few days... We can take him..."*

I sniffled and wiped my arm across my nose. "I..." Tears rolled down my face. "I'm..."

"Landon, it's okay. I know," she said before hugging me. Then, the floodgates opened, and I sobbed in her arms. "My sweet boy, I've always known. And it doesn't change a thing. Okay?"

"It doesn't?"

"Of course not. Look at me." She cupped my cheeks in both hands. "You are still the smart, talented boy I raised. Nothing is ever going to change my love for you."

"But what if—"

"Listen, even when you leave this house, I'll still watch over you whether you like it or not." She smiled.

I sighed. "You've missed so much already."

"My room... Upstairs... Can rest..."

I wondered if Mom could hear the voice, too.

"I haven't missed a thing." She wiped the tears from my cheek and held my hands in hers. "Even when I'm long gone, you might not be able to see me, but if you close your eyes and think of me, I promise I'll always be right there next to you. No matter where you are."

It was hard to catch my breath. "Pinky swear?"

She smiled and held up her pinky. I wrapped mine around hers. "Pinky swear," Mom said.

I wiped the remaining tears from my face before she finally stood. "One more thing." I hopped up and hugged her, taking in her mango perfume one last time. "I love you more than anything."

Mom kissed my head. "I love you too, Landon." She collected a few shirts off my floor, then turned to me from the doorway. "Dress warm today. It's going to snow."

My head tilted. "What?"

My eyes shot open.

Wednesday, January 15th

I stared at the ceiling, but it wasn't my bedroom. I propped onto my elbows. The sheets stuck to my sweaty back. I was in a bed wearing nothing but my underwear. A large warehouse-like window let the setting sun into the loft. A long glass desk sat under it. Vines hung over their pots and off the edge of the desk.

I looked at the side table. My phone sat atop a folded pair of sweats. I snatched it and poked the screen. An automated alert flashed at me.

BLIZZARD WARNING IN EFFECT UNTIL TOMORROW, THURSDAY, JANUARY 16th, 7 P.M.!

I swung my legs off the bed and rubbed my eyes. "Tomorrow's Thursday?" A bass drum had taken residence in my skull. I wondered if everything was a dream. Maybe I had spent too much time outside and caught the flu. Maybe I took too much cough medicine and passed out. I swiped the blizzard warning away and saw that I had sixty unread texts in my group chat with Lauren, Steven, and Tasha.

I can't handle that right now.

I pulled on the sweatpants and then the T-shirt that was left underneath. Footsteps pattered behind me.

"He's awake!" Caleb called over his shoulder before barreling up the rest of the stairs. He scooped me into his arms. "Are you okay? How're you feeling?"

Isaac raced up the stairs and hugged both Caleb and me.

"A little foggy," I said. "Kind of have a headache."

Isaac let go of us and trotted through the doorway next to the bed, returning with a bottle of ibuprofen. Isaac gently pressed the back of his hand to my forehead. "No more fever. Sit. I'll get you some water." He scuttered down the stairs as Caleb and I sat at the bed's edge.

"What happened?" I asked.

Caleb held my thigh. "I used your phone to call Isaac. I didn't know what else to do. I got you as far away as I could." Caleb looked at the floor. "I could barely stand when Isaac found us."

Fear filled my stomach again. Flashes of Victor's wooden smile pulsed in my mind.

"Isaac got us to the hospital. I was fine after a couple hours and some fluids, but they kept you overnight. You were in and out of sleep. Do you remember anything?"

"Those guys. Who were they?"

Caleb shrugged. "Isaac talked to the cops. Told them where to go, but they said the place was empty when they got there. They said we're lucky they let us go. If I see them on the street, I swear—"

Isaac glided up the steps and handed me a glass of water. "This should help." He opened the bottle and gave me two small red pills. "Feeling any better?"

I rolled my shoulders. "A little sore, like the day after a football game. But yeah, I feel okay." I popped the pills and guzzled the glass as if it were the first time I tasted water.

Isaac sat on the other side of me just as the stairs creaked.

Josh appeared at the top of the steps, holding his laptop under his arm. "Heard you were awake."

"Josh? What're you doing here?"

"Caleb called me from your phone. I was worried about my roomie."

"He's been here the whole time," Isaac said.

Josh smiled. "Not happy to see me?"

"I honestly didn't think I'd see any of you again," I said.

Josh leaned against the banister. "How're you holding up?"

"I'm... I don't know. I thought it was a dream," I said.

"I wish it was," Caleb said.

Josh's brow pinched. "So there's just a bunch of randos out there drugging people for fun?"

"This city's always had a dark side," Isaac said.

"I gave descriptions to the police, but they probably aren't doing shit about it," Caleb said.

I looked at him. "What about the drugs they gave us?"

Caleb scratched his cheek. "The doctors weren't sure what it was, but they knew it wasn't enough to cause damage. They said you'd sleep it off." I leaned on my knees, and Caleb grazed my back. "Landon, I used every muscle in my body to rip you from that bathroom. You kept saying, 'he needs help.' Do you remember that?"

The image of my best friend's blood filling the tub was seared in my mind. "Dan."

Caleb closed his eyes. "What about him?"

"Who's Dan?" Josh asked.

"He was there, in the bathtub. He was talking to me, but blood was just, like, pouring out of his neck—"

"The fuck?" Josh said. "And you knew this person?" The room went silent. Josh looked at each of us. "What? Did you kill someone or something?" He chuckled. Again, no one spoke, and Josh's brow furrowed. "Okay, fuck this. If ya'll killed someone, I'm out. I don't fuck with that shit."

Caleb shot up off the bed. "It's not like that!"

"Then what the fuck is it?" Josh gestured to Isaac. "Do you know?"

"It's not my story to tell," Isaac said.

Josh rolled his eyes and started down the stairs. "Okay. Good luck with everything. I'm out."

"It was self-defense!" Caleb shouted.

Josh stood still, staring.

"Landon's homophobic best friend Dan held a fucking gun to our heads on prom night, then almost beat me to death. So, I'm sorry if I don't want to rehash it."

Josh stepped back up the two stairs and placed his laptop on the bedside table. "Dude, Caleb, I'm sorry." He looked at us. "Landon, why didn't you tell me?"

I sat up straight. "'Cause this was supposed to be my fresh start. That's what I wanted. Imagine if the day we met, I told you I killed my best friend. You would've packed your shit and looked for a different roommate. I don't want to be the guy everyone stares at, not again. I wanted to leave Dan in Texas."

"You did," Caleb said.

"Then why am I still seeing him?"

Caleb sat beside me again. "It was the drugs, Landon."

"What if it wasn't? What if I'm just damaged? Fucked completely?"

"What are you talking about?" Caleb asked.

I stood and paced at the foot of the bed. "That wasn't the first time I saw Dan, but the drugs definitely made it worse."

Caleb watched me. "You told me the dreams stopped when you moved to New York."

"They did, but—"

"But what?"

All eyes were on me, and it made my stomach tighten. "But then we had our fight, and I came back, and... it got worse."

Caleb leaned forward, resting his arms on his legs. "Worse, how?"

"Like, I wasn't just seeing him in dreams anymore."

"You didn't tell me that part," Isaac said.

Caleb scratched the small patch of stubble on his chin. "Wait, what do you mean?"

"I've been seeing Dan as if he's standing right there in the room with me. I saw him at a party. I saw him on the sidewalk. But the tub was the first time he spoke to me. It was the first time I could touch him."

Caleb's brow creased. "Jesus Christ, Landon. Why didn't you tell me this?"

"I tried. I called you the first night I saw him. But I was drunk, so I thought—"

"Have you told your dad?" Caleb asked, standing.

"No. He'd make me come home."

Caleb huffed. "Maybe you should! The dreams were one thing, but this is fucking serious now."

The air in the room shifted.

Josh picked up his laptop and tiptoed down the stairs. "I'll give you guys a minute."

I wanted to curl up in Isaac's bed again and sleep away my problems.

Caleb reached a hand toward me. "Give me your phone."

"For what?" I asked.

"Calling Parker."

"Why?"

"To tell him we're coming home."

"What?" Isaac and I asked at the same time.

"I'm done searching," Caleb said. "Look where it got us."

"Caleb, we'll never see those guys again," I said.

He looked at me. "I don't want anything else to happen. Seeing you like that was terrifying enough. Fuck finding my dad. I've put you in danger enough."

I crossed to Caleb at the corner of the bed. "Nothing else is going to happen."

"You don't know that," Caleb said.

"Holy shit!" Josh yelled, making us all flinch. "I found something!"

Isaac hopped off the bed and hustled down the stairs.

Caleb watched him go, then looked at me. "You need to tell your dad."

"I know. But what if he makes me move back?"

Caleb took my hands in his. "Then we'll figure it out."

"I don't want to go back."

"Guys!" Isaac shouted. "Come look at this!"

"C'mon." I let go of one hand and led Caleb with the other. Josh sat at the kitchen island downstairs, staring at his open laptop. "What'd you find?" I asked.

Josh adjusted the screen. "I've been using AI for the search. It created an algorithm that scans the internet for Tommy's name in any form. Someone posted a picture of a sign-in sheet for an AA meeting on Facebook."

I squinted at the picture. "Alcoholics Anonymous?"

"That's not very anonymous," Isaac said.

Josh scoffed. "It's Facebook. Shit's like the wild west, idiots post everything."

Caleb looked at Josh. "Okay, so how does this help us?"

Josh's finger tapped the screen. "Look at the clipboard."

Someone had taped a label to the top of the clipboard in all caps. 'PROPERTY OF CECELIA'S CATHOLIC CHURCH.'

Josh started typing. "A quick search." The keys sounded like rain against a window. "Boom. Adams Street in Brooklyn." He moved closer to the screen. "Just over the bridge, across from Whitman Park."

"Glad he's getting help," Caleb said, pacing toward the couch and leaning against the back. "Good for him."

Isaac checked his phone. "It's still early. I'm sure the church is still open."

Caleb crossed his arms and stared at us. "I told you, I'm done."

"Why?" I shot back.

"Because psychos fucking drugged us! This is over."

"But we've never been so close. And I feel fine now," I said.

"That doesn't mean you are," Caleb said.

"Listen, we know he goes to that AA meeting at the church. We can at least ask if anyone there knows him," I said.

Caleb rolled his eyes. "Yeah, 'cause that worked so well the first time."

I chuckled. "It's a church. How bad could it be?"

Caleb pushed himself off the couch. "Why are you joking right now?"

"You said you wanted answers, right? Caleb, you've been waiting for this for so long. It's right there."

Caleb looked at Isaac, then me. "But—"

I moved away from the counter to hold Caleb's hands. "I'll tell my dad, okay? I promise. But can we find yours first?"

Isaac shrugged. "You came all this way."

"God damn it," Caleb whispered, pinching the bridge of his nose. "Fine. I'll go check it out." He pointed at me. "But you're staying here. Isaac can come with me."

Isaac's shoulders tensed, and he pulled air through his teeth. "Sorry, but I have to be on Zoom for a production meeting in like twenty minutes."

Caleb nodded. "Okay. Josh?"

Josh pointed at his computer. "This is kinda my lane, so I'm gonna stay in it."

Caleb rested his hands on his hips. "Great."

"Looks like you're stuck with me," I said.

Caleb grunted. "Fine. Just take it easy, don't do anything crazy." He started for the coat closet.

I followed behind him. "Like what?"

"The subway stop at the corner has been closed all day," Isaac shouted as Caleb handed me my coat.

"It looks like there's a shuttle bus going over the Brooklyn Bridge," Josh said.

"Oh, that's gonna be a nightmare," Isaac said. "I'll pay for a car." Isaac reached for his phone on the kitchen counter.

Caleb lurched forward with only one arm in his coat, and cupped his hand over Isaac's so he couldn't move the phone. "You've spent enough money on me. I'll take the bus, thank you." He pecked Isaac on the cheek, spun on his heels, and started for the elevator.

Josh's eyes met mine. Our thoughts felt connected. *What the hell was that?*

Isaac nibbled his lip. "Fine. But that leather coat isn't gonna be warm enough. Take the red one in the closet."

Caleb nodded, opened the closet door again, and slapped the elevator button before switching coats.

Isaac hugged me just as the elevator opened. "Be safe."

I studied his face, noticing the shards of gray speckled around the emerald in his eyes. "I will."

"I'll text you the address," Josh said.

Isaac watched us with his hands in his pockets as the doors closed.

Caleb flipped his hood up. It looked like fox fur. "I'm starting to miss the Texas heat."

TWENTY ONE

Caleb and I stood under a small bus stop enclosure. It creaked with every gust of wind. The walk made my feet numb. The sidewalks were already piled high with soft snow that made it into my sneakers with every step. I glanced at Caleb, who gripped his backpack strap over his shoulder. I respected him for not taking Isaac's offer to get a car. But I wondered if he regretted it now that our teeth chattered.

The bus pulled up after an excruciating five-minute wait. The heavy snow danced in the glow of the headlights. The massive vehicle looked like two buses sewn together with accordion-like material.

A small square screen beside the driver said 'TAP HERE' in red letters. The driver placed a hand over the screen. "No fares. Last stop is next."

I nodded and stepped onto the bus, noticing a skinny man entering through the back door with a hood covering his face. He sat at the farthest seat back.

A few people sat scattered, taking refuge from the cold. Caleb stopped and held onto the bar connected to the roof. I stood next to him, holding a bar attached to a seat. I watched the lights whiz by. The dusty white streets were mostly empty.

A kid, maybe sixteen at the oldest, sat toward the front, behind the driver. His puffy, blue, and black striped coat didn't look warm enough. He bobbed his head as he sat, music pumping from his EarPods. A bundled couple sat across from Caleb and me. The woman wearing a white fur coat sat in the aisle seat, cuddled into her man.

I could see Caleb staring at me from the corner of my eye. I turned to him. "What?"

Caleb adjusted his grip on the bar and leaned his head on his arm. "I was so scared you weren't gonna wake up. I wouldn't have been able to live with myself for doing that to you."

"You didn't have a choice."

Caleb sighed. "I know. I wanted to protect you, but I felt powerless again."

The bus hopped a bump and forced me into Caleb. He wrapped an arm around my waist to keep me steady.

He's always protecting me. "When do I get to protect you?" I asked.

"I never want to feel that scared again," Caleb said.

I reached for his free hand and wrapped my pinky around his. "Me either."

"I don't know what I would've done without Isaac's help."

"I told you."

"He's... really sweet, actually."

"Oh?"

"All we did was talk about you. He really cares for you."

I scoffed, then playfully pushed myself away from him. "Yeah, right."

Caleb smiled. "I'm serious!"

"Okay, so how does that make you feel?"

"Validated."

My brow furrowed. "What?"

"Because I know how easy it is to fall in love with you."

"Isaac's not in love with me."

"He could be someday."

"Says who?"

"He told me himself."

My cheeks warmed for the first time since I was back in Isaac's apartment. "What?"

"Getting to know him, I'm starting to realize just how similarly we feel about you."

"And how do you feel about him?"

"My mom wouldn't buy me any of those teen magazines when I was younger, so I'd just rip out the posters while we were in the store when no one was looking. I was obsessed with *Little Chef.*"

I covered my mouth. "Oh my god."

"So going from that to sitting on his couch, talking to him face to face, and holding his hand is fucking wild to me."

I tried not to squee. "You held hands!" The butterflies in my stomach fluttered too much to be jealous.

"Alright, folks." The driver's voice boomed from the speakers. "I'll be able to bring you across the bridge, but that has to be the last stop. The roads are getting too slippery with all this snow. I repeat, the next stop across the bridge will be the last."

We were over the water in a blink, speeding toward Brooklyn. It was my first time over the bridge. The moon lit up the east river. The whipping wind forced waves to crash at the shoreline. The city was a landscape of white, except for the purple lights at the top of the Empire State Building.

"You don't get that view in Texas," Caleb said. "No wonder you don't want to leave."

I pried my eyes away from the window to look at Caleb again. "What's gonna happen after?"

"After what?"

"After you meet your dad, and you get your answers."

Caleb shrugged. "Go back home, I guess. Give Parker the news. Finally move on. Find something new."

"Do you have to?"

"Go home? Parker's probably driving Miguel nuts, so yes."

"And then what? I don't see you again 'til I come home for summer break?"

Sitting with her boyfriend, the woman shuffled through her purse and pulled out a water bottle as the bus jerked to the left. The bottle slipped from her hand, fell to the floor, and rolled by us as the driver hit the gas again. My stomach lurched at the constant push and pull of the bus. Luckily, we were almost at the other end of the bridge, and I couldn't wait to get off, even if it meant diving into a pile of snow.

"Sorry about that, folks," the driver shouted from the front.

The woman in the fur coat popped up from her seat and chased after the water bottle as it rolled past the middle accordion section of the bus and toward the back. The bus's tires slipped again, making her stumble. She yelped, desperately reaching for something to hold onto. The woman caught Caleb's eye, and he crossed the accordion, holding out his arm to help her stay steady.

I stayed put in the front half of the bus, glued to the pole I held onto. Afraid I'd puke if I took a step in either direction.

The woman's boyfriend stayed in his seat but watched over his shoulder. I glanced toward Caleb again, but my eyes caught the passenger sitting at the back of the bus. Long, stringy, black hair dangled from the darkness under his hood, but the passing lights of the bridge revealed his scarred-up face.

Jasper, that Russian guy's goon. "Caleb!" I yelled. Suddenly, everyone's eyes were on me.

Jasper gripped the seat in front of him and slowly stood.

The bus tires lost traction again, and the back half of the bus swayed left and right, setting everyone off balance. The woman screamed, and her boyfriend stood, trying to stay upright. The force tossed Jasper into an empty seat while Caleb held onto a pole and cradled the woman.

The bus tires screeched, sounding like a demon rising from the snow. The driver floored the brake, but the traction couldn't catch. We were already on the decline into Brooklyn.

I wrapped my arms around the pole, held on as tightly as possible, and glanced at the front of the bus. We swerved left, then hard swerved right, but the bus picked up speed. The left side tires levitated for a moment, making everyone scream.

"HOLD ON TO SOMETHING!" the driver yelled. The bus violently veered to the left, hurdling me into the empty seats. I sat up just in time to see what was coming. The front of the bus smashed through the bridge's guardrail and nose-dived over the edge. The rail splintered and the metal scraped the sides of the bus, sounding like a million nails scratching a chalkboard. For a moment, there was no gravity. My stomach dropped like a trap door as the force lifted me out of the seats. I screamed as gravity took hold again. My forehead smacked a metal pole, and everything went black.

———

Even in the darkness, I felt like I was floating, as if my insides were made of helium. Maybe that was what death felt like: light and free. I was still aware of my thoughts, though. To my surprise, I wasn't panicking. I was just being. I was nowhere with no time limit or care. But then, a muffled sound pushed through the emptiness. I tried to focus on it, but it sounded so far away. A sliver of light poked through like a needle in a cushion, giving more weight to the sound. I became more aware of my breath. The noise got louder—a voice. Someone was yelling. I felt my heartbeat. It was slow at first but picked up speed. The light brightened. The voice got louder. It was Caleb calling my name.

My eyes opened, and I took a huge breath.

"Don't move!" Caleb yelled.

I rubbed my wet forehead. "What happened?" I wiped my hand on my coat and tried to sit up again, but I was seeing through clouds. I blinked and rubbed my eyes.

"Sit up very slowly," Caleb shouted.

Why does it sound like he's shouting from the sky?

A woman shouted from the sky, too. "No! Travis! Oh god!" Her screams mixed with cries.

"Okay, okay," I mumbled, propping up on my elbows. I blinked again and focused on my reflection in the bus window. A gasp hitched in my throat. I gently touched my forehead and winced. A throbbing pulsed from the gash at my hairline. Blood trickled down the left side of my face.

I looked between my legs. I had landed on the back of a set of seats. I peeked over the edge, and my heart plummeted to the deepest part of my stomach. The bus lightly swayed as it hung off the edge of the Brooklyn Bridge, thirty feet above a construction site. As soon as I realized we were still in the air, I clenched my eyes, preparing to hit the ground at any second, but the crash never came.

"Landon," Caleb called. "Are you okay?"

I gripped the edge of the seat, poked my head into the aisle, and looked up. The splintered metal from the guardrail had ripped through the accordion material and suspended the bus. Caleb looked down over the edge. He was still at the back half of the bus, which I assumed still had all its tires on the ground.

"I'm okay, I think!" I shouted up at him. The memory of Jasper's scarred face ripped through my mind. "Jasper!"

Caleb pointed down the aisle. "Look."

The bus's right-side windshield was smashed. I rubbed the moisture from my eyes before squinting. My jaw clenched, seeing Jasper's mangled body. He had fallen onto the bed of a truck, skewered by several PVC pipes. Unfortunately, the driver and the woman's boyfriend suffered the same fate. My stomach lurched, and I puked a burning spurt of bile that slid down the floor.

The bus jolted, slamming my heart against my ribcage, and a collective scream echoed through the bus.

"Landon, you have to climb. The bus is too heavy. It's ripping up here!"

"Fuck, fuck, fuck," I whispered.

Caleb dropped to his stomach and hung his arms over the edge of the splitting bus. "Landon, listen to me."

"I'm coming up," I yelled to him.

"No, wait!" He shouted. "The kid."

My brow furrowed, sending a bolt of pain through my skull. "What?"

He pointed down the aisle again. "I think he's scared. I can't give the bus more weight. You have to get him."

I looked down the nose of the bus, and my chest tightened. The kid in the puffy jacket sat on the back of a seat with his arms and legs wrapped around a pole.

Jesus Christ. "Okay," I said. My mind told my hands to move, but they weren't following orders.

"Just go slow, okay?" Caleb said calmly from above.

"Okay." I closed my eyes and breathed, slowly letting it out through pursed lips. I pushed myself up and slowly stood, finding my balance like a tightrope. There wasn't much space between the pairs of seats. I wiped my bloody hands on my coat before gripping the pole above me. I shuffled to the edge of the seats. One slip and I would have fallen straight down through the broken windshield.

I crouched, letting one leg hang off the edge, and slowly reached until I connected with the seats below me. "I'm coming," I said to the boy as I slowly descended the ladder of seats. When I leaned into the seats above the boy, his lips quivered. "What's your name?" I asked.

His eyes locked on me. "I'm scared."

"It's gonna be okay," I said, desperate to reassure him. "What's your name?"

He hesitated. "A... Aidan."

He looked so much younger than I thought he was. His hair was blonde and straight. Blood smeared across his cheek from a cut on his lip, and his eyes were bloodshot.

"Nice to meet you, Aidan. I'm Landon."

"La... Landon... I'm scared."

"See that guy up there?" I pointed a thumb over my shoulder. Aidan's eyes shuffled to Caleb, back to me, then nodded. "That's Caleb. He won't let anything happen to us, okay? He's like a super-hero. Do you like superheroes?" Aidan nodded. "Yeah? Who's your favorite?"

"Adam... Sh... Shock."

I smiled. "He's my favorite too." Aidan's breathing slowed. "Caleb is just like Adam Shock. He's gonna help you get off this bus. All you gotta do is climb, okay?"

Aidan shook his head. "I can't."

"Listen, I know you're scared. I am, too. But this bus could fall at any second, okay? We have to move. We need to get you back to your family. You want to see them, right?" Aidan nodded furiously. "They're probably wondering where you are right now, huh?" Aidan nodded again. "Let's get you home then," I whispered before forcing a smile. "Just reach up and grab the pole."

"Okay," Aidan said through gritted teeth. He loosened one hand's grip and reached for me. I caught his hand in mine and balanced Aidan as he stood.

"Now stand on that pole, and—"

Aidan's shoe squeaked, and his right foot slid out from under him. "Landon!"

I squeezed Aidan's wrist and his weight pulled me forward. My slick coat glided against the smooth plastic seats. My shoulder crashed against the pole, stopping our impending fall, and Aidan's weight graded the muscles in my shoulder. I screamed as the pain shot down the left side of my body.

Aidan held my wrist with his other hand, pulling my arm further.

"Aidan, grab the pole!"

"I'm scared!" He screamed.

My arm was a pendulum, shooting fire to my shoulder. "It's okay, just grab it!"

Aidan let go of my wrist and clamped onto the pole beside him.

"Now, put your foot on the seat," I said between breaths. "Slowly, okay?"

Aidan followed my directions, and I was able to let go. I pushed off the pole and turned to lay on my back, rubbing the burn from my muscles.

"You guys have to climb!" Caleb shouted.

I stared at the seat above me. "Aidan, you go first. I'll be right behind you." I needed to catch my breath. Aidan climbed by my row of seats and continued up the ladder.

"Landon?" Caleb shouted.

"I'm okay!" I called back with a cough. I rolled to my stomach and slowly pushed myself up. Pieces of glass twisted into my palms. Every breath reminded me of the metal taste on my tongue. I ducked into the aisle and reached for the pole above me.

Caleb's voice shot down the aisle and out the broken window. "Landon, it's ripping up here! You have to move!"

I reached for the next pole just as Caleb hoisted Aidan to safety. I was almost in the middle of the bus when I heard the accordion tear. The bus jerked. I screamed and tightened my grip. The pole under my foot was wet from my blood. One of the lights blew out, raining sparks on me.

"Don't let go!" Caleb cried out. "You're almost there!"

My foot finally found a dry spot to steady myself. I climbed two more rows. Caleb was on his stomach, still hanging his arms over the edge of the cracked floor. I could stand upright on the back of the last pair of seats, but the accordion had torn so much that I couldn't reach Caleb. He desperately swatted at my fingertips.

"You have to jump!" Caleb shouted.

"What?"

"You have to jump, Landon!"

I glanced at the accordion. The metal shards from the guardrail were pointed and sharp. The material wasn't going to hold for much longer. I could feel the blood pulsing through the veins in my neck. It was now or never.

The bus shook again, and the floor snapped and splintered deeper.

Caleb's eyes widened. "JUMP!"

I held my breath and crouched, using every muscle in my legs to launch me in the air. Caleb's palms slapped against my forearms and gripped me so tightly that I thought my bones would break.

The floor cracked like thunder, the accordion tore, then snapped like an overstretched rubber band, letting the front of the bus go. The wind rushed by, almost sucking me down with it, but Caleb held tight. It was hard to hear my own scream over the crunching metal destroying the construction site below.

Caleb lifted me enough to grab onto the edge of the splintered floor. He scooped me to my feet, pulled one arm over his shoulder, and led us through the side door. My knees gave out as soon as we touched the pavement. I crumbled, but Caleb led me down gently.

Aidan wrapped his arms around me from behind and squeezed. "Thank you," he mumbled between tears. "Thank you so much."

I nodded and watched him disappear into the accumulating crowd as sirens wailed in the distance.

Caleb crouched in front of me and held my face. "Are you okay?" Blood dripped from a small gash on his chin. "Landon? Talk to me."

My head floated, but I blinked at him. "That was just like—"

"Are you—"

"That scene from Jurassic Park 2, where—"

"Landon, I know the scene. Are—"

"The trailer is hanging off the cliff and—"

Caleb's lips met mine, and it felt like I'd been rebooted for the first time in decades. My bloody hands wrapped around the back of his neck, and I leaned into his kiss. Suddenly, things didn't hurt as badly.

Caleb cupped my face. "I told you not to do anything crazy," Caleb whispered.

"I'm sorry."

"I love you," Caleb said.

At first, I wasn't sure I heard him right. The ringing in my ears was too intense. But the more I focused on his eyes, the quieter everything got.

Caleb's voice was low and shaky. "I swear I'm done being stubborn. I'm done not communicating. I'm done missing you. My world is nothing without you in it, okay? I love you so fucking much."

A fire lit in my stomach as I held his wrists. "I love you more."

Caleb kissed me again as the red and blue lights approached.

TWENTY TWO

I sat on a skinny, uncomfortable bed behind a blue curtain. An ambulance brought us to the Brooklyn Hospital Center. Caleb used my phone to call Isaac while we were in the ambulance.

The nurses cleaned us up pretty quickly. Caleb got five stitches in his chin, and I got double that on my forehead.

Caleb stood between my legs. His thumb grazed the bandage on my forehead. "Does it hurt?"

"Not really. I think the meds are working."

Caleb's hands moved down my arms and around my waist. "They said they'd give us something to take home before we left. Or maybe Isaac can heal us with one of his crystals."

"Be nice." I cupped Caleb's chin and grazed his bandage. "Does *this* hurt?"

"It might if you keep touching it." I let my hand fall to his shoulder. "I don't love the idea of another scar on my face."

I wrapped my arms around his neck and pulled him closer. "The more scars, the better."

Caleb gave a crooked smile before kissing me.

The curtain pulled, screeching against its metal rod. Isaac stood there with his coat unzipped. A black scarf hung from around his neck. Josh flanked him and waved before Isaac rushed in, pulling Caleb and me into a hug. "Oh my God, are you guys okay? I was so worried." He studied our bandages. "What did the doctors say?"

Josh stepped in and closed the curtain.

"We're okay," I said. My hands were occupied, one interlocked with Caleb's and the other now in Isaac's grip. "Slight concussion—major exhaustion. I just wanna sleep."

Josh stepped closer. "No serious damage?"

"We got lucky," Caleb said, gently squeezing my hand.

My ear suddenly caught a familiar voice on the other side of the curtain. "I need to find my friend. He was in that bus crash on the bridge."

My eyes shot to Caleb. "Did you text Lauren?"

"Maybe."

The curtain rings scraped the pole so harshly that it made my wound sting. Lauren pushed by Josh, squeezed between me and Isaac —separating us—and hugged me. "Thank God," she said in my ear. She squeezed me so tight that it was hard to breathe.

"I'm okay," I said.

Lauren hugged Caleb, then examined his chin. "You're not okay. You were just in a serious accident. Who would be okay after that?"

Jasper's impaled flesh flickered in my mind. "I just need to rest. We both do."

Lauren's words flew at me like a jet. "We'll get you to your dorm. I'll get you some soup. I have to go to class tomorrow, but Steven said he can get on a plane. Tasha said she might be able to get out of class, but—"

I touched her arm. "Lauren, relax."

"I'm sorry, I was worried when I hadn't heard from you, and—"

"I know. I'm sorry. A lots been going on."

"Well, you need to fill me in. First, I see you kissing a celebrity online, then you tell me Caleb's back and then go awol? What is going on?"

Isaac cleared his throat, and Lauren whipped around to him and Josh.

"Oh," Lauren said. "Hi, sorry. Didn't realize you were—um. Hi. I'm Lauren."

Isaac held out his hand. "I'm—"

"I know," Lauren said, rapidly shaking Isaac's hand. She suddenly went quiet but kept shaking his hand, staring.

I leaned to look at her. "Lauren?"

She quickly let go of Isaac's hand.

Josh stayed close to the curtain. "I'm just the roommate. Not a celebrity."

"That's Josh," I said.

"Nice to finally meet you, Josh," Lauren said.

Josh's eyes hit the ground, and his hands jutted into his pockets. Was he blushing? "You too."

"You didn't have to come all this way," I told Lauren.

She turned to me and crossed her arms. "Are you kidding me? You almost died!"

I looked between her and Caleb. "Neither of you called my dad, right?"

"I should've," Lauren said.

"I don't need him freaking out," I said.

Lauren's forehead creased. "Landon, that's not okay. Your dad needs to know what's going on."

"He will," I said. "Just not yet."

"He's gonna start to catch on when he doesn't hear from you," Caleb said.

"Can we just get home first?"

Lauren parted the curtain and looked around. "I'll find a nurse. Be right back."

Isaac approached Caleb and me on the bed. "You guys can use my place for as long as you need." Isaac glanced over his shoulder. "You too, Josh."

"Thank you," Caleb said.

Isaac leaned on the bed next to me. "Thank god you guys are okay. I knew I should've paid for the car."

Caleb glanced at Isaac. "None of us thought this would happen."

Isaac sighed. "I'm just glad it's over."

I stared at the floor. "I don't think it is."

Isaac eyed me. "Huh?"

"Jasper was on the bus before it crashed," I said.

"What? How?" Isaac asked.

I glanced through the curtain to make sure Lauren wasn't close by. "I don't know. But I don't think it was a coincidence."

"Where is he now?" Josh asked.

Caleb stood and rolled his shoulders. "He didn't make it."

I nodded. "I'll never be able to unsee it."

Caleb wrapped his arm around me and gently rubbed my shoulder.

The curtain swiped, and the nurse who cleaned the blood from my face appeared with Lauren. She looked at Caleb and me. "Your discharge is ready." The nurse pointed a thumb over her shoulder. "Just sign them at the front desk, and you're good to go."

"Thanks," I said, hopping off the bed to put on my coat.

A woman with glasses at the bridge of her nose handed me a clipboard from behind the desk. "Just sign here and here." She looked up at Caleb. "And here's yours."

"How much is the bill?" Caleb asked.

"We'll send it to your address," she said.

A flash went off in my peripheral just as I signed the paper. A dozen people with cameras had gathered outside the glass doors, bobbing and weaving to get a look inside.

"Shit," Isaac said, flipping his hood up.

I shook my head, signed the paper, and returned the clipboard to the woman. "Is there another exit?"

"Yes." She pointed. "Go down this hall, take the first left, pass the rec room, and exit into the staff parking lot."

I nodded. "Thanks."

Lauren led the charge down the hall, and we followed.

Caleb lingered before turning the corner, adjusting his tattered backpack over his shoulder. He held his hand out for me to take before leading us around the corner. I could see the glass door at the end of the hall—no cameras on the other side. We passed the rec room door when Caleb stopped cold. The others were already at the exit, waiting.

I turned over my shoulder. "Caleb?"

He let go of my hand. "I thought I just—" He backed up and peeked through the rec room door before pushing inside.

I glanced at the others before jogging after him. I pushed through the door to find Caleb staring at a group of people putting on their coats and folding metal chairs. A man picked through the remaining donuts at a small table. His salt and pepper hair was slicked back, and his goatee was thick. Everyone exited, leaving Caleb and me alone with the man.

"Sorry guys, we just ended for the night. There's another meeting—"

"James Montes?" Caleb asked, stepping forward.

The man spun toward us and frantically looked around the room before moving closer. His sticker name tag said, Hello, My Name Is Tommy. "Where did you hear that name?"

Caleb stood as still as a statue. "When I heard your voice, I—"

"Who are you?" Tommy asked as his eyes darted around the room before settling on us.

"I knew it was you," Caleb whispered.

Tommy squinted. "Caleb?"

That's all the confirmation we needed. My heartbeat quickened.

"Glad to know you're still alive," Caleb said flatly.

Tommy rushed past us and stood at the entrance. "Did anyone follow you here?"

Caleb spun to look at him. "What?"

Tommy poked his head out the door. "You can't be here." He paced by us again and collected his things at the small table, knocking the box of doughnuts to the floor.

Caleb watched the man. "What are you talking about?"

"We can't do this here," Tommy said, zipping up his hoodie. He fished through his pockets until he found a flip phone. He hurried toward us and held it in front of Caleb. "Put your number in. I'll text you an address."

Caleb was a brick wall, unmoveable, staring at Tommy with a stern glare.

I took the phone and typed my number out.

Tommy snatched the phone back. "Go. We'll talk soon." He pushed the phone in his pocket and bolted out the door.

I put a hand on Caleb's arm, and he frowned. "Fucking typical," he said.

"Guys?" Isaac's voice called from behind us. He opened the door, and Josh and Lauren followed him into the rec room.

"We found him," I said.

Lauren's brow furrowed. "Who?"

"We went through hell to find him, and he can't even give his own son a fucking second to talk?" Caleb asked.

"You found him?" Josh asked.

"Holy shit!" Isaac exclaimed, bouncing on the balls of his feet. "What happened? Where is he?"

"Something's weird," I said.

"What do you mean?" Isaac asked.

"He was caught off guard, I think." I looked at Caleb and then back to our friends. "Said we couldn't do this here. He took my number to text us an address."

"Yeah, I don't know," Lauren said. "This sounds sketchy. Are you sure it was him?"

"I'm sure," Caleb growled.

My phone buzzed. "Guys." I slipped it out and stared at the screen. It was a text from an unknown number. "I live above the shoe repair shop at 30 Irving Place. Apartment 6D. Meet me there in an hour."

"That's near Union Square," Isaac said.

Josh looked at him. "Meaning he's been in our backyard this whole time."

"Of course he has," Caleb scoffed and started for the door. "You guys can go home. I'm gonna end this."

"You shouldn't go alone," Lauren said, following Caleb into the hall.

Isaac was the last one out. "I'm sure Tommy doesn't want all of us showing up at his doorstep."

"Isaac, take Landon home to rest. Please." Caleb's eyes pierced me. "I'll be fine. Everything's okay."

"No. We're not splitting up." I said.

"You need to go home to—"

"I feel fine, Caleb."

"I can do this on my own. Everything's okay," Caleb said.

"Stop saying everything's okay!" The air went still. The chirping of a heart monitor echoed. "Nothing is okay unless I know you're alive." My voice quivered. "I'm going with you."

Caleb's jaw tensed, and his eyes glistened. "Okay."

Isaac pulled out his phone. "I'll get us a car back," he said softly.

I hooked Lauren's arm on our way out. "I'll catch you up on the ride back."

———

Caleb and I stood outside 30 Irving Place, looking up the side of the building. I wondered how many times I could've walked by since moving to the city.

"How are you feeling?" I asked.

"Tired," Caleb said. "I just want answers. That's all I need for things to be simple again."

The fog from my mouth evaporated around my chilled face. I pushed the 6D button on the intercom nestled into the brick. Static called back at us.

"Is it broken?" I wondered.

Caleb pulled the handle, and the door opened with ease. "Must be."

The lobby was modest. No doorman, just a short hallway with mirrors on either side that led us to an elevator, and a door labeled 'STAIRS' in white letters.

As we ascended in the elevator, I couldn't stop thinking about how ready I was to go back to the simple life. I was ready to go back to class, to write silly stories that would never see the light of day.

The elevator opened to a skinny hallway, and I silently prayed for no more hoops to jump through. A citrus plugin cleansed the air. The beige carpet had a spring to it. I followed closely behind Caleb. 6D was the last door on the left.

Caleb gripped his backpack and stared at the door.

"You go this," I said.

Caleb nodded, took a breath, and knocked three times.

A shadow scurried around the bottom of the door. "Unzip your coats." Tommy's voice was muffled behind the door. "Show your waistbands." Caleb and I shared a look. "Hurry up!" Tommy said through the door.

We unzipped our coats and lifted our shirts. The bolt clicked, and a chain clacked against the wood. The door cracked open, and a bulging eye surveyed us. "Did anyone follow you?"

"No," I said. "We're alone."

The door swung open, and Tommy frantically gestured for us to come in. The apartment looked like a dorm room. Just big enough to fit a twin-sized bed, a desk, and a tall wardrobe in the corner. The room had no kitchen, just a single sink under the one small window. Tommy swung into the hall, checked left and right, then slammed the door. The long strands previously slicked back fell in front of his face in a messy clump. He pushed it back with his hand, but some strands refused to stay put. "Caleb," Tommy said, pointing at me. "Do you trust him?"

Caleb's brow furrowed. "With my life."

Tommy nodded. "Good. Okay. Good." His hands hugged his hips. "God, you've grown. Sorry, I don't have much room. You guys can sit on the bed if you want."

Caleb let his bag drop to the floor at the foot of the bed frame. "No thanks."

Tommy scratched his goatee. "You want water or anything? I only have one cup, so—"

"We're fine," Caleb said.

I leaned around Caleb. "I'm Landon, by the way. Caleb's—"

"Boyfriend," Caleb said.

The word almost knocked me out cold.

"Nice to meet you," Tommy said as he pulled the chair from his desk. "I'm—"

"We know," Caleb said flatly.

Tommy sat, leaned on his knees, and looked at Caleb. "You look banged up, kid. I thought I taught you to keep your hands up." Tommy chuckled lightly.

My forehead pulsed on cue. The numbing shot was wearing off.

Caleb squeezed the bridge of his nose. "Look, can we skip the small talk? Maybe jump to the reason why you abandoned your family?"

Tommy sighed. "It's not that simple, kid." His eyes flickered to me. His lips parted, but he didn't say anything.

I felt the tension rising. "I can leave you two alone if—"

Caleb tugged my shirt, forcing me to sit on the bed. "You're right. Nothing's been simple since you left," he said to Tommy. "I woke up that morning, and you were gone. No goodbye, no fucking note. Nothing but an empty closet."

Tommy leaned back in his chair. "That wasn't my intention. I didn't know—"

"What didn't you know?" Caleb's tone was sharp enough to cut glass. "I could fill an entire book with the shit you don't know."

I reached for Caleb's hand. "Hey—"

"No, he needs to hear this. Mom found out she was pregnant after you left. Did you know you have another son? His name's Parker, and he's the coolest, most loyal little kid on the planet. But you'd know that if you didn't leave us with a shitty person who cared more about getting high than making sure we were fed. So I stepped up and raised him to be nothing like our fucking parents."

Tommy's eyes hit the floor. "I'm sorry. If I'd—"

"I looked for you every fucking time I stepped outside. Every day,

I hoped you'd come back and save us from the hell my mom turned our lives into."

"Things got complicated," Tommy said.

Caleb stared with a furrowed brow. "What does that even mean?"

Tommy stood and hurried to the sink, grabbing his one plastic cup and filling it with water. He chugged it, wiped his mouth, and faced us. "I lived a double life for a long time."

Caleb and I glanced at each other.

"I was deep undercover when I met your mom," Tommy said.

"Undercover?" Caleb asked. "What, like, you're a cop?"

Tommy shook his head. "Not anymore."

"What're you saying?" Caleb asked.

I started to feel more and more uncomfortable, like I was a fly on the wall hearing things I shouldn't have been allowed to hear.

"I was in Narco," Tommy said. "I was given a new name and planted in Texas to get close to a few guys linked to the Russian Mafia."

Caleb laughed him off. "Russian Mafia in Texas? Is this a joke?"

"It was suspected that the Russians were running an underground drug ring linked to human trafficking. But we needed proof. It was my job to get in tight with them and report back. It was supposed to be in and out, but it took me years to get them to trust me enough to let me in the door."

Caleb scratched his head. His fake smile faded. "This isn't true." Caleb looked at me. "He was a mechanic my whole life."

"That was the part I had to play, kid," Tommy said.

Caleb shook his head. "No, this can't be true. Why would you meet someone and start a family?"

"That wasn't really part of the plan."

"So we were a mistake?"

Tommy sat in the desk chair again and leaned closer to Caleb. "No. You have to understand your mom didn't even know I was undercover. I didn't leave the house most nights until you were asleep. I loved you both so—"

Caleb huffed. "Then why the fuck did you leave?"

"I had no choice, damn it! The Russians were getting too suspicious. It was getting too hard to keep my two lives separate. It was only a matter of time before the Russians found where I lived and killed you in your fucking sleep." Tommy pressed his fingers against his leg, cracking his knuckles. "So I chose to save your goddamn life."

Caleb seemed to stop breathing.

"If they found you... I knew too much. You name it, and the Russian Mafia had their grimy fingers in it. And those scumbags left me undercover to rot. They never had enough evidence. They always wanted more. That bullshit went on for years."

It was almost too much to comprehend. Too far fetched. The man was obviously manic, but I wasn't sure if that meant he couldn't be trusted.

Caleb closed his eyes for a beat. "If you were undercover, why didn't the cops help us when you left?"

Tommy nodded. "No one knew about my family. Not even the feds."

"How is that possible?"

"I was good at keeping secrets until I started drinking."

"What are you talking about? We had a life. A house. I played with other kids on our street."

"We blended in. No one knew anything. But it wasn't part of the plan. I wasn't supposed to have a family," Tommy said.

"Jesus Christ. Is James Montes even your real name?"

Tommy sighed, and his eyes darted around the room. "No."

Caleb slowly sat next to me on the bed, staring forward. "My whole life has been a lie?"

Tommy sat up straight. "You're still my son. And I made sure you were legally documented."

Caleb's eyes shot to his father. "It doesn't matter! My name is made up, I... I have no lineage. My last name was probably picked from a fucking hat."

"Caleb, I didn't want to leave—"

"I don't believe you."

"You found the key, didn't you? That's how you're here?" Caleb's brow creased as Tommy continued. "It was the only thing I could think of. I didn't know if you'd catch on, but I hoped I'd have something in the box waiting for you by the time you did. For both of you."

I raised my hand. "I'm sorry. But I'm trying to fill in some gaps here. You had the deposit box but nothing in it?"

Tommy nodded. "I had it for emergencies. I didn't fill it until I had no other choice."

"But I was a kid. What if I didn't find the key?" Caleb asked.

"That was the only risk I could take."

Caleb stared at the floor. "You left your family for the Russian Mafia." Caleb shook his head. "This is ridiculous." He looked at Tommy. "Do you realize how ridiculous this sounds? Where's the proof? Huh?"

"You have it," Tommy said.

I cocked my head.

"Where the fuck did they take you? Huh?" Caleb asked.

Tommy slumped in the desk chair and crossed his arms. "I told you, they were in Texas. I was always nearby."

Caleb shrugged. "What does that mean?"

"I found you when I could." Tommy wiped a hand down his goatee. "I was able to watch from afar sometimes. But it killed me."

Caleb stood and paced in front of the bathroom door. "No fucking way."

Tommy watched his son. "Seeing you search for me—" his voice cut out. He stood and stepped closer to Caleb, attempting to touch his shoulder. Caleb avoided Tommy's advance with a step backward. Tommy sighed, and his brow wrinkled. "That was the worst pain I'd ever felt."

"No," Caleb said.

"The only way to cope was a bottle of Vodka every night." Tommy's voice quivered.

"You're lying!"

"Parker has red hair! How would I know that? Huh?" Tommy said.

Caleb stopped pacing and stared with wide eyes.

"I tried coming around more after he was born, but it was hard, Caleb. They were watching my every move."

"You watched everything our mom put us through and did nothing?" Caleb's voice trembled. "How could you let that happen?"

Tommy rubbed his forehead. "I didn't have a choice."

Caleb's lips curled around his teeth, and he nodded. "Right, 'cause we didn't exist."

"Everything I did was for you," Tommy said softly.

"More bullshit," Caleb said.

"Do you have the key?" Tommy asked.

Caleb stepped to the foot of the bed and reached for his backpack. "I'm done here. I got everything I needed. Let's go, Landon."

I stood.

"I have to give you something," Tommy said.

I met Caleb at the door.

"I don't want anything from you," Caleb said.

Tommy moved to the large wardrobe.

Caleb opened the door leading into the hall.

"Please, I need you to have it," Tommy said.

Caleb slammed the door shut again. "I needed to know my dad was still fucking ALIVE! I needed to know you still fucking cared."

Tommy sighed. "I did."

"Then why did you leave Texas? Why are you here?"

"Do you have the key?" Tommy asked slower.

Caleb stepped forward. "Answer me."

Tommy's jaw tightened. "My drinking got really bad."

"And?"

"And I made a mistake."

"What kind of mistake?" Caleb asked.

"One you can't come back from." Tommy rolled his eyes. "Son, I don't want to rehash this. Do you have—"

Caleb's arms slapped his legs. "Who cares about a fucking key!"

I placed a hand on Caleb's shoulder, nervous his shouting would attract neighboring attention. "Caleb, calm down."

"No," Caleb said flatly. "After what he's put us through, I want answers."

Caleb's skin was hot as lava.

"What did you do? Why did you leave?" Caleb demanded.

Tommy chewed his lip. "I got too drunk. And…" He took a breath. "I followed you one night when you were in high school."

Caleb's shoulders relaxed, and his arm hung limp.

"I was two bottles deep. I could barely see the road." Tommy's voice cracked. "Those back roads by the lake… They get so foggy at night."

"No," Caleb whispered so softly I barely caught it.

"I thought it was a deer." Tommy wiped his eyes. "I didn't see the bike til I got out to check."

Caleb covered his mouth with his hand and slowly shook his head. Tears formed in his eyes.

Tommy continued. "I panicked. The only thing I knew how to do was hide."

Caleb whimpered behind his hand.

"I took the Russian's money, and I ran." Tommy leaned against the wardrobe, letting more hair fall into his face. "I knew I couldn't risk seeing you again. Sending items to my deposit box was the only way I thought I could fix things."

Caleb's hand fell from his face. "What color was the bike?"

Tommy's brow creased. "What? What does that matter?"

"I need to know," Caleb said through gritted teeth.

Tommy's mouth fell agape as he focused. "I—Yeah. It was silv—"

Caleb let out the most visceral scream I had ever heard, shocking my entire system. Before I could even blink, Caleb turned into a blur of color. My brain couldn't register what was happening fast enough. But everything came back into focus just as I heard the crack of Caleb's fist against his father's jaw.

The force of Caleb's punch sent his father against the wall. Caleb's backpack hit the floor with a hard thud. He pounced again, able to connect another hook to Tommy's chin.

Tommy screamed and pushed his son with desperate force. Caleb slammed into me, and I wrapped my arms around his chest before he could attack again. His rage was his fuel. Caleb stepped forward, dragging me with him. He shoved his dad into the corner and took fist fulls of his shirt. The only way to prevent another punch was to let go of Caleb's waist and wedge myself between them.

I pushed my hands to his chest. "Stop!" It was like looking into the eye of a volcano.

"He killed Andy!" Caleb's face was drenched in sweat and tears.

Tommy wiped the blood from his lip. "What? You knew him?"

"He was my first boyfriend, you fucking prick!" Caleb sniffled and leaned all his weight against me. My arms folded, and Caleb's head dropped onto my shoulder. I struggled to keep him upright as he sobbed. "He... killed Andy," Caleb cried into my chest, heaving between each word.

Tommy hobbled to the sink and splashed water on his face.

Caleb lunged, but I kept my whole body against him. His eyes narrowed. "We were supposed to meet at Rocky Lake Park that night. I saw his bike in the street. I saw the blood and—" He took a breath and wiped his nose with his sleeve. "I never should've looked for you," Caleb sneered. "I hope you fucking *rot*." Goosebumps tickled my arm as Caleb brushed by. He opened the front door and walked out.

I stared at Tommy as a pit formed in my stomach, wishing Caleb had gotten different answers. I stepped out into the hall without a goodbye.

TWENTY THREE

Caleb paced as we waited for the elevator. "Fuck this." He pushed open the stairwell exit. I followed close behind until we reached the sidewalk. Caleb jogged through the parked cars and across the street.

"Caleb, wait up!"

Caleb paced, wiping away the moisture from his cheeks. "That mother fucker! How could someone hit a kid and just go on with life as if nothing fucking happened?" He let out another sob.

I pulled him into me, wrapping my arms around his waist. I rubbed his back as people passed us on the sidewalk. Caleb's tear-stained cheeks shone under the streetlights. I dried his face with my thumbs. "What should we do?"

"I need to call Andy's mom," Caleb said.

"Okay."

"She deserves to know the truth," Caleb said between sniffles. "I need to go back up there." He started for the street, but I grabbed him by the elbow. "He should be the one to have to tell Andy's mom."

"So, what, you're gonna force him?" I asked.

"I'll do whatever I have to."

"Maybe we should just call the police."

Caleb yanked his arm out of my grip. "Why would New York cops care about a Texas kid who was killed years ago?" I tried to form a sentence, but my brain had nothing in the tank. "Exactly."

"I just don't want you getting in trouble again."

Caleb sighed and glanced up at Tommy's building. "I forgot my bag." He looked at me. "I need to go back up anyway."

"Fine. But I'm not gonna let you beat the shit out of him."

"He deserves a lot worse. C'mon." Caleb shimmied through the parked cars, crossed the street, and entered Tommy's building again.

My heart pounded. I was worried what Caleb might do and if I could stop him if things got out of hand. Caleb took long strides from the elevator. Tommy's door was still cracked when I caught up.

Caleb pushed the door with his fingertips, and our eyes discovered Tommy at the same time. Caleb quickly covered my mouth before I could scream.

Tommy was face down in a pool of blood next to his bed. His limbs splayed in different directions. Chunks of pink and red matted his hair. My stomach flipped, and I gagged into Caleb's hand.

The sink spat on in the bathroom. Tommy's murderer grunted behind the door. Caleb poked his chin toward the elevator, lowered his hand, and mouthed "slowly." He took me by the hand.

Did the neighbors not hear anything? A struggle? A gunshot?

"Stop," Caleb whispered. "Do you hear that?"

A man's voice echoed in the stairwell, getting louder and speaking Russian.

Caleb stepped back, bumping into me. The stairwell handle jiggled before Caleb spun and shoved me back toward the apartment. "Go, go!" he whispered.

I tripped over my foot, stumbling back toward Tommy's door. I peeked around the molding. The bathroom door in his apartment was still shut, so I pulled Caleb in, and he softly closed the door.

I shrugged before mouthing, "Now what?"

Caleb's eyes scanned the tiny room before pointing to the bed. I glanced at the floor. There was enough space underneath for both of us, but I shook my head.

He clenched his jaw and pointed to the floor again. The voice in the hall was getting closer. Caleb swiftly locked the door.

I flattened myself on the floor and shimmied underneath the bed, leaving enough room to my right for Caleb. I pulled myself to the head of the bed, sliding my right cheek against the floor, breathing in the dust bunnies caught on my nose. Caleb's arm crawled up my body as someone pounded on the front door.

Caleb wrapped his left arm around my hip and pulled me closer to him. His breath was warm and rapid against my neck. Caleb's whisper was barely audible. "Do... not... move."

Tommy's dead eyes stared into mine. A perfect circle bored through his forehead, and a single stripe of blood ran down his skin, filling the puddle on the floor.

The front door rattled again before the bathroom door opened. Huge boots stepped over Tommy. The click of the latch was followed by an angry voice spouting in Russian. Two sets of feet walked in, surrounding the body. Two voices spoke back and forth. One sounded younger; the other was deeper.

Tommy's blood hadn't stopped. The puddle grew rapidly, and the flow forked, creating a thin stream closer to my face. I tried to move, but Caleb squeezed my hip, sending pins up my side. I closed my eyes and tucked my lips over my teeth as Tommy's blood pushed against my mouth and down my chin.

The thud of big boots forced my eyes open. Gorilla-like hands reached under Tommy's shoulders, and his corpse was dragged into the bathroom. His limp head streaked red across the floor. My jaw clenched so tightly I thought my teeth would crack.

The other sets of feet followed, and the bathroom door closed behind them. I pictured Tommy's body being tossed into the tub with every clunk that came from behind the door.

Caleb slid out from the bed, latched onto my ankle, and yanked, pulling me out from under the frame. Caleb twisted the knob of the front door just as the bathroom door swung open. Panic dropped into my stomach like a sledgehammer as we met eyes with Victor.

Victor screamed something in Russian as Caleb and I bolted

down the hall and through the stairwell door. Our heels pounded step after step. Caleb's unzipped coat caught the wind like a cape.

The slam of the stairwell door smashing the concrete wall above us rang through my head. I glanced up. The blonde behemoth Mikhail from Victor's apartment barreled down the stairs. His jumps from one landing to the next shook the railings.

"GO! GO!" Caleb yelled.

Sweat poured from my face, streaking Tommy's blood down my neck. I wiped my sleeve over my throat as we shot through the stairwell door into the lobby. We whizzed by the mirrored walls, but Mikhail was close behind. He smashed through the stairwell door, ripping the bottom hinges off the wall.

The frigid wind against my face hardened the streaks of sweat and blood. My shoes slipped on the snowy sidewalk, and my knee caught the concrete before I steadied myself. I chased behind Caleb.

"We need to hide!" Caleb yelled over his shoulder before rounding a corner.

Mikhail busted through the main door and slid into a parked car, setting off its alarm.

I scampered around the corner. "Inside!" I pointed to a small pharmacy storefront.

Caleb pressed himself against the door and pulled. "It's locked!"

I tried the darkened bagel shop next door. Locked. I slapped the glass. "Damn it!"

"There!" Caleb pointed to a roped-off sewer hole missing its cover at the end of the sidewalk. Big lights were set up, pointing down into the opening. A white ConEd truck was parked close by. Wires snaked out from the side of the truck and down into the hole.

Caleb slid to a stop at the end of the sidewalk and glanced around. I bumped into him, using his body to stabilize myself.

Mikhail grunted as he turned the corner, spotting us.

"We can outrun him," I said, pushing Caleb toward the hole in the ground. "Go!"

Caleb ducked under the rope and peeked into the hole. "I don't see anyone."

"Go. I'm right behind you."

Caleb sat, lowered his legs onto the ladder, and found his footing.

A chill shot up my spine as I sat in the wet snow. The metal bars on the way down made my hands numb—once I hit solid ground, I shook them back to life. "Where now?"

Caleb backed against the curved wall. He looked to his right. The power lines from the truck snaked between us. "This way."

We sprinted into unknown territory. I pulled my phone from my pocket and tapped the phone case twice, turning on the flashlight. The path curved to the left, so we followed until it ended. We hopped off the edge into dirty, ankle-deep water.

Caleb grabbed my hand and led the charge into the long stretch of darkness. A gust of air cut through us, bringing a stench like rotting pizza. "Call Josh," Caleb said. "Maybe he can find us a way out."

I nodded. As soon as the phone started ringing, I put it on speaker. "Come on, pick up," I whispered.

"Hey. How'd it go?" Josh's voice echoed through the sewer.

"Josh, are you by your computer?" I asked.

"Always."

"Okay, we need help."

"What'd you say? You're kind of breaking up."

"Shit," Caleb mumbled.

I glanced behind us. No Mikhail, yet. "I said we need help."

"Why do you sound out of breath?" Josh asked.

I sighed. "It's a lot to explain, but Victor's back."

"Who? You're cutting—" Josh's voice glitched. "Hello?"

Caleb's arm blocked me. "We should stop moving."

I pulled the phone closer to my mouth. "Can you hear me?"

"Yeah," Josh said.

"The Russian is back," I said.

"What do you mean back?"

"As in, he's fucking chasing us," Caleb said through his teeth.

"Where are you guys?"

"That's why I called you," I said. "We're underground; we need a way out."

"I'll track your phone to get your location."

"How?" I asked.

"They made us download the 'find your roommate' app at orientation. It's complete bullshit, but the software is decent." I could hear his fingers tapping the keyboard. "Found you." He cleared his throat. "You know you're—" His voice cut out. I stepped forward and raised my arm, hoping for a better signal. "—way, right?"

I put the phone to my face. "What'd you say?"

I could see my breath in the dim light. A chill rushed by, and then another, slowly turning into a current against our backs. I spun to a light in the distance.

Caleb looked at me. "We're on the subway tracks."

The train's horn blared down the tunnel, forcing us to cover our ears.

"RUN!" Caleb screamed.

I shined my light ahead. Caleb and I ran in sync. Soon, the sounds of our stomping shoes bled into the sounds of screeching metal. The train lights barreled closer.

I brought the phone to my ear. "Josh, help!"

"Working on it!" Josh yelled from the other end.

My throat burned. My chest tightened. The side of my stomach started to cramp.

"It's getting closer!" Caleb screamed.

"Okay, okay," Josh said. "Um"

My knees rattled with every crashing gallop. "HURRY UP!"

"A door! Coming up on your left!"

Caleb had a lead on me, but his foot got caught in a deep puddle. His ankle went limp, sending him to the ground, rolling over his shoulder. I tried to stop before smashing into him, but my shoes lost traction once I hit the water. I slid on my hip, feeling the stinging scrapes from pieces of rock and glass. My phone escaped my grip and bounced off the track into the darkness. I hopped to my feet and reached for Caleb. He tried to stand, but his ankle gave out.

I pulled Caleb's arm over my shoulders and stood with a grunt. "C'mon, Josh said there was a door." We hobbled forward. "We have to go faster!"

The train's horn blasted, and screeching brakes pierced my eardrums. I screamed and lifted Caleb as we stepped together. *I'm not letting us die like this.*

My eyes followed the left wall, and I could smell the smoke from the dying sparks shooting off the tracks. The horn shot through my chest, vibrating my bones.

The reflection off the silver door handle caught my attention—the perfect entry to the afterlife. I pulled Caleb over the rail and reached for the handle. I prayed to a God I didn't believe in that it wasn't locked. Then, with my eyes clenched, I tossed my weight against the door.

We toppled into a dimly lit, concrete corridor. Caleb landed on top of me. My palms burned, sliding against the cement, trying to catch us. The train whizzed by the door, pushing through a whirlwind of trash and debris. The cramp in my side flared as I took a breath, making me wince.

Caleb rolled off of me. My palms were stained with blood. I pushed myself to my knees. "Are you okay?" I asked between breaths.

Caleb sat against the wall. "I twisted my ankle." He pulled his pant leg up. His ankle had almost doubled in size.

"Shit," I wiped my sleeve across my forehead.

"You should go."

I tsked. "And let them find you here? Fuck no!"

"I'm only gonna slow—"

"Don't give me that cliched bullshit." I shook my head, getting a painful reminder I had fresh stitches. "I don't care how slow we have to go. I'm not leaving you alone. Especially now that we don't have phones." I stared at him. His eyes were completely bloodshot, and heavy bags formed under them. "Okay?"

He nodded. "Okay."

I helped Caleb to his feet and held his wrist to stabilize him. We started slow but eventually fell into a rhythm. We got to a brown-stained door at the other end of the corridor, and Caleb twisted the handle. I pushed it open with my foot, and two rats ran through our legs.

The room was lit only by the lights behind us. We moved forward, passing two stalls and a sink. I unlocked the door on the opposite wall and pulled it open, bringing much more light into the chilly bathroom.

"Where are we?" Caleb asked.

A man leaned against a metal beam with a black sign and white letters. "Union Square station." I looked left and right. "Where is everyone?"

"Snow's probably keeping everyone inside," Caleb said.

Did he think we were still in Texas? *New York is the city that never sleeps.* "Maybe we can use that guy's phone. Excuse me, sir!"

The man turned over his shoulder.

No fucking way.

Caleb straightened up. "John?"

The stocky bartender waved as we approached. "What the hell happened? You guys okay?"

"No," I said, leaning Caleb against the beam. Seeing John was kind of a relief, like seeing—

My brain stopped everything in my body. I froze with wide eyes. Like a whip, it cracked through my memory. At the bar, John asked if we were with Victor.

A bag was pulled over my face before I could turn and reach for Caleb. I screamed and thrashed until someone cracked me in the jaw. I wobbled. Someone was behind me, keeping the bag tight over my head; its plastic stuck to my mouth with every breath. I gripped and clawed at the person's hands, but eventually, the darkness took me.

TWENTY FOUR

My eyes burned when I woke up. I tried to stand, but my ankles were tied to the chair. A rope dug into my wrists behind my back. I shivered in just a T-shirt and blinked away the gloss. Caleb was tied to a chair to my right. His chin slumped against his chest. A trail of blood ran down his shirt from the stitches in his chin.

We sat in an empty, bricked room. Light shone through the square window at the top of the only door. A plastic sheet hung haphazardly on the wall to my left, stained with streaks of brownish red.

My head throbbed. My pulse pounded in my ears. "Caleb?" I whispered. "Caleb." My eyes hit the door, checking for unwanted attention. I tried to lift my leg, but the rope was too tight. "Caleb, wake up."

I used my whole body to hop myself closer to Caleb. The chair's wooden legs scraped the concrete. I glanced at the door between each hop until I was close enough to bump Caleb with my shoulder.

He groaned and slowly opened his eyes. "Where are we?"

"I don't know."

Caleb thrashed in his seat, but his limbs were tied too tightly to escape.

"Shhh, I don't know where they are."

Caleb looked at me—his chin stained with blood. "Who?"

"Whoever took us."

Caleb's brow wrinkled. "John. That piece of shit, he let this happen."

"I think he's with—"

A bang erupted from outside the room, making us flinch.

"We need to get out of here," Caleb said.

"How?"

"Can you reach my hands?" Caleb asked, leaning into me.

I reached, feeling the rope cut into my skin.

Caleb watched the door as I struggled. "See if you can untie me," he said.

I leaned against Caleb's chair, feeling the rope. It was thick and coarse, but I found a weak point in the knot under his wrists. I wiggled the rope, trying to loosen it, finally making enough space for Caleb to squeeze a hand through.

Caleb bent and unwrapped the rope from his ankles. As soon as he stood, he spun around to untie me. My wrists were red and tattered. He held my face in his hands. "Did they hurt you?"

"I don't think so. You?"

"No. I'm okay."

"I'm scared, Caleb."

He pressed his forehead against mine and closed his eyes. "I'm not gonna let anything happen to you, okay?"

I held his wrists and nodded. My breath was so shallow, scared to breathe too loudly.

Caleb limped to the door. He crept an eye through the small window, then ducked. "Someone's keeping watch," he whispered. Caleb stood with his back against the corner. "Lan, listen. I'm gonna need your help."

"Oh... Okay."

"Get the guy to come inside," he whispered.

"What?" I whispered through gritted teeth.

"Do you trust me?"

I swallowed hard. "Yes."

"Call for him."

My eye lingered on him before my brain started working. I rearranged our chairs, sat in mine, and held my arms behind my back. "Hey, we need help in here!" I shouted.

"Shut up!" A man's voice with a Russian accent called back.

I glanced at Caleb.

"Say something else," Caleb whispered.

I sighed. "I have to go to the bathroom!"

"Piss your pants!" The Russian shouted.

Caleb's hands signaled me to keep talking.

"No, like, I'm gonna be sick!" I shouted. "Please!"

The man mumbled in Russian. His steps skated across the dusty concrete. A face appeared in the square window. He wore a black beanie, and his cheeks were sunken. His eyes were bug-like, bulging from his face. His brow furrowed before the doorknob jiggled, unlocked, and popped ajar. The man pushed his head through. "Where's the other—"

Caleb rammed the door with his shoulder like a defensive lineman protecting his quarterback, sandwiching the man's head in the metal frame, and forcing him to crumble to his knees.

I jumped from my chair as Caleb pushed the man to the floor, closed the door, and stood over him. The guy reached for his head, letting out a groan.

Caleb scooped two fist fulls of the guy's jacket. "Where are we?"

The man looked around the room before focusing on Caleb's face. "Fuck... you."

Caleb grunted and shoved the man back down, forcing his head against the floor and knocking him out. Caleb checked the man's pockets and waistband. "Nothin'." He straightened up and wiped the blood dripping from his stitches. "You okay?" I nodded. Caleb held out a hand. "Let's get outta here."

I latched on tight, and he led us through the door. We were in the middle of an empty hallway; everything was brick and concrete, and most windows were boarded up. Lights flickered. The place looked like a tornado had ripped through it. Even the brick walls crumbled, leaving dust and debris all over the floor. I shivered again as a cold breeze danced across my exposed arms.

We tiptoed to the corner, our backs sliding against the wall. Caleb limped to the edge and peaked around the corner. Caleb's arm crossed my chest, keeping me in place. He held up two fingers, pointed his thumb over his shoulder, and then pointed a finger gun to the sky. The men were armed. My knees trembled.

"Let's try the other way," Caleb whispered. The corridor turned left about fifty feet in the other direction.

A voice called from our room. The man was awake and screaming in Russian. Caleb and I locked eyes before he shoved me forward just as we heard shuffling. I gripped Caleb's hand and bolted, forcing him to keep up.

I whipped around another corner. A slender puddle split the floor where my feet slipped from under me. The concrete smacked my cheek as I slid on my stomach, splashing the murky water in every direction. Caleb caught up and quickly collected me. We sprinted to the first door we saw. It was a copy of the one we had escaped from. He jiggled the handle.

"Try another," I said.

Caleb limped across the hall to the next door. "Locked."

I jogged past him, pulling at his shirt to follow me. "They're coming!"

My shoes squelched with every step. I nearly lost my footing again as I jumped over a broken pallet. I gulped the cold, fishy air. A cramp in my side pulsed.

"Go right!" Caleb shouted.why?"

I turned sharply. I would've thought we were outside if it weren't for the flickering fluorescents. The voices of men gained on us. My heart pounded as my arms pumped hard. A gunshot echoed through the building. I flinched as a large window pane shattered nearby.

"Keep going!" Caleb yelled.

My mind raced as fast as my pulse. *We need to find a way out; then, we'll be okay.*

I pushed through a swinging door and was hit with a wall of frigid air, as I stumbled into a makeshift meat locker. Large chunks of a dead animal hung on hooks around the room. The rotting stench singed my nostrils. My eyes caught a garage door ahead. The reflection of streetlights illuminated the three windows at the top.

My feet came to a halt. "That's it!" I looked over my shoulder but didn't see Caleb behind me. I returned to the swinging door and peered through the small circular window. A bald man tackled Caleb to the floor.

Caleb saw me staring as the man picked him up off the ground, keeping his arms locked behind his back. He struggled in the bald man's grip, trying to escape, but the man outweighed Caleb by a hundred pounds.

"Landon, run!"

I ducked to the side, pressing my back against the concrete wall, and wiped the blood from my lip. My jaw throbbed. I squeezed my eyes shut, and the fear on Caleb's face surfaced in my mind.

"Let me go!" Caleb yelled.

I heard his grunts as he struggled. I crouched under the door's window and peeked through to see two identical-looking men dressed in black surrounding Caleb. One of them punched Caleb in the stomach, sending him to his knees. I crouched again and rubbed my face. I wanted to scream. Instead, I took a deep breath and let it out slowly as my eyes welled.

A familiar Russian accent made my teeth grind. "Come out, red boy!" Victor shouted. I swore I could feel the wall vibrate from his voice.

"He's gone, you piece of shit," Caleb said before getting hit again. Hearing Caleb cough and gasp for air made my blood boil.

I spotted a metal hook stuck into the top of a wooden stool. I stayed crouched and started for it, stepping as quietly as possible.

"Come out now. I won't shoot boyfriend in pretty head."

A gun cocked, and my heart stopped. The hook was still six feet away, but I didn't want to risk anything happening to Caleb. I stepped toward the door and slowly pushed it open, returning to the stark hallway to face Victor and his goons.

"No," Caleb mumbled. "God damn it, I told you to run!"

"Cute," Victor said. He stepped to Caleb and squeezed his cheeks. Caleb grunted and pulled away. "He loves too much to leave behind." Victor laughed to himself. His gun was still cocked, and it dangled in his right hand.

My fingers tremored. I didn't want to move or even breathe too deep, fearing Victor would shoot me any second.

"I not have much fun in long time," Victor said, planting himself next to Caleb and crossing his wrists. His grip tightened on the gun. The bald man let Caleb's arms go but held him by the shoulders, keeping Caleb on his knees. The twins in black flanked the bald man on either side.

"I had fun. You did what I needed. It shame you saw aftermath. We almost let you go, but seeing such gets you—" Victor used his gun to pantomime a slice across his throat, then scratched the side of his head with the tip.

Just behind the group, Mikhail turned the corner and strutted toward us. His barrel chest stopped his arms from hanging close to his torso. John, the bartender, stepped out from behind him, and they joined the cluster.

John's gray hoodie was snug around his stout frame. He licked his lips and smiled at me.

Caleb saw John and tried to stand. "You mother fu—"

The bald man pushed Caleb's shoulders down, keeping him in place.

Victor tousled Caleb's hair. "Just like you, I looked for Tommy for long time. It tough when name change many times."

I looked at John. "So everything you told us at the bar was a lie?"

John grinned. "Mostly."

"You didn't know my dad at all, did you?" Caleb asked. I could see the fire in his eyes from where I stood.

John laughed. "Nope!"

My brow furrowed, and I swallowed hard, fighting back tears. "Was anything you told us true?"

John's eyes searched the ceiling. "I was planted there since Tommy left. He always seemed one step ahead of us till we met you fairies." John's forehead still leaked despite how cold it was in the building. "Anyone who came lookin' for Tommy was sent to Victor. I'm surprised you made it out alive." A sharp, deep laugh erupted from his throat, which made him cough.

"What is wrong with you?" I asked John. "Do you know what he put us through? You sent us to a psychopath!"

John shrugged. "The money was worth it."

Caleb thrashed. "Fuck you!" The bald man shoved him down again, and Caleb winced.

Victor looked at John and smiled. "Loyal man." He stroked the back of Caleb's head as he stared at me.

"You were having us followed," I said. My shoulders tensed, and my hands balled into fists. "That's why Jasper was on the bus."

Victor nodded. "We always close." He shrugged. "Where is Jasper? You know?"

"Dead," I sneered.

Victor smiled, then held his hands up. The gun pointed to the ceiling. "What is they say? Everyone's expendable?"

"Something like that," John chimed in.

Victor glanced down at Caleb. "You and pretty ginger boy did work for us. Led us to Tommy. What I wanted."

"Just so you could kill him?" Caleb struggled under the bald man's grip again. I could see the man's fingers digging into Caleb's shoulders.

Victor kneeled in front of Caleb and tsked three times in his face. "Such angry boy."

"Why?" I asked. "Why did you kill Tommy?"

Victor stayed crouched, looking over his shoulder at me. "He stole from us. Only punishment is death."

Caleb spit, hitting Victor's cheek. Victor's attention shot to Caleb, and he laughed before smacking Caleb with the butt of his gun. The crack echoed down the hall.

I stumbled forward. "Stop!"

Victor stood with a groan, stepped to the side, and wiped his cheek on the sleeve of his black windbreaker. "Americans, disrespectful."

Caleb looked up at him, both nostrils dripping blood. His breath heavied, and the fire in his eyes hadn't subsided.

I wanted to wake up from this nightmare.

Victor turned to me again. "Tommy knew. Knew our faces. We trust him. Then disappear with our money." He looked at Caleb as he paced in front of the group then stopped in front of John. Victor slithered behind the husky bartender and placed his empty hand on John's shoulder. "What was it I said earlier? Everyone's..."

John locked eyes with me, and a Cheshire-like smile took his face. "Expendable."

Victor bit his lip, raised his gun, and squeezed the trigger, sending a bullet through the back of John's head. Blood sprayed across the floor before his body crumbled.

The pop of the gun felt like an explosion. The shock sent me backward into the swinging door, tripping over my foot and landing on my tailbone. The door lightly swung, bumping my back. My eyes met Caleb's, but I could still see John's bloodied head in the corner of my vision.

Victor used a finger to wipe the bit of John's blood from his face. He examined his red finger, then put it in his mouth and sucked it clean. Victor crouched in front of John, examining the blood pooling around him.

"Why?" Caleb asked through clenched teeth.

Victor stood. "To prove point." He gave an eyebrow flick to the bald man, whose hands quickly moved to hold Caleb's head steady. Victor pressed the tip of his gun to the side of Caleb's temple. The hot metal hissed against his skin, making Caleb scream in agony.

I jumped to my knees. "Stop!" Caleb fell forward, catching himself with his hands. Victor stared at me. Wetness brimmed my eyes. "Please. I'm begging you, just let us go. We won't tell anyone anything, I swear."

Victor frowned, then let out a belly laugh. "Who would you tell?" Victor smiled down at me. "The police? Russian dollars keep police quiet. No one to help pretty red boy."

I stood, but my eyes clung to the floor, trying to find the right thing to say that wouldn't set Victor off. "We'll leave!" My wet eyes met Victor's. "You'll never see us in the city again. Ever."

Victor waved a finger at me. "Not fair trade."

I took a step. "Okay, okay. What can we do then?"

"You can't negotiate with a murderer," Caleb grunted.

Victor crouched next to Caleb, grabbed a fist full of hair, and yanked Caleb's head back, forcing him to look at me. "To you, how much is his life worth?" Victor asked.

I stuttered. "He... he's worth everything to me."

"But what amount of money?"

"What?"

"Fifty thousand?"

I froze, unable to answer. How was I supposed to put a price on the person I loved?

Victor let go of Caleb's hair and stood. "Maybe seventy-five?" He looked to Mikhail and the others, but they all shrugged. "Maybe, one hundred. What do guys think?" He looked at all of them. "Tommy's boy has debt to pay. We split it!" He turned back to me. "I give discount. One hundred thousand American dollars. Then you get Caleb."

I shook my head. "What? I don't have that."

Victor rushed me faster than I could blink. He pushed me against the brick wall and held his forearm against my throat, cutting off my air. I gripped his arm. Tears spilled over my lids.

Caleb jumped up. "Don't fucking touch him!" The bald man punched Caleb in the ribs, knocking his breath out.

"One hundred thousand," Victor hissed in my face. His spit splattered with each word, some even getting in my mouth as I gasped. He pushed harder on my throat. "I don't care how you get. If not back by sun up, Caleb gets bullet, just like fat bartender."

I nodded furiously, and Victor backed away. I fell to the floor, gasping and coughing.

"Bruno," Victor said, catching the bald man's attention. "Let lovers say goodbye." Bruno released his grip on Caleb.

He crawled to me on all fours and hugged me tightly before whispering. "Get to Isaac, okay?"

I shook my head across his shoulder. "I can't leave you."

"You have to, Landon. Victor's not gonna let up." Caleb was strangely calm, while I was a mess of tears.

"I don't know what to do," I whimpered.

Caleb rested his forehead on mine. "Get to Isaac, then back to Tommy's apartment," Caleb whispered.

"What?"

His voice was low. "You have to find my backpack. My gun is in it. Don't come back without it, okay?"

I nodded.

"Promise me?" Caleb asked.

"I promise."

Caleb held out his pinky, and I curled mine around it.

Victor clapped. "Mikhail, take him."

The blonde stepped with long strides. He pulled at Caleb's shirt, but we didn't let go of each other.

"Enough!" Victor yelled before Mikhail wrapped a large hand around Caleb's arm, ripping him away from me.

"No!" I screamed as Mikhail dragged Caleb around the corner.

"Bruno," Victor said to the bald man, "stay with red boy. Make sure he pays."

The bald man nodded, then stepped to me. I flinched as he grabbed me around the back of the neck.

Victor moved close to my ear. "If I get word of police, Caleb dies." Victor chuckled. "See you soon." He waved with his fingers, then motioned for the twins in black to follow him down the hall.

Bruno squeezed the back of my neck, leading me through the

swinging door, back into the meat-decaying air, and shoved me to the side. "Stay there." His voice was low and gruff, but he was American. He approached the garage door.

"H-hey, Bruno?"

The bald man glanced at me.

"We can help each other." My right hand trembled by my side. "I know Victor must treat you guys like shit."

Bruno quickly spun and slammed his fists into my chest. It felt like an 18-wheeler hit me. The force sent me to the floor. If Bruno didn't knock the breath out of me, my back smacking the concrete did. I gasped for air, but nothing came in. It felt like my throat was glued shut. Bruno stood over me, crouched, and spit next to my head. "You don't know shit! You're a pathetic, weak little fuck!" A vein bulged across the crown of his smooth head. "What the fuck do you know?"

I instinctively raised my arms to protect my face, thinking he might hit me again. But instead, he spat at me one more time before turning. My throat relaxed, and I was finally able to gulp some air. I coughed, slowly propping myself up.

There was no reasoning with the men who surrounded Victor. They were all as batshit as he was. Talking to Bruno wouldn't get him off my back. I didn't need or want an abusive chaperone to get back to Isaac. I thought about running as soon as Bruno opened the garage door, but I didn't think my lungs could hold out.

I watched as Bruno yanked a chain. It rattled and clicked, forcing the garage door to fold itself up. My eyes searched the room, desperate for inspiration. Finally, my gaze landed on the hook stuck in the wooden stool. *Fuck, fuck, fuck.* It was my only option. I popped to my feet. The chains rattled so loudly that Bruno didn't hear my footsteps. I gripped the sickle's handle and yanked it from the wood. With two strides, I reared the hook back and let out a guttural scream as I swung. My aim was suddenly as steady as a brain surgeon.

The pointed end of the sickle plunged through Bruno's jaw. He screamed and gargled as he reached for his face. I pulled the hook back with force, twisting Bruno's neck. Blood sprayed from his mouth, covering my face before we both dropped. He shivered a few times before his gargles quit.

My face fell into my hands. I couldn't get them to stop shaking. I screamed into my palms, then used my shirt to wipe Bruno's blood off my face. *What the fuck! Jesus fucking Christ, why is this happening?* My breaths were sharp and short. I pushed my hand through my hair and tugged a fistful. "Go, fucking go," I whispered to myself.

I looked at the garage door. It was open enough to duck under. I crawled past Bruno. The hook was still stuck in his face. I held my stomach, knowing I could vomit any second, ducked under the door, and slipped into the winter flurry.

TWENTY FIVE

Thursday, January 16th

The street was a construction mess. Scaffolding had been erected up the sidewalk, and cement blocks were placed to keep cars off the street. Planks of wood and metal rods were left abandoned in the snow. The entire street was a ghost town, but the smell of salty air blowing off the Hudson told me I was still in Manhattan.

I got to the corner, gripped a light post, and vomited. It burned my insides on the way up. My entire body shook after one lurch. The bile I spewed melted the snow on the ground. I hugged the post, desperate for stability. A sign flashed at me from a small bank window. It was 12:32 a.m.

Back by sun up.

My forehead pressed against the post as I sobbed and shivered. Pelting snow wet my hair. I didn't want to move. I wanted to lay in the street and drown in the bloody images that filled my thoughts. My knees wobbled, and I kneeled in the snow. After everything I saw, I was ready to freeze to death and end it all. I closed my eyes.

———

I woke up in my bedroom again. Everything looked the way I'd left it from Christmas. Boxes were packed and stacked by my closet door. Besides a few crumpled papers and lingering soda cans, my desk was empty. The window at the foot of my bed let in the coldest breeze Texas had ever produced. My toes tingled from the chill. I tiptoed to the window, and a breath caught in my throat. My street glistened with a sheet of bright snow.

Dozens of kids ran around the high school's courtyard, seemingly in a snowball war. Parents watched from the sidewalk, sipping from styrofoam cups. A large truck plowed the white powder from the street, emitting black smoke from its tailpipe as it slid by.

What the hell?

I slammed the window shut. Madison, Texas, had never seen a flake of snow, at least not in my lifetime. Why was everyone acting like it was normal? I searched my bed for my phone, wanting to check the news.

Three knocks rattled my thin bedroom door, sending my heart to the sky.

"Dad?"

No answer, just three more knocks. I stomped to the door and pulled it open. My eyes widened, then immediately clenched closed. "No!" I shouted.

Dan stood at my door, staring, his neck and white tuxedo jacket stained red.

I backed away until my legs hit my bed. I sat and shook my head, keeping my eyes closed. "What do you want?"

"Landon, it's okay," Dan said.

My eyes slowly opened. Dan stepped through the door. The blood no longer stained his tux. It was white and pristine. Even the wound where I had shot him in his neck was gone.

I stared at him. "Can't you just leave me alone?"

"That's not up to me," Dan said. His voice was the softest I'd ever heard it.

"What's that supposed to mean?"

"You have to let me go."

My breath calmed. I wiped my sweaty palms on my bare legs. "What?"

"You had no other choice. I know that now." His voice was ethereal, bouncing around the room as if we were in an empty gym. "You have to understand that too."

My jaw tightened, thinking back to prom night, and my eyes welled. "I told you I'd shoot if you didn't stop. You were killing him."

"None of this was your fault. You were only protecting the person you love."

"I loved you too!" I yelled, but my voice didn't echo. "You were my best friend. But you turned into this monster."

Dan slipped his hands into his pockets. "I lost my way."

"Why didn't you come to me? I could've helped you."

"I didn't think you'd understand."

I stood. "But you didn't even try!"

Dan's arms wrapped around my shoulders, pulling me into a tight hug. I could still smell the Axe body spray on him. "I wish I had," he said.

I hugged him back. My tears stained his shoulder. "I'm so sor—"

"You have nothing to be sorry for." Dan's calm voice rang in my ear, but I couldn't feel his breath. "You have to forgive yourself now."

"I ruined your family, your future."

"You saved a life. That's more important than anything I ever could've done."

A circle of warmth pressed against my chest, stopping my shivering.

Dan held my face and stared into my eyes. "He needs you again."

"Who?"

"Wake up!"

My eyes opened, and I grabbed my throbbing head. I pulled myself up with the help of the light post and glanced at the street signs. I was at the corner of Washington and Laight St. It was unfamiliar territory, but I just needed to find the nearest train.

I hugged my torso, attempting to keep myself warm. I drudged through the soft snow, looking for any subway entrance lamps in the darkness. I walked almost ten blocks before I spotted one. I didn't even notice which train line it was. I just descended the stairs to feel the warmth of being underground. The station was empty. Even the MTA worker who sat in the windowed cubicle was asleep. I ducked under the turnstile and slumped on a bench against the wall. My eyes couldn't stay open. It wasn't until I heard the screech of the train's brakes that I awoke and ran on. I stood under the heating vent as long as my legs held me up. The entire train car was empty.

My feet were numb by the time I reached Isaac's building. I pushed the glass door into the lobby, but it was locked. The front desk manager stared at me with wide eyes. A fake smile lit up my face as I waved to him. He reached out of sight and then brought a phone to his ear.

I rapidly knocked to get his attention. "Hey, hey! I'm here for Isaac!"

The man put the phone down, walked around the desk, and stood at the door. "Who are you?" His voice was muffled behind the glass, but the streets were so quiet I could hear him perfectly. "Why are you covered in blood?"

"It's not mine!" I said too quickly before realizing that was the most wrong thing to say. "It's from set! I was just filming close by. It's fake, I swear!" The lying came back so easily when I was desperate.

The man's brow furrowed. "Where's your coat? It's freezing."

"I accidentally left it with Isaac." My entire body shivered again, and my voice warbled. "Please call him. Tell him Landon's here."

"Do you know what time it is? I won't disturb Mr. Matthews at this—"

"PLEASE!" I shouted. "I need him. Just... please tell him I'm here. He'll know me, I promise."

The man scowled but backed away. He picked up the phone at the desk. After a moment, I could see his lips moving but couldn't make out his words. He glanced at me before the door buzzed. I pushed through and jogged to the elevator, smashing the button until the door opened. I leaned a shoulder against the wall as the elevator climbed.

Isaac was there in his pajamas when the doors opened. "I've been trying to call you guys. Where have—" Isaac gasped, finally noticing my appearance.

I collapsed in his arms, taking him down with me. Tears streaked Bruno's blood down my face, or was it John's? Tommy's? My own?

Isaac held me against him. "Jesus, Landon. What happened?"

The words caught in my throat, and only unintelligible sounds escaped.

Isaac held my face, fully supporting the weight of my head. "Landon, I can't understand you. What happened?"

I gulped and tried to take a bigger breath. "They...They have Caleb."

Isaac's face twisted. "Who has Caleb?"

"Victor."

"What?" Isaac let go of me. His eyes widened. "How?"

I wiped my cheeks on my arm, smearing red across my freckles. At first, I spoke quickly, but when I told Isaac about killing Bruno, my words felt heavy.

Isaac reached into his pocket. "We have to call the police."

"NO!" I shouted, making Isaac flinch. "Did you hear what I said? Victor has ties to the police. Caleb's dead if he finds out they got word of what's happening."

"Victor could be lying."

My eyes drooped. "I don't want to take that risk! We have to go back to Tommy's. Caleb said not to... to come back without... Sun up..." The more I spoke, the more tired I got.

Isaac snapped fingers in my face. "Landon? God, you're shaking." Isaac stood and ran to the kitchen.

My head swayed. All I could see was a streak of gray zipping around the apartment.

Isaac suddenly plopped in front of me, wrapping a fluffy blanket around my shoulders. He pushed two pills into my hand. "Here, take this. You're dehydrated as fuck." Isaac forced a bottle of cold water into my other hand. It was slippery with condensation. "Drink."

My mouth tasted like pennies and sand before guzzling the water.

Isaac held the butt end of a baguette in front of my face. "Eat this. You need something solid in your stomach."

I ripped a piece and shoved it in my mouth. I hadn't noticed my jaw throbbing again until I chewed. I pulled the blanket tighter. "We have to go," I said with a shaky voice. "We don't have time."

Isaac gripped my trembling hands. "This isn't working." Isaac helped me stand. The blanket fell behind me as Isaac led me to the stairs.

I looked at him. "What're you doing?"

"We need to warm you faster. Get your blood pumping again."

"How?"

"You need a hot shower."

My eyes hit the floor. "I'll be fine," I said.

"Landon, you wo—"

I pulled away from him and grabbed the banister. "No! We need to help Caleb!

"We can't help him if you can't walk."

"We don't have time!"

"All Victor cares about is the money. He'll wait for it."

"You don't know that!"

Isaac pinched the bridge of his nose, then squinted at me. "I'm sorry." He took a deep breath. "We *will* get him, Landon. I promise you. But I need you with me to do it."

I stared at him with wet eyes.

"Please, we can't walk around New York City with you looking like this. Eventually, someone's gonna notice," Isaac said.

My teeth ground together. Everything he said made sense. We didn't need any unwanted attention. I was being stubborn, taking a page out of Caleb's book.

Isaac placed himself under my arm and guided me up the stairs. The bathroom was black marble with white accents. At the far end was a large walk-in shower. Isaac rested me against the shower's glass, opened the door, walked inside, and pushed a button on the wall. Water rained from the ceiling. He hopped out completely dry and faced me. Warm steam swirled from the open door. Isaac poked a thumb over his shoulder. "The towels are hanging there on the wall. You gonna be okay?"

I shook my head. Everything rushed back into my thoughts, pushing out more tears and flashes of violence. I leaned into Isaac, and he wrapped his arms around me.

"You're okay," he said. "I have you."

I tried pulling my shirt at the collar, but it stuck to my body.

"Here," Isaac said, pulling my shirt up slowly from the bottom. Blood stained my pale skin underneath.

I kicked my shoes off, then unbuttoned my soaked jeans, pushing them down as Isaac kept me steady. I held his shoulders as I pulled my feet through, turning the jeans inside out. "Can you take my socks off, please?"

Isaac nodded, crouched, and peeled my socks off. As he stood, I started to push down my underwear, but Isaac grabbed my hand to stop me. "Hold on. I'll go."

"That's the last thing I want." I didn't want to make him uncomfortable, but the faster I got in the shower, the faster we could get to Caleb.

"Okay," Isaac whispered. He held me steady as I pushed my underwear down and off my feet. He then held my arm and walked me into the shower.

I reached under the stream, testing the temperature. "Stay with me?" I asked.

Isaac nodded and remained clothed. The only thing he removed was his phone from his pocket. He let me take my time stepping under the rain.

The water stung at first but eventually soothed my icy skin. My muscles thawed and loosened. The water trickled down my back as Isaac held me under my arms. My head rested on his shoulder, watching red swirl down the drain.

The steam entered my lungs, rejuvenating my breath. "I can't stop thinking about it," I said softly. Isaac reached for a bar of soap. "The last thing Caleb said to me was, 'I love you more than anything.'" I tried to hold back the tears by clenching my jaw every time my lip quivered. "That was the last thing my mom wrote in her suicide note." Every terrible scenario rushed through my head. "That has to be a sign this won't end well."

Isaac looked at me. I was a little more steady now that I was warm. "Don't think like that," Isaac said. "We'll give Victor the money, and that'll be that, okay?"

I nodded, but my optimism wasn't as bright.

Isaac ran the soap over my neck and shoulders, splashing away the blood of strangers. He eventually stepped out and draped a towel over the glass, allowing me to wash my hair now that my knees weren't rubber. I dried myself before wrapping the towel around my waist and entered his bedroom.

Isaac had changed into a black T-shirt and black jeans. He pulled a beanie over his curls. "I laid some clothes for you on the bed. If the shirt is too big, go through my drawers for one." His shoes squeaked toward me. "I'm gonna get the money. You okay staying here till I'm back?"

I nodded and held his hands. "What you're doing for us is—"

"I know we haven't known each other for that long," Isaac said, "but the universe brought you and Caleb into my life for a reason. Feels like I should follow through."

I didn't know what to say at first. I brought so much drama and chaos into Isaac's life. He had no obligation to me and even less obligation to Caleb. But for some reason, he stayed. "Thank you, Isaac."

"I'll be back soon. Get ready, and I'll have the doorman call up when I'm outside with the car."

"The car?"

Isaac pulled a set of keys from his pocket. "Yeah. My car's parked in the garage under the building."

"You've had a car this whole time? You could've been driving us around—"

"I don't like driving it. And gas is a waste of money."

Says the guy about to withdraw a hundred thousand dollars.

"Get dressed. Then let's get our boy."

Our boy.

———

I pulled the glass door and stepped outside. My shoes slid against the snowy sidewalk. One of Victor's men stripped me of my coat, so Isaac provided a replacement.

"Hey!" Isaac called through the open window of a black Prius.

I hopped in the passenger seat and clicked my seatbelt before glancing at the black duffle bag in the backseat. "Is that it?"

"That's all of it." Isaac hit the gas. The car's engine was silent.

"Banks are closed right now. How'd you get that much so quickly?"

"Secret safe stash. I can't trust the bank with *all* my money," Isaac said.

I had so many questions. I couldn't fathom owning a safe, never mind an extra hundred thousand dollars to keep in it. How much did he have left? It wasn't the right time to question it. "You remember Tommy's address?"

Isaac nodded.

It took less than ten minutes to drive there. There wasn't much traffic, assumingly because of the snow, but the constant stoplights wasted our time. I stayed silent the whole ride. My left leg wouldn't stop bouncing until Isaac's hand lightly gripped my thigh.

We pulled up to Tommy's building and parked across the street. Isaac grabbed the bag from the backseat and locked it in the trunk, out of sight of any passersby.

I jiggled the cold handle and pushed through the front door of Tommy's building. The single elevator took us to the sixth floor, and the doors opened to the familiar hallway.

Isaac caught up to me before I opened the apartment door. "Wait," he whispered. "Are you sure no one's in there?"

"Everyone I saw here, I saw at the warehouse before I got away."

Isaac sighed. I don't think he shared my confidence. "Okay."

I pushed my ear against the door and closed my eyes. *Nothing.* "You should stay out here," I whispered. "You shouldn't be forced to see this." Tommy's dead eyes staring back at me flashed through my memory.

"It's okay. I can handle it."

I hoped his stomach was stronger than mine. I twisted the knob and pushed. The smell of bleach was so strong it burned my nostrils. I hurried to the window above the sink and pushed it open. Isaac closed the door behind him and surveyed the room.

My eyes searched the floor. I pointed beside the bed. "He was right there. Tommy's blood was everywhere."

Isaac waved the air away from his face. "They must have a clean-up crew."

I pushed the bathroom door open. The tub was empty and spotless. I gripped my hair in one hand. "Jesus, what did they do with the body?"

"Is that Caleb's backpack?" Isaac asked, pointing to the foot of the bed.

I took a few steps and crouched. Caleb's bag had been turned upside down. I lifted it with ease. All that remained inside was the key on the stretchy coil, left on the floor under the bag. I removed the single picture Caleb had shown me when we started searching for Tommy.

I dropped the bag and leaned against the bed frame, stretching my legs across the tile. I stared at the picture. Little Caleb looked so happy. I swallowed hard. My eyes welled up, and I quickly wiped them. "Caleb said not to come back without a gun."

Isaac searched the desk drawers behind him. "Maybe there's something around here we can use?"

I tossed the picture back in the bag and joined Isaac at the desk, pulling open a deep drawer as Isaac moved to the wardrobe in the corner. The drawer was a mess of papers. Police files mostly. *Why did he keep all of this?* I reached the bottom of the drawers and found nothing to defend ourselves with.

"This is weird," Isaac said, stepping around to the side of the wardrobe.

I sat on the bed to look at him. "What?"

"The wardrobe goes all the way back to the wall, but look." He opened the doors to Tommy's hanging shirts. Isaac pushed the hangers aside and touched the wood panel behind them. "This doesn't match. There's more space back there."

My eyes widened. "Seriously?"

Isaac's fingers glided across the wood. "There must be a way to open it." Two fingers traced the perimeter of the panel but came up empty. He stepped back and stared at it, chewing his bottom lip. "Maybe if I—" Isaac placed both hands on the panel and pushed up. We heard something unlatch, and I flew off the bed. Isaac glided the panel to the left. "I can't believe that worked," Isaac whispered to himself.

"Holy shit!" Just behind the wood panel was a small black safe— A two-by-two-foot square. A number pad sat in the center of its face with a handle below it.

"What do you think's inside?" Isaac asked.

I shook my head. "No clue."

"Did Caleb ever mention a code or anything?"

I searched my memory. "No, I don't think so." I reached for the handle, hoping for a miracle. Still locked. "I don't think Caleb even knew about a safe."

Isaac leaned forward, inspecting the black box. He touched every corner and tried to move it, but it wouldn't budge. He pushed the 1 button, which called back with a loud beep. The small display above the numbers lit up with a digital 1 blinking in the first of five positions. "It's a five-number code," Isaac said.

I sighed. "Great. That could be anything." I sat on the bed again with my head in my hands. "We're wasting time."

"Wait!" Isaac shouted.

I looked to find him torso-deep in the back of the wardrobe

behind the panel he'd pushed aside. "There's something else back here," Isaac said with a muffled voice. He slithered back out holding a yellow tin lunchbox with a rusted handle. Isaac held it out to examine. The picture on the front was faded, but the word '*THUNDER-CATS*' was still visible. "This is weird," Isaac said.

I shot to my feet. "It's not, actually! Caleb has one just like it." I spotted a keyhole under the handle. "His doesn't have a lock, though."

Isaac squinted, bringing the box closer to his face. "I've never seen a lunchbox with a lock on it." He bit his bottom lip. "Ah, look." He flipped the box to show me. "The metal around the lock is scorched. Tommy must've added it himself."

A lightbulb exploded in my head. I snatched Caleb's backpack and pulled out the key on the stretchy coil. "Caleb said he had no idea what this was for."

"Try it." Isaac handed me the box, and something clacked the walls inside.

The mattress bounced as I sat again—the key fit like a glove. Isaac sat next to me as I popped the lid.

Inside the box was a stack of photos and a small thumb drive. At the top of the stack was a picture of a little boy blowing out birthday candles.

"Is that Caleb?" Isaac asked.

"Yeah."

I moved the photo to the back of the stack. The next one was of a woman covering her face and turning away from the camera. I assumed it was Caleb's mom because of the red hair. Every picture we went through was a snapshot of Caleb's young life. He was in most of them. Little Caleb raking leaves in the backyard, playing with action figures, climbing a swing set, and kicking the air in his karate uniform. I stared at the karate photo. If Parker and little Caleb stood beside each other, I'd think they were twins. I scanned the face of the next picture. Caleb was a little older and swimming in an above-ground pool.

I pulled the next photo, and my brow furrowed. "Wait, this one's the same as—" It was the picture of Tommy and Caleb standing in front of the beat-up silver car. I reached into Caleb's backpack, pulling out the matching picture. By then, the corner had been folded and crushed by the chaos of our journey so far. I compared the two pictures side by side before glancing at Isaac.

Isaac grabbed the stack of photos and quickly passed through them, flipping to see the back of each one. "There's a date written on all of these. Month, day, year."

"Tommy left this one in the deposit box back in Texas," I said, gesturing to the tattered picture in my hand.

Isaac plucked the identical photo from the stack and compared it to the tattered one. "What's so special about this one?"

I flipped the crumpled picture. No date was written, but a small circle had been drawn in the bottom right corner. "Weird." I flipped it again and compared the pictures side by side. "They're exactly the same."

"Except for the date," Isaac huffed. "Flip them again. Every picture has a date."

I raised an eyebrow. "Okay?"

Isaac pointed to the back of the worn-out picture. "Except Caleb's." He nibbled his bottom lip again. "This is the only picture that matches Caleb's. The date on Tommy's version has to mean something." He squinted and flipped Tommy's photo. "Look, this one's missing the year at the end of the date."

I studied the photos. On Tommy's version, 08/27 was written in the same handwriting as all the others. I looked at Isaac. "But this is already four numbers. The safe needs five."

Isaac's eyes somehow got brighter. "Hear me out. Tommy left the year out on purpose, obviously. But who might be the only person who knows what year this photo was taken? Caleb."

He's fucking brilliant. "Tommy definitely wanted Caleb to find this," I said.

"Exactly. Did Caleb tell you anything about this picture?"

"Just that it was taken on the first day of school the year his dad left."

"What year?"

My eyes searched the room. "I think he said it was almost ten years ago? But adding the year gives us more numbers than we need."

Isaac scratched his chin. "Maybe we don't need the zero? Who writes dates like that anyway?"

I nodded furiously. "Try it."

Isaac hopped off the bed and poked at the keypad. The buttons glowed red, and three rapid-fire beeps followed. "Okay. Maybe it was eleven years ago." Three rapid-fire beeps and red buttons sent Isaac back to the bed. "I really thought that would work."

I rubbed my forehead. "Yeah, something's not right. Everything Tommy left for Caleb has had a purpose."

"But it wasn't the code," Isaac said.

"We're missing something."

Isaac's eyes shot to my lap. Caleb's tattered photo was still face down. Isaac tapped the drawn circle. "That has to mean something, then."

I picked up the photo by its corner, and the light caught its face, making the picture translucent momentarily.

Isaac gasped. "Hold it up to the light!"

I followed his instructions, and there it was. The circle on the back was drawn over the black mailbox at the bottom corner of the picture. The house's numbers had been peeled off, and all that remained was a number symbol on the side of the mailbox. "The code needs a hashtag!"

Isaac hopped to the safe, but his finger stopped short of typing on the keypad.

"Wait," I said. "If we add a hashtag, does that count as one of the five spaces?"

Isaac reached into his pocket. "I'll Google it." He peered at the front of the safe. The words 'SealedTight' were branded at the bottom. Isaac's phone lit up his face. "Whoa, this safe is old. Okay yes. It says the hashtag does count as one of the spaces, and if..." His voice trailed off.

"What?"

"If you punch in the wrong code three times, the safe will lock itself for an hour."

My head fell into my hand. "Fuck. We have one shot left."

"If everything has a purpose and the hashtag counts as one of the spaces, the date on the matching picture has to be it."

I held the two pictures side by side again, staring at the date written. "You're right. It has to be." I sat up straight with a newfound confidence. "Tommy didn't write the year because we don't need it! Hashtag, zero, eight, two, seven. That's five!"

Isaac faced the safe again but hesitated. "But how do you know the hashtag comes first?"

I groaned at the ceiling. He was right. "Fifty-fifty shot. Hashtag before or after the numbers?"

Isaac took a breath. "That date was the only one missing a year. Maybe the hashtag comes after?"

I nodded. "I trust you."

Isaac readied his finger. My heart hammered my chest.

The numbers beeped under Isaac's touch. "Zero, eight, two, seven. Hashtag."

The safe let out a flat line instead of three rapid beeps, and the numbers flashed green. The latch unhooked, and the door swung open. Isaac and I erupted with cheers before he grabbed my face and kissed me.

We both stared inside.

"Caleb said not to come back without a gun." Isaac glanced at me. "There's your gun."

My jaw tensed. Seeing the black handgun reminded me we weren't playing a game. "Can you take it?"

"Sure."

I picked up Caleb's backpack and shoved the lunchbox inside.

Isaac pulled a manilla folder from the bottom of the safe and stared at its contents. "Whoa."

I was too panicked to care. Caleb was still in trouble, still counting on me. I dropped the backpack at Isaac's feet. "Put everything in the bag. We gotta go."

TWENTY SIX

I gave Isaac the cross streets I remembered—corner of Washington and Laight St. We were stopped at a red light when I glanced at the gun in Isaac's lap. "Is it loaded?"

Isaac placed a hand over the gun, leaving the other on the steering wheel. "Yeah."

"How do you know?"

"Gun safety gets taken pretty seriously on any set. I've handled a few prop guns," Isaac said, tucking the gun into his waistband behind him. "I checked it before we left the apartment."

"Is shooting a prop gun similar to shooting a real one?"

"In almost every way."

"What's the difference?"

He glanced at me as the light turned green. "This one won't be shooting blanks."

Caleb's lucky backpack sat between my legs. I gripped the strap with both hands. It was the closest I'd felt to Caleb since being dragged in separate directions.

"What's on your mind?" Isaac asked, touching my leg.

My head rested against the window, focusing on a melting

snowflake. "Everything," I said. "Are they hurting Caleb? Will they actually let us go once they have the money? Is he even still alive?"

"Of course he is. And they will. They're getting what they want."

I looked at Isaac with narrow eyes. "You don't know these people." My voice cracked. "Victor tortured us! I watched him shoot a man in the head for no fucking reason! That shit doesn't just evaporate from your memory."

Isaac gently squeezed my thigh. "I'm sorry."

"Have you ever lost someone you cared about?" I asked.

"My grandma died when I was fourteen."

I rolled my eyes, focusing out the window again. "That's different. Every death I've experienced made me go fucking crazy."

"You're not crazy, Landon."

"Show me another nineteen-year-old who's been through this because I'd love some fucking advice right about now." Isaac removed his hand from my leg. "I'm sorry," I said.

Isaac glanced at me. The streetlights skated across his face. "Never apologize for how you feel." He used both hands to turn the wheel, and the car came to a stop. "This is it," Isaac said, pointing at the street sign. The windshield wipers scraped the glass. "I've never seen Manhattan so dead."

I looked through Isaac's window. The brick building looked blue under the moonlight. I hadn't noticed it before, but 'Volkov Meats' was painted across the side of the building.

Isaac turned the car off and looked at me. "Before we feed ourselves to the wolves, do you have a plan?"

"I think I should go in alone," I said.

Isaac's face twisted. "What? Why?"

"They might recognize you."

He shrugged. "I don't think a bunch of Russian guys will know who I am."

"Bruno was American," I said, shaking my head. "The other guys could be too. They might know you."

Isaac leaned back against the door. "Then I don't think you should go in with the money. You need some sort of leverage."

"What're you thinking?"

Isaac sat up straight. "You make sure Caleb is safe first, then lead them out here to get the money and exchange it on the street. That also might stop them from pulling anything on us since we're in public."

"Okay."

Isaac reached behind him. "Take the gun."

"What if they search me?" I tried to think of every scenario. "Keep it, and stay down. You know how to use it. It's better with you. You're sure you can do this?"

Isaac nodded. "I'm sure."

I kissed him deeply. My lips moved between his before our tongues met as if it were the last time we'd ever kissed.

"Be safe," Isaac whispered.

I pecked his lips again, then hopped out of the car. I turned the corner, walked through my fogged breath, and zipped my coat.

I passed between the cement blocks and followed the sidewalk under the familiar scaffolding. The garage door was still cracked enough to duck under. My shoes slid on the snow, blown inside. Bruno's body lay in the same spot. His legs dusted in white. The sickle still stuck in his flesh. Everything seemed as I'd left it. Hopefully that meant no one came looking for me.

I pushed through the swinging door back into the empty hall. My sneakers slid again, but not from the snow. John's body was gone, but his blood had pooled against the wall and snaked under the door. I stepped softly. Every hallway looked the same, scattered with random closed doors.

Caleb's scream echoed through the cold building. His voice hit me like a sonar pulse. I jogged, following his voice. I cut left and followed the flickering lights. "Slaughter House" looked professionally painted on the wall ahead of me, with an arrow pointing the way. I followed the arrows to a large open room filled with conveyor belts and big metal bins. Oversized hooks hung from thick chains. Massive crates, each stacked three high, were scattered around. A rusty stench filled the air. Victor's wooden laugh chiseled my ears. I crouched behind a crate.

Tall work-lights lit a corner of the room. Caleb slumped in a metal chair, his bloodied chin resting on his chest and his arms limp. Victor paced behind the chair, his hands clasped behind his back as if walking through a museum—the gun grip protruded from Victor's waistband.

The twins watched.

I stood, accidentally knocking over an empty beer bottle that rolled into Victor's view.

Victor stopped pacing. "Mikhail?"

I crouched again and hugged my knees.

"Red boy?" A gun snapped. "Show yourself!"

Victor's voice ripped through my chest, forcing me to my feet. I stepped from behind the crate with my hands up.

Victor smiled. "Ah! There is Red Boy!"

My jaw tightened. "Caleb? Are you okay?"

Caleb slowly raised his head. "You came back." A weak smile showed off a bloody row of teeth.

My heart shattered, and my fists tightened. "I have the money," I said through clenched teeth.

Victor pushed his gun into his pants and clapped. "Great! Good boy." He leaned to look around me. "Where is Bruno?"

"I got away," I said with a flat tone.

Victor stepped around Caleb, waving his finger in the air. "Not polite thing." He shook his head, mumbling something in Russian.

"Give me Caleb, and I'll give you the money," I said. My right knee trembled, so I shifted weight, hoping to calm the shake.

Victor crossed his arms. "Where is money?"

"In my car, outside."

Victor motioned for the twins to approach him. He spoke to them in Russian. One of the twins listened and glared at me, and I finally spotted their one difference—A cleft lip scar that extended up one's nose.

"Not two-person job," the scarred twin said.

Victor sneered something in Russian and pulled the scarred man's gun from its holster under his arm. It was silver with a black grip. Victor removed the clip, emptied the chamber, and hucked the gun over a stack of crates, ricocheting echoes around the room. Victor slapped the scarred man across the face and pushed him toward me, spouting more Russian words I couldn't understand.

My heart raced. After seeing Victor shoot John without warning, I thought the scarred twin would meet the same fate. "Let Caleb go, and—"

"You don't give orders!" Victor bent at the waist to scream toward me. "I do!" The force of his voice pushed me back a step. He straightened and pulled the gun from his waistband. He scratched his chin along the barrel and pointed a finger at the scarred twin now standing to my left. "Just like Dmitriy, you not very good listener."

"I did what you asked," I mumbled.

"NO! I said bring money. I don't see money!"

My voice wavered. "I told you, it's outside. Just—"

Victor let out a spartan-like scream and smacked Caleb across the jaw with his gun's handle. Caleb spat blood and returned his chin to his chest.

I lunged forward, but Dmitriy caught my arm. The other twin rushed to help keep me in place. The pressure around my shoulder blades felt like being stabbed with a blunt knife.

Caleb coughed, and a string of blood hit his shirt.

"Ivan," Victor called out. "You and Dmitriy take red boy to get MY money, or Caleb gets bullet in head." Victor could've said all that in Russian, but he wanted me to know the consequences of not playing by *his* rules.

The twins tugged at me. "Caleb!" I caught his eyes as the twins spun around and dragged me back down the hall. I thrashed in their arms. "Caleb!"

The twins spoke back and forth in Russian in aggressive tones as they led me down the hall. I kept looking over my shoulder, thinking Caleb would somehow escape and run after us. They forced me around a corner, and we were back at John's blood splatter. Ivan pushed me through the swinging door. More snow had collected inside, covering more of Bruno's lifeless body.

"Der'mo!" Dmitriy shouted. "Bruno!"

Ivan pulled the gun from his waist and pointed it at me. "You stupid fuck." His accent was less severe than Victor's and Dmitriy's. My hands raised. "You're fucking dead," Ivan sneered. "Victor will kill you for this. You know that, right?"

I swallowed hard. "As if he wasn't going to already?"

"I can't wait to watch." Ivan motioned his gun toward the garage door. "Walk. If you try to escape, I'll shoot you dead in the street."

Dmitriy crouched to examine Bruno's face as I ducked under the door.

I kept my hands in the air. The rabid wind bit at my fingertips. Ivan kept his gun against my back. Snow crunched under our feet. My heart pounded in my chest as I spotted the headlights of Isaac's car peeking out from the corner of the building. I prayed Isaac was ready. If Dmitriy hadn't opposed Victor, we would've been outgunned.

"Where are you taking us?" Ivan asked.

I pointed. "The car up ahead." Ivan pushed me between my shoulder blades, and my feet almost slid out from under me. The steam from my mouth erupted in short bursts. Nothing had gone the way I imagined. I knew if I was going to survive, the twins couldn't bring me back to Victor. Ivan said it himself: Victor would kill me once he knew I'd murdered Bruno. The twins weren't going to keep that a secret. I needed to get them off my back. Isaac was my only hope.

We turned the corner and walked along the side of the car. I expected to meet eyes with Isaac, but the car was empty. All the blood drained from my head. *Did someone find him? Did he chicken out and run? Did he go looking for help? Where the fuck is he?*

"It's in the trunk," I said, hitting the button above the license plate. The trunk popped, and the duffle bag was still there. I gripped it at both ends but didn't lift.

Ivan grunted and pushed the barrel of his gun into my spine. "What're you waiting for?"

The street was silent. There was no more hope. Nothing else to fall back on. It was two against one.

The snow crunched behind us. "Let him go," Isaac said.

My shoulders dropped.

The twins turned to face Isaac, but Ivan kept his gun on me. "You're an even bigger idiot than I though, Landon." He snapped his fingers. "Dmitriy, get the fucker."

Dmitriy slowly stepped to Isaac with his hands raised. "Give me gun. You don't want this."

Isaac straightened his arms, pointing the barrel at Dmitriy.

"Shoot him!" I shouted before Ivan twisted his gun into my skin.

"Stop!" Isaac said, stepping backward. "I'll shoot you, stop!"

Dmitriy lunged for Isaac, taking him by the wrist. The two grappled, trying to overpower each other. Dmitriy took Isaac down and smashed his wrist to the street, and a shot fired, causing Ivan to spin toward the pair to point his gun at them.

I lifted the duffle from both ends, covering my chest. "Hey!"

Before I could blink, Ivan spun back to me and fired a shot. The bullet pierced the bag, forcing me against the lip of the trunk. Ivan's eyes widened when I stood and swung the bag as hard as possible. It connected, hitting Ivan's arm and knocking his gun onto the snowy pavement. Ivan and I watched as the handgun slid into the open gutter.

Ivan let out a guttural screech and rushed me. I tossed the bag to Ivan, who instinctively caught it, giving me an opening. I balled my fists, jabbing Ivan in the throat, crunching his trachea. Ivan dropped the bag and staggered, holding his throat with both hands. His eyes narrowed, and he rushed me again.

I sidestepped his advance, and the snow worked in my favor. Ivan lost traction and slipped just as he reached for me. His face smacked the car's tail light, knocking him out face down in the snow.

Isaac was still wrestling with the scarred twin. I hopped over Ivan's body and searched the open trunk. The streetlight reflected a tire iron propped on its side. I snatched it; the cold metal burned my palm, but I gripped it tightly. I skated a path in the snow and held the tire iron with both hands before I swung it into Dmitriy's back. His yelp bounced off the buildings. Another hard swing caught Dmitriy above the ear, knocking him off Isaac and onto his back. His eyes were closed, and blood dripped from his ear, tainting the untouched snow.

Isaac looked up at me with glossy eyes and a red face. His heavy breaths ejected little clouds. He glanced at Dmitriy before sitting up.

I crouched beside Isaac, set the tire iron down, and cupped his face. "You okay?"

"I couldn't shoot," Isaac whispered. His voice warbled. "I'm... I'm sorry, I tried, I just couldn't. I'm sorry."

"It's okay. We're okay."

"Not much of a superhero, huh?"

I kissed him softly, then stood. "You should leave, Isaac." I wanted to give him one last chance to get out of the hellscape my life had become. I picked up the tire iron, shuffled back to the trunk, and tossed it inside. "I'm in over my head. I don't want you getting hurt."

Isaac scooped Tommy's gun from the snow and pushed it into his coat pocket. "I'm not leaving you alone. I don't want you getting hurt, either."

I moved closer to him. "What if this gets out, huh? What if someone sees you and snaps a picture?"

"It's like four in the morning."

"It doesn't matter! Your career is over if someone recognizes you holding a gun or fighting in the street." I was pushing him away, hoping he'd bite. "You get that, right?"

Steam pushed from Isaac's nostrils. "I don't care."

"Don't be an idiot." I turned and started for the car.

Isaac caught me by the wrist, and pulled me back. "I'm serious. I don't care."

"Go. Home."

Isaac shook his head. "No."

"Look, I am so grateful for everything you've done, but it's not worth it, Isaac."

"Everything is worth it if I have you."

My stomach dropped. I had been knocked in the head too many times that night. I could've jumbled his words.

"Everything I've done with you has been worth it. Everything from falling in the Hudson to now. I can't stand the thought of being without you, so I'm not going anywhere."

I stepped to him. "You're so fucking stubborn."

"You're right," Isaac said, leaving clouds of breath in the inch between our faces. "I won't fail you again. The next time you say shoot, I'll shoot. I promise."

There was no more time to argue. Caleb needed us. My brow creased. "Fine. Help me move these guys. Grab his legs," I said. "I'll get the other one. We can bring them inside."

I nudged Ivan with my foot. He was still face down in the snow, his arms askew. I nudged him again, but he didn't move.

Isaac grunted, dragging Dmitriy's body through the snow and onto the sidewalk. I rushed to kick fresh powder over the red stains left on the trail.

I was unsure how to move Ivan. What if he woke up? I crouched and struggled to flip the twin on his back. I flinched when I saw his face. Ivan's eyes were open. Blood froze around his upper lip. His nose was crooked and protruding up between his eyes. The hit to the tail-light killed him instantly. I grabbed the duffle of money, slung it across my chest, and stood, wrapping my arms around Ivan's ankles.

As I turned the corner, Isaac ducked under the garage door and pulled Dmitriy under. Isaac helped me do the same with Ivan. The garage became an icy tomb for both animals and men.

I pointed to Bruno. "That's the one I told you about." Fresh powder now covered his lower half.

Isaac glanced but didn't keep his eyes on Bruno long. "Now what?"

"Victor isn't gonna like me coming back without his guys."

"That's why we have this," Isaac said, pulling the gun from his pocket.

"If you see Victor make any moves, shoot him," I said. "He won't hesitate, so you can't either."

Isaac swallowed. "I won't."

"Follow me. Stay quiet." I said, and Isaac nodded. I pushed through the swinging door, looking down to avoid the puddle of blood I had gotten to know too well. "Be ready for anything," I said.

I led the way with quiet steps. Isaac tiptoed behind me, gripping the gun with both hands. We turned the corner, and Isaac quickly raised the gun. Standing ahead of us was the man Caleb smashed with the door. A bandage covered the side of the man's forehead, and his cheek was swollen. His hands flew up, dropping a styrofoam cup of coffee.

Isaac glanced at me. "Shoot?"

"No," I whispered. I showed the bandaged man my hands and took a step forward. "Listen to me. Three of your friends are dead. We'll let you go if you don't say a word and leave right now."

Isaac held the gun steady.

"Do you understand?" I asked with a sharp tone. The man nodded furiously, still keeping his hands up. I gently pushed Isaac's arm down. "Let him go."

The man flew by us, keeping his hands raised until he disappeared around the corner. Isaac and I exchanged a glance and continued forward.

"Where are we going?" Isaac asked.

"Just follow the arrows. It's not far."

Isaac moved but poked his head through the first open door he saw. He backed away, covering his mouth. "Jesus fuck."

Two bodies were strewn over a metal table at the center of the room. I stepped inside and slowly approached the bodies. "It's Tommy and John." The corpses were stripped, and Tommy's hands were no longer attached to his arms. Red goo dripped off the edge of the table from a bloody cleaver.

Isaac covered his nose with the bend of his arm. "What the fuck are they doing to them?"

A butcher knife was stuck in John's ribs. "I don't know."

"Look." Isaac pointed to a worn wooden table at the back wall. Various tools and knives had been laid out.

"I should take some—"

"Shh." Isaac stared at me, his brow tense. "Boots."

Mikhail's massive frame sidestepped through the door. His shirt, arms, and hands were stained red. The giant's eyes widened, and he dashed toward us.

Isaac aimed the gun at Mikhail.

"Shoot!" I screamed.

Isaac fired a shot. The pop made my ear ring. The bullet ripped through the side of Mikhail's stomach. He grunted, taking the ammo as if it were a paintball.

Mikhail swung his massive hand, grabbed Isaac's wrist, and crushed it against the wall. Isaac screamed, dropping the gun. It bounced before landing under the metal table.

I dropped the duffel bag and jumped onto Mikhail's back, wrapping my scrawny arms around his thick neck and squeezing as hard as I could. Mikhail twisted left and right, trying to swat me away. I held tight to cut off his air supply, but his arms were long enough to reach over his head and latch onto my coat. Mikhail yanked me over his shoulder.

The room spun. I saw the ceiling before my head nicked the edge of metal table on the way down. I stared at the flickering bulbs as a searing heat shot up my back. Mikhail's hand cast a shadow over my face as he reached to pull the butcher knife from John's ribs.

Mikhail flipped the table with ease. I covered my face as the table with John and Tommy's bodies toppled onto me. I tried to pull myself free, to stretch out my neck to breathe, but John's dead weight trapped my left arm. I pushed at the dead man's shoulder.

Mikhail turned his attention back to Isaac and lifted him by his curls. Isaac winced in pain and scratched at Mikhail's forearm. The giant let go, only to wrap his mammoth grip around Isaac's throat. He pushed Isaac against the wall and lifted him with one arm. Isaac's sneakers dangled, his heels tapping against the wall as he thrashed.

I stared up at them. "Stop!"

Mikhail raised the butcher knife with his free hand. Isaac caught Mikhail's solid arm and resisted as best he could. Mikhail's bicep bulged as the knife inched closer and closer to Isaac's shoulder.

Tears pushed from my eyes as I screamed. Then I spotted Tommy's gun on the floor and stretched for it. My fingertips grazed the handle.

Isaac gargled and screamed. The knife punctured his skin, and Mikhail slowly pushed the blade deeper into his shoulder.

I wriggled and pushed, freeing my left arm. My fingers snaked over the handle and gripped the gun. I pointed at Mikhail and squeezed the trigger.

Click.

Click.

Nothing.

I screamed and squeezed again. The trigger was jammed. I slid the gun away and pulled myself out from under John's weight. My hands burned against the cement floor. I bounced up to one knee, then bolted with my head down. I dove, driving my shoulder into the side of Mikhail's knee, and a bone popped in my ear. Mikhail's left leg gave out from under him. A deep growl emanated from his throat as he dropped Isaac.

Isaac's legs crumbled as he hit the floor. He held his throat, coughing specs of blood.

Even with Mikhail on one knee, he was just as tall as I was.

My self-defense training kicked in. One foot forward, even weight distribution, fists up. Jab. Cross.

Punching Mikhail's face felt like punching a cinder block. He smiled after two hits to the mouth. A single drop of red leaked from his lip, and he licked it away. I swung at him again, but he caught my arm. His massive hand squeezed my forearm so tightly it felt like my bones were getting shoved into a meat grinder. The pain forced me to my knees. Mikhail reared back. I clenched my eyes, preparing for the inevitable asteroid that would decapitate me. The last thing I heard was Isaac's scream as I braced for impact. But Mikhail's grip loosened instead.

Mikhail let go of me and pawed at his throat. His mouth opened and closed like a fish out of water. The sharp end of the bloody butcher knife stuck out from under his chin before Isaac ripped it back out from behind. With another visceral war cry, Isaac plunged the knife through the back of Mikhail's neck again. The blade forced another path of destruction, poking out from under Mikhail's Adam's apple. The giant man's eyes rolled back before collapsing—his shoulders now drenched in his own mess.

Isaac froze, staring. I saw the flip in his eyes. At that moment, he was me, and Mikhail was Dan. Blood freckled Isaac's perfect face. His hands dripped with what was left of Mikhail. Isaac's chest rose and fell rapidly as he took it all in with wide, wet eyes. I knew he'd replay that nightmare in his head for the rest of his life.

TWENTY SEVEN

Mikhail's blood pooled around his broad shoulders. The long blade still poked through his skin.

I forced myself to look away and run to Isaac. "Fuck, are you okay?" I hugged him tightly.

He sucked air through his teeth and winced.

"Sorry, sorry," I said, unwrapping my arms. "Can I see it?"

Isaac unzipped his jacket and peeled it from his shoulder.

I gently pulled at the neck of his shirt. Mikhail had carved through a good chunk. The wound was deep but clean. "Can you move it?"

Isaac wiggled his hand and fingers. "Everything seems okay. Just a little hard to lift it."

I searched my coat pockets, producing a few unused tissues, and held them against Isaac's wound. "Keep pressure on it."

Isaac nodded and replaced my hand with his. I helped him zip his coat.

I picked up the duffle bag and slung it over my shoulder. Isaac stood over Mikhail, staring, his chest heaving. I touched Isaac's shoulder, and he jumped.

He looked at me with watery eyes. "I had to, right?"

I hugged him again. "Yes. He would've killed us." I softly pushed our foreheads together. "You saved my life." Isaac sighed. I wanted to scream, but I couldn't fall apart while Caleb and Isaac were still in danger. "You're gonna be okay." I held his head against my shoulder. I was tired of improvising. We survived by chance all night, by mere fucking luck. "We need to end this."

Isaac wiped his face. "Where's the gun?"

"It jammed."

"So now what?"

"We pray Victor takes the money."

We left Mikhail's body where it was and followed the arrows back to the slaughterhouse. The duffle bag dug into my shoulder, feeling heavier by the second. I shuffled past the metal bins and stacked crates, finding Victor where I left him. I dropped the bag in the pool of light.

"Thought I heard you coming," Victor said, sipping from a bottle of whiskey. He looked me up and down. Then his eyes slowly shifted to Isaac, who flanked me from the darkness. "How you come back without my men but with stranger?"

I pointed to the bag. "He's the reason you have this." My eyes met Caleb's. He was on his knees next to Victor, facing me. I could hear his teeth chattering. I looked at Victor. "That's what you wanted, right? Now, let him go!"

"Where are my men?" Victor asked.

"They're dead, asshole," Isaac stated. "Do the smart thing. Take the money."

Not helping. I should've told him to stay quiet.

Victor tossed his head back, and his laugh filled the room. He pulled the gun from his waistband and waved it around. "You're new," he said before wiping a tear from his eye. "So I tell you. I make rules. Victor. No one else." He giggled to himself one last time.

"Yes," I said, nodding. "We followed the rules. You have your money."

Victor paced in front of Caleb, walking toe to heel as if on a tightrope. He waved a finger in the air. "Ah, ah, but no men."

I glanced over my shoulder at Isaac, then back to Victor. "What?"

"My men were not part of deal," Victor said.

I cleared my throat. "Victor, please, I—"

Victor spiked the whiskey bottle, splashing the alcohol all over the floor. "NEW RULE!" Victor screamed.

My breath quickened, and I clenched my jaw to keep my head from spinning.

Victor grinned. "New. Rule." His voice calmed. "Based on old saying." Victor raised his gun to his lips and nibbled the edge. "Eye for eye, yes?" Victor turned to Caleb.

"NO!" Isaac screamed.

Victor's arm stiffened. My eyes caught Caleb's just as Victor squeezed the trigger.

POP!

"Caleb!" My throat burned, screaming his name. Caleb didn't make a sound when he hit the floor face down. My knees buckled, and I kneeled on the concrete. I couldn't get a full breath, my lungs pulsed in short bursts as if filled with water. I had failed the person I loved most in the world.

Victor whipped around to me, his face sprinkled with Caleb's blood. I bolted. "I'LL KILL YOU!"

The Russian pointed the smoking barrel at my face, breaking my stride. My nose wrinkled, and my jaw stayed tight as snot and tears covered my face.

Victor eyed Isaac. "Take one step and Red Boy dies." Victor's eyes dashed between us, and he licked his lips repeatedly.

"We gave you everything you wanted." My voice trembled.

"And still could not save boyfriend." Victor's shoulders bounced with his laugh.

I closed my eyes, realizing it was the end. Victor wouldn't let us live. He was right; I failed the one person who needed me. Saving Caleb a second time was inevitably impossible. My luck ran out. A memory of Caleb handing me the football the first time we met flashed behind my eyes. The sun made him look so angelic. He was the best thing that ever happened to me, but I was his worst. I was his death.

"Wait!" Isaac called out.

"Right! How rude." Victor said. "I let you say one last thing before Red Boy dies."

Isaac mumbled something inaudible.

Victor kept the gun at my face but looked at Isaac. "What?"

"The video," Isaac said a little louder.

"Speak up, stranger!" Victor shouted.

"On the pier," Isaac said.

The self defense video I showed Isaac on the pier. My eyes shot open. It was now or never. I leaned my body to the right and quickly reached for Victor's gun, but my technique still wasn't perfect. Victor's finger twisted, and he yelped before a shot fired. One of the work-lights shattered and knocked over two more standing lights, causing a ripple effect. Wires were ripped from their ports, erupting with sparks.

The gun dropped and skidded across the slick floor. Another bulb exploded, sending sparks to the ground, igniting the pool of whiskey. Flames danced beside us, spreading under our feet.

Victor backed away as a stack of crates crackled and caught fire, lighting up the room. He bumped a makeshift table and swiped another glass bottle.

"Look out!" Isaac shouted.

Victor sped toward me with the bottle raised above his head, snarling like a rabid animal. A bang cracked the air, echoing through us. A bullet exploded through Victor's knee, and he crumbled under his weight, sending him crashing to the floor. The bottle smashed at my feet.

Caleb stood behind the flames, pointing Victor's gun. His left arm was limp and covered in red and black goo.

My heart sank. I couldn't keep my eyes off of him. Everything was so blurry, I was sure my mind was playing tricks again.

Caleb moved slowly, never dropping his aim on Victor. Glass

crunched under Victor's hand as he pushed himself to rest on his good knee.

"Isaac," Caleb said with a grizzly tone. "Get your money."

Isaac ran to the duffle and grabbed it by the handles.

Caleb limped closer to Victor.

Victor growled as he straightened his back, gripping his leg. He eyed Caleb, then smiled wide. "Like cockroach." Victor's chuckle turned into a full belly laugh.

"Laugh all you want," Caleb said through his teeth. "It's over. You lost."

"Everyone expendable," Victor said, chuckling again. "I am cog in wheel. Piece of puzzle." Victor stared down at his palms. He looked pleased with the color of his own blood. "One way or other, debt will be paid." Victor sucked the blood off his finger. Another laugh showed his red teeth.

Heat blared as the flames rose, flickering in the reflection of Caleb's eyes. He cocked the gun with his thumb. "No. This ends now," Caleb said.

"WEAK!" Victor sneered. "Pretty boy not have balls." Victor wheezed out another laugh. "Victor not scared of pretty boy."

"You should be," Caleb whispered.

It felt like a cannon exploded next to my face. The pop ricocheted through my ears and up into the ceiling. A single bullet was all it took, erupting through Victor's eye and out the other side. The force snapped his head back before his body crashed to the concrete. The contents of Victor's head on the floor looked like painted spikes leaving his skull.

Caleb's arm fell, and we finally locked eyes.

Tears streamed my face as I crashed into him with a hug. "I thought you were dead."

Caleb held me with one arm, leaning his face into my neck. "It's over now."

"Guys, the fire's spreading!" Isaac called out. "We need to go!"

Flames touched the ceiling now. More wood crackled and popped around us.

Caleb tossed the gun and pulled me toward Isaac. "Go!"

Isaac led the charge, following the arrows.

Caleb winced with every heavy limp. We passed Mikhail's kill room, getting closer to the garage exit. Glass shattered behind us. We reached the swinging door and pushed through. Snow now covered Bruno's body completely.

"Under here," Isaac said as he ducked under the garage door.

Something exploded in the distance as Caleb rolled into the snowy street. I crawled through, my hands sinking in the powder. I popped to my feet and pushed the garage handle, closing it tight. I could already smell the smoke. Someone was gonna notice soon enough.

We jogged to Isaac's car and helped Caleb into the backseat. Hues of red and yellow painted the sky as we sped away, sloshing snow in our wake.

Caleb let air out through his teeth. His body trembled. "Heat." His tone was still stern.

Isaac twisted a knob, forcing hot air from the vents. Caleb scratched at his legs. His eyes stayed locked on the back of Isaac's seat.

"Oh, here." Isaac reached for Caleb's bag resting on the passenger side floor. "Your lucky pack." Isaac passed it back to me, and I placed it in Caleb's lap.

Caleb gripped the lone strap in his right hand and squeezed. He stared down at it before bringing it to his face. His shoulders relaxed, his fingers quit scratching, and he let go, whimpering into his bag.

Isaac and I met eyes in the rearview mirror before I touched Caleb's shoulder. He dropped the bag and practically leaped into my arms, sobbing.

———

A shirtless Caleb sat on a stool next to Isaac's kitchen sink. I dabbed the bullet's exit wound in Caleb's shoulder with a peroxide-soaked paper towel. "You need a doctor," I said.

"We all do," Isaac agreed, wincing as he peeled the tissue off his stab wound.

"We need to lay low," Caleb said. "If we go to the hospital now, they're gonna ask too many questions. We can go, just not yet."

"I've stopped the bleeding for now," I said, pressing a cloth to Caleb's shoulder.

Isaac pulled out his phone. "We should tell Josh it's over."

I nodded. "Good idea."

"Check the news first. They have to have found the fire by now," Caleb said.

Isaac's thumb swiped, and his brow creased, staring at his screen. "It's live," he said, placing the phone on the counter for us to see.

A woman in a beige peacoat shivered in frame. The scene of flashing fire trucks behind her couldn't cover up the whipping flames kissing the sky. The reporter held a bulky microphone to her face. "As you can see behind me, these first responders are attempting to gain control of this warehouse fire on the west side of Lower Manhattan. Authorities say they do not yet know the cause of the fire that has already claimed most of the building. Currently, the police have not found any eyewitnesses to the events and told us the few CCTVs in the area were obstructed by the storm."

"We got lucky," Isaac said.

Caleb leaned his elbows on the counter and massaged his forehead with one hand.

"Think they can link anything back to us?" Isaac asked.

"I don't know, that's a lot of fire damage," I said.

We watched the screen; the news showed different angles of the burning warehouse.

I looked at Caleb and was reminded of the interaction between Victor and Dmitry. "They took your gun," I said. Caleb reached for his backpack on the counter and rummaged through it. "I saw Victor toss it. It's the one you had at home, right? Silver with a black grip?"

"Can they link it to you, Caleb?" Isaac asked.

"I hadn't registered it yet." Caleb's head tilted. "What's this?" He pulled the *Thundercats* lunchbox from his backpack.

"We found it when we went back to Tommy's place," I said. "The key in your bag opened it."

Caleb's wide eyes shot to me before he ripped the lunchbox open. He slowly picked up the stack of pictures and flipped through a couple. "He saved all these?" He passed through some more, and his bottom lip quivered.

"There was a thumb drive in there, too," Isaac said. He pointed to the counter behind me. "Landon, hand me my laptop."

I placed the computer next to Isaac's phone. He opened the screen and Caleb handed him the USB. Once plugged in, a video player immediately popped up on the desktop.

Caleb's jaw fell. "What is this?"

I shrugged. "Play it."

Caleb pressed the spacebar to start the video.

The footage showed Tommy sitting back in a chair, and then he came into focus on the screen. His eyes weren't bloodshot and droopy. His skin was smoother. His hair hadn't grown a gray speck yet. His goatee was short and thinner around his chin. His face was fuller. He stared at the camera and smiled, but it faded quickly as he shook his head. He pushed a hand through his thick hair. "Hi, Caleb. I hope we're watching this together right now. But if you're watching this alone, then my nightmare came true. They found me. Consider this my last will and testament if that's the case." He reached out of frame and returned with a clear plastic cup of water. He sipped it and took another breath. Tommy continued explaining why he left, just as he did to us in his apartment.

The video cut to him wearing a different shirt but in the same spot against the wall. "Caleb, if you're the one watching this, I hope you know that being your dad was the greatest privilege of my life. Keeping these secrets rips me apart every day." The video cut again. Tommy's clothes hadn't changed, but a lit cigarette now hung from his lips. "I'm lucky I made it this far. I regret a lot, everything actually. Except you." The cigarette tip glowed. He blew the smoke out the side of his mouth. "Taking the money was the only thing I could think of to make it up to you. I'm sorry for all the hoops you had to jump through to get it. I wanted to make sure it was you and not them. No one else's hands could touch it."

Caleb straightened in his stool and looked at me. "What is he talking about?"

Tommy's voice pulled Caleb's attention back to the screen. "Once you figure out the code, you'll find a manilla folder in my safe with stock and bond certificates worth almost a hundred and fifty thousand dollars at the time of this recording. Might be even more by the time you watch this."

Caleb reached into his bag, pulled out the folder, opened it, and fingered through the sheets of paper. They all looked like birth certificates, except each had a drawing of a western-looking town at the top or an old portrait of a white-bearded man.

Tommy continued. "It doesn't matter how, as I said, I have regrets. But this money is clean, I promise. And it's yours."

"This can't be real," Caleb said.

Tommy took another drag of his cigarette. "I hope this money can help take care of that little boy. I hope he's just like you." Tommy put out his cigarette, and stared at the camera with glossy eyes. "Take care, kid."

Caleb stared at the black screen. "I... I can't. It's blood money." Caleb wiped the moisture from under his eye and turned to me. "What if Parker asks questions? He's gonna notice things are suddenly different."

"Tell him the truth like you always do," I said.

"How can a preteen process all of this adult bullshit?"

Isaac gently scratched Caleb's back. "Maybe a little truth now and a little more truth later?"

Caleb reached to hold Isaac's hand. "He's already dealt with so much."

"You guys deserve this," I said, shuffling through the certificates. "Every single one is in your name. This money is legally yours."

Caleb squeezed my hand. "I'll think about it, okay?"

Isaac's phone lit up, and he swiped it from the counter. "Josh is on his way over."

"I should call Parker," Caleb said, "and tell him everything's okay."

Isaac handed his phone to Caleb, but Caleb placed it in front of me. "Call your dad first."

"It's okay, call Par—"

"Landon, he should know you're okay."

My brow pinched before I took the phone and walked upstairs. I sat at the edge of Isaac's bed, looking out onto a street just coming alive. The sun started to beam across the floor through the window. I typed the numbers and held the phone to my ear.

A groggy voice answered.

"Hey, Dad, it's me. Sorry for the early call."

"Landon? Who's phone is this? Are you okay?"

I pressed the edge of my fist to my lips, choking back a sob. "It's so nice to hear your voice."

"Son, what's going on?"

I pinched the bridge of my nose to stop my eyes from watering, but it didn't work. "I should've listened to you before." I cleared my throat.

Dad grunted. I could hear the shuffling of his bedsheets. "Landon, are you okay?"

Tears spilled over my lids. "I haven't been okay for a long time." My voice warbled. "I have to tell you something." I sniffled and wiped my nose on my arm. "Everything, actually."

TWENTY EIGHT
NEW YORK CITY

Eighteen Months Later

The air was just starting to cool after a blistering summer. The day of Isaac's *Adam Shock* premiere was an incredibly sunny one. Isaac's team had us hulled up in a hotel lobby on the Upper East Side before hitting the red carpet. I sat on a black velvet couch with pinstripe cushions, holding my phone at eye level to FaceTime with Steven and Tasha before the film screening.

"Wait, the limos are fake?" Steven asked, staring with wide eyes from the screen.

"Yeah," I said. "All the limos that drop off the celebrities on red carpets are apparently all the same ten limos. They make everyone wait nearby until one is ready."

"Damn," Steven said. "What else is Hollywood hiding from us?"

Tasha rolled her eyes. "Girl, don't even get me started."

"Are you nervous?" Steven's phone was propped on his desk, and he leaned away to apply eyeliner. In solidarity, he decided to put on a full face of makeup for the premiere.

"I'm terrified," I said.

"But it's gonna be so glamorous!" Tasha said with a smile. "You took your meds, right?"

I huffed. "Yes, Mom."

"Then you'll be golden," she said.

"It's our first public appearance with Isaac. He told me the press will probably ask us a ton of questions."

"You're making history!" Steven said. "Hollywood's first gay superhero movie, and the star brings his TWO boyfriends to the premiere? It's iconic!"

Tasha made a high-pitched squeal. "You're gonna break the internet!"

The thought of millions of people seeing my pictures online made me sweat. I don't know if it was something I'd ever get used to.

"You better still hang out with me when I get there!" Steven said. He had transferred to The New School for fashion and was set to move into the dorms in a week. "Think Isaac can set me up with someone?"

I laughed. "I'll ask, but no promises."

"Everyone's in New York now!" Tasha said. "I'm coming for Halloween this year, and you bitches are taking me out. And I need to meet Lauren's new man. Are we sure he's straight this time?"

"I've met him. Josh is, unfortunately, very straight." Steven leaned into the camera. "Wait, where is Lauren?"

"Her and Josh are meeting us at the theater." I glanced over my shoulder. Isaac, Caleb, and Parker were standing by the lobby entrance. Isaac spotted me and waved me over. "I gotta go," I said. "I think we're next to get picked up. I love you both! Wish me luck!"

Tasha waved at the camera. "Good luck, baby! Love you!"

Steven patted his face with a makeup sponge. "Love you, girl. Go slay with your boys! See you so soon!"

I waved and hung up.

My boys looked so dapper in their Zelda originals. Parker was a little less formal but still looked like a rock star. He wore tight black jeans with Converse sneakers. A black blazer fit snugly over a bedazzled *Adam Shock* T-shirt Zelda made with Swarovski crystals. Parker said he wouldn't take it off for the rest of his life.

Isaac kissed me as I entered their circle. Parker was glued to Isaac's arm. The little guy couldn't stop smiling. He was probably the most excited kid in New York City.

Isaac's manager approached us. Her blonde hair was pulled into a tight bun, and her white power suit screamed, 'New York lesbian in charge.' She held an iPad and scrolled briefly before looking at me. "Hey, Landon. How's the book coming?"

"Slowly but surely," I said.

"He won't let us read it," Isaac said, bumping me with his shoulder.

My cheeks warmed. "It's not ready." It wasn't easy writing about my mom, but I wanted her life to be remembered long after I was gone. Blending fact with fiction was my way of keeping her memory alive.

"Alright, you guys are up next," Isaac's manager said. "The limo door will be opened for you when you get to the red carpet. I will be directing you where to stand for pictures and which media you'll talk to."

I held up a hand. "We don't *have* to talk to them, do we?"

Isaac turned to me. "No NDAs this time. Everyone will know you guys are my boyfriends."

Isaac's manager pursed her lips. "Most of the questions will be directed to Isaac, but they might ask you a few," she said, looking between Caleb and me.

Parker's smile beamed at us. "I'll answer questions for you," he said with a squeak in his voice.

I gave Parker a fist bump. "Always my wingman."

"There will be a section where Isaac will be photographed alone. I'll be with you three by the entrance while that's happening, okay?" She smiled at Isaac. "Get ready; your first premiere at Radio City is a big deal."

"Thanks," Isaac said.

Parker suddenly pointed across the room, and our eyes followed.

"It's Cameron Wesker!" Parker said as he bounced and tugged on Isaac's sleeve. Cameron played the superhero, Biohazard, Adam Shock's mentor in the film. Parker pulled at the lanyard around his neck and looked up at Isaac. "Think he'll sign my premiere pass?"

Isaac smiled. "He'd be honored, I'm sure."

"C'mon!" Parker said before bolting away.

Caleb leaned into Isaac. "You know this is the best day of his life, right? He's never gonna stop talking about this."

"That's the goal," Isaac said before kissing Caleb's lips. Our curly-haired boyfriend kissed me, too, then jogged to Parker, who had already started chatting with Cameron. The kid had more confidence in his pinky finger than I had in my entire body.

Caleb wrapped an arm around my waist. "When Isaac met Parker last year and promised to take him to the premiere, I thought he was just being nice."

I leaned my head on Caleb's shoulder. "Parker deserves this. And so do you."

Caleb decided to keep the inheritance from Tommy once we were sure the warehouse fire burned away any link to us. Isaac introduced Caleb to his financial advisor to help settle any debts Caleb had to his name and to manage the nearly three hundred thousand dollars the stocks and bonds were worth. Caleb and Parker used the money to move to New York and start a new chapter. Isaac and I helped them find a small two-bedroom apartment in the west village, the first place they could call their own.

"A lot's changed since that day in detention," Caleb said. I wrapped my arms around his waist and squeezed.

———

The leather seats crunched as we sat in the limo. Parker slid down the long seat and reached for a champagne bottle in a bucket of ice.

"Hey," Caleb called out to his brother. "Is that bottle heavy?"

Parker gave the bottle a little shake. "Yeah,"

"That means it's expensive. Put it back. Nice try, though."

Parker returned the bottle to its ice bath and turned his attention to the small screen in the wall behind the driver's seat. "Cool!"

"Do not press anything," Caleb said, sliding down the seat.

I could already hear the screaming fans erupting from outside when the limo stopped. The red carpet jutted out from the street and under the marquee of Radio City Music Hall. Huge spotlights danced a ballet of black, red, and yellow, Adam Shock's signature colors. Isaac's face was on every poster.

Isaac glanced out the window. A hundred bodies waited to see who appeared next. "You're about to get a lot more Instagram followers," he said to us.

Caleb's eyebrows perked. "I'm suddenly glad I don't have Instagram."

"Whoa," Parker said as he observed the spectacle. His face pressed against the window.

I squeezed Isaac's hand. "You ready?"

Isaac turned to us. "I've never felt more ready. Having you guys with me makes any crowd a cakewalk."

Caleb held Isaac's hand over mine, and the ring he'd got us for Christmas clinked against the one he'd recently given Isaac. All three of us wore the ring on our right hands. "You got this, babe."

Isaac kissed Caleb. "I love you." Then, he leaned and kissed me too. "And I love you."

"We love you too," Caleb said.

Parker rolled his eyes. "Am I gonna have to deal with you guys kissing all night?"

"Okay, they better open this door before I get emotional," Isaac said, wiping his hands on his pants. He looked at us and smiled. "Let's go turn some heads."

The door opened, and a wave of screams filled the limo. Isaac popped out first and offered his hand to help me out. The flashes from the cameras were blinding. It was suddenly clear why I always saw celebrities wearing sunglasses on the red carpet in my mom's tabloids.

My heart calmed. I pretended Mom held my arm and walked me

down the red carpet. Of course, none of it was for me, but it was still an exciting experience. My mom would've loved being there all dressed up. I don't think she ever saw that kind of life for me, but I hoped she was proud.

Isaac was directed forward, moving us to the closest reporter. A dark-skinned woman wearing a red dress pushed a microphone at Isaac. "Meredith Skinner with Total Film. How are you, Isaac?" Her wide smile was infectious.

Isaac buttoned his blazer. "I am fantastic! This is a dream come true."

Meredith's eyes trickled to Caleb and me. "Who are your handsome dates this evening?"

My cheeks burned. I wasn't expecting to be acknowledged so soon.

Isaac's smile somehow got wider as he gestured to us. "My amazing boyfriends, Landon and Caleb. And, of course, Adam Shock's biggest fan." Parker gladly took the spotlight, stepping in front of Isaac. Isaac placed his hands on Parker's shoulders. "This is Caleb's little brother, Parker."

Parker beamed up at the much taller Meredith. "I'm the most important one. You can ask me as many questions as you want!"

The crowd laughed at Parker's endearing confidence, and the cameras continued to flash at rapid speed.

Holding their hands that day, I had never felt more grateful to be alive. I'd been through more than I thought I was capable of handling. And somehow, I landed exactly where I was supposed to. With them.

THANK YOU FOR READING MY BOOK!

As a new author, reviews can be such a huge help to get new eyes on the page! I'd love to see what you have to say about *Land On Him*. Please leave a review on Amazon and Goodreads!

To stay up to date with me and to get exclusives about my next book, please join my Newsletter at www.matthewrcorr.com and follow me across Social Media @matthewrcorr

<u>COMING SOON!</u>

This bloody new book series follows Final Boy Anderson "Ander" Thorne, a charismatic gay influencer whose dancing videos garner millions of views. Ander's world shifts when he and his friends find themselves entangled in a series of gruesome murders, served up one by one. Each book features a new location, fresh characters beside Ander, and a new Slasher who dons a unique mask. Each story also comes with its own set of rules. And if they survive, characters from previous books may reappear. Ander's mission? Unravel the mystery and stop the Slasher before all his friends are dead.

ACKNOWLEDGMENTS

I can't believe this book is finally here and in your hands! It was honestly such a bumpy journey, and I wasn't sure it would ever be released. After almost a year of recovery from two emergency eye surgeries within a month of each other, I'm very grateful to say that things are better and that my doctor and everyone in his office are excellent at what they do. I honestly wouldn't be doing this right now if they hadn't helped to get my sight back.

I also wouldn't be here without my boyfriends, Ryan and Kyle. They kept me going through the entire recovery process, pretty much doing everything for me while I was out of commission. Ryan, your patience with me is impeccable. Thank you for being kind, caring, and loving me with all your heart. Kyle was responsible for creating my new cover for this book, and it was such a blast getting to work together on something creative for the first time. Thank you for not killing me after my thousands of notes. If it weren't for you two, I'd probably be a sack of potatoes on the street by now. I love you both more than anything.

Thank you to all my family and friends for constantly asking when the next book comes out. Thank you for keeping me accountable! All of the support I get from you all means the world to me.

Once again, my team of Beta Readers was crucial in forming this book into what it is now. I am grateful to you all. Thank you, Alyssa Venora, Dana Semmel, Justine Melvin, Christian Krenek for your amazing feedback. And a special shout out to beta reader Brandy (Eva) Lovell for giving me Isaac's name. <3

The last thank you goes out to my readers. To all of you who stood with me and waited patiently for this book. I hope you enjoy this one. If you wrote a review or posted on your socials about this book, thank you, it means the world to me and is such a huge help!

New York City is my favorite place in the world. I feel very grateful to have spent my whole adult life here. I hope my love for this city shows in the book. One of my life goals was to write a book set in New York City so I'm kind of giddy that it's here. I wanted this story to feel like a treasure hunt, moving from one clue to the next with a bunch of roadblocks in between. As every good sequel should be, I wanted it to be bigger and bolder than the original. It was also important to me to showcase polyamory naturally and healthily, to show that non-monogamous relationships are genuine and thriving, just like mine! I'm so excited for the future, with my first series on the way next. I hope you stick around for it!

ABOUT THE AUTHOR

Matthew Corr was born and raised in beautiful New England. Coming out as gay in high school in his small town fueled his big city dreams. Matthew moved to New York City, where he gained a degree in musical theatre. After countless performances on stages across the country, his passion for writing finally stepped into the spotlight. Matthew is a huge nerd for film and everything Marvel related. He currently lives in Brooklyn, NY. To learn more about Matthew, and the release of his next book, please visit www.matthewrcorr.com or @matthewrcorr

www.ingramcontent.com/pod-product-compliance
Lightning Source LLC
Chambersburg PA
CBHW030548310726
48979CB00010B/2076/J